1.000

Michael Moorcock is astonishing. His enormous output includes around fifty novels, innumerable short stories and a rock album. Born in London in 1939, he became editor of *Tarzan Adventures* at sixteen, moving on later to edit the *Sexton Blake Library*. He has earned his living as a writer/editor ever since, and is without doubt one of Britain's most popular and most prolific authors. He has been compared with Tennyson, Tolkien, Raymond Chandler, Wyndham Lewis, Ronald Firbank, Mervyn Peake, Edgar Allan Poe, Colin Wilson Anatole France, William Burroughs, Edgar Rice Burroughs, Charles Dickens, James Joyce, Vladimir Nabokov, Jorge Luis Borges, Joyce Cary, Ray Bradbury, H. G. Wells, George Bernard Shaw and Hieronymus Bosch, among others.

'No one at the moment in England is doing more to break down the artificial divisions that have grown up in novel writing — realism, surrealism, science fiction, historical fiction, social satire, the poetic novel — than Michael Moorcock'.

'He is an ingenious and energetic experimenter, restlessly original, brimming over with clever ideas'
Robert Nye, *The Guardian*

Michael Moorcock

The End of All Songs

VOLUME THREE OF A TRILOGY
'The Dancers at the End of Time'

A MAYFLOWER BOOK

GRANADA
London Toronto Sydney New York

Published by Granada Publishing Limited
in 1977, 1980
Reprinted 1978, 1979

ISBN 0 583 12105 5

First published in Great Britain by
Hart-Davis, MacGibbon Ltd 1976
Copyright © Michael Moorcock 1976

Granada Publishing Limited
Frogmore, St Albans, Herts AL2 2NF
and
3 Upper James Street, London W1R 4BP
866 United Nations Plaza, New York, NY 10017, USA
117 York Street, Sydney, NSW 2000, Australia
100 Skyway Avenue, Rexdale, Ontario, M9W 3A6, Canada
PO Box 84165, Greenside, 2034 Johannesburg, South Africa
61 Beach Road, Auckland, New Zealand

Granada ®
Granada Publishing ®

Printed in Canada

For John Clute
– and Tom Disch

Acknowledgements

Apart from Alfred Austin's, all verses quoted in the text are the work of Ernest Wheldrake. The majority are from *Posthumous Poems*, published in 1881 and never reprinted.

The fire is out, and spent the warmth thereof,
(This is the end of every song man sings!)
The golden wine is drunk, the dregs remain,
Bitter as wormwood and as salt as pain;
And health and hope have gone the way of love
Into the drear oblivion of lost things,
Ghosts go along with us until the end;
This was a mistress, this, perhaps, a friend.
With pale, indifferent eyes, we sit and wait
For the dropt curtain and the closing gate:
This is the end of all the songs man sings.

Ernest Dowson
Dregs
1899

Contents

CHAPTER ONE

IN WHICH JHEREK CARNELIAN AND
MRS AMELIA UNDERWOOD COMMUNE, TO
SOME DEGREE, WITH NATURE

'I really do think, Mr Carnelian, that we should at least *try* them raw, don't you?'

Mrs Amelia Underwood, with the flat of her left hand, stroked thick auburn hair back over her ear and, with her right hand, arranged her tattered skirts about her ankles. The gesture was almost petulant; the glint in her grey eye was possibly wolfish. There was, if nothing else, something over-controlled in the manner in which she perched primly upon her block of virgin limestone and watched Jherek Carnelian as he crouched, elbows and knees pressed in the sand of a Palaeozoic beach, and sweated in the heat of the huge Silurian (or possibly Devonian) sun.

Perhaps for the thousandth time he was trying to strike two of his power-rings together to make a spark to light the heap of half-dried ferns he had, in a mood of ebullience long since dissipated, arranged several hours before.

'But you told me,' he murmured, 'that you could not bear to consider ... There! Was that a spark? Or just a glint?'

'A glint,' she said, 'I think.'

'We must not despair, Mrs Underwood.' His optimism

1

was uncharacteristically strained. Again he struck ring against ring.

Around him were scattered the worn and broken fragments of fronds which he had earlier tried to rub together at her suggestion. As power-ring clacked on power-ring, Mrs Underwood winced. In the silence of this Silurian (if it was Silurian) afternoon the sound had an effect upon her nerves she would not previously have credited; she had never seen herself as one of those over-sensitive women who populated the novels of Marie Corelli. She had always considered herself robust, singularly healthy. She sighed. Doubtless the boredom contributed something to her state of mind.

Jherek echoed her sigh. 'There's probably a knack to it,' he admitted. 'Where are the trilobites?' He stared absently around him at the ground.

'Most of them have crawled back into the sea, I think,' she told him coldly. 'There are two brachiopods on your coat.' She pointed.

'Aha!' Almost affectionately he plucked the molluscoidea from the dirty black cloth of his frock-coat. Doubtfully, he peered into the shells.

Mrs Underwood licked her lips. 'Give them to me,' she commanded. She produced a hat-pin.

His head bowed, Pilate confronting the Pharisees, he complied.

'After all,' she told him as she poised the pin, 'we are only missing garlic and butter and we should have a meal fit for a French gourmet.' The utterance seemed to depress her. She hesitated.

'Mrs Underwood?'

'Should we say grace, I wonder?' She frowned. 'It might help. I think it's the colour ...'

'Too beautiful,' he said eagerly. 'I follow you. Who could destroy such loveliness?'

'That greenish, purplish hue pleases you?'

'Not you?'

'Not in *food*, Mr Carnelian.'

'Then in what?'

'Oh ...' Vaguely. 'In – no, not even in a picture. It brings to mind the excesses of the Pre-Raphaelites. A morbid colour.'

'Ah.'

'It might explain your affinities ...' She abandoned the subject. 'If I could conquer ...'

'A yellow one?' He tried to tempt her with a soft-shelled creature he had just discovered in his back pocket. It clung to his finger; there was the sensation of a kiss.

She dropped molluscs and hat-pin, covered her face with her hands and began to weep.

'Mrs Underwood!' He was at a loss. He stirred the pile of fronds with his foot. 'Perhaps if I were to use a ring as a prism and direct the rays of the sun through it we could ...'

There came a loud squeak and he wondered at first if one of the creatures were protesting. Another squeak, from behind him. Mrs Underwood removed her fingers to expose red eyes which now widened in surprise.

'Hi! I say – Hi, there!'

Jherek turned. Tramping through the shallows, apparently oblivious of the water, came a man dressed in a seaman's jersey, a tweed Norfolk jacket, plus-fours, heavy woollen stockings, stout brogues. In one hand he clutched a stick of a peculiarly twisted crystalline nature. Otherwise he appeared to be a contemporary of Mrs Underwood's. He was smiling. 'I say, do you speak English of any kind?' He was bronzed. He had a full moustache and signs of a newly sprouting beard. He beamed at them. He came to a stop, resting his knuckles on his hips. 'Well?'

Mrs Underwood was confused. 'We speak English, sir. Indeed we are – at least I am – English, as you must be.'

'Beautiful day, isn't it?' The stranger nodded at the sea. 'Nice and calm. Must be the early Devonian, eh? Have you been here long?'

'Long enough, sir.'

'We are marooned,' Jherek explained. 'A malfunction

of our time-craft. The paradoxes were too much for it, I suspect.'

The stranger nodded gravely. 'I've sometimes experienced similar difficulties, though happily without such drastic results. You're from the nineteenth century, I take it.'

'Mrs Underwood is. I hail from the End of Time.'

'Aha!' The stranger smiled. 'I have just come from there. I was fortunate enough to witness the complete disintegration of the universe — briefly, of course. I, too, am originally from the nineteenth century. This would be one of my regular stops, if I were journeying to the past. The peculiar thing is that I was under the impression I was going forward — beyond, as it were, the End of Time. My instruments indicate as much. Yet here I am.' He scratched his sandy hair, adding, in mild disappointment, 'I was hoping for some illumination.'

'You are on your way, then, to the future?' Mrs Underwood asked. 'To the nineteenth century?'

'It seems that I must be. When did you leave?'

'1896,' Mrs Underwood told him.

'I am from 1894. I was not aware that anyone else had hit upon my discovery during that period ...'

'There!' exclaimed Jherek. 'Mr Wells was right!'

'Our machine was from Mr Carnelian's period,' she said. 'Originally, I was abducted to the End of Time, under circumstances which remain mysterious. The motives of my abductor continue to be obscure, moreover. I ...' She paused apologetically. 'This is of no interest to you, of course.' She moistened her lips. 'You would not, I suppose, have the means of lighting a fire, sir?'

The stranger patted the bulging pockets of his Norfolk jacket. 'Somewhere. Some matches. I tend to carry as many necessities as possible about my person. In the event of being stranded ... Here we are.' He produced a large box of vestas. 'I would give you the whole box, but ...'

'A few will do. You say you are familiar with the early Devonian.'

4

'As familiar as one can be.'

'Your advice, then, would be welcome. The edibility of the molluscs, for instance?'

'I think you'll find the *myalina subquadrata* the least offensive, and very few are actually poisonous, though a certain amount of indigestion is bound to result. I, myself, am a slave to indigestion.'

'And what do these *myalina* look like?' Jherek asked.

'Oh, like mussels, really. You have to dig for them.'

Mrs Underwood took five matches from the box and handed it back.

'Your time-craft, sir, is functioning properly?' Jherek said.

'Oh, yes, perfectly.'

'And you are returning to the nineteenth century?'

'To 1895, I hope.'

'Then you could take us with you?'

The stranger shook his head. 'It's a single-seater. The saddle barely accommodates me, since I began to put on weight. Come, I'll show you.' He turned and began to plod through the sand in the direction from which he had come. They followed.

'Also,' added the stranger, 'it would be unwise for me to try to take people from 1896 to 1895. You would meet yourselves. Considerable confusion would result. One can tamper just a little with the Logic of Time, but I hesitate to think what would happen if one went in for such blatant paradoxes. It would seem to me that if you have been treating the Logic so cavalierly it is no wonder – I do not moralize, you understand – that you find yourselves in this position.'

'Then you verify the Morphail Theory,' Jherek said, trudging beside the time-traveller. 'Time resists paradox, adjusting accordingly – refusing, you might say, to admit a foreign body to a period to which it is not indigenous?'

'If a paradox is likely to occur. Yes. I suspect that it is all to do with consciousness, and with our *group* understanding of what constitutes Past, Present and Future.

5

That is, Time, as such, does not exist . . .'

Mrs Underwood uttered a soft exclamation as the stranger's craft came in sight. It consisted of an open frame of tubular lengths of brass and ebony. There was ivory here and there, as well as a touch or two of silver, copper coils set into the top of the frame, immediately above a heavily sprung leather saddle of the sort normally seen on bicycles. Before this was a small board of instruments and a brass semi-circle where a lever might normally fit. Much of the rest of the machine was of nickel and crystal and it showed signs of wear, was much battered, dented and cracked in places. Behind the saddle was strapped a large chest and it was to this that the stranger made at once, undoing the brass buckles and pushing back the lid. The first object he drew out of the trunk was a double-barrelled shot-gun which he leaned against the saddle; next he removed a bale of muslin and a solar topee, and finally, using both hands, he hauled up a large wickerwork basket and dumped it in the sand at their feet.

'This might be useful to you,' he said, replacing the other objects in the trunk and securing the straps. 'It's the best I can offer, short of passage home. And I've explained why that's impossible. You wouldn't want to come face to face with yourselves in the middle of Waterloo Circus, would you?' He laughed.

'Don't you mean Piccadilly Circus, sir?' enquired Mrs Underwood with a frown.

'Never heard of it,' said the time-traveller.

'I've never heard of Waterloo Circus,' she told him. 'Are you sure you're from 1894?'

The stranger fingered the stubble on his chin. He seemed a little disturbed. 'I thought I'd merely gone full circle,' he murmured. 'Hm – perhaps this universe is not quite the same as the one I left. Is it possible that for every new time-traveller a new chronology develops? Could there be an infinite number of universes?' He brightened. 'This is a fine adventure, I must say. Aren't you hungry?'

Mrs Amelia Underwood raised her beautiful brows.

6

The stranger pointed at the basket. 'My provisions,' he said. 'Make what use of them you like. I'll risk finding some food at my next stop – hopefully 1895. Well, I must be on my way.'

He bowed, brandishing his quartz rod significantly. He climbed onto his saddle and placed the rod in the brass groove, making some adjustments to his other controls.

Mrs Underwood was already lifting the lid of the hamper. Her face was obscured, but Jherek thought he could hear her crooning to herself.

'Good luck to you both,' said the stranger cheerfully. 'I'm sure you won't be stuck here forever. It's unlikely, isn't it? I mean, what a find for the archeologists, ha, ha! Your bones, that is!'

There came a sharp click as the stranger moved his lever a notch or two and almost immediately the time machine began to grow indistinct. Copper glowed and crystal shimmered; something seemed to be whirling very rapidly above the stranger's head and already both man and machine were semi-transparent. Jherek was struck in the face by a sudden gust of wind which came from nowhere and then the time-traveller had gone.

'Oh, look, Mr Carnelian!' cried Mrs Amelia Underwood, brandishing her trophy. 'Chicken!'

CHAPTER TWO

IN WHICH INSPECTOR SPRINGER TASTES
THE DELIGHTS OF THE SIMPLE LIFE

For the following two days and nights a certain tension, dissipating before the advent of the time-traveller but since restored, existed between the lovers (for they *were* lovers – only her upbringing denied it) and they slept fitfully, the pair of them, on either side of a frond-fondled limestone rock, having to fear nothing but the inquisitive attentions of the little molluscs and trilobites whose own lives now were free from danger, thanks to the hamper, crammed with cans and bottles enough to sustain a good-sized expedition for a month. No large beasts, no unexpected turn of the weather, threatened our Adam and our Eve; Eve, alone, knew inner conflict: Adam, simple bewilderment; but then he was used to bewilderment, and sudden moods or twists of fate had been the stuff of his existence until only recently – yet his spirits were not what they had been.

They rose somewhat, those spirits, at dawn this morning – for the beauty, in its subtlety, excelled any creation of *fin de cosmos* artifice. A huge half-sun filled the horizon line so that the sky surrounding it shone a thousand shades of copper, while its rays, spread upon the sea, seemed individually coloured – blues, ochres, greys, pinks – until they reached the beach and merged again, as if at apex, to make the yellow sand glare rainbow white, turn the limestone to shimmering silver and make individual leaves and stems of the fronds a green that seemed near-sentient, it was so alive; and there was a human figure at the core of this vision, outlined against the pulsing semi-circle of dark scarlet, the velvet dress murky red amber, the auburn hair a-flame, the white hands and neck reflecting the hues, delicate hint of the palest of poppies. And there was music, sonorous – it was her voice; she declaimed a favourite verse, its subject a trifle at odds with the ambience.

> *Where the red worm woman wailed for wild revenge,*
> * While the surf surged sullen 'neath moon-silver'd*
> *   sky,*
> *Where her harsh voice, once a sweet voice, sang,*
> * Now was I.*
> *And did her ghost on that grey, cold morn,*
> * Did her ghost slide by?*

Rapt, Jherek straightened his back and pushed aside the frock-coat which had covered him through the night; to see his love thus, in a setting to match the perfection of her beauty, sent all other considerations helter-skelter from his head; his own eyes shone: his face shone. He waited for more, but she was silent, tossing back her locks, shaking sand from her hem, pursing those loveliest of lips.

'Well?' he said.

Slowly, through iridescence, the face looked up, from shadow into light. Her mouth was a question.

'Amelia?' He dared the name. Her lids fell.

'What is it?' she murmured.

'Did it? Was it her ghost? I await the resolution.'

The lips curved now, perhaps a touch self-consciously, but the eyes continued to study the sand which she stirred with the sharp toe of her partly unbuttoned boot. 'Wheldrake doesn't say. It's a rhetorical question . . .'

'A very sober poem, is it not?'

A sense of superiority mingled with her modesty, causing the lashes to rise and fall rapidly for a moment. 'Most good poems are sober, Mr Carnelian, if they are to convey – significance. It speaks of death, of course. Wheldrake wrote much of death – and died, himself, prematurely. My cousin gave me the *Posthumous Poems* for my twentieth birthday. Shortly afterwards, she was taken from us, also, by consumption.'

'Is all good literature, then, about death?'

'Serious literature.'

'Death is serious?'

'It is final, at any rate.' But she shocked herself, judging this cynical, and recovered with: 'Although really, it is only the beginning – of our real life, our eternal life . . .'

She turned to regard the sun, already higher and less splendid.

'You mean, at the End of Time? In our own little home?'

'Never mind.' She faltered, speaking in a higher, less natural tone. 'It is my punishment, I suppose, to be denied, in my final hours, the company of a fellow Christian.' But there was some insincerity to all this. The food she had consumed during the past two days had mellowed her. She had almost welcomed the simpler terrors of starvation to the more complex dangers of giving herself up to this clown, this innocent (oh, yes, and perhaps this noble, manly being, for his courage, his kindness went without question). She strove, with decreasing success, to recreate that earlier, much more suitable, mood of resigned despondency.

'I interrupted you.' He leaned back against his rock. 'Forgive me. It was so delicious, to wake to the sound of your voice. Won't you go on?'

She cleared her throat and faced the sea again.

What will you say to me, child of the moon,
* When by the bright river we stand?*

10

*When forest leaves breathe harmonies to the night
    wind's croon.
Will you give me your hand, child of the moon?
Will you give me your hand?*

But her performance lacked the appropriate resonance,
certainly to her own ears, and she delivered the next verse
with even less conviction.

*Will you present your pyre to me, spawn of the sun,
    While the sky is in full flame?
While the day's heat the brain deceives, and the
    drugged bees hum.
Will you grant me your name, spawn of the sun?
Will you grant me your name?*

Jherek blinked. 'You have lost me entirely, I fear ...' The
sun was fully risen, the scene fled, though pale gold light
touched sky and sea still, and the day was calm and sultry.
'Oh, what things I could create with such inspiration, if
only my power rings were active. Vision upon vision, and
all for you, Amelia!'

'Have you no literature, at the End of Time?' she asked.
'Are your arts only visual?'

'We converse,' he said. 'You have heard us.'

'Conversation has been called an art, yet ...'

'We do not write it down,' he said, 'if that is what you
mean. Why should we? Similar conversations often arise –
similar observations are made afresh. Does one discover
more through the act of making the marks I have seen you
make? If so, perhaps I should ...'

'It will pass the time,' she said, 'if I teach you to write
and read.'

'Certainly,' he agreed.

She knew the questions he had asked had been innocent,
but they struck her as just. She laughed. 'Oh, dear, Mr
Carnelian. Oh, dear!'

He was content not to judge her mood to but to share

it. He laughed with her, springing up. He advanced. She awaited him. He stopped, when a few steps separated them. He was serious now, and smiling.

She fingered her neck. 'There is more to literature than conversation, however. There are stories.'

'We make our own lives into stories, at the End of Time. We have the means. Would you not do the same, if you could?'

'Society demands that we do not.'

'Why so?'

'Perhaps because the stories would conflict, one with the other. There are so many of us – there.'

'Here,' he said, 'there are but two.'

'Our tenancy in this – this Eden – is tentative. Who knows when ...?'

'Logically, if we are torn away, then we shall be borne to the End of Time, not to 1896. And what is there, waiting, but Eden, too?'

'No, I should not call it that.'

They stared, now, eye to eye. The sea whispered. It was louder than their words.

He could not move, though he sought to go forward. Her stance held him off; it was the set of her chin, the slight lift of one shoulder.

'We could be alone, if we wished it.'

'There should be no choice, in Eden.'

'Then here, at least ...' His look was charged, it demanded; it implored.

'And take sin with us, out of Eden?'

'No sin, if by that you mean that which give your fellows pain. What of me?'

'We suffer. Both.' The sea seemed very loud, the voice faint as a wind through ferns. 'Love is cruel.'

'No!' His shout broke the silence. He laughed. 'That is nonsense! Fear is cruel! Fear alone!'

'Oh, I have so much of that!' She called out, lifting her face to the sky, and she began to laugh, even as he seized her, taking her hands in his, bending to kiss that cheek.

12

Tears striped her; she wiped them clear with her sleeve, and the kiss was forestalled. Instead she began to hum a tune, and she placed a hand on his shoulder, leaving her other hand in his. She dipped and led him in a step or two. 'Perhaps my fate is sealed,' she said. She smiled at him, a conspiracy of love and pain and some self-pity. 'Oh, come, Mr Carnelian, I shall teach you to dance. If this is Eden, let us enjoy it while we may!'

Brightening considerably, Jherek allowed her to lead him in the steps.

Soon he was laughing, a child in love and, for the moment, not the mature individual, the man whose command could conquer.

Disaster (if it was disaster) delayed, they pranced, beside the Palaeozoic seaside, an improvised polka.

But it was only delayed. Both were expectant, fulfillment, consummation, hovered. And Jherek sang a wordless song; within moments she would be his bride, his pride, his celebration.

The song was soon to die on his lips. They rounded a clump of flimsy vegetation, a pavement of yellow rock, and came to a sudden and astounded stop. Both glared, both felt vitality flow from them to be replaced by taut rage. Mrs Underwood, sighing, withdrew into the stiff velvet of her dress.

'We *are* fated,' she murmured. 'We *are*!'

They continued to glare at the unwitting back of the one who had frustrated their idyll. He remained unaware of their wrath, their presence.

The shirtsleeves and trousers rolled up to elbow and knee respectively, the bowler hat fixed firmly on the heavy head, the briar pipe between the lips, the newcomer was paddling contentedly in the amniotic ocean.

As they watched, he took a large white handkerchief from the pocket of his dark, serge trousers (waistcoat and jacket, shoes and socks, lay neat and incongruous on the beach behind), shook it out, tied a small knot at each corner, removed his hat and spread the handkerchief over

13

his cropped and balding scalp. This accomplished, he began to hum – 'Pom te pom, pom pom pom, te pom pom' – wading a little further through the shallow water, pausing to raise a red and goose-pimpled foot and to brush at two or three wheat-coloured trilobites which had begun to climb his leg.

'Funny little beggars,' he was heard to mutter, but did not seem to mind their curiosity.

Mrs Underwood was pale. 'How is it possible?' A vicious whisper. 'He has pursued us through Time!' With one hand, she unclenched the other. 'My respect for Scotland Yard, I suppose, increases ...'

Forgetting his private disappointment in favour of his social responsibilities (he had developed proprietorial feelings toward the Palaeozoic) Jherek called:

'Good afternoon, Inspector Springer.'

Mrs Underwood reached a hand for his arm, as if to forestall him, but too late. Inspector Springer, the almost seraphic expression fading to be replaced by his more familiar stern and professional mask, turned unwillingly.

Bowler forgotten in his left hand, he removed his pipe from his lips. He peered. He blinked. He heaved a sigh, fully the equal of their own most recent sighs. Happiness fled away.

'Good 'eavens!'

'Heavens, if you prefer.' Jherek welcomed correction, for he still studied the mores of the nineteenth century.

'I *thought* it was 'eaven.' Inspector Springer's slap at an exploring trilobite was less tolerant than before. 'But now I'm beginning to doubt it. More like 'ell ...' He remembered the presence of Mrs Underwood. He stared mournfully at a wet trouser leg. 'The other place, I mean.'

There was a tinge of pleased malice in her tone: 'You think yourself dead, Inspector Springer?'

'The deduction fitted the facts, madam.'

Not without dignity, he placed the bowler on top of the knotted handkerchief. He peered into the pipe and, satisfied that it had gone out, slipped it into a pocket. Her irony was wasted; he became a trifle more confidential.

'An 'eart-attack, I presumed, brought about by the stress of recent events. I was jest questioning them foreigners – the little anarchists with only one eye – or three, if you look at it another way – when it seemed to me they vanished clear away.' He cleared his throat, lowered his voice a fraction. 'Well, I turned to call me sergeant, felt a bit dizzy meself, and the next thing I knows, 'ere I am in 'eaven.' He seemed, then, to recall his previous relationship with the pair. He straightened, resentful. 'Or so I deduced until you turned up a minute ago.' He waded forward until he stood on glinting sand. He began to roll down his trousers. He spoke crisply. 'Well then,' he demanded, 'what is the explanation? Briefly, mind. Nothing fancy.'

'It is simple enough.' Jherek was glad to explain. 'We have been hurled through Time, that is all. To a pre-Dawn Age. That is, to a period before Man existed at all. Millions of years. The Upper or—?' He turned to Mrs Underwood for help.

'Probably the Lower Devonian,' she said. She was off-hand. 'The stranger confirmed it.'

'A warp in Time,' Jherek continued. 'In which you were caught, as we were. Admitting no large paradoxes, Time ejected us from your period. Doubtless, the Lat were so ejected. It was unfortunate that you were in the proximity ...'

Inspector Springer covered his ears, heading for his boots as if towards a haven. 'Oh, Gawd! Not again. It *is* 'ell! It *is*!'

'I am beginning to share your view, Inspector.' Mrs Underwood was more than cool. She turned on her heel and started to walk in the direction of the frond forest at the top of the beach. Normally her conscience would sharply rule out such obvious tricks, but she had been thwarted; she had become desperate – she gave Jherek the impression that he was to blame for Inspector Springer's arrival, as if, perhaps, by speaking of sin he had

15

called forth Satan into Eden.

Frozen, Jherek was trapped by the manoeuvre as neatly as any Victorian beloved. 'Amelia,' was all he could pipe.

She did not, of course, reply.

Inspector Springer had reached his boots. He sat down beside them; he pulled free, from one of them, a grey woollen sock. He addressed the sock as he tried to pull it over his damp foot. 'What I can't work out,' he mused, 'is whether I'm technically still on duty or not.'

Mrs Underwood had come to the frond forest. Determinedly she disappeared into the rustling depths. Jherek made up his mind to stumble in wretched pursuit. The host in him hesitated for only a second:

'Perhaps we'll see you again, Inspector?'

'Not if I —'

But the high-pitched scream interrupted both. A glance was exchanged. Inspector Springer forgot differences, obeyed instincts, leapt to his feet, hobbling after Jherek as he flung himself forward, racing for the source of the scream.

But already Mrs Underwood was flying from the forest, outrage and horror remoulding her beauty, stopping with a gasp when she saw salvation; mutely, she pointed back into the agitated foliage.

The fronds parted. A single eye glared out at them, its three pupils fixed steadily, perhaps lecherously, upon the panting form of Mrs Underwood.

'Mibix,' said a guttural, insinuating voice.

'Ferkit,' replied another.

CHAPTER THREE

A LOWER DEVONIAN TEA

Swaggering, in torn and mephitic striped pyjamas, a three foot high humanoid, with a bulbous nose, pear-shaped head, huge protuberant ears, facial whiskers, a silver dinner-fork in one hand and a silver dinner knife in the other, emerged from the ferns.

Jherek, too, had once worn the pyjamas of the Nursery; had suffered the regime of that robot survivor from the Late Multitude Cultures. He recognized Captain Mubbers, leader of the Lat brigand-musicians. He had seen him twice since the Nursery – at the Café Royal, and later, in custody together, at Scotland Yard.

Captain Mubbers grunted at Jherek with something like grudging neutrality, but when his three pupils focussed on Inspector Springer he uttered an unpleasant laugh.

Inspector Springer would accept no nonsense, even when five more Lat joined their leader and shared his amusement. 'In the name of Her Majesty the Queen,' he began. But he hesitated; he was off-guard.

'Ood ja shag ok gongong pish?' Captain Mubbers was contemptuous. 'Klixshat efang!'

Inspector Springer was used to this sort of thing; he

remained apparently impassive, saying ponderously:

'That's insulting behaviour to a police officer. You're doing yourself no good at all, my lad. The sooner you understand that English law ...' Abruptly, he was baffled. 'This still would be England, wouldn't it?' Mrs Underwood was enlisted.

'I'm not altogether sure, Inspector.' She spoke without sympathy, almost with relish. 'I haven't recognized anything.'

'It's a bit too warm for Bognor, certainly. I could be outside my jurisdiction.' Inspector Springer sensed escape. The notebook he had begun to extract from his back pocket was now returned. Beneath his disturbed moustache there appeared a strained grin. It was weak. He had lost the day to the Lat. He continued, lame. 'You think yourself lucky, my lad. If you ever set foot in the Metropolitan area again —'

'Hrunt!' Derisively, Captain Mubbers waved his remaining man forward. He came cautiously from the bushes, pupils a-dart for Springer's forces. And Jherek relaxed a fraction, knowing the Lat would be wary of decisive action until they were convinced the three were without allies.

Inspector Springer seemed ill at ease with his new and self-appointed diplomatic status. 'By the looks of it,' he told the Lat, 'we're all in the same boat. It's no time to be raking up old scores, lads. You can see the sense of that, surely?'

Questioningly, Captain Mubbers looked up at Jherek and Mrs Underwood. 'Kaprim ul shim mibix clom?' he asked, with a nod of his head in the policeman's direction.

Jherek shrugged. 'I'm inclined to agree with the inspector, Captain Mubbers.'

'Ferkit!' exclaimed one of the other Lat. 'Potkup mef rim chokkum! Shag ugga?' He started forward, brandishing a fish-fork marked with the prominent 'N' of the Café Royal.

'Thurk!' commanded Captain Mubbers. He leered unctuously at Mrs Underwood; he offered her an unwholesome bow. He took a step closer, murmuring: 'Dwap ker niknur, fazzy?'

'Really!' Mrs Underwood lost all her carefully restored composure. 'Mr Carnelian! Inspector Springer! How can such suggestions ...? Oh!'

'Kroofrudi.' Captain Mubbers was unrepentant. Significantly, he patted his elbow. 'Kwot-kwot?' He glanced back at the frond forest. 'Nizzle uk?'

Inspector Springer's sense of decency was offended. He listed forward, one boot still in his hand. 'Law or no law ...'

'Fwik hrunt!' spat Captain Mubbers. The others laughed, repeating the witticism to one another; but the policeman's objection had lowered the tension.

Mrs Underwood said firmly: 'They are probably hungry. We have some biscuits back at our camp. If we were to lead them there ...'

'At once,' said Jherek, and he began to walk. She linked her arm in his, an action which served to confuse both Jherek and Captain Mubbers.

Inspector Springer kept step with them. 'I must say, I could do with a nice Rich Tea!'

'I think I've eaten most of those.' Jherek was regretful. 'But there's a whole box of Fig Rolls.'

'Ho, ho!' Inspector Springer performed a cryptic wink. 'We'll let *them* 'ave the Fig Rolls, eh?'

Puzzled, but temporarily passive, the Lat trailed behind.

Relishing the delicate touch of her arm against his rib, Jherek wondered if a police inspector and seven aliens could constitute the 'society' Mrs Underwood claimed as the influence upon the 'morality' and 'conscience' thwarting the full expression of his love for her. He felt, in his heart, that she would so define the group. Resignation, once more, slid into the space so recently left by anticipation.

They reached the rock and the hamper; their home. Kettle in hand, he set off for the spring they had discovered. Mrs Underwood prepared the primus.

Alone for a moment, Jherek reflected that their provisions would soon expire, with eight fresh mouths to fill. He foresaw, indeed, a dispute in which the Lat would attempt to gain possession of the food. It would mean some relief, at least. He smiled. It might even mean a War.

A little later, when the primus stove had been pumped and lit and the kettle settled on its flame, he studied the Lat. It seemed to him that their attitude towards Mrs Underwood had altered a fraction since they had first seen her in the frond forest. They sat in a semi-circle on the sand, a short distance away from the rock in whose shadow the three humans crouched. Their manner, while still what she would probably have called 'insulting', was tinged with caution; perhaps awe; perhaps they were daunted by the easy way in which she had taken command of events. Could it be that she reminded them of that invulnerable old robot, Nurse? They had learned to fear Nurse. Certainly their position – cross-legged, hands on knees – recalled Nurse's demands upon her charges.

The kettle began to steam. Inspector Springer, with a courtly gesture to Mrs Underwood, reached for the handle. Accepting the metal tea-pot from his hostess, he poured on the water. The Lat, like witnesses at a religious ritual (for Inspector Springer certainly conveyed this mood – he the priest, Mrs Underwood the priestess) were grave and wary. Jherek, himself, shared some of their feelings as the ceremony advanced with formal grace.

There were three tin cups and a tin basin. These were laid out on the top of the hamper (which contained many such comforts). A can of milk was set beside them, and a box of sugar, with a spoon.

'A minute or two to let it brew,' intoned Inspector Springer. In an aside, he told Jherek: 'It's what I've been missing most of all.'

Jherek could not guess if he meant the tea itself or the ritual involved.

From a box at her side, Mrs Underwood made a selection of biscuits, arranging them in a pattern upon a tin plate.

And at length the tea was poured. The milk was added. The sugar was added.

Inspector Springer was the first to sip.

'Ah!' The sense of occasion remained. 'That's better, eh?'

Mrs Underwood handed the large bowl to Captain Mubbers. He sniffed it, blew at it, then sucked up half the contents in a single inhalation.

'Gurp?' he enquired.

'Tea,' she told him. 'I hope it's to your taste. We have nothing stronger.'

'Tee-ee!' Captain Mubbers, quick to mine innuendo from the least promising vein, glanced sidelong (with two of his pupils) at his companions. They sniggered. 'Kroof-rudi.' He held out the cup for more.

'That's for all of you to share,' she said firmly. She waved, to indicate his men. 'All of you.'

'Frit hrunti?' He seemed unwilling.

She took the bowl from him and gave it to the man next to him.

'Grotchit snirt.' Captain Mubbers snorted and touched his comrade's elbow with his own. 'Nootchoo?'

The Lat was amused. The tea burbled as he exploded with laughter.

Inspector Springer cleared his throat. Mrs Underwood averted her eyes. Jherek, feeling a need to extend some sort of friendship to the Lat, bubbled his tea and laughed with them.

'Not you, Mr Carnelian,' she said. 'You, surely, know better. Whatever else, you are not a savage.'

'They offend your morality?'

'Morality, no. Merely my sensibilities.'

'It strikes you as unaesthetic.'

'Your analysis is accurate.'

She had withdrawn from him again. He swallowed the stuff down. To him, it seemed crude, in taste and texture.

But he accepted her standard; to serve it, and to win her approval, was all he desired.

The biscuits, one by one, were consumed.

Inspector Springer was the first to finish; he withdrew a large white handkerchief from his pocket and dabbed at his moustache. He was thoughtful. He voiced Jherek's concern of a short while before:

'Of course,' he said, 'this grub isn't going to last for ever now, is it?'

'It will not last very long at all,' said Mrs Underwood.

'And the Lat will try to steal it,' added Jherek.

'They'll 'ave a job there.' Inspector Springer spoke with the quiet confidence of the professional protector of property. 'Being English, we're more fair-minded, and therefore we'll keep strict control of the supplies. Not, I suppose, that we can let them starve. We shall 'ave to eke 'em out – learn to live off the land. Fish and stuff.'

'Fish?' Mrs Underwood was uncertain. 'Are there fish?'

'Monsters!' he told her. ''Aven't you seen 'em? Sort of sharks, though a bit smaller. Catch one o' those beggars and we could eat for a fortnight. I'll put me mind to it.' He had brightened again and seemed to be enjoying the challenges offered by the Lower Devonian. 'I think I spotted a bit o' line in the 'amper. We could try using snails for bait.'

Captain Mubbers indicated that his bowl was empty.

'Crotchnuk,' he said ingratiatingly.

'No more,' she said firmly. 'Tea-time is over, Captain Mubbers.'

'Crotchnuk mibix?'

'All gone,' she said, as if to a child. She took the lid from the pot and showed him the sodden leaves. 'See?'

His hand was swift. It seized the pot. The other dived into the opening, scooping out the tea-leaves, cramming them into his mouth. 'Glop-pib!' he spluttered approvingly. 'Drexy glop-pib!'

Fatalistically, Mrs Underwood allowed him to complete his feast.

CHAPTER FOUR

A FRESH QUEST – ON THE TRAIL
OF THE HAMPER

'But, Inspector, you told us that the hamper could not be removed without bringing you instantly to wakefulness!' Mrs Amelia Underwood was within an ace of tapping her foot; there was a note to her voice which Jherek recognized.

Inspector Springer also recognized it. He blushed as he held up the wrist to which was attached a severed thong. 'I tied it to the 'amper,' he said lamely. 'They must o' cut it.'

'How long have you been asleep, Inspector?' Jherek asked.

''Ardly at all. A few winks 'ere, a few there. Nothin' to speak of.'

'They were hearty winks!' She drew in a sharp breath as she stared around her in the grey pre-dawn. 'Judging by your snores. I heard them all night.'

'Oh, come now, ma'am ...'

'They could be miles away,' said Jherek. 'You should see them run, when they want to. You did not sleep well either, Mrs Underwood?'

'Only the inspector, it seems, enjoyed a satisfying rest.'

She glared at the policeman. 'If you want your house burgled, tell the police you're going on holiday. That's what my brother always used to say.'

'That's 'ardly fair, ma'am ...' he began, but he knew he was on shaky ground. 'I took every precaution. But these foreigners – with their *knives* —' again he displayed the severed thong – 'well, 'ow can you anticipate ...?'

She inspected the surrounding sand, saying mournfully. '*Look* at all these footprints. Do you remember, Mr Carnelian, when we would rise in the morning and go down to the sea and there wouldn't be a mark on the beach? Not a sign of another soul! It's so *spoiled* now.' She was pointing. 'There – a fresh trail. Leading inland.'

Certainly, the ground was disturbed. Jherek detected the broad footprints of the departing Lat.

'They'll be carrying the 'amper,' offered Inspector Springer, 'so they'll be slowed down a bit.' He clutched his midriff. 'Ooh, I 'ate to start the day on an empty stomach.'

'That,' she said with satisfaction, 'is entirely your fault, Inspector!'

She led the way forward while Jherek and Inspector Springer, tugging on their coats, did their best to keep pace with her.

Even before they had entered a large stretch of frond-forest and were labouring uphill, Mrs Underwood's quick eye detecting a broken branch or a crushed leaf as signposts to the route of the thieves, the sun had risen, splendid and golden, and begun to beat its hottest. Inspector Springer made much use of his handkerchief on the back of his neck and his forehead, but Mrs Underwood would not let them pause.

The hill grew steeper. It was virtually sheer. Still she led; still she allowed them no rest. They panted – Jherek cheerfully and Inspector Springer with loud resentment. At two stages he was heard to breathe the word 'Women' in a desperate, incantatory fashion, and at a third he appended another word, in a voice which was entirely inaudible. Jherek, in contrast, was enjoying the exertion, the sense of adventure, though he had no belief that they could catch Captain Mubbers and his men.

She was a score of yards ahead of them, and higher. 'Nearly at the top,' she called.

Inspector Springer was not encouraged. He stopped, leaning against the stem of a fern which rose fifteen feet over his head and rustled as it took the weight of his bulky frame.

'It would be best,' Jherek said, passing him, 'if we were to remain as close together as possible. We could so easily become separated.'

'She's a bloomin' mad woman,' grunted the inspector. 'I knew it all along.' But he laboured after Jherek, even catching him up as he clambered over a fallen trunk which left a smear of green on the knees of his trousers. Jherek sniffed. 'Your smell! I wondered — I haven't quite smelt anything like it before? It *is* you. Very odd. Pleasant, I suppose ...'

'Gur!' said Inspector Springer.

Jherek sniffed again, but continued to climb, now using his hands and his feet, virtually on all fours. 'Certainly pungent ...'

'Cor! You cheeky little b —'

'Excelsior!' It was Mrs Underwood's voice, though she could no longer be seen. 'Oh, it's magnificent!'

Inspector Springer caught hold of Jherek's ankle. 'If you've any further personal comments, I'd be more than grateful if you'd keep them to yourself.'

'I'm sorry, Inspector.' Jherek tried to free his foot. He frowned. 'I certainly meant no offence. It's simply that such smells — perspiration, is it? — are uncommon at the End of Time. I love it. Really.'

'Ugh!' Inspector Springer let go of Jherek's foot. 'I 'ad you marked right from the start, too. Bloomin' cream puff. Café Royal — Oscar Wilde — should 'ave trusted me own judgement ...'

'I can see them!' Mrs Underwood's voice again. 'The

quarry's in sight!'

Jherek pressed past a low branch and saw her through the dappled fronds.

'Ouch!' said Inspector Springer from behind him. 'Cor! If I ever get back to London and if I ever lay 'ands on you ...'

The belligerence seemed to give him energy, enabling him, once more, to catch up. They arrived, shoulder to shoulder, to stand at Mrs Underwood's side. She was flushed. Her eyes shone. She pointed.

They stood on the edge of a cliff that was almost sheer, its sides dotted with clumps of vegetation. Some hundreds of feet below them the cliff levelled out to a broad, stony beach, touching the wide, placid waters of a creek whose brilliant blue, reflecting the sky, was in beautiful and harmonious contrast with the browns, greens and yellows of the flanking cliffs.

'It is simple,' she said, 'and it is magnificent! Look, Mr Carnelian! It goes on forever. It is the world! So much of it. All virgin. Not even a wild beast to disturb its vast serenity. Imagine what Mr Ruskin would say to all this. Switzerland cannot compare ...' She was smiling now at Jherek. 'Oh, Mr Carnelian – it *is* Eden. It is!'

'Hm,' said Inspector Springer. 'It's pretty enough scenery. But where's our little friends? You said—'

'There!'

Tiny figures could be seen on the beach. There was activity. They were at work.

'Making something, by the look of it,' murmured Inspector Springer. 'But what?'

'A boat, probably.' She spread an arm. 'You'll observe there is just a small area of beach – a sort of cove, really. The only way to continue is across the water. They will not turn back, for fear of our pursuit.'

'Aha!' Inspector Springer rubbed his hands together. 'So we've got 'em, ripe. We'll nab 'em before they can ever—'

'They are seven,' she reminded him. 'We are three. And

26

one of us a woman.'

'Yes,' he said. 'That's true.' He lifted his bowler between thumb and forefinger, scratching his head with his little finger. 'But we're bigger. And we 'ave the advantage of surprise. Surprise is often worth more than any amount of 'eavy artillery ...'

'So I gather from the *Boys' Own Paper*,' she said sourly. 'But I would give much, at this moment, for a single revolver.'

'Not allowed to carry them in the ordinary way, ma'am,' he said portentously. 'If we had received information ...'

'Oh, really, Inspector!' She was exasperated. 'Mr Carnelian? Have you any suggestions?'

'We might frighten them off, Mrs Underwood, long enough for us to regain the hamper.'

'And have them chase and overwhelm us? No. Captain Mubbers must be captured. With a hostage, we can hope to return to our camp and bargain with them. I had hoped to maintain civilized behaviour. However ...'

She inspected the cliff edge. 'They descended here. We shall do the same.'

'I've never 'ad much of an 'ead for 'eights.' Inspector Springer watched dubiously as she swung herself over the edge and, clinging to tufts of foliage and outcroppings of rock, began to climb downwards. Jherek, concerned for her safety, yet acknowledging her leadership, watched her carefully, then he followed her. Grumbling, Inspector Springer blundered in the rear. Little showers of stones and loose earth fell on Jherek's head.

The cliff was not so steep as Jherek had imagined, and the descent became noticeably easier after the first thirty feet so that at times they could stand upright and walk.

It seemed to Jherek that the Lat had seen them, for their activity became more frenetic. They were building a large raft, from the stems of the bigger ferns which grew near the water, using strips of their torn up pyjamas to hold the rather fleshy trunks together. Jherek knew little of such matters, but it seemed to him that the raft would quickly become water-logged and sink. He wondered if the Lat could swim. Certainly, he could not.

'Ah! We are too late!' Mrs Underwood began to let herself slide down the cliff, ripping her already tattered dress in several places, careless of modesty, as she saw Captain Mubbers order their hamper placed in the middle of the raft. The six Lat, under the command of their captain, lifted the raft and began to bear it towards the brackish waters of the creek.

Jherek, anxious to remain close to her, copied her example, and was soon sliding without control after her.

'Stop!' she cried, forgetting her plans to capture Captain Mubbers. 'We wish to bargain!'

Startled, perhaps, by the wild descent, the Lat began to run with their raft until they were up to their waists in water. Captain Mubbers jumped aboard. The raft tilted. He flung himself upon the hamper, to save it. The raft swung out at an angle and the Lat began to flounder after it, pulling themselves aboard as best they could, but two were left behind. Their shrieks could be heard by the human beings, who had almost reached the bottom of the cliff.

'Ferkit!'

'Kroofrudi!'

'Nukgnursh!'

Captain Mubbers and his men had left their paddles on the beach. With their hands, they tried to force the raft back towards the land.

'Quickly!' cried Mrs Underwood, a general still. 'Seize them. There are our hostages!'

The raft was now many yards from the shore, though Captain Mubbers seemed determined not to abandon his men.

Jherek and Inspector Springer waded into the shallows and grabbed at the two Lat, who were now almost up to their necks in the waters of the creek. They splashed; they tried to kick, but were gradually herded back to where Mrs Underwood, blazing and determined, awaited them (it was evident that they were much more nervous of Mrs Underwood than of those they recognized as her minions).

'Knuxfelp!' cried Captain Mubbers to his men. 'Groo hrunt bookra!' His voice grew fainter.

The two Lat reached the beach, dodged past Mrs Underwood, and began to make for the cliff. They were in a state of panic.

'Blett mibix gurp!' screamed one of the hysterical Lat as he fell over a stone. His comrade helped him to his feet, glaring behind him at the drifting raft. It was then that he suddenly transfixed – all three pupils focussed on the raft. He ignored Jherek and Inspector Springer as they ran up and laid hands on him. Jherek was the first to look back.

There was something in the water, besides the raft. A glittering green, insect-like body, moving very rapidly.

'Gawd!' breathed Inspector Springer. 'It must be over six feet long!'

Jherek glimpsed antennae, white-grey claws, spiny and savage, a rearing, curling tail, armed with brown tusks, paddle-shaped back legs, all leaping half-out of the thick waters, attacking the raft.

There were two loud snapping noises, close together, and the front claws had each grasped a Lat. They struggled and screamed. The tusky tail swung up and round, clubbing them unconscious. Then the gigantic scorpion (for it resembled nothing else) had returned to the depths, leaving debris behind, a bobbing wickerwork hamper, green pulpy logs to which the surviving Lat clung.

Jherek saw a trail in the distant water, near the middle of the creek. He knew that this must be another such beast; he waded forward, offering his arms to the desperate Lat and shouting:

'Oh, what a jolly adventure, after all! The Duke of Queens could not have arranged a more sensational display! Just think, Mrs Underwood – none of this was engineered. It is all happening spontaneously – quite naturally. The scorpions! Aren't they superbly sinister, sweet sister of the sphynx?'

'Mr Carnelian!' Her voice was more than urgent. 'Save yourself. More of the creatures come from all sides!'

It was true. The surrounding water was thick with gigantic scorpions. They converged.

Jherek drew Captain Mubbers and another Lat back to the shore. But a third was too slow. He had time to cry one last 'Ferkit!' before the claws contracted and the great tail thumped and he became a subject of contention between the scorpion who had caught him and those of the scorpion's comrades who were disappointed at their own lack of success.

Mrs Underwood reached his side. There was alarm and disapproval on her features. 'Mr Carnelian — you frightened me so. But your bravery ...'

He raised both eyebrows.

'It was superb,' she said. Her voice had softened, but only momentarily. She remembered the hamper. It was the only thing left afloat, and apparently was without interest for the scorpions, who continued to dispute the ownership of the rapidly disintegrating corpse which occasionally emerged above the surface of the creek. There was foam, and there was blood.

The hamper bobbed up and down in the eddy created by the warring water scorpions; it had almost reached the middle of the creek.

'We must follow its drift,' she said, 'and hope to catch up with it later. Is there a current? Inward or outward? Where is the sea?'

'We must watch,' said Jherek. 'With luck, we can plot its general course at least.'

Something fishy appeared above the surface near the hamper. A brown, glistening back, with fins, slid from view almost immediately.

'The sharks,' said Inspector Springer. 'I told you about them.'

The hamper, which made this world a true Eden, rose under the back of at least one large finny creature. It turned over.

'Oh!' cried Mrs Underwood.

They saw the hamper sink. They saw it rise again. The lid had swung open, but still it bobbed.

Quite suddenly, Mrs Underwood sat down on the shingle and began to cry. To Jherek, the sound diminished all those which still issued from that savage Lower Devonian creek. He went to her. He seated himself beside her and he put a slim arm around her lonely shoulders.

It was then that a small power-boat, its motor whining, rounded the headland. It contained two black-clad figures, one seated at the wheel, the other standing up with a boathook in its hands. The craft made purposefully for the hamper.

CHAPTER FIVE

AT THE TIME CENTRE

Mrs Underwood stopped crying and began to blink.

'It's getting to be like bloomin' Brighton,' said Inspector Springer disapprovingly. 'It seemed so unspoiled at first. What a racket that boat makes!'

'They have saved the hamper,' said she. The two figures were hauling it aboard. The boat was rocked by the squirming movements of the large fish. A few objects fell from the hamper. The two figures seemed abnormally anxious to recover the objects, taking great trouble to pursue and scoop up a tin mug which had gone adrift. This done, the boat headed in their direction.

Jherek had seen nothing quite like the costumes of the newcomers; though they bore some resemblance to certain kinds of garments sometimes worn by space-travellers; they were all of a piece, shining and black, pouched and quilted, belted with broad bands containing what were probably tools. They had tight-fitting helmets of the same material, with goggles and ear-pieces, and there were black gauntlets on their hands.

'I don't like the look of 'em,' muttered the inspector. 'Divers, ain't they?' He glanced back at the hills. 'They could be up to no good. Why 'aven't they showed themselves before?'

'Perhaps they didn't know we were here,' said Jherek reasonably.

'They're showing an uncommon interest in our 'amper. Could be the last we'll see of it.'

'They are almost upon us,' said Mrs Underwood quietly. 'Let us not judge them, or their motives, until we have spoken. Let us hope they have some English, or at worst French.'

The boat's bottom crunched on the shingle; the engine was cut off; the two passengers disembarked, pulling the little vessel clear of the water, removing the hamper and carrying it between them to where Mrs Underwood, Jherek Carnelian, Inspector Springer, Captain Mubbers and the three surviving Lat awaited them. Jherek noted that they were male and female, but of about the same height. Little of their faces could be seen above the high collars and below the goggles. When they were a couple of yards away they stopped and lowered the hamper. The female pushed back her goggles, revealing a heart-shaped face, large blue-grey eyes, as steady as Mrs Underwood's, and a full mouth.

It was unsurprising that Mrs Underwood took her for French.

'*Je vous remercie bien ...*' she began.

'Aha!' said the woman, without irony, 'You are English, then.'

'Some of us are,' said Inspector Springer heavily. 'These little ones are Latvians.'

'I am Mrs Persson. May I introduce Captain Bastable.' The man saluted; he raised his own goggles. His face was tanned and handsome; his blue eyes were pale.

'I am Mrs Underwood. This is Mr Carnelian, Inspector Springer, Captain Mubbers — I'm afraid I've no idea of the other names. They do not speak English. I believe they are space-travellers from the distant future. Are they not, Mr Carnelian?'

33

'The Lat,' he said. 'We were never entirely clear about their origins. But they did come in a space-ship. To the End of Time.'

'You are from the End of Time, sir?' Captain Bastable spoke in the light, clipped tones familiar to Jherek as being from the nineteenth century.

'I am.'

'Jherek Carnelian, of course,' said Mrs Persson. 'A friend of the Duke of Queens, are you not? And Lord Jagged?'

'You know them?' He was delighted.

'I know Lord Jagged slightly. Oh, I remember – you are in love with this lady, your – Amelia?'

'My Amelia!'

'I am not "your Amelia", Mr Carnelian,' she said firmly. And she became suspicious of Mrs Persson.

Mrs Persson was apologetic. 'You are from 1896. I was forgetting. You will forgive me, I hope, Mrs Underwood. I have heard so much about you. Your story is one of the greatest of our legends. I assure you, we are honoured to meet you in the flesh.'

Mrs Underwood frowned, guessing sarcasm, but there was none.

'You have heard —?'

'We are only a few, we gossip. We exchange experiences and tales, as travellers will, on the rare occasions when we meet. And the Centre, of course, is where we all congregate.'

The young man laughed. 'I don't think they're following you, Una.'

'I babble. You will be our guests?'

'You have a machine here?' said Mrs Underwood, hope dawning.

'We have a base. You have not heard of it? You are not yet members of the Guild, then?'

'Guild?' Mrs Underwood drew her eyebrows together. 'No.'

'The Guild of Temporal Adventurers,' explained Captain Bastable. 'The GTA?'

'I have never heard of it.'

'Neither have I,' said Jherek. 'Why do you have an association?'

Mrs Persson shrugged. 'Mainly so that we can exchange information. Information is of considerable help to those of us whom you could call "professional time-travellers".' She smiled self-deprecatingly. 'It is such a risky business, at best.'

'Indeed it is,' he agreed. 'We should love to accept your invitation. Should we not, Mrs Underwood?'

'Thank you, Mrs Persson.' Mrs Underwood was still not at ease, but she had control of her manners.

'We shall need to make two trips. I suggest, Oswald, that you take the Lat and Inspector Springer back with you and then return for us three.'

Captain Bastable nodded. 'Better check the hamper first. Just to be on the safe side.'

'Of course. Would you like to look, Mrs Underwood, and tell me if anything is missing?'

'It does not matter. I really think —'

'It is of utmost importance. If anything is lost from it, we shall search meticulously until it is found. We have instruments for detecting almost everything.'

She peered in. She sorted. 'Everything here, I think.'

'Fine. Time merely tolerates us, you know. We must not offend.'

Captain Bastable, the Lat and Inspector Springer, were already in their boat. The motor whined again. The water foamed. They were away.

Mrs Persson watched it disappear before turning back to Jherek and Mrs Underwood. 'A lovely day. You have been here some while?'

'About a week, I would say,' Mrs Underwood smoothed at her ruined dress.

'So long as one avoids the water, it can be very beautiful. Many come to the Lower Devonian simply for the rest. If it were not for the eurypterids — the water scorpions – it would be perfect. Of all Palaeozoic periods, I find it the nicest. And, of course, it is a particularly friendly age, permitting more anachronism than most. This is your first visit?'

'The first,' said Mrs Underwood. Her expression betrayed what propriety restrained her from stating, that she hoped it would be the last.

'It can be dull.' Mrs Persson acknowledged the implication. 'But if one wishes to relax, to re-plot one's course, take bearings – there are few better at this end of Time.' She yawned. 'Captain Bastable and I shall be glad to be on our way again, as soon as our caretaking duties are over and we are relieved. Another fortnight should see us back in some twentieth century or other.'

'You seem to suggest that there are more than one?' said Jherek. 'Do you mean that different methods of recording history apply, or —?'

'There are as many versions of history as there are dedicated time-travellers.' Mrs Persson smiled. 'The difficulty lies in remaining in a consistent cycle. If one cannot do so, then all sorts of shocks are likely – environmental readjustment becomes almost impossible – madness results. How many fashions in insanity, do you think, have been set by mentally disturbed temporal adventures? We shall never know!' She laughed. 'Captain Bastable, for instance, was an inadvertent traveller (it sometimes happens), and was on the borders of madness before we were able to rescue him. First one finds it is the future which does not correspond, and this is frightening enough, if you are not expecting it. But it is worse when you return – to discover that your past has changed. You two, I take it, are fixed to a single band. Count yourselves lucky, if you do not know what to expect of multiversal time-travelling.'

Jherek could barely grasp the import of her words and Mrs Underwood was lost completely, though she fumbled with the notion: 'You mean that time-traveller we met, who referred to Waterloo Circus, was not from my time at all, but one which corresponded ...?' She shook her head.

'You cannot mean it. My time no longer exists, be-cause ...?'

'Your time exists. Nothing ever perishes, Mrs Under-wood. Forgive me for saying so, but you seem singularly ill-prepared for temporal adventuring. How did you come to choose the Lower Devonian, for instance?'

'We did not choose it,' Jherek told her. 'We set off for the End of Time. Our ship was in rather poor condition. It deposited us here – although we were convinced we went forward.'

'Perhaps you did.'

'How can that be?'

'If you followed the cycle round, you arrived at the end and continued on to the beginning.'

'Time is cyclic, then?'

'It can be.' She smiled. 'There are spirals, too, as it were. None of us understands it very well, Mr Carnelian. We pool what information we have. We have been able to create some basic methods of protecting ourselves. But few can hope to understand very much about the nature of Time, because that nature does not appear to be constant. The Chronon Theory, for instance, which was very popu-lar in certain cultures, has been largely discredited – yet seems to apply in societies which accept the theory. Your own Morphail Theory has much to recommend it, al-though it does not allow for the permutations and com-plications. It suggests that Time has, as it were, only one dimension – as if Space had only one. You follow me, Mr Carnelian?'

'To some extent.'

She smiled. 'And "to some extent" is all I follow my-self. One thing the Guild always tells new members – "There are no experts where Time is concerned". All we seek to do is to survive, to explore, to make occasional discoveries. Yet there is a particular theory which suggests that with every one discovery we make about Time, we create two new mysteries. Time can never be codified, as Space can be, because our very thoughts, our information

37

about it, our actions based on that information, all contribute to extend the boundaries, to produce new anomalies, new aspects of Time's nature. Do I become too abstract? If so, it is because I discuss something which is numinous – unknowable – perhaps truly metaphysical. Time is a dream – or a nightmare – from which there is never any waking. We who travel in Time are dreamers who occasionally share a common experience. To retain one's identity, to retain some sense of meaning in one's own life, that is all the time-traveller can hope for – it is why the Guild exists. You are lucky that you are not adrift in the multiverse, as Captain Bastable was, for you can become like a drowning man who refuses to float, but flounders – and every wave which you set up in the Sea of Time has a habit of becoming a whole ocean in its own right.'

Mrs Underwood had listened, but she was disturbed. She lifted the lid of the hamper and opened an air-tight tin, offering Mrs Persson a brandy-snap.

They munched.

'Delicious,' said Mrs Persson. 'After the twentieth, the nineteenth century has always been my favourite.'

'From what century are you originally?' Jherek asked, to pass the time.

'The twentieth – mid-twentieth. I have a fair bit to do with that ancestor of yours. And his sister, of course. One of my best friends.' She saw that he was puzzled. 'You don't know him? Strange. Yet, Jagged – your genes ...' She shrugged.

He was, however, eager. Here could be the answer he had sought from Jagged.

'Jagged has refused to be frank with me,' he told her, 'on that very subject. I would be grateful if you could enlighten me. He has promised to do so, on our return.'

But she was biting her lip, as if she had inadvertently betrayed a confidence. 'I can't,' she said. 'He must have reasons – I could not speak without first having his permission ...'

'But there is a motive,' said Mrs Underwood sharply. 'It seems that he deliberately brought us together. We have had more than a hint – that he could be engineering some of our misfortunes ...'

'And saving us from others,' Jherek pointed out, to be fair. 'He insists disinterest, yet I am certain ...'

'I cannot help you speculate,' said Mrs Persson. 'Here comes Captain Bastable with the boat.'

The small vessel was bouncing rapidly towards them, its engine shrieking, the water foaming white in its wake. Bastable made it turn, just before it struck the beach, and cut off the engine. 'Do you mind getting a bit wet? There are no scorpions about.'

They waded to the boat and pulled themselves aboard after dumping the hamper into the bottom. Mrs Underwood scanned the water. 'I had no idea creatures of that size existed ... Dinosaurs, perhaps, but not insects – I know they are not really insects, but ...'

'They won't survive,' said Captain Bastable as he brought the engine to life again. 'Eventually the fish will wipe them out. They're growing larger all the time, those fish. A million years will see quite a few changes in this creek.' He smiled. 'It's up to us to ensure we make none ourselves.' He pointed back at the water. 'We don't leave a trace of oil behind which isn't detected and cleaned up by one of our other machines.'

'And that is how you resist the Morphail Effect,' said Jherek.

'We don't use that name for it,' interjected Mrs Persson, 'but, yes – Time allows us to remain here as long as there are no permanent anachronisms. And that includes traces which might be detected by future investigators and prove anachronistic. It is why we were so eager to rescue that tin cup. All our equipment is of highly perishable material. It serves us, but would not survive in any form after about a century. Our existence is tentative – we could be hurled out of this age at any moment and find ourselves not only

39

separated, perhaps for ever, but in an environment incapable, even in its essentials, of supporting human life.'

'You run great risks, it seems,' said Mrs Underwood. 'Why?'

Mrs Persson laughed. 'One gets a taste for it. But, then, you know that yourself.'

The creek began to narrow, between lichen-covered banks, and, at the far end, a wooden jetty could be seen. There were two other boats moored beside it. Behind the jetty, in the shadow of thick foliage, was a dark mass, manmade.

A fair-haired youth, wearing an identical suit to those worn by Mrs Persson and Captain Bastable, took the mooring rope Mrs Persson flung to him. He nodded cheerfully to Jherek and Mrs Underwood as they jumped onto the jetty. 'Your friends are already inside,' he said.

The four of them walked over lichen-strewn rock towards the black, featureless walls ahead; these were tall and curved inward and they had a warm, rubbery smell. Mrs Persson took off her helmet and shook out her short dark hair; she had a pleasant, boyish look. Her movements were graceful as she touched the wall in two places, making a section slide back to admit them. They stepped inside.

There were several box-shaped buildings in the compound, some quite large. Mrs Persson led them towards the largest. There was little daylight, but a continuous strip of artificial lighting ran the entire circumference of the wall. The ground was covered in the same slightly yielding black material and Jherek had the impression that the entire camp could be folded in on itself within a few seconds and transported as a single unit. He imagined it as some large time-ship, for it bore certain resemblances to the machine in which he had originally travelled to the nineteenth century.

Captain Bastable stood to one side of the entrance allowing first Mrs Persson and then Mrs Underwood to enter. Jherek was next. Here were panels of instruments, screens, winking indicators, all of the primitive, fascinating kind which Jherek associated with the remote past.

'It's perfect,' he said. 'You've made it blend so well with the environment.'

'Thank you.' Mrs Persson's smile was for herself. 'The Guild stores all its information here. We can also also detect the movements of time-vessels along the megaflow, as it's sometimes termed. We did not, incidentally, detect yours. Instead there was a sort of rupture, quickly healed. You did not come in a ship?'

'Yes. It's somewhere on the beach where we left it, I think.'

'We haven't found it.'

Captain Bastable unzipped his overalls. Underneath them he wore a simple grey military uniform. 'Perhaps it was on automatic return,' he suggested. 'Or if it was malfunctioning, it could have continued on, moving at random, and be anywhere by now.'

'The machine was working badly,' Mrs Underwood informed him. 'We should not, for instance, be here at all. I would be more than grateful, Captain Bastable, if you could find some means of returning us – at least myself – to the nineteenth century.'

'That wouldn't be difficult,' he said, 'but whether you'd stay there or not is another matter. Once a time-traveller always a time-traveller, you know. It's our fate, isn't it?'

'I had no idea ...'

Mrs Persson put a hand on Mrs Underwood's shoulder. 'There are some of us who find it easier to remain in certain ages than others – and there are ages, closer to the beginnings or the ends of Time, which rarely reject those who wish to settle. Genes, I gather, have a little to do with it. But that is Jagged's speciality and he has doubtless bored you as much as he has bored us with his speculations.'

'Never!' Jherek was eager.

Mrs Persson pursed her lips. 'Perhaps you would care

for some coffee,' she said.

Jherek turned to Mrs Underwood. He knew she would be pleased. 'Isn't that splendid, dear Mrs Underwood. They have a stall here. Now you must really feel at home!'

CHAPTER SIX

DISCUSSIONS AND DECISIONS

Captain Mubbers and his men were sitting in a line on a kind of padded bench; they were cross-legged and tried to hide their knees and elbows, exposed since they had destroyed their pyjamas; all were blushing a peculiar plum colour and averted their eyes when the party containing Mrs Persson and Mrs Underwood entered the room. Inspector Springer sat by himself in a sort of globular chair which brought his knees close to his face; he tried to sip from a paper cup, tried to rise when the ladies came in, succeeded in spilling the coffee on his serge trousers; his grumble was half-protest, half-apology; he subsided again. Captain Bastable approached a black machine, marked with letters of the alphabet. 'Milk and sugar?' he asked Mrs Underwood.

'Thank you, Captain Bastable.'

'Mr Carnelian?' Captain Bastable pressed some of the letters. 'For you?'

'I'll have the same, please.' Jherek looked around the small relaxation room. 'It's not like the stalls they have in London, is it, Captain Bastable?'

'Stalls?'

'Mr Carnelian means coffee stalls,' explained Mrs Underwood. 'I think it's his only experience of drinking coffee, you see.'

'It is drunk elsewhere?'

'As is tea,' she said.

'How crude it is, my understanding of your subtle age.' He accepted a paper cup from Captain Bastable, who had already handed Mrs Underwood her own. He sipped conscientiously, expectantly.

Perhaps they noticed his expression of disappointment. 'Would you prefer tea, Mr Carnelian?' asked Mrs Persson. 'Or lemonade? Or soup?'

He shook his head, but the smile was weak. 'I'll forgo fresh experience for the moment. There are so many new impressions to assimilate. Of course, I know that this must seem familiar and dull to you – but to me it is marvellous. The chase! The scorpions! And now these huts!' He glanced towards the Lat. 'The other three are not, then, back yet?'

'The others ...?' Captain Bastable was puzzled.

'He means the ones the scorpions devoured,' Mrs Underwood began. 'He believes ...'

'That they will be reconstituted!' Mrs Persson brightened. 'Of course. There is no death, as such, at the End of Time.' She said apologetically to Jherek: 'I am afraid we lack the necessary technology to restore the Lat to life, Mr Carnelian. Besides, we do not possess the skills. If Miss Brunner or one of her people were on duty during this term – but, no, even then it would not be possible. You must regard your Lat as lost forever, I fear. As it is, you can take consolation that they have probably poisoned a few scorpions. Happily, there being so many scorpions, the balance of nature is not noticeably changed, and thus we retain our roots in the Lower Devonian.'

'Poor Captain Mubbers,' said Jherek. 'He tries so hard and is forever failing in his schemes. Perhaps we could arrange some charade or other – in which he is monumentally successful. It would do his morale so much good.

Is there something he could steal, Captain Bastable? Or someone he could rape?'

'Not here, I'm afraid.' But Captain Bastable blushed as he controlled his voice, causing Mrs Persson to smile and say, 'We are not very well equipped for the amusement of space-travellers, I regret, Mr Carnelian. But we shall try to get them back to their original age – your age – as near to their ship as possible. They'll soon be pillaging and raping again with gusto!'

Captain Bastable cleared his throat. Mrs Underwood studied a cushion.

Mrs Persson said: 'I forgot myself. Captain Bastable, by the way, Mrs Underwood, is almost a contemporary of yours. He is from 1901. It *is* 1901, isn't it, Oswald?'

He nodded, fingering his cuff. 'Thereabouts.'

'What puzzles me, more than anything,' continued Mrs Persson, 'is how so many people arrived here at the same time. The heaviest traffic in my experience. And two parties without machines of any kind. What a shame we can't speak to the Lat.'

'We could, if we wished,' said Jherek.

'You know their language?'

'Simpler. I have a translation pill, still. I offered them before, but no one seemed interested. At the Café Royal. Do you remember, Inspector?'

Inspector Springer was as sullen as Captain Mubbers. He seemed to have lost interest in the conversation. Occasionally a peculiar, self-pitying grunt would escape his throat.

'I know the pills,' said Mrs Persson. 'Are they independent of your cities?'

'Oh, quite. I've used them everywhere. They undertake a specific kind of engineering, I gather, on those parts of the brain dealing with language. The pill itself contains all sorts of ingredients – but entirely biological, I'm sure. See how well I speak *your* language!'

Mrs Persson turned her eyes upon the Lat. 'Could they give us any more information than Inspector Springer?'

'Probably not,' said Jherek. 'They were all ejected at about the same time.'

'I think we'll keep the pill, therefore, for emergencies.'

'Forgive me,' said Mrs Underwood, 'if I seem insistent, but I should like to know our chances of returning to our own periods of history.'

'Very poor, in your own case, Mrs Underwood,' said Captain Bastable. 'I speak from experience. You have a choice – inhabit some period of your future, or "return" to a present which could be radically changed, virtually unrecognizable. Our instruments have been picking up all kinds of disruptions, fluctuations, random eddies on the megaflow which suggest that heavier than usual distortions and re-creations are occurring. The multiversal planes are moving into some sort of conjunction —'

'It's the Conjunction of the Million Spheres,' said Mrs Persson. 'You've heard of it?'

Jherek and Mrs Underwood shook their heads.

'There's a theory that the conjunction comes when too much random activity occurs in the multiverse. It suggests that the multiverse is, in fact, finite – that it can only sustain so many continua – and when the maximum number of continua is attained, a complete re-organization takes place. The multiverse puts its house in order, as it were.' Mrs Persson began to leave the room. 'Would you care to see some of our operations?'

Inspector Springer continued to sulk and the Lat were still far too embarrassed to move, so Amelia Underwood and Jherek Carnelian followed their hosts down a short connecting tunnel and into a room filled with particularly large screens on which brilliantly coloured display models shifted through three dimensions. The most remarkable was an eight-arrowed wheel, constantly altering its size and shape. A short, swarthy, bearded man sat at the console below this screen; occasionally he would extend a moody finger and make an adjustment.

'Good evening, Sergeant Glogauer.' Captain Bastable

46

bent over the bearded man's shoulder and stared at the instruments. 'Any changes?'

'Chronoflows three, four and six are showing considerable abnormal activity,' said the sergeant. 'It corresponds with Faustaff's information, but it contradicts his automatic reconstitution theory. Look at number five prong!' he pointed to the screen. 'And that's only measuring crude. We can't plot the paradox factors on this machine – not that there would be any point in trying at the rate they're multiplying. That kind of proliferation is going on everywhere. It's a wonder *we're* not affected by it. Elsewhere, things are fairly quiescent at present, but there's a lot more activity than I'd like. I'd propose a general warning call – get every Guild member back to sphere, place and century of origin. That might help stabilization. Unless it's got nothing at all to do with us.'

'It's too late to know,' said Mrs Persson. 'I still hold with the reaction theory on the Conjunction, but where it leaves us – how we'll be affected – is anyone's guess.' She shrugged and was cheerful. 'I suppose it helps to believe in reincarnation.'

'It's the sense of insecurity that I mind,' said Glogauer.

Jherek made a contribution. 'They're very pretty. It reminds me of some of the things the rotting cities still do.'

Mrs Persson turned back from where she was inspecting a screen. 'Your cities, Mr Carnelian, are almost as bewildering as Time itself.'

Jherek agreed. 'They are almost as old, I suppose.'

Captain Bastable was amused. 'It suggests that Time approaches senility. It's an attractive metaphor.'

'We can do without metaphors, I should have thought,' Sergeant Glogauer told him severely.

'It's all we have.' Captain Bastable permitted himself a small yawn. 'What would be the chances of getting Mrs Underwood and Mr Carnelian here back to the nineteenth century?'

'Standard line?'

Captain Bastable nodded.

'Almost zero, at present. If they didn't mind waiting ...'

'We are anxious to leave.' Mrs Underwood spoke for them both.

'What about the End of Time?' Captain Bastable asked Glogauer.

'Indigenous? Point of departure?'

'More or less.'

The sergeant frowned, studying surrounding screens. 'Pretty good.'

'Would that suit you?' Captain Bastable turned to his guests.

'It was where we were heading for, originally,' Jherek said.

'Then we'll try to do that.'

'And Inspector Springer?' Mrs Underwood's conscience made her speak. 'And the Lat?'

'I think we'll try to deal with them separately – they arrived separately, after all.'

Una Persson rubbed her eyes. 'If there were any means of contacting Jagged, Oswald. We could confer.'

'There is every chance he has returned to the End of Time,' Jherek told her. 'I would willingly bear a message.'

'Yes,' she said. 'Perhaps we will do that. Very well. I suggest you sleep now, after you've had something to eat. We'll make the preparations. If everything goes properly, you should be able to leave by morning. I'll see what the power situation is like. We're a bit limited, of course. Essentially this is only an observation post and a liaison point for Guild members. We've very little spare equipment or energy. But we'll do what we can.'

Leaving the charting room, Captain Bastable offered Mrs Underwood his arm. She took it.

'I suppose this all seems a bit prosaic to you,' he said. 'After the wonders of the End of Time, I mean.'

'Scarcely that,' she murmured. 'But I do find it rather confusing. My life seemed so settled in Bromley, just a few months ago. The strain ...'

'You *are* looking drawn, dear Amelia,' said Jherek from behind them. He was disturbed by Captain Bastable's attentions.

She ignored him. 'All this moving about in Time cannot be healthy,' she said. 'I admire anyone who can appear as phlegmatic as you, Captain.'

'One becomes used to it, you know.' He patted the hand which enfolded his arm. 'But you are bearing up absolutely wonderfully, Mrs Underwood, if this is your first trip to the Palaeozoic.'

She was flattered. 'I have my consolations,' she said. 'My prayers and so on. And my Wheldrake. Are you familiar with the poems of Wheldrake, Captain Bastable?'

'When a boy, they were all I read. He can be very apt. I follow you.'

She lifted her head and, as they moved along that black, yielding corridor, she began to speak in slow, rounded tones:

> For once I looked on worlds sublime,
>   And knew pure Beauty, free from Time,
>   Knew unchained Joy, untempered Hope;
>   And coward, then, I fled!

Captain Bastable had been speaking the same words beneath his breath. 'Exactly!' he said, adding:

> Detected now beneath the organ's note,
>   The organ's groan, the bellows' whine;
>   And what the Sun made splendid,
>   Bereft of Sun is merely fine!

Listening, Jherek Carnelian felt a peculiar and unusual sensation. He had the impulse to separate them, to interrupt, to seize her and to carry her away from this handsome Victorian officer, this contemporary who knew so much better than did Jherek how to please her, to comfort her. He was baffled.

49

He heard Mrs Persson say: 'I do hope our arrangements suit you, Mr Carnelian. Is your mind more at ease?'

He spoke vaguely. 'No,' he said, 'it is not. I believe I must be "unhappy".'

CHAPTER SEVEN

EN ROUTE FOR THE END OF TIME

'The capsule has no power of its own,' Una Persson explained. Morning light filtered through the opening in the wall above them as the four stood together in the Time Centre's compound and inspected the rectangular object, just large enough for two people and resembling, as Mrs Underwood had earlier remarked, nothing so much as a sedan chair. 'We shall control it from here. It is actually safer than any other kind of machine, for we can study the megaflow and avoid major ruptures. We shall keep you on course, never fear.'

'And be sure to remind Lord Jagged that we should be glad of his advice,' added Captain Bastable. He kissed Mrs Underwood's hand. 'It has been a very great pleasure, ma'am.' He saluted.

'It has been a pleasure for me to meet a gentleman,' she replied, 'I thank you, sir, for your kindness.'

'Time we were aboard, eh?' Jherek's joviality was of the false and insistent sort.

Una Persson seemed to be enjoying some private glee. She hugged one of Oswald Bastable's arms and whispered in his ear. He blushed.

Jherek climbed into his side of the box. 'If there's anything I can send you from the End of Time, let me know,' he called. 'We must try to keep in touch.'

'Indeed,' she said. 'In the circumstances, all we time-travellers have is one another. Ask Jagged about the Guild.'

'I think Mr Carnelian has had his fill of adventuring through time, Mrs Persson.' Amelia Underwood was smiling and her attitude towards Jherek had something possessive about it, so that Jherek was bewildered even more.

'Sometimes, once we have embarked upon the exercise, we are not allowed to stop,' Una Persson said. 'I mention it, only. But I hope you are successful in settling, if that is what you wish. Some would have it that Time creates the human condition, you know – that, and nothing else.'

They had begun to shout, now that a loud thrumming filled the air.

'We had best stand clear,' said Captain Bastable. 'Occasionally there is a shock wave. The vacuum, you know.' He guided Mrs Persson towards the largest of the black huts. 'The capsule finds its own level. You have nothing to fear on that score. You won't be drowned, or burned, or compressed.'

Jherek watched them retreat. The thrumming grew louder and louder. His back pressed against Mrs Underwood's. He turned to ask her if she were comfortable but before he could speak a stillness fell and there was complete silence. His head felt suddenly light. He looked to Mrs Persson and Captain Bastable for an answer, but they were gone and only a shadowy, flickering ghost of the black wall could be seen. Finally this, too, disappeared and foliage replaced it. Something huge and heavy and alive moved towards them, passed through them, it seemed, and was gone. Heat and cold became extreme, seemed one. Hundreds of colours came and went, but were pale, washed out, rainy. There was dampness in the air he breathed; little tremors of pain ran through him but were past almost before his brain could signal their presence.

Booming, echoing sounds – slow sounds, deep and sluggish – blossomed in his ears. He swung up and down, he swung sideways, always as if the capsule were suspended from a wire, like a pendulum. He could feel her warm body pressed to his shoulders, but he could not hear her voice and he could not turn to see her, for every movement took infinity to consider and perform, and he appeared to weigh tons, as though his mass spread through miles of space and years of time. The capsule tilted forward, but he did not fall from his seat; something pressed him in, securing him: grey waves washed him; red rays rolled from toe to head. The chair began to spin. He heard his own name, or something very like it, being called by a high, mocking voice. Words piped at him; all the words of his life.

He breathed in and it was as if Niagara engulfed him. He breathed out; Vesuvius gave voice.

Scales slipped by against his cheek and fur filled his nostrils and flesh throbbed close to his lips, and fine wings fluttered, great winds blew; he was drenched by a salty rain (he became the History of Man, he became a thousand warm-blooded beasts, he knew unbearable tranquillity). He became pure pain and was the universe, the big slow-dancing stars. His body began to sing.

In the distance:

'*My dear – my dear – my dearest dear ...*'

His eyes had shut. He opened them.

'My dear!'

Was it Amelia?

But, no – he could move – he could turn and see that she was slumped forward, insensible. Still the pale colours swam. They cleared.

Green oak trees surrounded a grassy glade; cool sunlight touched the leaves.

He heard a sound. She had tumbled from the capsule and lay stretched, face-forward, upon the ground. He climbed from his seat, his legs trembling, and went to her, even as the capsule made a wrenching noise and was gone.

'Amelia!' He touched soft hair, stroked the lovely neck, kissed the linen exposed by the torn velvet of her sleeve. 'Oh, Amelia!'

Her voice was muffled. 'Even these circumstances, Mr Carnelian, do not entitle you to liberties. I am not unconscious.' She moved her head so that her steady grey eyes could see him. 'Merely faint. Perhaps a trifle stunned. Where are we?'

'Almost certainly at End of Time. These trees are of familiar workmanship.' He helped her to her feet. 'I think it is where we originally came across the Lat. It would be logical to return me here, for Nurse's sanctuary is not far distant.' He had already recounted his adventures to her. 'The Lat spaceship is probably also nearby.'

She became nervous. 'Should we not seek out your friends?'

'If they have returned. Remember, the last we saw of them was in London, 1896. They vanished – but did they return? Our destinations were the same. Almost certainly the Morphail Effect sent them home – but we know that Brannart's theories do not apply to all the phenomena associated with Time.'

'We'll not be served by further speculation,' she pointed out. 'You have your power-rings, still?'

He was impressed by her sense. 'Of course!' He stroked a ruby, turning three of the oaks into a larger version of the power-boat of the Palaeozoic, but translucent, of jade. 'My ranch awaits us – rest or roister, as we will!' He bowed low as, with a set expression upon her beautiful features, she advanced towards the boat. He brought up the rear. 'You do not think the jewelled propeller vulgar?' He was eager for her praise. 'It seemed a refinement.'

'It is lovely,' said she, distantly. With considerable dignity, she entered the vessel. There were benches, quilted with cloth-of-gold. She chose one near the centre of the craft. Joining her, he lounged in the prow. A wave of a hand and the boat began to rise. He laughed. He was his old self again. He was Jherek Carnelian, the son of a

54

woman, the darling of his world, and his love was with him.

'At last,' he cried, 'our aggravations and adventures are concluded. The road has been a weary one, and long, yet at its end what shall we find but our own little cottage complete with cat and kettle, cream, crumpets, cranberries, kippers, cauliflower, crackers, custard, kedgeree for tea, sweet, my dear Amelia, sweet tranquillity! Oh, you shall be happy. You shall!'

Stiffly though she sat, she seemed more amused than insulted. She seemed pleased to recognize the landscapes streaming by below, and she did not chide him for his use of her Christian name, nor for his suggestions which were, of course, improper.

'I knew it!' he sang. 'You have learned to love the End of Time.'

'It does have certain attractions,' she admitted, 'after the Lower Devonian.'

CHAPTER EIGHT

ALL TRAVELLERS RETURNED: A
CELEBRATION

The jade air-car reached the ranch and hovered. 'You see,'
said Jherek, 'it is almost exactly as you last saw it, before
you were torn away from me and tumbled back through
Time. It retains all the features you proposed, familiar
comforts of your own dear Dawn Age. You will be happy,
Amelia. And anything else you wish, it shall be yours. Remember – my knowledge of your needs, your age, is much
more sophisticated now. You will not find me the náive
who courted you so long, it seems, ago!'

'It is the same,' she said, and her voice was wistful, 'but
we are not.'

'I am more mature,' he agreed, 'a better mate.'

'Ah!' She smiled.

He sensed ambiguity. 'You do not love another? Captain Bastable ...'

She became wicked. 'He is a gentleman of excellent
manners. And his bearing – so soldierly ...' But her eyes
laughed at her words. 'A match any mother would approve. Were I not already married, I should be the envy
of Bromley – but I am married, of course, to Mr Underwood.'

Jherek made the car spiral down towards the rose-gardens and the rockeries he had created for her, and he said with some nervousness: 'He said he would – what? – "divest" you!'

'Divorce. I should have to appear in court – millions of years from here. It seems,' (turning so that he should not see her face), 'that I shall never be free.'

'Free? Free? No woman was ever more free. Here is humanity triumphant – Nature conquered – all desires may be fulfilled – of enemies, none. You can live as you please. I shall serve you. Your whims shall be mine, dearest Amelia!'

'But my conscience,' she said. 'Can I be free from that?'

His face fell. 'Oh, yes, of course, your conscience. I was forgetting it.' The car sank to the lawn. 'You did not leave it, then, behind? In Eden?'

'There? I had greater need of it, did I not?'

'I thought you suggested otherwise.'

'Then condemn me as fickle. All women are so.'

'You contradict yourself, but apparently without relish.'

'Ha!' She was the first to leave the craft. 'You refuse to accuse me, Mr Carnelian? You will not play the game? The old game?'

'I did not know there was a game, Amelia. You are disturbed? The set of your shoulders reveals it. I am confused.'

She rounded on him, but her face was softening. Her eyes held disbelief, fast fading. 'You do not try me for my femininity? I am not accused of womanliness?'

'All this is meaningless.'

'Then perhaps there is a degree of freedom here, at the End of Time, mixed with all your cruelties.'

'Cruelties?'

'You keep slaves. Casually, you destroy anything which bores you. Have you no consideration for these time-travellers you capture? Was I not captured so – and put in a menagerie? And Yusharisp – bartered for me. Even in my age such barbarities are banished!'

He accepted her admonishment. He bowed his head. 'Then you must teach me what is best,' he said. 'Is this "morality"?'

She was overwhelmed, suddenly, by the enormity of her responsibility. Was it salvation she brought to Paradise, or was it merely guilt? She hesitated. 'We shall discuss it, in the fullness of time,' she told him.

They set foot upon the crazy paving of the path, between low yew-hedges. The ranch – Gothic red brick reproduction of her ideal Bromley villa – awaited them. A parrot or two perched on chimneys and gables; they seemed to flute a welcome.

'It is as you left it,' he said. He was proud. 'But, elsewhere, I have built for you a "London", so that you shall not be homesick. It still pleases you, the ranch?'

'It is as I remember it.'

He understood that he read disappointment in her tone. 'You compare it now with the original, I suppose.'

'It has the essentials of the original.'

'But remains a "mere copy", eh? Show me . . .'

She had reached the porch, ran a hand over the painted timber, fondled a still-blooming rose (for none had faded since she had vanished), touched the flower to her nose. 'It has been so long,' she murmured. 'I needed familiarity, then.'

'You do not need it now?'

'Ah, yes. I am human. I am a woman. But perhaps there are other things which come to mean more. I felt, in those days, that I was in hell – tormented, mocked, abused – in the company of the mad. I had no perspective.'

He opened the door, with its stained-glass panels. Potted plants, pictures, carpets of Persian design, dark paint, were revealed in the gloom of the entrance hall.

'If there are additions . . .' he began.

'Additions!' She was half amused. She inspected the what-nots and the aspidistras with a disdainful eye. 'No more, I think.'

'Too cluttered, now?' He closed the door and caused

light to blossom.

'The house could be bigger. More windows, perhaps. More sun. More air.'

He smiled. 'I could remove the roof.'

'You could, indeed!' She sniffed. 'Yet it is not as musty as I supposed it would be. How long is it since you departed it?'

'That's difficult. We can only find out by conferring with our friends. They will know. My range of scents has much improved since I visited 1896. I agree that it was an area in which I was weak. But my palette is altogether enriched.'

'Oh, this will do, Mr Carnelian. For the present, at any rate.'

'You cannot voice your disquiet?'

She turned kind eyes on him. 'You possess a sensitivity often denied by your behaviour.'

'I love you,' he said simply. 'I live for you.'

She coloured. 'My rooms are as I left them? My wardrobe remains intact?'

'Everything is there.'

'Then I will rejoin you for lunch.' She began to mount the stairs.

'It will be ready for you,' he promised. He went into the front parlour, staring around him at this Collins Avenue of the mind, peering through the windows at the gentle green hills, the mechanical cows and sheep with their mechanical cow-boys and shepherds, all perfectly reproduced to make her feel at home. He admitted to himself that her response had bewildered him. It was almost as if she had lost her taste for her own preferred environment. He sighed. It had seemed so much easier, when her ideas were definite. Now that she herself found them difficult to define, he was at a loss. Antimacassars, horsehair furniture, red, black and yellow carpets of geometrical pattern, framed photographs, thick-leaved plants, the harmonium with which she had eased her heart, all now (because she seemed to have disapproved) accused him as a brute who

59

could never please any woman, let alone the finest woman who had ever breathed. Still in the stained rags of his nineteenth-century suit, he slumped into an armchair, head on hand, and considered the irony of his situation. Not long since, he had sat in this house with Mrs Underwood and made tentative suggestions for its improvement. She had forbidden any change. Then she had gone and all that he had left of her was the house itself. As a substitute, he had come to love it. Now it was she who suggested improvements (of almost exactly the kind he had proposed) and he felt a deep reluctance to alter a single potted palm, a solitary sideboard. Nostalgia for those times when he had courted her and she had tried to teach him the meaning of virtue, when they had sung hymns together in the evenings (it had been she, again, who had insisted upon a daily time-scale similar to that which she had known in Bromley), filled him – and with nostalgia came trepidation, that his hopes were doomed. At every stage, when she had been close to declaring her love for him, to giving herself to him, she had been thwarted. It was almost as if Jagged watched them, deliberately manipulating every detail of their lives. Easier to think that, perhaps, than to accept an arbitrary universe.

He rose from the chair and, with an expression of defiance (she had always insisted that he follow her conventions) created a hole in the ceiling through which he might pass and enter his own room, a haven of glittering white, gold and silver. He restored the floor to completeness and his ruby ring cleansed his body of Palaeozoic grime, placed wafting robes of white spider-fur about him, brought ease to his mind as it dawned on him that his old powers (and therefore his old innocence) were restored to him. He stretched himself and laughed. There was certainly much to be said for being at the mercy of the primeval elements, to be swept along by circumstances one could not in any way control, but it was good to return, to feel one's identity expand again, unchecked. Creatively, he knew that he would be capable of the best entertainments he had yet given his world. He felt the need for company, for old friends to whom he could retail his adventures. Had his mother, the magnificent Iron Orchid, yet returned to the End of Time? Was the Duke of Queens as vulgar as ever, or had his experiences taught him taste? Jherek became eager for news.

In undulating white, he left his room and began to cross the landing, crammed with nooks which in turn were crammed with little china figurines, china vases, china flowers, china animals, to the stairs. His emerald power-ring brought him delicate scents, of Lower Devonian ferns, of nineteenth-century streets, of oceans and of meadows. His step grew lighter as he descended to the dining room. 'All things bright and beautiful,' he sang, 'all creatures great and small ...'

A turn of his amber ring and an ethereal orchestra accompanied him. The amethyst – and peacocks stepped behind him, his train in their prim beaks, their feathers at full flourish. He passed an embroidered motto – he still could not read it, but she had told him its sense (if sense it were!): 'What Mean These Stones?' he carolled. 'What Mean These – tra-la-la – Stones?'

His spider-fur robes began to brush ornaments from the shelves at the side of the stairs. With scarcely any feelings of guilt at all, he widened the steps a little, so that he could pass more freely.

The dining room, dark, with heavy curtains and brown, gloomy furniture, dampened his spirits for only a second. He knew what she had once demanded – partially burned animal flesh, near-tasteless vegetables – and he ignored it. If she no longer dictated her pleasures, then he would offer his own again.

The table bloomed exotic. A reminder of their recent adventures – a spun-sugar water-scorpion glittering as a centre-piece – two translucent scarlet jellies, two feet high, in the image, to the life, of Inspector Springer. A couple of herds of animated marzipan cows and sheep (to satisfy her relish for fauna) grazing, in miniature, at the bases of

61

the jellies. Everywhere: fronds of yellow, blue, pink, white, lilac and purple, of savoury, brittle pastry. Not a typical table, for Jherek usually chose for colour and preferred to limit himself to two, with one predominating — perhaps not a tasteful table, even — but a jolly one, that he hoped she would appreciate. Great green pools of gravy; golden mounds of mustards; brown, steaming custards, and pies in a dozen pastel shades; bowls of crystals — cocaine in the blue, heroin in the silver, sugar in the black — and tottering pyramids of porridge — a dish for any mood, to satisfy every appetite. He stood back, grinning his pleasure. It was unplanned, it was crowded, but it had a certain zest, he felt, that she would appreciate.

He struck the nearby gong. Her feet were already upon the stairs.

She entered the room. 'Oh!'

'Lunch, my lovely Amelia. Flung together, I fear, but all quite edible.'

She eyed the little marzipan ruminants.

He beamed. 'I knew you'd like those. And Inspector Springer? Does he not amuse you?'

Fingers flew to lips; a sound escaped her nostrils. The bosom rose and then was slow to fall; she was almost as red as the jelly.

'You are distressed.'

Eruption. She doubled, gasping.

'Fumes?' He stared wildly. 'Something poisonous?'

'Oh, ho, ho ...' She straightened, hand at back of hip. 'Oh, ho, ho!'

He relaxed. 'You *are* amused.' He pulled back her chair, as she had trained him to do. She slumped down, still shaking, picking up a spoon. 'Oh, ho, ho ...'

He joined in. 'Oh, ho, ho.'

It was thus, before they had put a morsel to their mouths, that the Iron Orchid found them. They saw her in the doorway, after some time. She was smiling. She was resplendent.

'Dear Jherek, wonder of my womb! Astonishing Amelia,

ancestress without compare! Do you hide from us all? Or are you just returned? If so, you are the last. All travellers are back – even Mongrove, you know. He has returned from space – gloomier, if anything, than before. We speculated. We expected your return. Jagged was here – he said that he sent you on, but that only the machine arrived, bereft of passengers. Some would have it – Brannart Morphail in particular – that you were lost forever in some primitive age – destroyed. I disbelieved, naturally. There was talk, earlier, of an expedition, but nothing came of it. Today, at My Lady Charlotina's, there was a rumour of a fluctuation – a time-machine had been sensed for a second or two on one of Brannart's instruments. I knew it must be you!'

She had chosen red for her chief colour. Her crimson eyes glittered with maternal joy at her son restored to her. Her scarlet hair curled itself here and there about her face, as if in ecstasy, and her poppy-coloured flesh seemed to vibrate with pleasure. As she moved, her perspex gown, almost the colour of clementines, creaked a little.

'You know there is to be a celebration?' she said. A party so that we may all hear Mongrove's news. He has consented to appear, to speak. And the Duke of Queens, Bishop Castle, My Lady Charlotina – we shall be there to give our tales. And now you and Mrs Underwood? Where have you been, you rogues? Hiding here, or adventuring through History?'

Mrs Underwood began: 'We have had a tiring experience, Mrs Carnelian, and I think . . .'

'Tiring? Mrs What? Tiring? I'm not certain of the meaning. But Mrs Carnelian – that is excellent. I never thought – yes, excellent. I must tell the Duke of Queens.' She cruised for the door. 'But I'll interrupt your meal no longer. The theme for the celebration is of course 1896 —' a gesture to Mrs Underwood – 'and I know you will both surpass yourselves! Farewell!'

Mrs Underwood implored him: 'We are not going?'

'We must!'

63

'It is expected?'

He knew secret glee in his own cunning. 'Oh, indeed it is,' he said.

'Then, of course, I shall go with you.'

He eyed her crisp cream dress, her pinned auburn hair. 'And the beauty of it is,' he said, 'that if you go as you are, the purity of your conception will outshine all others!'

She snapped a branch from a savoury frond.

CHAPTER NINE

THE PAST IS HONOURED: THE FUTURE REAFFIRMED

First there came a broad plane, a vast, level carpet of pale green; the jade power-boat sped low over this — then avenues approached — spaced to have their entrances arranged around the perimeter of a semi-circle; each avenue leading inwards to a hub. The air-car selected one. Cypresses, palms, yews, elders, redwoods, pines, shoe and plane trees, sped by on either side — their variety proclaiming that the Duke of Queens had not lost his vulgar touch (Jherek wondered, now, if he would have it otherwise). The focus became visible, ahead, but they heard the music before they recognized details of the Duke's display.

'A waltz!' cried Mrs Underwood (she had renounced the sensible day dress for fine blue silk, white lace, a flounce or two, even the suggestion of a bustle, and the hat she wore was two feet across at the brim; on her hands, lace gloves, and in them a blue and white parasol). 'Is it Strauss, Mr Carnelian?'

In the tweeds she had helped him make, he leaned back against the side of the car, his face half-shaded by his cap. One hand fingered his watch-chain, the other steadied the briar-wood pipe she had considered fitting ('a manlier, more mature air, altogether,' she had murmured with satisfaction, after the brogues were on his feet and the cravat adjusted, 'your figure would be envied anywhere' and then she had become a fraction confused). He shook his head. 'Or Starkey, or Stockhausen. I was never as familiar as I should have been with the early primitives. Lord Jagged would know. I hope he is there.'

'He became almost garrulous at our departure,' she said. 'I wonder if he regrets that now, as people sometimes do. I remember once that the brother of a girl I knew at school kept us company for an entire vacation. I thought he disliked me. He seemed disdainful. At the end of the holiday he drove me to the station, was taciturn, even surly. I felt sorry for him, that he should be burdened. I entered the train. He remained on the platform. As the train left, he began to run beside it. He knew that I should probably never see him again. He was red as a raspberry as he shouted his parting remark.' She inspected the silver top of her parasol.

He could see that there was a small, soft smile on her lips, which was all that was visible to him of her face, beneath the brim of the hat.

'His remark?'

'Oh!' She looked up and, for an instant, the eye which met his was merry. 'He said "I love you, Miss Ormont", that was all. He could only declare himself when he knew I should not be able to confront him again.'

Jherek laughed. 'And, of course, the joke was that you were not this Miss Ormont. He confused you with another.'

He wondered why both tone and expression changed so suddenly, though she remained, it seemed, amused. She gave her attention back to the parasol. 'My maiden name was Ormont,' she said. 'When we marry, you see, we take the name of our betrothed.'

'Excellent! Then I may expect, one day, to be Jherek Underwood?'

'You are devious in your methods of clinging to your

points, Mr Carnelian. But I shall not be trapped so simply. No, you would not become Jherek Underwood.'

'Ormont?'

'The idea is amusing, even pleasant.' She checked herself. 'Even the hottest of radicals has never suggested, to my knowledge, such a reversal.' Smiling, she chewed her underlip. 'Oh, dear! What dangerous thoughts you encourage, in your innocence!'

'I have not offended?'

'Once, you might have done so. I am shocked at myself, for not feeling shocked. What a bad woman I should seem in Bromley now!'

He scarcely followed, but he was not disturbed. He sank back again and made the pipe come alight for the umpteenth time (she had not been able to tell him how to keep it fuming). He enjoyed the Duke's golden sunshine, the sky which matched, fortuitously, his loved one's dress. Other air-carriages could be seen in other avenues, speeding for the hub – red and gold, plush and gilt, a fanciful reproduction of the Duke's only prolonged experience with the nineteenth century.

Jherek touched her hand. 'Do you recognize it, Amelia?'

'It is overpoweringly huge.' The brim of the hat went up and up, a lace glove touched her chin. 'It disappears, look, in clouds.'

She had not seen. He hinted: 'But if the proportions were reduced ...'

She tilted her head, still craning. 'Some sort of American Building?'

'You have been there!'

'I?'

'The original is in London.'

'Not the Café Royal?'

'Don't you see – he has taken the décor of the Café Royal and added it to your Scotland Yard.'

'Police headquarters – with red plush walls!'

'The Duke comes near, for once, to simplicity. You do not think it too spare?'

'A thousand feet high! It is the tallest piece of plush, Mr Carnelian, I may ever hope to see. And what is that at the roof – now the clouds part – a darker mass?'

'Black?'

'Blue, I think.'

'A dome. Yes, a hat, such as your policemen wear.'

She seemed out of breath. 'Of course.'

The music grew louder. He waved his pipe in time. But she was puzzled. 'Isn't it a little slow – a little drawn out – for a waltz. It's as if it were played on those Indian instruments – or were they Arabic? More than a flavour of the Oriental, at any rate. High-pitched, too, in a way.'

'The tapes are from one of the cities, doubtless,' said Jherek. 'They are old – possibly faulty. This is not authentic, then?'

'Not to my time.'

'We had best not tell the Duke of Queens. It would disappoint him, don't you think?'

She shrugged compliance. 'Yet it has a rather grating effect. I hope it does not continue throughout the entire reception. You do not know the instruments used?'

'Electronics or some such early method of music-making. You would know better ...'

'I think not.'

'Ah.'

A degree of awkwardness touched the atmosphere and, for a moment, both strove to find a new subject and restore the mood of relaxation they had been enjoying till now. Ahead, at the base of the building, was a wide, shadowy archway, and into this other air-cars were speeding – fanciful vehicles of every description, and most based on Dawn Age technology or mythology: Jherek saw a hobby-horse, its mechanical copper legs making galloping motions in the air, a Model T, its owner seated on the section where the long vertical bar joined the short horizontal one, and he heard the distinctive sound of a clipper ship, but it had disappeared before he could see it properly. Some of the vessels moved with considerable speed, others made more stately progress, like the large, grey and white car – it could be nothing else but a London Pigeon – immediately in front of them as the archway loomed.

'It seems the whole world attends,' said Jherek.

She fingered the complicated lace on her bodice. She smoothed a pleat. The music changed; the sound of slow explosions and of something being dragged through sand surrounded them as their car entered a great hall, its ceiling suported by fluted arches, in which, evidently, they were to park. Elaborately dressed figures floated from their own air-cars towards a doorway into the hall above; voices echoed.

'It dwarfs King's Cross!' exclaimed Mrs Underwood. She admired the mosaics, finely detailed, multicoloured, on walls and arches. 'It is hard to believe that it has not existed for centuries.'

'In a sense it has,' said Jherek, aware that she made an effort to converse. 'In the memories of the cities.'

'This was made by one of your cities?'

'No, but the advice of the cities is sought on such matters. For all that they grow senile, they still remember a great deal of our race's history. Is the interior familiar to you?'

'It resembles nothing so much as the vault of a Gothic cathedral, much magnified. I do not think I know the original, if one exists. You must not forget, Mr Carnelian, that I am no expert. Most aspects of my own world, most areas of it, are unknown to me. My experiences of London were not so varied, I would gather, as yours have been. I led a quiet life in Bromley, where the world is small.' She sighed as they left the car. 'Very small,' she said, almost under her breath. She adjusted her hat and tossed her head in a manner he found delightful. At that moment she seemed at once more full of life and of melancholy than he had ever seen her. He hesitated for a fraction of a second before offering her his arm, but she took it readily, smiling, the sadness melting, and together they ascended to the doorway above.

'You are glad, now, that you have come?' he murmured.

'I am determined to enjoy myself,' she told him.

Then she gasped, for she had not expected the scene they entered. The entire building was filled not by separated floors, but by floating platforms and galleries, rising higher and higher into the distance, and in these galleries and upon these platforms stood groups of people, conversing, eating, dancing, while other groups, or individuals, drifted through the air, from one platform to another, as, in her own world, people might cross the floor of a ballroom. High, high above, the furthest figures were tiny, virtually invisible. The light was subtle, supplying brilliance and shade, and shifting almost imperceptibly the whole time; the colours were vibrant, of every possible shade or tone, complementing the costumes of the guests, which ranged from the simplest to the most grotesque. Perhaps by some clever manipulation of the acoustics of the hall, the voices rose and fell in waves, but were never loud enough to drown any particular conversation, and, to Mrs Underwood, seemed orchestrated, harmonized into a single yet infinitely variegated chorus. Here and there, along the walls, people stood casually, their bodies at right angles to those of the majority, as they used power-rings to adjust their gravity, enabling them to convert the dimensions of the hall (or at least their experience of those dimensions) to an impression of length rather than height.

'It reminds one of a medieval painting,' she said. 'Italian, are they? Of heaven? My father's house ... Though the perspective is better ...' Aware that she babbled, she subsided with a sigh, looking at him with an expression showing amusement at her own confusion.

'It pleases you, though?' He was solicitous, yet he could see that she was not unhappy.

'It is wonderful.'

'Your morality is not offended?'

'For today, Mr Carnelian, I have decided to leave a

great deal of my morality at home.' Again, she laughed at herself.

'You are more beautiful than ever,' he told her. 'You are very fine.'

'Hush, Mr Carnelian. You will make me self-conscious. For once, I feel in possession of myself. Let me enjoy it. I will –' she smiled – 'permit the occasional compliment – but I should be grateful if you will forgo declarations of passion for this evening.'

He bowed, sharing her good humour. 'Very well.'

But she had become a goddess and he could not help it if he were astonished. She had always been beautiful in his eyes, and admirable, too. He had worshipped her, in some ways, for her courage in adversity, for her resistance to the ways of his own world. But that had been bravery under siege and now, it seemed, she single-handedly gave siege to that same society which, a few months before, had threatened to engulf and destroy her identity. There was a determination in her bearing, a lightness, an air of confidence, that proclaimed to everyone what he had always sensed in her – and he was proud that his world should see her as the woman he knew, in full command of herself and of her situation. Yet there was, as well, a private knowledge, an intimate understanding between them, of the resources of character on which she drew to achieve that command. For the first time he became conscious of the depth of his love for her and, although he had always known that she had loved him, he became confident that her emotion was as strong as his own. Like her, he required no declaration; her bearing was declaration enough.

Together, they ascended.

'Jherek!'

It was Mistress Christia, the Everlasting Concubine, clad in silks that were almost wholly transparent, they were so fine, and plainly influenced by the murals she had had described to her by one of those who had visited the Café Royal. She had let her body fill out, her limbs had rounded and she was slightly, deliciously, plump.

'May it be Amelia?' she asked of Mrs Underwood, and looked to both for confirmation.

Mrs Underwood smiled assent.

'I have been hearing of all your adventures in the nineteenth century. I am so jealous, of course, for the age seems wonderful and just the sort of period I should like to visit. This costume is not of my own invention, as you have guessed. My Lady Charlotina was going to use it, but thought it more suitable for me. Is it, Amelia, authentic?' She whirled in the air, just above their heads.

'Greek .. ?' Amelia Underwood hesitated, unwilling to contradict. Then, it seemed, she realized the influence. 'It suits you perfectly. You look lovely.'

'I would be welcome in your world?'

'Oh, certainly! In many sections of society you would be the centre of attention.'

Mistress Christia beamed and bent, with soft lips, to kiss Mrs Underwood upon her cheek, murmuring, 'You look magnificent, of course, yourself. Did you make the dress or did you bring it from the Dawn Age? It must be an original.'

'It was made here.'

'It is still beautiful. You have the advantage over us all! And you, too, Jherek look the very picture of the noble, Dawn Age hero. So manly! So desirable!'

Mrs Underwood's hand tightened a fraction on Jherek's arm. He became almost euphoric.

Yet Mistress Christia was sensitive, too. 'I shall not be the only one to envy you today, Amelia.' She permitted herself a wink. 'Or Jherek, either.' She looked beyond them. 'Here is our host!'

The Duke of Queens had been a soldier, during his brief stay in 1896. But never had there been a scarlet tunic so thoroughly scarlet as the one he sported, nor buttons so golden, nor epaulettes so bright, nor belt and boots so mirror-gleaming. He had doffed his beard and assumed Dundreary sidewhiskers; there was a shako a-tilt on his massive head; his britches were dark blue and striped with yellow. His gloves were white and one hand rested upon the pommel of his sword, which dripped with braid. He saluted and bowed. 'Honoured you could attend,' he said.

Jherek embraced him. 'You have been coached, dear friend! You look so handsome!'

'All natural,' declared the Duke with some pride. 'Created through exercise, you know, with the help of some time-travellers of a military persuasion. You heard of my duel with Lord Shark?'

'Lord Shark! I thought him a misanthrope entirely. To make Mongrove seem as gregarious as Gaf the Horse in Tears. What lured him from his grey fortress?'

'An affair of honour.'

'Indeed?' said Amelia Underwood. 'Insults, was it, and pistols at dawn?'

'I offended him. I forget how. But I was remorseful at the time. We settled with swords. I trained for ages. The irony was, however . . .'

He was interrupted by Bishop Castle, in full evening dress, copied from Mr Harris, doubtless. His handsome, rather ascetic, features were framed by a collar that was perhaps a little taller than normally fashionable in 1896. He had disdained black and the coat and trousers were, instead, bottle-green; the waistcoat brown, the shirt cream-coloured. His tie matched his coat and the exaggeratedly high top-hat on his head.

'Jesting Jherek, you have been hidden too long!' His voice was slightly muffled by the collar covering his mouth. 'And your Mrs Underwood! Gloom vanishes. We are all united again!'

'Is it mannerly to compliment your costume, Bishop Castle?' A movement of her parasol.

'Compliments are the colour of our conversation, dear Mrs Underwood. We are fulfilled by flattery; we feed on praise; we spend our days in search of the perfect peal of persiflage that will make the peacock in us preen and say

73

"Behold – I beautify the world!" In short, exquisite butterfly in blue, you may so compliment me and already do. May I in turn honour your appearance; it has detail which, sadly, few of us can match. It does not merely attract the eye – it holds it. It is the finest creation here. Henceforth there is no question but that you shall lead us all in fashion. Jherek is toppled from his place!'

She lifted an appreciative eyebrow; his bow was sweeping and all but lost him his hat, while his head virtually disappeared from view for a moment. He straightened, saw a friend, bowed again, and drifted away. 'Later,' he said to them both, 'we must reminisce.'

Jherek saw amusement in her eyes as she watched Bishop Castle rise to a nearby gallery. 'He is a voluble cleric,' she said. 'We have bishops not unlike him in 1896.'

'You must tell him, Amelia. What greater compliment could you pay?'

'It did not occur to me.' She hesitated, her self-assurance gone for a second: 'You do not find me callow?'

'Ha! You rule here already. Your good opinion is in demand. You have the authority both of bearing and of background. Bishop Castle spoke nothing but the truth. Your praise warmed him.'

He was about to escort her higher when the Duke of Queens, who had been in conversation with Mistress Christia, turned back to them. 'Have you been long returned, Jherek and Amelia, to the End of Time?'

'Hardly a matter of hours,' said she.

'So you remained behind in 1986. You can tell us what became of Jagged?'

'Then he is not yet back?' She glanced to Jherek with some alarm. 'We heard . . .'

'You did not meet him again in 1896? I assumed that was his destination.' The Duke of Queens frowned.

'He could be there,' said Jherek, 'for we have been adventuring elsewhere. At the very Beginning of Time, in fact.'

'Lord Jagged of Canaria conceals himself increasingly,'

74

complained the Duke, brushing at a braid. 'When challenged, he proves himself a master of sophistry. His mysteries cease to entertain because he confuses them so.'

'It is possible,' said Amelia Underwood, 'that he has become lost in Time; that he did not plan this disappearance. If we had not been fortunate, we should still be stranded now.'

The Duke of Queens was embarrassed by his own pettishness. 'Of course. Oh, dear — Time has become such a talking point and it is not one, I fear, which interests me greatly. I have never had Lord Jagged's penchant for the abstract. You know what a bore I can be.'

'Never that,' said Jherek affectionately. 'And even your vulgarities are splendid.'

'I hope so,' he said with modesty. 'I do my best. You like the building, Jherek?'

'It is a masterpiece.'

'More restrained than usual?'

'Much.'

The Duke's eye brightened. 'What an arbiter we make of you, Jherek! It is only because of your past innovations, or because we respect your experience, too?'

Jherek shrugged. 'I have not considered it. But Bishop Castle claims that art has a fresh leader.' He bowed to his Amelia.

'You like my Royal Scotland Yard, Mrs Underwood?' The Duke was eager.

'I am most impressed, Duke of Queens.' She appeared to be relishing her new position.

He was satisfied. 'But what is this concerning the Beginning of Time? Shall you bring us more ideas, scarcely before we can assimilate the old ones?'

'Perhaps,' said Jherek. 'Molluscs, you know. And ferns. Rocks. Hampers. Water-scorpions. Time Centres. Yes, there would be enough for a modest entertainment of some sort.'

'You have tales for us, too!' Mistress Christia had returned. 'Adventures, eh?'

75

Now more of the guests had sighted them and began to drift towards them.

'I think some, at least, will amuse you,' said Amelia Underwood. Jherek detected a harder edge to her voice as she prepared to face the advancing crowd, but she had lost that quality when she next spoke. 'We found many surprises there.'

'Oh, this is delightful!' cried Mistress Christia. 'What an enviable pair you are!'

'And brave, too, to risk the snares and vengeances of Time,' said the Duke of Queens.

Gaf the Horse in Tears, a Gibson Girl to the life, a Sailor hat upon his up-pinned hair, leaned forward. 'Brannart told us you were doomed, gone forever. Destroyed, even.'

Sharp-featured Doctor Volospion, in a black, swirling cape and a black, wide-brimmed hat, his eyes glittering from the shadows of his face, said softly: 'We did not believe him, of course.'

'Yet our time-travellers disappear – vanishing from our menageries at an astonishing rate. I lost four Adolf Hitlers alone, just recently.' Sweet Orb Mace was splendid in rubashka, tarboosh, pantaloons and high, embroidered boots. 'And one of them, I'm sure, was real. Though rather old, admittedly ...'

'Brannart claims these disappearances as proof that Time is ruptured.' Werther de Goethe, a saturnine Sicilian brigand, complete with curling moustachios which rather contradicted the rest of the impression, adjusted his cloak. 'He warns that we stand upon a brink, that we shall all, soon, plunge willy-nilly into disordered chronological gulfs.'

There was a pause in the babble, for Werther's glum drone frequently had this effect, until Amelia said:

'His warnings have some substance, it would seem.'

'What?' The Duke of Queens laughed heartily 'You are living denials of the Morphail Effect!'

'I think not.' She was modest, looked to Jherek to speak,

76

but he gave her the floor. 'As I understand it, Brannart Morphail's explanations are only partial. They are not false. Many theories describe Time – and all are provable.'

'An excellent summary,' said Jherek. 'My Amelia relates what we have learned, darling of Dukes, at the Beginning of Time. More scientists than Brannart concern themselves with investigating Time's nature. I think he will be glad of the information I bring. He is not alone in his researches, he'll be pleased to know.'

'You are certain of it?' asked Amelia, who had flickered an eye at his recent 'my' (though without apparent displeasure).

'Why should he not be?'

She shrugged. 'I have only encountered the gentleman in dramatic circumstances, of course ...'

'He is due?' asked Jherek of the Duke.

'Invited – as is the world. You know him. He will come late, claiming we force him against his will.'

'Then he might know the whereabouts of Jagged.' He appraised the hall, as if mention of the name would invoke the one he most wished to see. Many he recognized, not famous for their gregariousness, were here, even Lord Shark (or one of his automata, sent in his place) who styled himself 'The Unknown'; even Werther de Goethe, who had sworn never to attend another party. Yet, so far, that last member of the End of Time's misanthropic triumvirate, Lord Mongrove, the bitter giant, in whose honour this celebration was being held, was not in evidence.

Her arm was still in his. A touch drew his attention. 'You are concerned for Jagged's safety?' she asked.

'He is my closest friend, devious though he seems. Could he not have suffered our fate? More drastically?'

'If so, we shall never know.'

He drove this worry from his mind; it was not his business, as a guest, to brood. 'Look,' he said, 'there is My Lady Charlotina!'

She had seen them, from above, and now flew to greet

77

them, her golden robe-de-style, with its crystal beads, its ribbons and its roses, fluttering with the speed of her descent.

'Our hero and heroine happily restored to us. Is this the final scene? Are sleigh-bells to ring, blue-bloods to sing, catharsis achieved, tranquillity regained? I have missed so much of the plot. Refresh me – regale us all. Oh, speak, my beauties. Or are we to witness a re-enactment?'

Mrs Underwood was dry. 'The tale is not yet finished, I regret, My Lady Charlotina. Many clues remain to be unravelled – threads are still to be woven together – there is no clearly seen pattern upon the fabric – and perhaps there never will be.'

My Lady Charlotina's disbelieving laughter held no rancour. 'Nonsense – it is your duty to bring about resolution soon. It is cruel of you both to keep us in such suspense. If your timing is not exact, you will lose your audience, my dears. First there will be criticism of fine points, and then – you could not risk this – uninterest. But you must bring me up to date, before I judge. Give me merely the barest details, if that is what you wish, and let gossip colour the tale for you.'

Smiling broadly, Amelia Underwood began to tell of their adventures at the Beginning of Time.

CHAPTER TEN

IN WHICH THE IRON ORCHID
IS NOT QUITE HERSELF

Jherek still sought for Jagged. Leaving Amelia to spin a yarn untangled by his interruptions, he drifted a good distance roofward, until his love and the circle surrrounding her were a pattern of dots below.

Jagged alone could help him now, thought Jherek. He had returned expecting revelation. If Jagged had been playing a joke on them, then the joke should be made clear; if he manipulated a story for the world's entertainment – then the world, as My Lady Charlotina had said, was entitled to a resolution. The play continued, it seemed, though the author had been unable to write the final scenes. He recalled, with a trace of rancour, that Jagged had encouraged him to begin this melodrama (or was it a farce and he a sad fool in the eyes of all the world? Or tragedy, perhaps?) and Jagged therefore should provide help. Yet if Jagged were vanished forever, what then?

'Why,' said Jherek to himself, 'I shall have to complete the play as best I can. I shall prove that I am no mere actor, following a road laid by another. I shall show I am a playwright, too!'

Li Pao, from the twenty-seventh century, had overheard him. Insistently clad in blue overalls, the ex-member of the People's Governing Committee, touched Jherek to make him turn.

'You consider yourself an actor in a play, Jherek Carnelian?'

'Hello, Li Pao. I spoke confused thoughts aloud, that is all.'

But Li Pao was greedy for a discussion and would not be guided away from the subject. 'I thought you controlled your own fate. This whole love-story business, which so excites the woman, did it not begin as an affectation?'

'I forget.' He spoke the truth. Emotions jostled within him, each in conflict with the other, each eager for a voice. He let none speak.

'Surely,' Li Pao smiled, 'you have not come to believe in your rôle, as the ancient actors were said to do, and think your character's feelings are your own? That would be most droll.' Li Pao leaned against the rail of his drifting gallery. It tilted slightly and began to sink. He brought it back until he was again level with Jherek.

'However, it seems likely,' Jherek told him.

'Beware, Jherek Carnelian. Life becomes serious for you. That would never do. You are a member of a perfectly amoral society: whimsical, all but thoughtless, utterly powerful. Your actions threaten your way of life. Do I see a ramshackle vessel called Self-Destruction heaving its battered bulwarks over the horizon? What's this, Jherek? Is your love genuine, after all?'

'It is, Li Pao. Mock me, if you choose, but I'll not deny there's truth in what you say. You think I conspire against my own peace of mind?'

'You conspire against your entire society. What your fellows could see as your morbid interest in morality actually threatens the status quo — a status quo that has existed for at least a million years, in this form alone! Would you have all your friends as miserably self-conscious as me?' Li Pao was laughing. His lovely yellow face shone like a small sun. 'You know my disapproval of your world and its pleasures.'

'You have bored me often enough ...' Jherek was amiable.

'I admit that I should be sad to see it destroyed. It is reminiscent of that Nursery you discovered, before you disappeared. I should hate to see these children face to face with reality.'

'All this –' the sweep of an arm – 'is not "reality"?'

'Illusion, every scrap. What would happen to you all if your cities were to close down in an instant, if your heat and your light – the simplest of animal needs – were taken from you? What would you do?'

Jherek could see little point in the question. 'Shiver and stumble,' he said, 'until death came. Why do you ask?'

'You are not frightened by the prospect?'

'It is no more real than anything else I experience or expect to experience. I would not say that it is the most agreeable fate. I should try to avoid it, of course. But if it became inevitable, I hope I should perish with good grace.'

Li Pao shook his head, amused. 'You are incorrigible. I hoped to convince you, now that you, of all here, have rediscovered your humanity. Yet perhaps fear is no good thing. Perhaps it is only we, the fearful, who attempt to instil our own sense of urgency into others, who avoid reality, who deceive others into believing that only conflict and unhappiness lead us to the truth.'

'It is a view expressed even at the End of Time, Li Pao.' The Iron Orchid joined them, sporting an oddly wrought garment, stiff and metallic and giving off a glow; it framed her face and her body, which was naked and of a conventional, female shape. 'You hear it from Werther de Goethe. From Lord Shark. And, of course, from Mongrove himself.'

'They are perverse. They adopt such attitudes merely to provide contrast.'

'And you, Li Pao?' asked Jherek. 'Why do you adopt them?'

'They were instilled into me as a child. I am conditioned, if you like, to make the associations you describe.'

'No instincts guide you, then?' asked the Iron Orchid. She laid a languid arm across her son's shoulders. Apparently absent-minded, she stroked his cheek.

'You speak of instincts? You have none, save the seeking of pleasure.' The little Chinese shrugged. 'You have need of none, it could be said.'

'You do not answer her question.' Jherek Carnelian found himself a fraction discomfited by his mother's attentions. His eyes sought for Amelia, but she was not in sight.

'I argue that the question is meaningless, without understanding of its import.'

'Yet ...?' murmured the Iron Orchid, and her finger tickled Jherek's ear.

'My instincts and my reason are at one,' said Li Pao. 'Both tell me that a race which struggles is a race which survives.'

'We struggle mightily against boredom,' she said. 'Are we not inventive enough for you, Li Pao?'

'I am unconvinced. The prisoners in your menageries – the time-travellers and the space-travellers – they condemn you. You exploit them. You exploit the universe. This planet and perhaps the star around which it circles draws its energy from a galaxy which, itself, is dying. It leeches on its fellows. Is that just?'

Jherek had been listening closely. 'My Amelia said something not dissimilar. I could understand her little better, Li Pao. Your world and hers seem similar in some respects and, from what I know of them, menageries are kept.'

'Prisons, you mean? This is mere sophistry, Jherek Carnelian, as you must realize. We have prisons for those who transgress against society. Those who occupy them are there because they gambled – normally they staked their personal freedom against some form of personal gain.'

'The time-travellers often believe they stake their lives, as do the space-travellers. We do not punish them. We look after them.'

'You show them no respect,' said Li Pao.

The Iron Orchid pursed her lips in a kind of smile. 'Some are too puzzled, poor things, to understand their fate, but those who are not soon settle. Are *you* not thoroughly settled, Li Pao? You are rarely missed at parties. I know many other time-travellers and space-travellers who mingle with us, scarcely ever taking up their places in the menageries. Do we use force to keep them there, my dear? Do we deceive them?'

'Sometimes.'

'Only as we deceive one another, for the pleasure of it.'

Once more, Li Pao preferred to change ground. He pointed a chubby finger at Jherek. 'And what of "your Amelia"? Was she pleased to be manipulated in your games? Did she take pleasure in being made a pawn?'

Jherek was surprised. 'Come now, Li Pao. She was never altered physically – and certainly into nothing fishy.'

Li Pao put his finger to a tooth and sighed.

The Iron Orchid pulled Jherek away, still with her arm about his shoulders. 'Come, fruit of my loins. You will excuse us, Li Pao?'

Li Pao's bow was brief.

'I have seen Mrs Underwood,' the Iron Orchid said to Jherek, as they flew higher to where only a few people drifted. 'She looks more beautiful than ever. She was good enough to compliment me on my costume. You recognize the character?'

'I think not.'

'Mrs Underwood did, when I reminded her of the legend. A beautiful little story I had one of the cities tell me. I did not hear all the story, for the city had forgotten much, but enough was gained to make the costume. It is the tale of Old Florence and the Night of Gales and of the Lady in the Lamp, who tended to the needs of five hundred soldiers in a single day! Imagine! Five hundred!' She licked purple lips and grinned. 'Those ancients! I have it in mind to re-enact the whole story. There are soldiers here, too, you know. They arrived fairly recently and are in the menagerie of the Duke of Queens. But there are only twenty or so.'

'You could make some of your own.'

'I know, flesh of my flesh, but it would not be quite the same. It is your fault.'

'How, maternal, eternal flower?'

'Great stock is placed on authenticity, these days. Reproductions, where originals can be discovered, are an absolute anathema. And they become scarcer, they vanish so quickly.'

'Time-travellers?'

'Naturally. The space-travellers remain. But of what use are they?'

'Morphail has spoken to you, headiest of blooms?'

'Oh, a little, my seed. But all is Warning. All is Prophecy. He rants. You cannot hear him; not the words. I suppose Mrs Underwood shall be gone soon. Perhaps then things will return to a more acceptable pattern.'

'Amelia remains with me,' said Jherek, detecting, he thought, a wistful note in his mother's voice.

'You keep her company exclusively,' said the Iron Orchid. 'You are obsessed. Why so?'

'Love,' he told her.

'But, as I understand it, she makes no expression of love. You scarcely touch!'

'Her customs are not as ours.'

'They are crude, then, her customs!'

'Different.'

'Ah!' His mother was dismissive. 'She inhabits your whole mind. She affects your taste. Let her steer her own course, and you yours. Who knows, later those courses might again cross. I heard something of your adventures. They have been furious and stunning. Both of you need to drift, to recuperate, to enjoy lighter company. Is it you, bloom of my womb, keeping her by your side, when she would run free?'

'She is free. She loves me.'

'I say again – there are no signs.'

'I know the signs.'

'You cannot describe them?'

'They lie in gesture, tone of voice, expression in the eyes.'

'Ho, ho! This is too subtle for me, this telepathy! Love is flesh touched against flesh, the whispered word, the fingernail drawn delicately down the spine, the grasped thigh. There is no throb, Jherek, to this love of yours. It is pale – it is mean, eh?'

'No, giver of life. You feign obtuseness, I can tell. But why?'

Her glance was intense, for her, but cryptic.

'Mother? Strongest of orchids?'

But she had twisted a power-ring and was falling like a stone, with no word of reply. He saw her drop and disappear into a large crowd which swarmed at about the halfway point, below.

He found his mother's behaviour peculiar. She exhibited moods he had never encountered before. She appeared to have lost some of her wit and substituted malice (for which she had always had a delicious penchant, but the malice needed the wit to make it entertaining); she appeared to show a dislike for Amelia Underwood which she had not shown earlier. He shook his head and fingered his chin. How was it, that she could not, as she had always done in the past, delight in his delight? With a shrug, he aimed himself for a lower level.

A stranger sped to greet him from a nearby gallery. The stranger was clad in sombrero, fancy vest, chaps, boots and bandoliers, all in blinding red.

'Jherek, my pod, my blood! Why fly so fast?'

Only the eyes revealed identity, and even this confused him for a second before he realized the truth.

'Iron Orchid. How you proliferate!'

'You have met the others, already?'

'One of them. Which is the original?'

'We could all claim that, but there is a programme. At a certain time several vanish, one remains. It matters not which, does it? This method allows one to circulate better.'

'You have not yet met Amelia Underwood?'

'Not since I visited you at your ranch, my love. She is still with you?'

He decided to avoid repetition. 'Your disguise is very striking.'

'I represent a great hero of Mrs Underwood's time. A bandit king – a rogue loved by all – who came to rule a nation and was killed in his prime. It is a cycle of legend with which you must be familiar.'

'The name?'

'Ruby Jack Kennedy. Somewhere ...' she cast about ... 'you should find me as the treacherous woman who, in the end, betrayed him. Her name was Rosie Lee.' The Iron Orchid dropped her voice. 'She fell in love, you know, with an Italian called "The Mouser", because of the clever way he trapped his victims ...'

He found this conversation more palatable and was content to lend an ear, while she continued her delighted rendering of the old legend with its theme of blood, murder and revenge and the curse which fell upon the clan because of the false pride of its patriarch. He scarcely listened until there came a familiar phrase (revealing her taste for it, for she was not to know that one of her alter egos had already made it): 'Great stock is placed on authenticity, these days. Do you not feel, Jherek, that invention is being thwarted by experience? Remember how we used to stop Li Pao from giving us details of the ages we sought to recreate? Were we not wiser to do so?'

She had only half his attention. 'I'll admit that our entertainments lack something in savour for me, since I journeyed through Time. And, of course, I myself could be said to be the cause of the fashion you find distressing.'

She, in her own turn, had given his statements no close attention. She glared discontentedly about the hall. 'I believe they call it "social realism",' she muttered.

'My "London" began a specific trend towards the re-creation of observed reality . . .' he continued, but she was waving a hand at him, not because she disagreed, but because he interrupted a monologue.

'It's the spirit, my pup, not the expression. Something has changed. We seem to have lost our lightness of touch. Where is our relish for contrast? Are we all to become antiquarians and nothing more? What is happening to us, Jherek. It is – darkening . . .'

This particular Iron Orchid's mood was very different from that of the other mother, already encountered. If she merely desired an audience while she rambled, he was happy to remain one, though he found her argument narrow.

Perhaps the argument was the only one held by this facsimile, he thought. After all, the great advantage of self-reproduction was that it was possible to hold as many different opinions as one wished, at the same time.

As a boy, Jherek remembered, he had witnessed some dozen Iron Orchids in heated debate. She had enjoyed a phase where she found it easier to divide herself and argue, as it were, face to face, than to attempt to arrange her thoughts in the conventional manner. This facsimile, how-ever, was proving something of a bore (always the danger, if only one opinion were held and rigorously maintained), though it had that quality which saves the bore from snubs or ostracism – and, unfortunately, encourages it to retain the idea that it is an interesting conversationalist – it had a quality of pathos.

Pathos, thought Jherek, was not normally evident in his mother's character. Had he detected it in the facsimile he had previously encountered? Possibly . . .

'I worship surprises, of course,' she continued. 'I embrace variety. It is the pepper of existence, as the ancients said. Therefore, I should be celebrating all these new events. These "time-warps" of Brannart's, these disappearances, all these comings and goings. I wonder why I should feel – what is it? – "disturbed"? – by them. Disturbed? Have you ever known me "disturbed", my egg?'

He murmured: 'Never ...'

'Yes, I am disturbed. But what is the cause? I cannot identify it. Should I blame myself, Jherek?'

'Of course not ...'

'Why? Why? Joy departs; Zest deserts me – and is this replacement called Anxiety? Ha! A disease of time-travellers, of space-voyagers to which we, at the End of Time, have always been immune. Until now, Jherek ...'

'Softest of skins, strongest of wills, I do not quite ...'

'If it has become fashionable to rediscover and become infected by ancient psychoses, then I'll defy fashion. The craze will pass. What can sustain it? This news of Mongrove's? Some machination of Jagged's? Brannart's experiments?'

'Symptoms both, the latter two,' he suggested. 'If the universe is dying ...'

But she had been steering towards a new subject, and again she revealed the obsession of her original. Her tone became lighter, but he was not deceived by it. 'One may also, of course, look to your Mrs Underwood as an instigator ...'

The statement was given significant emphasis. There was the briefest of pauses before the name and after it. She goaded him to defend her or deny her, but he would not be lured.

Blandly he replied. 'Magnificent blossom, Li Pao would have it that the cause of our confusion lay within our own minds. He believes that we hold Truth at bay whilst embracing Illusion. The illusion, he hints, begins to reveal itself for what it is. That is why, says Li Pao, we know concern.'

She had become an implacable facsimile. 'And you, Jherek. Once the gayest of children! The wittiest of men! The most inventive of artists! Joyful boy, it seems to me that you turn dullard. And why? And when? Because Jagged encouraged you to play Lover! To that primitive...'

'Mother! Where is your wit? But to answer, well, I am sure that we shall soon be wed. I detect a difference in her regard for me.'

'A conclusion? I exult!'

Her lack of good humour astonished him. 'Firmest of metals, do not, I pray, make a petitioner of me. Must I placate a virago when once I was assured of the good graces of a friend?'

'I am more than that, I hope, blood of my blood.'

It occurred to him that if he had rediscovered Love, then she had rediscovered Jealousy. Could the one never exist without the presence of the other?

'Mother, I beg you to recollect ...'

A sniff from beneath the sombrero. 'She ascends, I see. She has her own rings, then?'

'Of course.'

'You think it wise, to indulge a savage —?'

Amelia hovered close to, in earshot now. A false smile curved the lips of the shade, this imperfect doppelganger. 'Aha! Mrs Underwood. What beautiful simplicity of taste, the blue and white!'

Amelia Underwood took time to recognize the Iron Orchid. Her nod was courteous, when she did so, but she refused to ignore the challenge. 'Overwhelmed entirely by the brilliant exoticism of your scarlet, Mrs Carnelian.'

A tilt of the brim. 'And what rôle, my dear, do you adopt today?'

'I regret we came merely as ourselves. But did I not see you earlier, in that box-like costume, then later in a yellow gown of some description? So many excellent disguises.'

'I think there is one in yellow, yes. I forget. Sometimes I feel so full of rich ideas, I must indulge more than one. You must think me coarse, dear ancestor.'

'Never that, lushest of orchids.'

Jherek was amused. It was the first time he had heard

Mrs Underwood use such language. He began to enjoy the encounter, but the Iron Orchid refused further sport. She leaned forward. Her son was blessed with an ostentatious kiss; Amelia Underwood was pecked. 'Brannart has arrived. I promised him an account of 1896. Surly he might be, but rarely dull. For the moment, then, dear children.'

She began to pirouette downwards. Jherek wondered where she had seen Brannart Morphail, for the hunchbacked, club-footed scientist was not in evidence.

Amelia Underwood settled on his arm again. 'Your mother seems distraught. Not as self-contained as usual.'

'It is because she divides herself too much. The substance of each facsimile is a little thin.' He explained.

'Yet it is clear that she regards me as an enemy.'

'Hardly that. She is not, you see, herself . . .'

'I am complimented, Mr Carnelian. It is a pleasure to be taken seriously.'

'But I am concerned for her. She has never been serious in her life before.'

'And you would say that I am to blame.'

'I think she is perturbed, sensing a loss of control in her own destiny, such as we experienced at the Beginning of Time. It is an odd sensation.'

'Familiar enough to me, Mr Carnelian.'

'Perhaps she will come to enjoy it. It is unlike her to resist experience.'

'I should be glad to advise her on how best to cope.'

He sensed irony, at last. He darted a glance of enquiry. Her eyes laughed. He checked a desire to hug her, but he touched her hand, very delicately, and was thrilled.

'You have been entertaining them all,' he said, 'down there?'

'I hope so. Language, thanks to your pills, is no problem. I feel I speak my own. But ideas can sometimes be difficult to communicate. Your assumptions are so foreign.'

'Yet you no longer condemn them.'

'Make no mistake – I continue to disapprove. But nothing is gained by blunt denials and denunciations.'

'You triumph, as you know. It is that which the Iron Orchid finds uncomfortable.'

'I appear to be enjoying some small social success. That, in turn, brings embarrassment.'

'Embarrassment?' He bowed to O'Kala Incarnadine, as Queen Britannia, who saluted him.

'They ask me my opinion. Of the authenticity of their costumes.'

'The quality of imagination is poor.'

'Not at all. But none is authentic, though most are fanciful and many beautiful. Your people's knowledge of my age is sketchy, to say the least.'

By degrees, they were drifting towards the bottom of the hall.

'Yet it is the age we know most about,' he said. 'Mainly because I have studied it and set the fashion for it, of course. What is wrong with the costumes?'

'As costumes, nothing. But few come close to the theme of "1896". There is a span, say, of a thousand years between one disguise and another. A man dressed in lilac ducks and wearing a crusty (and I must say delicious looking) pork pie upon his head announced that he was Harald Hardrede.'

'The prime minister, yes?'

'No, Mr Carnelian. The costume was impossible, at any rate.'

'Could he have been this Harald Hardrede, do you think? We have a number of distinguished temporal adventurers in the menageries.'

'It is unlikely.'

'Several million years have passed, after all, and so much now relies on hearsay. We are entirely dependent upon the rotting cities for our information. When the cities were younger, they were more reliable. A million years ago, there would have been far fewer anachronisms at a party of this kind. I have heard of parties given by our ancestors (your descendants, that is) which drew on all the resources of the cities in their prime. This masque must be feeble in comparison. There again, it is pleasant to use one's own imagination to invent an *idea* of the past.'

'I find it wonderful. I do not deny that I am stimulated by it, as well as confused. You must consider me narrow-minded ...'

'You praise us too much. I am overjoyed that you should find my world at last acceptable, for it leads me to hope that you will soon agree to be my —'

'Ah!' she exclaimed suddenly, and she pointed. 'There is Brannart Morphail. We must give him our news.'

CHAPTER ELEVEN

A FEW QUIET MOMENTS IN THE MENAGERIE

'... And thus it was, mightiest of minds, that we returned,' concluded Jherek, reaching for a partridge tree which drifted past – he picked two fruits, one for himself and one for Mrs Underwood, at his side. 'Is the information enough to recompense for my loss of your machine?'

'Scarcely!' Brannart had added another foot or two to his hump since they had last met. Now it towered, taller than his body, tending to overbalance him. Perhaps to compensate, he had increased the size of his club foot. 'A fabrication. Your tale defies logic. Everywhere you display ignorance of the real nature of Time.'

'I thought we brought fresh knowledge, um, Professor,' said she, half-distracted as she watched a crocodile of some twenty boys and girls, in identical dungarees, float past, following yet another Iron Orchid, a piping harlequin, towards the roof. Argonheart Po, huge and jolly, in a tall white chef's hat (he had come as Captain Cook), rolled in their wake, distributing edible revolvers. 'It would suggest, for instance, that it is now possible for me to return to the nineteenth century, without danger.'

'You still wish to return, Amelia?' What was the lurch

in the region of his navel? He dissipated the remainder of his partridge.

'Should I not?'

'I assumed you were content.'

'I accept the inevitable with good grace, Mr Carnelian – that is not necessarily contentment.'

'I suppose it is not.'

Brannart Morphail snorted. His hump quivered. He began to tilt, righted himself. 'Why have you two set out to destroy the work of centuries? Jagged has always envied me my discoveries. Has he connived with you, Jherek Carnelian, to confuse me?'

'But we do not deny the truth of your discoveries, dear Brannart. We merely reveal that they are partial, that there is not one Law of Time, but many!'

'But you bring no proof.'

'You are blind to it, Brannart. We are the proof. Here we stand, immune to your undeniably exquisite but not infallible Effect. It is a fine Effect, most brilliant of brains, and applies in billions, at least, of cases – but occasionally . . .'

A large green tear rolled down the scientist's cheek. 'For millennia I have tried to keep the torch of true research alight, single-handed. While the rest of you have devoted your energies to phantasies and whimsicalities, I have toiled. While you have merely exploited the benefits built up for you by our ancestors, I have striven to carry their work further, to understand that greatest mystery of all . . .'

'But it was already fairly understood, Brannart, most dedicated of investigators, by members of this Guild I mentioned . . .'

'. . . but you would thwart me even in that endeavour, with these fanciful tales, these sensational anecdotes, these evidently concocted stories of zones free from the influence of my beloved Effect, of groups of individuals who prove that Time has not a single nature but several . . . Ah Jherek! Is such cruelty deserved, by one who has sought to be only a servant of learning, who has never interfered

– criticized a little, perhaps, but never interfered – in the pursuits of his fellows?'

'I sought merely to enlighten ...'

My Lady Charlotina went by in a great basket of lavender, only her head visible in the midst of the mound. She called out as she passed. 'Jherek! Amelia! Luck for sale! Luck for sale!' She had made the most, it was plain, of her short spell of temporal tourism. 'Do not bore them too badly, Brannart. I am thinking of withdrawing my patronage.'

Brannart sneered. 'I play such charades no longer!' But it seemed that he did not relish the threat. 'Death looms, yet still you dance, making mock of the few who would help you!'

Mrs Underwood understood. She murmured: 'Wheldrake knew, Professor Morphail, when he wrote in one of his last poems —

> *Alone, then, from my basalt height*
> *I saw the revellers rolling by –*
> *Their faces all bemasked,*
> *Their clothing all bejewelled –*
> *Spread cloaks like paradise's wings in flight,*
> *Gowns grown so hell-fire bright!*
> *And purple lips drained purple flasks,*
> *And gem-hard eyes burned cruel.*
> *Were these old friends I would have clasped?*
> *Were these the dreamers of my youth?*
> *Ah, but old Time conquers more than flesh!*
> *(He and his escort Death.)*
> *Old Time lays waste the spirit, too!*
> *And Time conquers Mind,*
> *Time conquers Mind –*
> *Time Rules!'*

But Brannart could not respond to her knowing, sympathetic smile. He looked bemused.

'It is very good,' said Jherek dutifully, recalling Captain

Bastable's success. 'Ah, yes ... I seem to recall it now.' He raised empty, insincere eyes towards the roof, as he had seen them do. 'You must quote me some of Wheldrake's verses, too, some day.'

The sidelong look she darted him was not unamused.

'Tcha!' said Brannart Morphail. The small floating gallery in which he stood swung wildly as he shifted his footing. He corrected it. 'I'll listen to nonsense no longer. Remember, Jherek Carnelian, let your master Lord Jagged know that I'll not play his games! From henceforth I'll conduct my experiments in secret! Why should I not? Does he reveal his work to me?'

'I am not sure that he is with us at the End of Time. I meant to enquire ...'

'Enough!'

Brannart Morphail wobbled away from them, stamping impatiently on the floor of his platform with his monstrous boot.

The Duke of Queens spied them. 'Look, most honoured of my guests! Wakaka Nakooka has come as a Martian Pastorellan from 1898.'

The tiny black man, himself a time-traveller, turned with a grin and a bow. He was giving birth to fledgeling hawks through his nose. They fluttered towards the floor, now littered with at least two hundred of their brothers and sisters. He swirled his rich cloak and became a larger than average Kopps' Owl. With a flourish, off he flew.

'Always birds,' said the Duke, almost by way of apology. 'And frequently owls. Some people prefer to confine themselves by such means, I know. Is the party entertaining you both?'

'Your hospitality is as handsome as ever, most glamorous of Dukes.' Jherek floated beside his friend, adding softly: 'Though Brannart seems distraught.'

'His theories collapse. He has no other life. I hope you were kind to him, Jherek.'

'He gave us little opportunity,' said Amelia Underwood. Her next remark was a trifle dry. 'Even my quotation from

Wheldrake did not seem to console him.'

'One would have thought that your discovery, Jherek, of the Nursery and the children would have stimulated him. Instead, he ignores Nurse's underground retreat, with all its machinery for the control of Time. He complains of trickery, suggests we invented it in order to deceive him. Have you seen your old school-chums, by the by?'

'A moment ago,' Jherek told him. 'Are they enjoying their new life?'

'I think so. I give them less discipline than did Nurse. And, of course, they begin to grow now that they are free of the influence of the Nursery.'

'You have charge of them?'

The Duke seemed to swell with self-esteem. 'Indeed I have – I am their father. It is a pleasant sensation. They have excellent quarters in the menagerie.'

'You keep them in your menagerie, Duke?' Mrs Underwood was shocked. 'Human children?'

'They have toys there – playgrounds and so on. Where else would I keep them, Mrs Underwood?'

'But they grow. Are not the boys separated from the girls?'

'Should they be?' The Duke of Queens was curious. 'You think they will breed, eh?'

'Oh!' Mrs Underwood turned away.

'Jherek.' The Duke put a large arm around his friend's shoulders. 'While on the subject of menageries, may I take you to mine, for a moment – at least until Mongrove arrives? There are several new acquisitions which I'm sure will delight you.'

Jherek was feeling overwhelmed by the party, for it had been a good while since he had spent so much time in the company of so many. He accepted the Duke's suggestion with relief.

'You will come too, Mrs Underwood?' The Duke asked from politeness, it appeared, not enthusiasm.

'I suppose I should. It is my duty to inspect the conditions under which those poor children are forced to live.'

'The nineteenth century had certain religious attitudes towards children, I understand,' said the Duke conversationally to her as he led them through a door in the floor. 'Were they not worshipped and sacrificed at the same time?'

'You must be thinking of another culture,' she told him. She had recovered something of her composure, but there was still a trace of hostility in her manner towards her flamboyant host.

They entered a classic warren of passages and halls, lined with force-bubbles of varying sizes and shapes containing examples of thousands of different species, from a few viruses and intelligent microcosmic life to the gigantic two-thousand-foot-long Python Person whose spaceship had crashed on Earth some seven hundred years before. The cages were well-kept and reproduced, as exactly as was possible, the environments of those they contained. Mrs Underwood had, herself, experience of such cages. She looked at these with a mixture of disgust and nostalgia.

'It seemed so simple, then,' she murmured, 'when I thought myself merely damned to Hell.'

The Duke of Queens brushed at his fine Dundrearies. 'My homo-sapiens collection is somewhat sparse at present, Mrs Underwood – the children, a few time-travellers, a space-traveller who claims to be descended from common stock (though you would not credit it!). Perhaps you would care to see it after I have shown you my latest non-human acquisitions?'

'I thank you, Duke of Queens, but I have little interest in your zoo. I merely wished to reassure myself that your children are reasonably and properly looked after; I had forgotten, however, the attitudes which predominate in your world. Therefore, I think I shall —'

'Here we are!' Proudly the scarlet duke indicated his new possessions. There were five of them, with globular bodies into which were set a row of circular eyes (like a coronet, around the entire top section of the body) and a small triangular opening, doubtless a mouth. The bodies were supported by four bandy limbs which seemed to serve as legs as well as arms. The colour of these creatures varied from individual to individual, but all were nondescript, with light greys and dark browns proliferating.

'Is it Yusharisp and some friends?' Jherek was delighted to recognize the gloomy little alien who had first brought them the news of the world's doom. 'Why has not Mongrove . . .?'

'These are from Yusharisp's planet,' explained the Duke of Queens, 'but they are not him. They are five fresh ones! I believe they came to look for him. In the meantime, of course, he has been home and returned here.'

'He is not aware of the presence of his friends on our planet?'

'Not yet.'

'You'll tell him tonight?'

'I think so. At an appropriate moment.'

'Can they communicate?'

'They refuse to accept translation pills, but they have their own mechanical translators, which are, as you know, rather erratic.'

Jherek pressed his face against the force-bubble. He grinned at the inmates. He smiled. 'Hello! Welcome to the End of Time!'

China-blue eyes glared vacantly back at him.

'I am Jherek Carnelian. A friend of Yusharisp's,' he told them agreeably.

'The leader, the one in the middle, is known as Chief Public Servant Shashurup,' the Duke of Queens informed him.

Jherek made another effort. He waved his fingers. 'Good afternoon, Chief Public Servant Shashurup!'

'Why-ee (skree) do you continue-oo too-too-to tor(roar)-ment us?' asked the CPS. 'All we a(kaaar)sk(skree) is (hiss) that-tat-tat you do-oo-oo us(ushush) the cour(kur-kur-kur) tesy-ee of com-com-communicat(tate-tate)ing our requests

99

to your representat(tat-tat)ives!' He spoke wearily, without expectation of answer.

'We have no "representatives", save ourselves,' said Jherek. 'Is there anything wrong with your environment? I'm sure that the Duke of Queens would be only too pleased to make any adjustments you saw fit ...'

'Skree-ee-ee,' said CPS Shashurup desperately. 'It is not(ot-ot) in our nat(tate-tate)ure to (skree) make(cake-cake) threat(et-et-et)s, but we must warn you (skree) that unless we are re(skree)lea(skree)sed our peo(pee-pee)ple will be forced to take steps to pro(pro-pro)tect us and secure(ure-ure) our release. You are behaving childishly! It is imposs(oss-oss)ible to believe(eve-eve-eve) that a race grown so old can still(ill-ill) skree-skree yowl eek yaaaarrrrk!'

Only Mrs Underwood showed any genuine interest in the Chief Public Servant's attempts to communicate with them. 'Shouldn't you release them, Duke of Queens?' she asked mildly. 'I thought it was argued that no life-form was kept here against its will.'

'Ah,' said the Duke, dusting at his braid, 'that is so, by and large. But if I let them go immediately, some rival will acquire them. I have not yet had time to display them as mine, you see.'

'Then how long must they remain prisoners?'

'Prisoners? I do not understand you, Mrs Underwood. But they'll stay here until after this party for Mongrove, at least. I'll conceive a special entertainment later, at which I may display them to full advantage.'

'Irr-re-re-sponsible oaf(f-f-f)!' cried CPS Shashurup, who had overheard some of this. 'Your people already suck(uck-uck) the universe dry and we do not complain(ain-ain-ain). Oh, but we shall see (skree-skree-skree) a change when we are free (ee-ee-ee-ee)!'

The Duke of Queens glanced at his index-finger's nail, in which a small, perfect picture formed. It showed him the party above.

'Ah, Mongrove has arrived at last. Shall we return?'

CHAPTER TWELVE

IN WHICH LORD MONGROVE REMINDS US OF INEVITABLE DOOM

'Truly, my dear friends, I, too, disbelieved, as you do ...' moaned Mongrove from the centre of the hall, '... but Yusharisp showed me withered planets, exhausted stars – matter collapsing, disintegrating, fading to nothing ... Ah, it is bleak out there. It is bleak beyond imagining.' His great, heavy head dropped towards his broad, bulky chest and a monstrous sigh escaped him. Massive hands clasped themselves together just above his mighty stomach. 'All that is left are ghosts and even the ghosts fade. Civilizations that, until recently, spanned a thousand star-systems, have become merely a whisper of static from a detector screen. Gone without trace. Gone without trace. As *we* shall go, my friends.' Mongrove's gaze upon them was a mixture of sympathy and accusation. 'But let my guide Yusharisp, who risked his own life to come to us, to warn us of our fate, and to whom none but I would listen, tell you in his own words.'

'Scarce(skree)ly – scarcely any life survives in the universe,' said the globular alien. 'The process of collapse continues faster than (roar) I predicted. This is partially (skree) the fault of the people of this planet. Your cities (yelp) draw their energy from the easiest available (skree-skree) source. Now they (roar) suck raw energy from disintegrating novae, from already (skree) dying suns. It is the only reason why (skree) you still (yelp) survive!'

Bishop Castle stood at Jherek's left shoulder. He leaned to murmur: 'In truth I become quickly bored with boredom. The Duke of Queens' efforts to make entertainment from that alien are surely useless, as even he must see now.' But he lifted his head and dutifully cried: 'Hurrah! Hurrah!' and applauded.

Mongrove lifted a hand. 'Yusharisp's point is that we are contributing to the speed with which the universe perishes. If we were to use less energy for pursuits like – like this party – we could slow down the rate of collapse. It is all running out, dear friends!'

My Lady Charlotina said, in a loud whisper, 'I thought Mongrove shunned what he called "materialism". This talk smacks of it, if I'm not mistaken. But, then, I probably am.' She smiled to herself.

But Li Pao said firmly: 'He echoes only what I have been saying for years.'

An Iron Orchid, in red and white checks and a simple red and white domino, linked arms with Bishop Castle. 'The world does grow boring, I agree, most concise of clerics. Everyone seems to be repeating themselves.' She giggled. 'Especially me!'

'It is even in our power, thanks to our cities, to preserve this planet,' continued Mongrove, raising his voice above what had become a general babble of conversation. 'Yusharisp's people sent us their finest minds to help. They should have arrived by now. When they do, however, there is just a chance that there will still be time to save our world.'

'He must be referring to those we have just seen in the Duke's menagerie,' said Mrs Underwood. She gripped Jherek's arm. 'We must tell Lord Mongrove where they are!'

Jherek patted her hand. 'We could not. It would be in

very bad taste to spoil the Duke's surprise.'

'Bad taste?'

'Of course.'

She subsided, frowning.

Milo de Mars went by, leaving a trail of perfectly symmetrical gold six-pointed stars in her wake. 'Forgive me, Lord Mongrove,' she fluted, as the giant petulantly brushed the metallic things aside.

'Oh, what self-satisfied fools you are!' cried Mongrove.

'Should we not be? It seems an excellent thing to be,' said Mistress Christia in surprise. 'Is it not what, we are told, the human race has striven for, all these millions of years? Is it not contentment?' She twirled her Grecian gown. 'Is that not what we have?'

'You have not earned it,' said Li Pao. 'I think that is why you will not make efforts to protect it.'

Amelia smiled approval, but Jherek was puzzled. 'What does he mean?'

'He speaks of the practical basis of the morality you were so anxious to understand, Mr Carnelian.'

Jherek brightened, now that he realized they touchd upon a subject of interest. 'Indeed? And what is this practical basis?'

'In essence – that nothing is worth possessing unless it has been worked for.'

He said, with a certain slyness, 'I have worked hard to possess you, dearest Amelia.'

Again amusement threatened to get the better of her. The struggle showed on her face for only a moment before she was once more composed. 'Why, Mr Carnelian, will you always insist on confusing the issue with the introduction of personal matters?'

'Are such matters less important?'

'They have their place. Our conversation, I thought was a trifle more abstract. We discussed morality and its usefulness in life. It was a subject dear to my father's heart and the substance of many a sermon.'

'Yet your civilization, if you'll forgive me saying so, did

not survive for any great length of time. A couple of hundred years saw its complete destruction.'

She was nonplussed, but soon found an answer: 'It is not to do with the survival of civilizations, as such, but with personal satisfaction. If one leads a moral life, a useful life, one is happier.'

He scratched his head beneath the tweed cap. 'It seems to me that almost everyone at the End of Time is happier, however, than were those I encountered in your Dawn Age era. And morality is a mystery to us, as you know.'

'It is a mindless happiness – how shall it survive the disaster Lord Mongrove warns us about?'

'Disaster, surely, is only that if one believes it to be important. How many here, would you say, believe in Mongrove's doom?'

'But they will.'

'Are you certain?'

She cast an eye about her. She could not say that she was certain.

'But are you not afraid, even a little?' she asked him.

'Afraid? Well, I would regret the passing of all this variety, this wit. But it has existed. Doubtless something like it will exist again.'

She laughed and she took his arm. 'If I did not know you better, Mr Carnelian, I should mistake you for the wisest and most profound of philosophers.'

'You flatter me, Amelia.'

Mongrove's voice continued to boom from the babble, but the words were indistinct. 'If you will not save yourselves, think of the knowledge you could save – the inherited knowledge of a million generations!'

An Iron Orchid, in green velvet and brocade, glided by beside Brannart Morphail, who was discoursing along lines very similar to Mongrove's, though it was evident he did not listen to the gloomy giant. With some alarm, Jherek heard her say: 'Of course, you are completely right, Brannart. As a matter of fact, I have it in mind to take a trip through time myself. I know you would disapprove, but it is possible that I could be of use to you ...'

Jherek heard no more of his mother's remarks. He shrugged, dismissing them as the expression of a passing foible.

Sweet Orb Mace was making love to Mistress Christia, the Everlasting Concubine, in a most interesting fashion. Their intertwined bodies drifted amongst the other guests. Elsewhere, Orlando Chombi, Kimick Rentbrain and O'Kala Incarnadine linked hands in a complicated aerial dance, while the recently re-styled Countess of Monte Carlo extended her substance until she was thirty feet tall and all but invisible; this, it seemed, for the entertainment of the Nursery children, who gathered around her and laughed with delight.

'We have a duty to our ancestors!' groaned Mongrove, now, for the moment, out of sight. Jherek thought he was buried somewhere in the sudden avalanche of blue and green roses tipped from Doctor Volospion's Pegasus-drawn platform. 'And to those (skree) who follow us ...' added a piping but somewhat muffled voice.

Jherek sighed. 'If only Jagged would reveal himself, Amelia! Then, I am sure, any confusion would be at an end.'

'He might be dead,' she said. 'You feared as much.'

'It would be a difficult loss to bear. He was my very best friend. I have never known anyone, before, who could not be resurrected.'

'Mongrove's point – that no one shall be resurrected after the apocalypse.'

'I agree the prospect is more attractive, for then none should feel a loss.' They drifted towards the floor, still littered with the feebly fluttering fledgeling hawks. Many had already expired, for Wakaka Nakooka had forgotten to feed them. Absently, Jherek dissipated them, so that they might descend and stand there, looking up at a party grown less sedate than when first they had arrived.

'I thought you were of the opinion that we should live forever, Amelia?' he said, still peering upwards.

'It is my *belief*, not my opinion.'

He failed to distinguish the difference.

'In the Life Beyond,' she said. She tried to speak with conviction, but her voice faltered, adding to herself: 'Well, yes, perhaps there is still a Life Beyond, hard though it is to imagine. Ah, it is so difficult to retain one's ordinary faith . . .'

'It is the end of everything!' continued Mongrove, from somewhere within the mountain of roses. 'You are lost! Lost! You will not listen! You will not understand! Beware! Oh, beware!'

'Mr Carnelian, we should try to make them listen to Lord Mongrove, surely!'

Jherek shook his head. 'He has nothing very interesting to say, Amelia. Has he not said it before? Is not Yusharisp's information identical to that which he first brought, during the Duke's African party. It means little . . .'

'It means much to me.'

'How so?'

'It strikes a chord. Lord Mongrove is like the prophet to whom none would listen. In the end his words were vindicated. The Bible is full of such stories.'

'Then surely, we have no need for more?'

'You are deliberately obtuse!'

'I assure you that I am not.'

'Then help Mongrove.'

'His temperament and mine are too dissimilar. Brannart will comfort him, and Werther de Goethe, too. And Li Pao. He has many friends, many who will listen. They will gather together and agree that all but themselves are fools, that only they have the truth, the right to control events and so on. It will cheer them up and they'll doubtless do little to spoil the pleasure of anyone else. For all we know, their antics will prove entertaining.'

'Is "entertainment" your only criterion?'

'Amelia, if it pleases you, I'll go this moment to Mongrove and groan in tune with him. But my heart will not be in it, love of my life, joy of my existence.'

She sighed. 'I would not have you live a lie, Mr Carnelian. To encourage you towards hypocrisy would be a sin, I know.'

'You have become somewhat sober again, dearest Amelia.'

'I apologize. Evidently, there is nothing to be done, in reality. You think Mongrove postures?'

'As do we all, according to his temperament. It is not that he is insincere, it is merely that he chooses one particular rôle, though he knows many other opinions are as interesting and as valuable as his own.'

'A few short years are left . . .' came Mongrove's boom, more distant now.

'He does not wholly believe in what he says?'

'Yes and no. He chooses wholly to believe. It is a conscious decision. Tomorrow, he could make an entirely different decision, if he became bored with this rôle (and I suspect he *will* become bored, as he realizes how much he bores others).'

'But Yusharisp is sincere.'

'So he is, poor thing.'

'Then there is no hope for the world.'

'Yusharisp believes that.'

'You do not?'

'I believe everything and nothing.'

'I never quite understood before . . . is that the philosophy of the End of Time?'

'I suppose it is.' He looked about him. 'I do not think we shall see Lord Jagged here, after all. Lord Jagged could explain these things to you, for he enjoys discussing abstract matters. I have never much had the penchant. I have always preferred to make things rather than to talk. I am a man of action, you see. Doubtless it is something to do with being the product of natural childbirth.'

Her eyes, when next she looked at him, were full of warmth.

CHAPTER THIRTEEN

THE HONOUR OF AN UNDERWOOD

'I am still uncertain. Perhaps if we began again?'

Amiably, Jherek disintegrated the west wing.

They were rebuilding his ranch. The Bromley-Gothic redbrick villa had vanished. In its place stood something altogether larger, considerably lighter, having more in common with the true Gothic of medieval France and Belgium, with fluted towers and delicately fashioned windows.

'It is all, I think, a trifle too magnificent,' she said. She fingered her fine chin. 'And yet, it would only seem grandiose in Bromley, as it were. Here, it is almost simple.'

'If you will try your own amethyst power-ring ...' he murmured.

'I have still to trust these things ...' But she twisted and thought at the same time.

A fairy-tale tower, the ideal of her girlhood, stood there. She could not bring herself to disseminate it.

He was delighted, admiring its slender hundred-and twenty-feet, topped by twin turrets with red conical roofs. It glittered. It was white. There were tiny windows.

'Such an elegant example of typical Dawn Age architecture!' he complimented her.

'You do not find it too fanciful?' She was shy of her achievement, but pleased.

'A model of utility!'

'Scarcely that ...' She blushed. Her own imagination, made concrete, astonished her.

'More! You must make more!'

The ring was turned again and another tower sprang up, connected to its fellow by a little marble bridge. With some hesitation she disseminated the original building he had made at her request, replacing it with a main hall and living apartments above. She gave her attention to the landscape around. A moat appeared, fed by a sparkling river. Formal gardens, geometric, filled with her favourite flowers, stretched into the distance, giving place to rose bowers and undulating lawns, a lake, with cypresses and poplars and willows. The sky was changed to a pale blue and the small clouds in it were never whiter; then she added subtle colours, pinks and yellows, as of the beginnings of a sunset. All was as she had once dreamed of, not as a respectable Bromley housewife, but as a little girl, who had read fairy stories with a sense that she consulted forbidden texts. Her face shone as she contemplated her handiwork. A new innocence bloomed there. Jherek watched, and revelled in her pleasure.

'Oh, I should not ...'

A unicorn now grazed upon the lawn. It looked up, its eyes mild and intelligent. Its golden horn caught the sunlight.

'It is everything I was told could never be. My mother admonished me, I remember, for entertaining silly fancies. She said no good would come of them.'

'And so you still think, do you not?'

She glanced his way. 'So I *should* think, I suppose.'

He said nothing.

'My mother argued that little girls who believed in fairy tales grew up to be shallow, vain and, ultimately, disappointed, Mr Carnelian. The world, I was told, was harsh and terrible and we were put into it in order that we should be tested for our worthiness to dwell in Heaven.'

'It is a reasonable belief. Though unrewarding, I should have thought, in the long run. Limiting, at least.'

'Limitations were regarded as being good for one. I have expressed that opinion myself.'

'So you have.'

'Yet there are no more cruelties here than there were in my world.'

'Cruelties?'

'Your menageries.'

'Of course.'

'But you do not, I now understand, realize that you are cruel. You are not hypocrites in that particular way.'

He was euphoric. He was enjoying listening to her voice as he might enjoy the peaceful buzz of an insect. He spoke only to encourage her to continue.

'We keep more prisoners in my society, when you think of it,' she said. 'How many wives are prisoners of their homes, their husbands?' She paused. 'I should not dare think such radical ideas at home, much less utter them!'

'Why not?'

'Because I would offend others. Disturb my friends. There are social checks to one's behaviour, far greater than any legal or moral ones. Have you learned that, yet, from my world, Mr Carnelian?'

'I have learned something, but not a great deal. You must continue to teach me.'

'I saw the prisons, when you were incarcerated. How many prisoners are there through no fault of their own? Victims of poverty. And poverty enslaves so many more millions than you could ever contain in your menageries. Oh, I know. I know. You could have argued that, and I should not have been able to deny it.'

'Ah?'

'You are kind to humour me, Mr Carnelian.' Her voice grew vague as she looked again upon her first creation. 'Oh, it is so beautiful!'

He came to stand beside her and when he put an arm about her shoulder, she did not resist.

Some time went by. She furnished their palace with simple, comfortable furniture, refusing to clutter the rooms. She made tapestries and brocades for floors and walls. She re-introduced a strict pattern of day and night. She created two large, long-haired black and white cats, and the parklands around the palace became populated with deer, as well as unicorns. She longed for books, but he could find her none, so in the end she began to write one for herself and found this almost as satisfactory as reading. Yet, still, he must court her. Still she refused the fullest expression of her affections. When he proposed marriage, as he continued to do, frequently, she would reply that she had given an oath in a ceremony to remain loyal to Mr Underwood until death should part them.

He returned, time after time, to the reasonable logic that indeed Mr Underwood was dead, had been dead for many millennia, that she was free. He began to suspect that she did not care a fig for her vows to Mr Underwood, that she played a game with him, or, failing that, waited for him to take some action. But as to what the action should be, she gave him no clue.

This idyll, pleasurable though it was, was marred not only by his frustration, but also by his concerns for his friend, Lord Jagged of Canaria. He had begun to realize to what extent he had relied on Jagged to guide him in his actions, to explain the world to him, to help him shape his own destiny. His friend's humour, his advice, indeed, his very wisdom, were much missed. Every morning, upon awaking, he hoped to see Lord Jagged's air-car upon the horizon, and every morning he was disappointed.

One morning, however, as he lounged alone upon a balcony, while Mrs Underwood worked at her book, he saw a visitor arrive, in some kind of Egyptianate vessel of

111

ebony and gold, and it was Bishop Castle, his high crown nodding on his handsome head, a tall staff in his left hand, his three golden orbs bobbing at his belt, stepping gracefully from air-car to balcony and kissing him lightly upon the forehead, complimenting him on the white linen suit made for him by Mrs Underwood.

'Things have settled, since the Duke's party,' the bishop informed him. 'We return to our old lives with some relief. A great disappointment, Mongrove, didn't you think?'

'The Duke of Queens sets great store by his entertainment value. I cannot think why.'

'He is out of touch with everyone else's taste. Scarcely a recommendation in one who desires to be the most popular of hosts.'

'It is not,' Jherek added, 'as if he were himself interested in this alien's prophecies. He probably hoped that Mongrove would have had some adventures on his trip through the universe — something with a reasonable amount of sensation in it. Yet Mongrove may be relied upon to ruin even the best anecdote.'

'It is why we love him.'

'To be sure.'

Mrs Underwood, in rose-pink and yellow, entered the room behind the balcony. She extended a hand. 'Dear Bishop Castle. How pleasant to see you. You will stay for lunch?'

'If I do not inconvenience you, Mrs Underwood.' It was plain that he had done much research.

'Of course not.'

'And what of my mother, the Iron Orchid?' asked Jherek. 'Have you seen her of late?'

Bishop Castle scratched his nose with his crook. 'You had not heard, then? She seeks to rival you, Jherek, I am sure. She somehow inveigled Brannart Morphail into allowing her the use of one of his precious time-craft. She has gone!'

'Through time?'

'No less. She told Brannart that she would return with proof of his theories, evidence that you manufactured the tales you told him! I am surprised no one has yet informed you.' Bishop Castle laughed. 'She is so original, your beautiful mother!'

'But she may be killed,' said Mrs Underwood. 'Is she aware of the risks?'

'Fully, I gather.'

'Oh!' cried Jherek. 'Mother!' He put his hand to his lips; he bit the lower one. 'It is you, Amelia, she seeks to rival. She thinks she is outdone by you!'

'She spoke of a time for her return?' Mrs Underwood asked Bishop Castle.

'Not really. Brannart might know. He controls the experiment.'

'Controls! Ha!' Jherek put his head in his hands.

'We may only pray – excuse me – hope – that she returns safely,' said Mrs Underwood.

'Time cannot defeat the Iron Orchid!' Bishop Castle laughed. 'You are too gloomy. She will be back soon – doubtless with news of exploits to rival yours – which is what she hopes for, I am sure.'

'It was luck, only, that saved us both from death,' Mrs Underwood told him.

'Then the same luck will come to her aid.'

'You are probably right,' said Jherek. He was despondent. First his best friend gone, and now his mother. He looked at Mrs Underwood, as if she would once again vanish before his eyes, as she had done before, when he had first tried to kiss her, so long ago.

Mrs Underwood spoke rather more cheerfully, in Jherek's view, than the situation demanded. 'Your mother is not one to perish, Mr Carnelian. For all you know, it was merely a facsimile that was sent through time. The original could still be here.'

'I am not sure that is possible,' he said. 'There is something to do with the life essence. I have never properly understood the theory concerning transmigration. But I do not think you can send a doppelganger through time, not without accompanying it.'

'She'll be back,' said Bishop Castle with a smile.

But Jherek, worrying for Lord Jagged, becoming convinced that he had perished, lapsed into silence and was a poor host during lunch.

Several more days passed, without incident, with the occasional visit from My Lady Charlotina or the Duke of Queens or Bishop Castle, again. The conversation turned often to speculation as to the fate of the Iron Orchid, as was inevitable, but if Brannart Morphail had news of her he had passed none of it on, even to My Lady Charlotina who still chose to play patron to him and give him his laboratories in her own vast domicile at Below-the-Lake. Neither would Brannart tell anyone the Iron Orchid's original destination.

In the meanwhile, Jherek continued to pay court to Amelia Underwood. He learned the poems of Wheldrake (or at least, those she could remember) from her and found that they could be interpreted in reference to their own situation – *'So close these lovers were, yet was their union sundered by the world'* – *'Cruel Fortune did dictate that they/Should ever singly pass that way'*, and so on – until she professed a lack of interest in he who had been her favourite poet. But it seemed to Jherek Carnelian that Amelia Underwood began to warm to him a little more. The occasional sisterly kiss became more frequent, the pressure of a hand, the quality of a smile, all spoke of a thaw in her resolve. He took heart. Indeed, so settled had become their domestic routine, that it was almost as if they were married. He hoped that she might slip, almost accidentally, into consummation, given time.

Life flowed smooth and, save for the nagging fear at the back of his mind that his mother and Lord Jagged might never return, he experienced a tranquillity he had not enjoyed since he and Mrs Underwood had first shared a house together; and he refused to remember that whenever he had come to accept such peace, it had always been interrupted by some new drama. But, as the uneventful days continued, his sense of inevitable expectation increased, until he began to wish that whatever it was that was going to happen would happen as soon as possible. He even identified the source of the next blow – it would be delivered by the Iron Orchid, returning with sensational information, or else by Jagged, to tell them that they must go back to the Palaeozoic to complete some overlooked task.

The blow did come. It came one morning, about three weeks after they had settled in their new home. It came as a loud and repetitive knocking on the main door. Jherek stumbled from his bed and went to stand on his balcony, leaning over to see who was disturbing them in this peculiar manner (no one he knew ever used that door). On the bijou drawbridge was grouped a party of men all of whom were familiar. The person knocking on the main door was Inspector Springer, wearing a new suit of clothes and a new bowler hat indistinguishable from his previous ones; gathered around him was a party of burly police officers, some ten or twelve; behind the police officers, looking self-important but a little wild-eyed, stood none other than Mr Harold Underwood, his pince-nez on his nose, his hay-coloured hair neatly parted in the middle, wearing a suit of good, dark worsted, an extremely stiff, white collar and cuffs, a tightly knotted tie and black, polished boots. In his hand he held a hat, similar to Inspector Springer's. Behind this party, a short distance away, in the ornamental garden, there buzzed a huge contraption consisting of a number of inter-connected wheels, ratchets, crystalline rods and what seemed to be padded benches – an open, box-like structure, but bearing a close similarity to the machine Jherek had first seen in the Palaeozoic. At the controls sat the bearded man in plus-fours and Norfolk jacket who had given them his hamper. He was the first to see Jherek. He waved a greeting.

From a nearby balcony there came a stifled shriek: 'Harold!'

Mr Underwood looked up and fixed a cold eye upon his wife, in negligee and slippers of a sort not normally associated with a Bromley housewife.

'Ha!' he said, his worst fears confirmed. Now he saw Jherek, peering down at him. 'Ha!'

'Why are you here?' croaked Jherek, before he realized he would not be understood.

Inspector Springer began to clear his throat, but Harold Underwood spoke first.

'Igrie gazer,' he seemed to say. 'Rijika batterob honour!'

'We had better let them in, Mr Carnelian,' said Mrs Underwood in a faint voice.

CHAPTER FOURTEEN

VARIOUS ALARUMS, A GOOD DEAL
OF CONFUSION, A HASTY EXCURSION

'I 'ave, sir,' said Inspector Springer with heavy satisfaction, 'been invested with Special Powers. The 'Ome Secretary 'imself 'as ordered me to look into this case.'

'The new machine – my, um, Chronomnibus – was requisitioned,' said the time-traveller apologetically from the background. 'As a patriot, though strictly speaking not from this universe ...'

'Under conditions of utmost secrecy,' continued the Inspector, 'we embarked upon our Mission ...'

Jherek and Mrs Underwood stood on their threshold and contemplated their visitors.

'Which is?' Mrs Underwood was frowning pensively at her husband.

'To place the ringleaders of this plot under arrest and return forthwith to our own century so that they – that's you, of course, among 'em – may be questioned as to their motives and intentions.' Inspector Springer was evidently quoting specifically from his orders.

'And Mr Underwood?' Jherek asked politely. 'Why is he here?'

' 'E's one o' the few 'oo can identify the people we're

after. Anyway, 'e volunteered.'

She said, bemusedly: 'Have you come to take me back, Harold?'

'Ha!' said her husband.

Sergeant Sherwood, sweating and, it seemed, only barely in control of himself, fingering his tight, dark blue collar, emerged from the ranks of his constables (who, like him, seemed to be suffering from shock) and, saluting, stood beside his leader.

'Shall we place these two under arrest, sir?'

Inspector Springer licked his lips contemplatively. ''Ang on a mo, sergeant, before putting 'em in the van.' He reached into his jacket pocket and produced a document, turning to Jherek. 'Are you the owner of these premises?'

'Not exactly,' said Jherek, wondering if the translation pills he and Amelia had taken were doing their job properly. 'That is to say, if you could explain the meaning of the term, perhaps I could . . .'

'Are you or are you not the owner . . .'

'Do you mean did I create this house?'

'If you built it, too, fair enough. All I want to know . . .'

'Mrs Underwood created it, didn't you, Amelia?'

'Ha!' said Mr Underwood, as if his worst suspicions were confirmed. He glared coldly at the fairy-tale palace.

'This lady built it?' Inspector Springer became pettish. 'Now, listen 'ere . . .'

'I gather you are unfamiliar with the methods of building houses at the End of Time, Inspector,' said Mrs Underwood, making some effort to save the situation. 'One has power-rings. They enable one —'

Inspector Springer raised a stern hand. 'Let me put it another way. I 'ave 'ere a warrant to search your premises or, indeed, any premises I might regard as 'avin' upon them evidence in this matter, or 'arbourin' suspected criminals. So, if you will kindly allow me and my men to pass . . .'

'Certainly.' Jherek and Amelia stepped aside as Inspec-

118

tor Springer led his men into the hall. Harold Underwood hesitated a moment, but at last crossed the threshold, as if into the netherworld, while the time-traveller hung back, his cap in his hands, murmuring disconnected phrases. 'Awfully embarrassing ... had no idea ... a bit of a joke, really ... regret the inconvenience ... Home Secretary assured me ... can see no reason for intrusion ... would never have agreed ...' But at Jherek's welcoming gesture, he joined the others. 'Delightful house ... very similar to those structures one finds in the, um ... fifty-eighth century, is it? ... Glad to find you arrived back safely ... am still a trifle at sea, myself ...'

'I have never seen such a large time-machine,' said Jherek, hoping to put him at ease.

'Have you not?' The time-traveller beamed. 'It is unusual, isn't it? Of course, the commercial possibilities have not escaped me, though since the Government took an interest, everything has been shrouded in secrecy, as you can imagine. This was my first opportunity to test it under proper conditions.'

'It would be best, sir, I think,' cautioned Inspector Springer, 'to say no more to these people. They are, after all, suspected alien agents.'

'Oh, but we have met before. I had no idea, when I agreed to help, that these were the people you meant. Believe me, Inspector, they are almost undoubtedly innocent of any crime.'

'That's for me to decide, sir,' reproved the policeman. 'The evidence I was able to place before the 'Ome Secretary upon my return was sufficient to convince 'im of a plot against the Crown.'

'He seemed somewhat bewildered by the whole affair. His questions to me were not exactly explicit ...'

'Oh, it's *bewildering*, right enough. Cases of this kind often are. But I'll get to the bottom of it, given time.' Inspector Springer fingered his watch-chain. 'That's why there is a police force, sir. To solve bewildering cases.'

'Are you certain that you are within your jurisdiction,

Inspector . . .' began Mrs Underwood.

'I 'ave ascertained from the gentleman 'ere,' Inspector Springer indicated the time-traveller, 'that we are still on English soil. Therefore . . .'

'Is it really?' cried Jherek. 'How wonderful!'

'Thought you'd get away with it, eh?' murmured Sergeant Sherwood, eyeing him maliciously. 'Made a bit of a mistake, didn't you, my lad?'

' 'Ow many others staying 'ere?' Inspector Springer enquired as he and his men tramped into the main hall. He looked with disgust upon the baskets of flowers which hung everywhere, upon the tapestries and the carpets and the furniture, which was of the most decadent sort of design.

'Only ourselves.' Mrs Underwood glanced away from the grim eye of her husband.

'Ha!' said Mr Underwood.

'We have separate apartments,' she explained to the inspector, upon whose ruddy features there had spread the suggestion of a leer.

'Well, sir,' said Sergeant Sherwood, 'shall we take this pair back first?'

'To the nineteenth century?' Jherek asked.

'That is what he means,' the time-traveller replied on the sergeant's behalf.

'This would be your opportunity, Amelia.' Jherek's voice was small. 'You said that you wished, still, to return . . .'

'It is true . . .' she began.

'Then . . .?'

'The circumstances . . .'

'You two 'ad better stay 'ere,' Inspector Springer was telling two of the constables, 'to keep an eye on 'em. We'll search the premises.' He led his men off towards a staircase. Jherek and Amelia sat down on a padded bench.

'Would you care for some tea?' Amelia asked her husband, the time-traveller and the two constables.

'Well . . .' said one of the constables.

'I think that'd be all right, ma'am,' said the other.

Jherek was eager to oblige. He turned a power-ring and produced a silver tea-pot, six china cups and saucers, a milk-jug and a hot-water jug, a silver tea-strainer, six silver spoons and a primus stove.

'Sugar, I think,' she murmured, 'but not the stove.'

He corrected his error.

The two police constables sat down together quite suddenly, goggling at the tea. Mr Underwood remained standing, but seemed rather more stiff than he had been. He muttered to himself. Only the time-traveller reacted in a normal fashion.

Mrs Underwood seemed to be suppressing amusement as she poured the tea and handed out the cups. The constables accepted the tea, but only one of them drank any. The other merely said, 'Gord!' and put his cup on the table, while his companion grinned weakly and said: 'Very good, very good,' over and over again.

From above there came a sudden loud cracking sound and a yell. Puzzled, Jherek and Amelia looked up.

'I do hope they are not damaging ...' began the time-traveller.

There was a thunder of boots and Inspector Springer, Sergeant Sherwood and their men came tumbling, breathless, back into the hall.

'They're attacking!' cried Sergeant Sherwood to the other two policemen.

' 'Oo?'

'The enemy, of course!' Inspector Springer answered, running to peer cautiously out of the window. 'They must know we've occupied these premises. They're a cunning lot, I'll grant you that.'

'What happened up there, Inspector?' asked Jherek, carrying forward a cup of tea for his guest.

'Something took the top off the tower, that's all!' Automatically the inspector accepted the tea. 'Clean off. Some kind of 'igh-powered naval gun, I'd say. 'Ave you got any sea near 'ere?'

'None, I fear. I wonder who could have done that.' Jherek looked enquiringly at Amelia. She shrugged.

'The Wrath of God!' announced Mr Underwood helpfully, but nobody took much notice of his suggestion.

'I remember once, some flying machine of the Duke of Queens' crashed into my ranch,' Jherek said. 'Did you notice a flying machine, Inspector?'

Inspector Springer continued to peer through the window. 'It was like a bolt from the blue,' he said.

'One minute the roof was there,' added Sergeant Sherwood, 'the next it was gone. There was this explosion — then — bang! — gone. It got very 'ot for a second, too.'

'Sounds like some sort of ray,' said the time-traveller, helping himself to another cup of tea.

Inspector Springer proved himself a reader of the popular weeklies by the swiftness with which he accepted the notion. 'You mean a Death Ray?'

'If you like.'

Inspector Springer fingered his moustache. 'We were fools not to come armed,' he reflected.

'Ah!' Jherek remembered his first encounter with the brigand-musicians in the forest. 'That's probably the Lat returned. They had weapons. They demonstrated one. Very powerful they were, too.'

'Those Latvians. I might 'ave guessed!' Inspector Springer crouched lower. ''Ave you any means of telling 'em you're our prisoners?'

'None at all, I fear. I could go and find them, but they could be hundreds of miles away.'

''undreds? Oh, Lor!' exclaimed Sergeant Sherwood. He looked at the ceiling, as if he expected it to fall in on him. 'You're right, Inspector. We should've put in for some pistols.'

'The Day of Doom is here!' intoned Harold Underwood, raising a finger.

'We must introduce him to Lord Mongrove,' Jherek said, inspired. 'They would get on very well, don't you think, Amelia?'

But she did not reply. She was staring with a mixture of sympathy and resignation at her poor, mad husband. 'I am to blame,' she said. 'It is all my doing. Oh, Harold, Harold.'

There came another loud report. Cracks began to appear in the walls and ceiling. Jherek turned a power-ring and re-formed the palace. 'I think you'll find the roof's back on, Inspector, should you wish to continue your tour.'

'I'll receive a medal for this, if I ever get back,' said Inspector Springer to himself. He sighed.

'I'd suggest, sir,' said his sergeant, 'that we make the most of what we've got and return with these two.'

'You're probably right. We'll do a dash for it. Better put the gyves on 'em, eh?'

Two constables produced their handcuffs and advanced towards Jherek and Amelia.

At that moment an apparition appeared at the window and drifted through. It was Bishop Castle, completely out of breath, looking extremely excited, his huge mitre askew. 'Oh, the adventures, my dears! The Lat have returned and are laying waste to *everything*! Murder, pillage, rape! It's marvellous! Ah, you have company ...'

'I believe you've met most of them,' Jherek said. 'This is Inspector Springer, Sergeant Sherwood ...'

Bishop Castle subsided slowly to the floor, nodding and smiling. Blinking, the constables backed away.

'They have taken *prisoners*, too. Just as they took us prisoner, that time. Ah, boredom is banished, at last! And there has been a *battle* – the Duke of Queens magnificent, in charge of our aerial fleet (it did not last more than a few seconds, unfortunately, but it did look pretty), and My Lady Charlotina as an amazon, in a *chariot*. Amusement returns to our dull world! Dozens, at least, are *dead*!' He waved his crook apologetically at the company. 'You must forgive the interruption. I am so sorry. I forget my manners.'

'I know you,' said Inspector Springer significantly. 'I

arrested you before, at the Café Royal.'

'So pleased to see you again, Inspector.' It was plain that Bishop Castle had not understood a word that Inspector Springer had said. He popped a translation pill into his mouth. 'You decided to continue your party, then, at the End of Time?'

'End of Time?' said Harold Underwood, showing fresh interest. 'Armageddon?'

Amelia Underwood went to him. She tried to sooth him. He shook her off.

'Ha!' he said.

'Harold. You're being childish.'

'Ha!'

Despondently, she remained where she was, staring at him.

'You should see the *destruction*,' continued Bishop Castle. He laughed. 'Nothing at all is left of Below-the-Lake, unless Brannart's laboratories are still there. But the menagerie is completely gone, and all My Lady Charlotina's apartments – the lake itself – all gone! It'll take her hours to replace them.' He tugged at Jherek's sleeve. 'You must return with me and see the spectacle, Jherek. That's why I came away, to make sure you did not miss it all.'

'Your friends aren't going anywhere, sir. And neither, I might add, are you.' Inspector Springer signalled his constables forward.

'How wonderful! You'd take us prisoners, too! Have you any weapons, like the Lats? You must produce something, Inspector, to rival their effects, unless you wish to be absolutely outshone!'

'I thought these Latvians were on your side,' said Sergeant Sherwood.

'Indeed, no! What would be the fun of that?'

'You say they're destroying everything. Rape, pillage, murder?'

'Exactly.'

'Well, I never . . .' Inspector Springer scratched his head.

'So you're merely the foils of these people, instead o' the other way about?'

'I think there's a misunderstanding, Inspector,' said Mrs Underwood. 'You see ...'

'Misunderstanding!' Suddenly Harold Underwood lurched towards her. 'Jezebel!'

'Harold!'

'Ha!'

There came another boom, louder than the previous ones, and the ceiling vanished to reveal the sky.

'It can only be the Lat,' said Bishop Castle, with the air of an expert. 'You really must come with me. Jherek and Amelia, unless you want to be destroyed before you have enjoyed any of the fun.' He began to lead them towards his air-car at the window. 'There'll be nothing left of our world, at this rate!'

'Do they really mean to destroy you all?' asked the time-traveller, as they went by.

'I gather not. They originally came for prisoners. Mistress Christia, of course,' this to Jherek, 'is now a captive. I think it's their habit to go about the galaxy killing the males and abducting the females.'

'You'll let them?' Mrs Underwood enquired.

'What do you mean?'

'You won't stop this?'

'Oh, eventually, I suppose we'll have to. Mistress Christia wouldn't be happy in space. Particularly if it has become as bleak as Mongrove reports.'

'What do you say, Amelia? Shall we go and watch? Join in?' Jherek wanted to know.

'Of course not.'

He suppressed his disappointment.

'Perhaps you wish *me* to be abducted by those creatures?' she said.

'Indeed, no!'

'Perhaps it would be better to return in my Chronomnibus,' suggested the time-traveller, 'at least until —'

'Amelia?'

125

She shook her head. 'The circumstances are too shameful for me. Respectable society would be closed to me now.'

'Then you will stay, dearest Amelia?'

'Mr Carnelian, this is no time to continue with your pesterings. I will accept that I am an outcast, but I still have certain standards of behaviour. Besides, I am concerned for Harold. He is not himself. And for that, we are to blame. Well, perhaps not you, really — but I must accept a large share of guilt. I should have been firmer. I should not have admitted my love—' and she burst into tears.

'You do admit it, then, Amelia!'

'You are heartless, Mr Carnelian,' she sobbed, 'and scarcely tactful ...'

'Ha!' said Harold Underwood. 'It is just as well that I have already begun divorce proceedings ...'

'Excellent!' cried Jherek.

Another boom.

'My machine!' exclaimed the time-traveller, and ran outside.

'Take cover, men.' Inspector Springer called. They all lay down.

Bishop Castle was already in his air-car, surrounded by a cloud of dust. 'Are you coming, Jherek?'

'I think not. I hope you enjoy yourself, Bishop Castle.'

'I shall. I shall.' The air-car began to rise, Charon's barge, into the upper atmosphere.

Only Mr and Mrs Underwood and Jherek Carnelian remained standing, in the ruins of the palace. 'Come,' said Jherek to them both, 'I think I know where we can find safety.' He turned a power-ring. His old air-car, the locomotive, materialized. It was in gleaming red and black now, but lime-coloured smoke still puffed from its stack. 'Forgive the lack of invention,' he said to them, 'but as we are in haste ...'

'You would save Harold, too?' she said, as Jherek helped her husband aboard.

126

'Why not? You say you are concerned for him.' He grinned cheerfully, while overhead a searing, scarlet bolt of pure energy went roaring by, 'Besides, I wish to hear the details of this divorce he plans. Is that not the ceremony that must take place before we can be married?'

She made no reply to this, as she joined him on the footplate. 'Where are we going, Mr Carnelian?'

The locomotive began to puff skyward. 'I'm full of old smokies,' he sang, 'I'm covered in dough. I've eaten blue plovers and I'm snorting up coke!' Mr Underwood clutched the rail and stared down at the ruins they left behind. His knees were shaking. 'It's a railroad song, from your own time,' Jherek explained. 'Would you like to be the fireman?'

He offered Mr Underwood the platinum shovel. Mr Underwood accepted the shovel without a word and, mechanically, began to stoke coal into the fire-chamber.

'Mr Carnelian! Where are we going?'

'To certain safety, dearest Amelia. To certain safety, I assure you.'

CHAPTER FIFTEEN

IN WHICH JHEREK CARNELIAN AND MRS UNDERWOOD FIND SANCTUARY OF SORTS, AND MR UNDERWOOD MAKES A NEW FRIEND

'You are not disturbed, dearest Amelia, by this city?'

'I find the place improbable. I failed to realize, listening only to talk of such settlements, how vast and how, well, how unlike cities they were!'

Mr Underwood stood some distance away, on the other side of the little plaza. Green globes of fuzzy light, about the size of tennis balls, ran up and down his outstretched arms; he watched them with childlike delight; behind him the air was black, purple, dark green shot with crimson, as chemicals expanded and contracted in a kind of simulation of breathing, giving off their vapours; bronze sparks showered nearby, pinkish energy arced from one tower to another; steel sang. The city murmured to itself, almost asleep, certainly drowsy. Even the narrow rivulets of mercury, criss-crossing the ground at their feet, seemed to be running slowly.

'The cities protect themselves,' Jherek explained. 'I have seen it before. No weapon can operate within them, no weapon can harm them from without, because they can always command more energy than any weapon brought against them, you see. It was part of their original design.'

'This resembles a manufactory more than it does a township,' she remarked.

'It is actually,' he told her, 'more in the nature of a museum. There are several such cities on the planet; they contain what remains of our knowledge.'

'These fumes – are they not poisonous?'

'Not to Man. They could not be.'

She accepted his assurance, but continued wary, as he led them from the plaza, through an arcade of lurid yellow and mauve metallic fronds, faintly reminiscent of those they had seen in the Palaeozoic; a strange greyish light fell through the fronds and distorted their shadows. Mr Underwood wandered some distance behind them, softly singing.

'We must consider,' she whispered, 'how Harold is to be saved.'

'Saved for what?'

'From his insanity.'

'He seems happier in the city.'

'He believes himself in Hell, no doubt. Just as I once believed. Inspector Springer should never have brought him.'

'I am not altogether sure that the inspector is quite himself.'

'I agree, Mr Carnelian. All this smacks of political panic at home. There is thought to be considerable interest in Spiritualism and Freemasonry among certain members of the Cabinet, at the present time. There is even some talk that the Prince of Wales . . .'

She continued in this vein for a while, mystifying him entirely. Her information, he gathered, was gleaned from a broadsheet which Mr Underwood had once acquired.

The arcade gave way to a chasm running between high, featureless buildings, their walls covered with chemical stains and peculiar semi-biological growths, some of which palpitated; ahead of them was something globular, glowing and dark, which rolled away from them as they advanced and, as they reached the end of the chasm, vanished. Here the vista widened and they could see across a plain littered with half-rotted metal relics to where, in the distance, angry flames spread themselves against an invisible wall.

'There!' he said. 'That must be the Lat's weapons at work. The city throws up its defences. See, I told you that we should be safe, dear Amelia.'

She glanced over her shoulder to where her husband sat upon a structure that seemed part of stone and part of some kind of hardened resin. 'I wish you would try to be more tactful, Mr Carnelian. Remember that my husband is within earshot. Consider his feelings, if you will not consider mine!'

'But he has relinquished you to me. He said as much. By your customs that is sufficient, is it not?'

'He divorces me, that is all. I have a right to choose or reject any husband I please.'

'Of course. But you choose me. I know.'

'I have not told you that.'

'You have, Amelia. You forget. You have mentioned more than once that you love me.'

'That does not mean – would not mean – that I would necessarily marry you, Mr Carnelian. There is still every chance that I may return to Bromley – or at least to my own time.'

'Where you will be an outcast. You said so.'

'In Bromley. Not everywhere.' But she frowned. 'I can imagine the scandal. The newspapers will have published something, to be sure. Oh, dear.'

'You seemed to be enjoying life at the End of Time.'

'Perhaps I would continue to do so, Mr Carnelian, were I not haunted, very definitely, by the Past.' Another glance over her shoulder. 'How is one ever to relax?'

'This is a fluke. It is the first time anything like it has ever occurred here.'

'Besides, I would remind you that, according to Bishop Castle (not to mention the evidence of our own eyes) your world is being destroyed about your ears.'

'For the moment, only. It can soon be replaced.'

'Lord Mongrove and Yusharisp would have us believe otherwise.'

'It is hard to take them seriously.'

'For you, perhaps. Not for me, Mr Carnelian. What they say makes considerable sense.'

'*Opportunities for redemption must therefore be few in such an ambience as you describe,*' said quite another voice, a low, mellow, slightly sleepy voice.

'There are none,' said Mr Underwood, 'at least that I know of.'

'*That is interesting. I seem to recall something of the theory, but most of the information I would require was stored elsewhere, in a sister city, whose co-ordinates I cannot quite recollect. I am of a mind to believe, however, that you are either a manifestation of this city's delusions (which proliferate notoriously, these days) or else that you are deluded yourself, a victim of too much morbid fascination with ancient mythologies. I could be mistaken — there was a time when I was infallible, I think. I am not sure that your description of this city tallies with the facts which remain at my command. You could argue, I know, that I myself am deluded as to the truth, yet my evidence would seem to tally with my instincts, whereas you, yourself, make intellectual rather than instinctive assumptions; that at least is what I gather from the illogicalities so far expressed in your analysis. You have contradicted yourself at least three times since you sat down on my shell.*'

It was the compound of rock and resin that spoke. 'One form of memory bank,' murmured Jherek. 'There are so many kinds, not always immediately recognizable.'

'*I think,*' continued the bank, '*that you are still confused and have not yet ordered your thoughts sufficiently to communicate properly with me. I assure you that I will function much more satisfactorily if you phrase your remarks better.*'

Mr Underwood did not seem offended by this criticism.

'I think you are right,' he said. 'I am confused. Well, I am mad, to be blunt.'

'*Madness may only be the expression of ordinary emotional confusion. Fear of madness can cause, I believe, a retreat into the very madness one fears. This is only superficially a paradox. Madness may be said to be a tendency to simplify, into easily grasped metaphors, the nature of the world. In your own case, you have plainly been confounded by unexpected complexities, therefore you are inclined to retreat into simplification – this talk of Damnation and Hell, for instance – to create a world whose values are unambivalent, unequivocal. It is a pity that so few of my own ancestors survive for they, by their very nature, would have responded better to your views. On the other hand it may be that you are not content with this madness, that you would rather face the complexities, feel at ease with them. If so, I am sure that I can help, in a small way.*'

'You are very kind,' said Mr Underwood.

'*Nonsense. I am glad to be of service. I have had nothing to do for the best part of a million years. I was in danger of growing "rusty". Luckily, having no mechanical parts, I can remain dormant for a long time without any especially deleterious effects. Though, as part of a very complex system, there is much information I can no longer call upon.*'

'Then you are of the opinion that this is not the afterlife, that I am not here as punishment for my sins, that I shall not be here for eternity, that I am not, as it were, dead.'

'*You are certainly not dead, for you can still converse, feel, think and experience physical needs and discomforts ...*'

The bank had a penchant for abstract conversation which seemed to suit Mr Underwood, though Jherek and Amelia became quickly bored listening to it. 'It reminds me of an old schoolmaster I once had,' she whispered, and she grinned. 'It is just what Harold needs really, at present.'

The vivid splashes of light no longer spread across the horizon and the scene darkened. No sun could be observed in the lurid sky, across which clouds of queerly coloured gases perpetually drifted. Behind them, the city seemed to stir, shuddering with age and strain, groaning almost complainingly.

'What would happen to you if your cities collapsed?' she asked him.

'That is impossible. They are self-perpetuating.'

'There is no evidence of that.' Even as she spoke, two of the metallic structures fell into the dust and became dust themselves.

'Yet they are,' he told her. 'In their own way. They have been like this for millennia, somehow surviving. We see only the surface. The essence of the cities is not so tangible, and that is as robust as ever.'

She accepted what he said with a shrug. 'How long must we remain here, then?'

'You sought escape from the Lat, did you not? We remain here until the Lat leave the planet.'

'You do not know when that will be?'

'It will be soon, I am sure. Either they will become bored with the game or we will. Then the game will end.'

'With how many dead?'

'None, I hope.'

'You can resurrect everyone?'

'Certainly.'

'Even the denizens of your menageries?'

'Not all. It depends how solidly they have made an impression on our own memories, you see. Our rings work from our minds, to achieve the reconstructions.'

She did not pursue the topic. 'We seem as thoroughly marooned now at the End of Time as we did at the Beginning,' she said moodily. 'How few are our moments of ordinary living ...'

'That will change. These are particularly agitated days.

Brannart explained that the chronological fluctuations are unusually persistent. We must all agree to stop travelling through time for a while, then everything will be back to normal.'

'I admire your optimism, Mr Carnelian.'

'Thank you, Amelia.' He began to walk again. 'This is the very city where I was conceived, the Iron Orchid told me. With some difficulty, it seems.'

She looked back. Mr Underwood still sat upon the memory bank, deep in conversation. 'Should we leave him?'

'We can return for him later.'

'Very well.'

They stepped upon thin silver surfaces which creaked as they crossed, but did not crack. They ascended a flight of ebony stairs, towards an ornamental bridge.

'It would seem fitting,' said Jherek, 'if I were to propose formally to you here, Amelia, as my father proposed to my mother.'

'Your father?'

'A mystery my mother chooses to perpetuate.'

'So you do not know who —'

'I do not.'

She pursed her lips. 'In Bromley such a fact would be sufficient to put a complete bar on marriage, you know.'

'Truly?'

'Oh, yes.

'But we are not in Bromley,' she added.

He smiled. 'Indeed, we are not.'

'However ...'

'I understand.'

'Please, continue ...'

'I was saying that it would seem fitting that I should ask you, here in this city where I was conceived, for your hand in marriage.'

'Should I ever be free to give it, you mean?'

'Exactly.'

'Well, Mr Carnelian, I cannot say that this is sudden. But . . .'

'Mibix dug frishy hrunt!' said a familiar voice, and across the bridge came marching Captain Mubbers and his men, armed to the teeth and looking not a little put out.

CHAPTER SIXTEEN

THE SKULL BENEATH THE PAINT

When Captain Mubbers saw them he stopped suddenly, aiming his instrument-weapon at Jherek.

Jherek was almost pleased to see him. 'My dear Captain Mubbers ...' he began.

'Mr Carnelian! He is armed!'

Jherek could not quite understand the point of her excitement. 'Yes. The music they produce is the most beautiful I have ever heard.'

Captain Mubbers plucked a string. There came a grinding noise from the bell-shaped muzzle of his weapon; a slight fizzle of blue sparks appeared for a moment around the rim. Captain Mubbers uttered a deep sigh and threw the thing to the flagstones of the bridge. Similar grindings and fizzlings came from the other instruments held by his men.

Popping a translation pill into his mouth (he had taken to carrying them everywhere just recently) Jherek said:

'What brings you to the city, Captain Mubbers?'

'Mind your own smelly business, sonny jim,' said the leader of the space-invaders. 'All we armjoint want to do now is find a shirt-elastic way out!'

'I can't understand why you wanted to come in, though ...' He glanced apologetically at Mrs Underwood, who could not understand anything that was being said. He offered her a pill. She refused. She folded her arms in an attitude of resignation.

'Spoils,' said another of the Lat.

'Shut it, Rokfrug,' Captain Mubbers ordered.

But Rokfrug continued:

'The knicker-patch place seemed so rotten-well protected that we thought there was bound to be something worth having here. Just our shirt-elastic luck —'

'I said shut it, arse-brain!'

But Captain Mubbers' men seemed to be losing faith in his authority. The crossed their three eyes in a most offensive manner and made rude gestures with their elbows.

'Weren't you already sufficiently successful elsewhere?' Jherek asked Rokfrug. 'I thought you were doing extremely well with the destruction, the rape and so on ...'

'Pissing right we were, until ...'

'Cork your hole, bum-face!' shouted his leader.

'Oh, elbow-off!' retorted Rokfrug, but seemed aware that he had gone too far. His voice became a self-pitying mumble as Captain Mubbers gazed disapprovingly back at him. Even his fellows plainly thought Rokfrug's language had put him beyond the pale.

'We're under a bit of a strain,' said one of them, by way of apology.

'Who wouldn't be?' Captain Mubbers kicked petulantly at his abandoned weapon. 'All the farting trouble we went to to get knicker-patching back to our ship in the first place ...'

'... and everything we laid waste to crapping re-appearing,' complained Rokfrug, evidently glad to find a point of agreement with his captain.

'... and all our puking prisoners suddenly disappearing ...' added another.

'What's the point of it?' Captain Mubbers asked Jherek

plaintively. 'When we sighted this planet we thought looting it'd be as easy as wiping your bum.'

'Ever since,' said Rokfrug, 'we've been buggered about. These people haven't got the shirt-elastic they were born with. No common sense. How can you terrorize people who keep laughing at you? Besides, the scenery keeps changing . . .'

'It's a Planet of Illusions,' said Captain Mubbers portentously. His pupils darted about in his single eye. 'I mean, this is probably another of their traps.' He focussed on Jherek. 'Is it? You seem a decent sort of bugger, basically. Is it?'

'I don't think anyone's been deliberately misleading you,' Jherek told him. 'In fact, there seems to have been an effort to accommodate you. What exactly happened? Who stopped you?'

'Well, it was half-and-half. Partly we just ran out of farting steam,' Rokfrug said. 'Then these soppy little round buggers arrived. They —'

Mrs Underwood was tapping Jherek urgently on the arm.

He turned, at last, to look at her. Plodding up the steps behind them, grim-faced and triumphant, was Inspector Springer, Sergeant Sherwood and the party of constables.

'Gee noo fig tendej vega!' said Inspector Springer.

'Flow hard!' exclaimed Mrs Underwood.

It was time for Jherek to swallow a fresh pill.

'Led us straight to 'em, didn't you?' Inspector Springer waved his men forward. 'Shackle 'em, lads!'

The constables, moving like automata, pressed forward to arrest the unresisting Lat.

'I knew you'd arrange a meeting sooner or later,' Inspector Springer told Jherek. 'That's why I let you get away.'

'But how were you able to follow us, Inspector?' Mrs Underwood asked.

'Commandeered a vehicle,' Sergeant Sherwood told her importantly.

'Whose?'

'Oh – 'is ...' A thumb was jerked backward.

Both Jherek and Amelia turned and looked below. There stood the Duke of Queens, wearing a bright pastel blue uniform not dissimilar in cut to Sergeant Sherwood's. As they saw him he gave a cheerful wave of his bright yellow truncheon and blew his silver whistle.

'Good heavens!' she exclaimed.

'We've made 'im an honorary constable, 'aven't we, Inspector?' said Sergeant Sherwood.

'There's no 'arm in 'umorin' 'em, sometimes.' Inspector Springer smiled to himself. 'If it's to your advantage.'

'Kroofrudi hrunt!' said Captain Mubbers as he was led away.

The city shuddered and groaned. A sudden darkness came and went. Jherek noticed that everyone's skins seemed ghastly pale, almost blue, and the light gave their eyes a peculiar flat sheen, so that they were like the eyes of statues.

'Cripes,' said Sergeant Sherwood. 'What was that?'

'The city —' Mrs Underwood whispered. 'It is so still. So silent.' She moved closer to Jherek. She gripped his arm. He was pleased to comfort her. 'Does this often happen?'

'To my knowledge, no ...'

Everyone had stopped moving, even the Duke of Queens, below. The Lat grunted nervously to one another. The mouths of the majority of the constables hung open.

Another great shudder. Somewhere in the distance a piece of metal rattled and then fell with a crash, but that was the only sound.

Jherek pressed her towards the stair. 'We had better get to the ground, I think. If that *is* the ground.'

'An earthquake?'

'The world is too old for earthquakes, Amelia.'

They hurried down the steps and their action lent motion to the others, who followed.

'Harold must be found,' said Mrs Underwood. 'Is there danger, Mr Carnelian?'

'I do not know.'

'You said the city was safe.'

'From the Lat.' He could scarcely bear to look at her deathly-pale skin. He blinked, as if blinking would dispel the scene, but the scene remained.

They reached the Duke of Queens. The Duke stroked his beard, which had gone a seedy sort of purple colour. 'I stopped by at your palace, Jherek, but you had gone on. Inspector Springer told me that he, too, was looking for you, so we followed in your wake. It took a while to find you. You know what these cities are like.' He fingered his whistle. 'Wouldn't you say this one was behaving a bit oddly, at present, though?'

'Collapsing?'

'Possibly – or undergoing some sort of radical change. The cities are said to be capable of restoring themselves. Could that be it?'

'There is no evidence ...'

The Duke nodded. 'Yet it can't be breaking down. The cities are immortal.'

'Breaking down superficially, perhaps.'

'One hopes that is all it is. You do look sickly, Jherek, my darling.'

'We all do, I think. The light.'

'Indeed.' The Duke replaced his whistle in his pocket. 'Those aliens of mine escaped, you know. While the Lat were on the rampage. They got to their own ship, with Yusharisp and Mongrove.'

'They've left?'

'Oh, no! They're spoiling everything. The Lat must be annoyed. They look a bit annoyed, don't they? Yusharisp and company have taken over!' The Duke laughed, but the sound was so unpleasant, even to his own ears, that he stopped. 'Ha, ha ...'

The city seemed to lurch, as if the entire structure slipped downhill. They recovered their balance.

'We'd better proceed to the nearest exit,' said one of the constables in a hollow voice. 'Walking, not running. As long as nobody panics, we'll be able to evacuate the premises in no time at all.'

'We've got what we came for,' agreed Sergeant Sherwood. His uniform had turned a luminous grey. He kept brushing at it, as if he thought the colour was dust clinging to the material.

'Where did we leave the whatsit?' Inspector Springer removed his bowler hat and wiped the inner band with a handkerchief. He looked enquiringly at the Duke of Queens. 'Attention there, Special Constable!' His grin was unspontaneous and horrible. 'The airship thing?' There had never been jocularity so false.

For a moment the Duke of Queens was so puzzled by the inspector's manner that he merely stared.

'The airship, ho, ho, ho, what brought us 'ere!' Inspector Springer replaced his hat and swallowed rapidly two or three times.

The Duke was vague. 'Over there, I think.' He rotated slowly, gesturing with his truncheon (which had turned brown), seeking his bearings. 'Or was it that way?'

'Cor blimey!' said Inspector Springer in disgust.

'Mibix?' Captain Mubbers spoke absently, as one whose mind is on other things. He returned to chewing on the metal of his hand-cuffs.

The ground made a moaning sound and shivered.

'Harold.' Mrs Underwood plucked at Jherek's sleeve. He noticed that the white linen of his suit had become a patchy green. 'We must find him, Mr Carnelian.'

As Jherek and Amelia began to run back to where they had left her husband Inspector Springer also broke into a trot, closely followed by his men, carrying the muttering but unresisting Lat between them, and lastly by the Duke of Queens who was beginning to cheer up at the prospect of action. Action, sensation, was his lifeblood; he wilted without it.

As Jherek and Amelia ran, they heard the piercing eery

141

tones of the Duke's whistle and his lusty voice crying:
'Halloo! View halloo!'

Tiny whispering noises issued from the ground, with
each step that they made. Something hot and organic
seemed at one point to be pulsing beneath their feet. They
reached the plain of rotting metal. Harold Underwood
could be distinguished through the murky semi-darkness,
still deep in conversation with his friend, the rock. He
looked up. 'Ha!' His tone was kindlier. 'So you are all
here, now. It says something, does it not, for our earthly
hypocrisies?' Evidently the rock had made no real impression on his convictions.

The plain gasped, gave way and became a mile-wide pit.

'I think I'd better make a new air-car,' said the Duke of
Queens, coming to a sudden halt.

Harold Underwood crossed to the lip of the pit and
stared down. He scratched his hay-coloured hair, disturbing the parting. 'So there's another level, at least,' he
mused. 'I suppose one should be relieved.' He made to investigate further but did not demur when his wife gently
drew him back.

The Duke of Queens was twisting all his rings. 'Do our
rings not work in the city itself?' he asked Jherek.

'I can't remember.'

At their backs a building silently burst. They watched
the debris float by overhead. Jherek noticed that all their
skins now had a mottled, glossy appearance, like mother-
of-pearl. He moved closer to Amelia, who still clutched her
husband (the only member of the party who seemed
serene). They began to move away from the pit, skirting
the city proper.

'*It is rare that the city's power is overtaxed,*' said Harold
Underwood's rocky confidante. '*Who could need such
energy?*'

'You know what is causing this upheaval, then?' Jherek
enquired of it.

'*No, no. A conversion problem, perhaps. Who can say?
You could try the central philosophy department. Except*

I believe I am all that is left of it. Unless I am the whole of it. Who is to say which is a fragment and which the whole? And is the whole contained in every fragment or a fragment in the whole, or are whole and fragment different, not in terms of size or capacity, but in essential qualities ...?'

Regretting his impoliteness, Jherek continued on past the rock. 'It would be wonderful to discuss these points,' he apologized, 'but my friends ...'

'The circle is the circle,' Harold Underwood said. 'We shall be back again, no doubt. Farewell, for the moment.' Humming to himself, he allowed Jherek and Amelia to lead him off.

'Indeed, indeed. The nature of reality is such that nothing can, by definition, be unreal, if it exists, and since anything can exist if it can be conceived of, then all that we say is unreal is therefore real ...'

'Its arguments are sometimes very poor,' Harold Underwood said in an undertone, as if apologizing. 'I do not believe that it has quite the authority it claims. Well, well, well, who would have believed that Dante, a Catholic, could have been so accurate, after all! ' He smiled at them. 'But then, I suppose, we must forget these sectarian differences now. Damnation certainly broadens the mind, eh?'

Mrs Underwood gasped. 'Was that a joke, Harold?'

He beamed.

Something alive, perhaps an animal, ran swiftly across their path and into the heart of the city.

'We are at the edge,' said the Duke of Queens. 'Yet nothing but blackness seems to exist beyond. Perhaps it is some optical trick? A malfunctioning force-screen?'

'No,' said Jherek, who was ahead of him. 'The city still sheds a little light. I can see – but it is a wasteland.'

'There is no sun.' Amelia peered forward. 'There are no stars. That is what it is.'

'The planet is dead, do you mean?' The Duke of Queens joined them. 'Yes, it is a desert out there. What can have become of our friends?'

'I suppose it is too late to say that I, of course, forgive you everything, Amelia,' Harold Underwood said suddenly.

'What, Harold?'

'It does not matter now. You were, of course, this man's mistress. You did commit adultery. It is why you are both here.'

With some reluctance, Amelia Underwood withdrew her gaze from the lifeless landscape. She was frowning.

'I was right, was I not?' her husband continued.

Dazed, she glanced from Jherek Carnelian to Harold Underwood. Jherek was turning, a bemused half-smile on his lips.

She gestured helplessly. 'Harold, is this the time . . .?'

'She loves me,' said Jherek.

'Mr Carnelian!'

'And you are his mistress?' Harold Underwood put a gentle hand to her face. 'I do not accuse you, Amelia.'

She gave a deep sigh and tenderly touched her husband's wrist. 'Very well, Harold. In spirit, yes. And I do love him.'

'Hurrah!' cried Jherek. 'I knew. I knew! Oh, Amelia. This is the happiest day of my life.'

The others all turned to stare at them. Even the Duke of Queens seemed shocked.

And from somewhere in the sky overhead a booming voice, full of gloomy satisfaction, shouted:

'I told you so. I told you all. See – it is the end of the world!'

CHAPTER SEVENTEEN

SOME CONFUSION CONCERNING THE EXACT NATURE OF THE CATASTROPHE

The large, black egg-shaped air-boat containing, in an indentation at the top, Lord Mongrove settled to the ground nearby. A look of profound and melancholy gratification lay upon the giant's heavy features. In robes of funereal purple he stepped from the boat, his right hand drawing their attention to the desolation beyond the city, where not even a wind whispered or stirred the barren dust to a semblance of vitality.

'It has all gone,' intoned Mongrove. 'The cities no longer sustain our follies. They can barely sustain themselves. We are the last survivors of humanity – and there is some question as to whether *we* shall continue to exist for much longer. Well, at least most of the time-travellers have been returned and the space-travellers given ships, for all the good it will do them. Yusharisp and his people did their best, but they could have done much more, Duke of Queens, if you had not been so foolish as to trap them for your menagerie ...'

'I wanted to surprise you,' said the Duke somewhat lamely. He was unable to take his eyes away from the desolation. 'Do you mean that it's completely lifeless out there?'

'The cities are oases in the desert that is our Earth,' Mongrove confirmed. 'The planet itself crumbles imminently.'

Jherek felt Mrs Underwood's hand seeking his. He took it, grasping it firmly. She smiled bravely up at him.

The Duke continued to fiddle with his useless power-rings. 'I must say one feels a certain sense of loss,' he said, half to himself. 'Is My Lady Charlotina gone? And Bishop Castle? And Sweet Orb Mace? And Argonheart Po? And Lord Shark the Unknown?'

'Everyone, save those here.'

'Werther de Goethe?'

'Werther, too.'

'A shame. He would have enjoyed this scene so much.'

'Werther flirts with Death no longer. Death grew impatient. Death took him, perforce.' Lord Mongrove uttered a great sigh. 'I am meeting Yusharisp and the others here, shortly. We shall know, then, how much longer we have.'

'Our time is limited, then?' said Mrs Underwood.

'Probably.'

'Gord!' said Inspector Springer, upon whom the import of Mongrove's words was just beginning to dawn. 'What bad luck!' He removed his bowler again. 'I suppose there's no chance at all of getting back now? You wouldn't 'ave seen a large time-machine about, eh? We *were* 'ere on official business . . .'

'Nothing exists beyond the cities,' Mongrove reiterated. 'I believe your time-travelling colleague was prevailed upon to help in the general exodus. We thought you dead, you see.'

For an instant, at their backs, the city shrieked, but subsided quickly. Scarlet clouds, like blood in water, swirled into the atmosphere. It was as if the city had been wounded.

'So he's returned . . .' continued Inspector Springer. 'That's for sure, eh?'

'I regret that the evidence would suggest as much. If he

was unlucky, he might have been caught up in the general destruction. It happened very quickly. Atoms, you know, dissipating. As our atoms will doubtless dissipate, eventually. As the city's will. And the planet's. Joining the universe.'

'Oo, blimey!' Sergeant Sherwood screwed up his face.

'Hm.' Inspector Springer rubbed his moustache. 'I don't know what the 'Ome Secretary's going to say. There's nobody to explain ...'

'And we'll never know, either,' Sergeant Sherwood pointed out. 'This is a fine turn up.' He seemed to be accusing the inspector. 'What price promotion now?'

'I think it's high time you reconciled yourselves to your fate,' suggested Harold Underwood. 'Earthly ambition should be put aside. We are, after all, here for eternity. We must begin considering repentance.'

'Do be quiet, Mr Underwood, there's a good chap.' Inspector Springer's shoulders had slumped somewhat.

'It could be that there is still a chance of salvation, Inspector.'

''Ow do you mean, sir?' asked Sergeant Sherwood. 'Salvation?'

'I have been considering the possibility that one may be granted the Kingdom of Heaven, even after one has been consigned here, if one can work out, satisfactorily, exactly why one was placed here ...'

''Ere?'

'In Hell.'

'You think this is —'

'I know it, Sergeant!' Harold Underwood's smile was radiant. Never had he been so relaxed. It was plain that he was absolutely happy. Amelia Underwood contemplated him with some relief and affection.

'I am reminded of John Bunyan's uplifting moral tale, *The Pilgrim's Progress*,' began Mr Underwood, flinging a friendly arm around Sergeant Sherwood's shoulders. 'If you recall the story ...' They wandered off together, along the perimeter.

'Would that we were all so deluded, at this moment,' said Mrs Underwood. 'Shall there be no chance of escape, ultimately, Lord Mongrove?'

'Yusharisp and his people are currently looking into the problem. It could be that, with careful use of the resources at our command, we could keep a small artificial vessel of some kind going, for a few hundred years. We should have to ration all provisions most carefully. It might even be that some would not be able to join the vessel, that a selection would have to be made of those most likely to survive ...'

'A sort of new Ark, then?' she suggested.

The reference was meaningless to Lord Mongrove, but he was polite. 'If you like. It would entail living in the most rigorous and uncomfortable conditions. Self-discipline would be all-important, of course, and there would be no place for amusement of any sort. We would use what we could from the cities, store the information we could glean, and wait.'

'For what?' asked the Duke of Queens, appalled.

'Well, for some kind of opportunity ...'

'What kind?'

'We cannot be sure. No one knows what will happen after the dissipation. Perhaps new suns and planets will begin to form. Oh, I know it is not very hopeful, Duke of Queens, but it is better than complete extinction, is it not?'

'Indeed,' said the Duke of Queens with some dignity, 'it is not! I hope you have no intention of selecting *me* for this – this drifting menagerie!'

'The selection will be arranged justly. I shall not be the arbiter. We must draw lots, I suppose.'

'This is *your* plan, Lord Mongrove?' asked Jherek.

'Well, mine and Yusharisp's.'

'It appeals to you?'

'It is not a question of what appeals, Jherek Carnelian. It is a question of realities. There are no more options. Will you not understand that? *There are no more op-*

tions!' Mongrove became almost kindly. 'Jherek, your childhood is over. Now it is time for you to become an adult, to understand that the world is no longer your cockle.'

'Don't you mean oyster?' Inspector Springer asked.

'I think he does,' agreed Mrs Underwood, with some distaste. The thought of sea-food was still inclined to make her feel queasy.

'It would help,' said Mongrove sternly, 'if I were not interrupted. I speak of the most serious matters. We may be moments away from total obliteration!' He looked up. 'Ah, here are our saviours.'

With a sort of wheezing noise the familiar asymmetrical mound that was Yusharisp's spaceship started to descend, to land near to Mongrove's egg. Almost immediately a tiny squeaking began and a mould-covered door opened in the side of the ship. From the door issued Yusharisp (at least, it was probably Yusharisp) followed by his colleagues.

'So(skree) many sur(skree)vivors!' exclaimed Yusharisp. 'I suppose (skree) that we (roar) should be grateful! We, the survivors of (skree) Pweeli, greet (roar) you, and are glad to kreee yelp mawk ...' Yusharisp lifted one of his feet and began to fiddle with something at the side of his body.

Another Pweelian (probably CPS Shashurup) said: 'I take it (skree) that Lord Mongrove (roar) has informed you that the end (skree) is with us and that (roar) you must now (skree) place yourselves under our discipline (skree) if you wish to (roar) extend your chances of living (skree) (roar) ...'

'A most distasteful idea,' said the Duke of Queens.

The Pweelian said, with a note of satisfaction in his voice: 'It is not (skree) long since, Duke (roar) of Queens, that we were (roar) forced to subject ourselves to your will without (skree) any justification whatso(skree)ever!'

'That was entirely different.'

'Indeed(skree) it was!'

149

The Duke of Queens subsided into a sulk.

'As far (skree) as we can ascertain (skree),' continued Yusharisp, 'your cities are still continuing to (roar) function, though they have been hard-pressed. Indeed, surprisingly, there is (skree) every evidence that (yelp) they will remain functional long enough (roar) to (skree) allow us good time in which to prepare evacuation (yelp). If a means of harnessing their energies can be found ...'

Helpfully, Jherek lifted a hand on which power-rings gleamed. 'These harness the energies of the city, Yusharisp. We have used them for a good many millions of years, I believe.'

'Those toys (yelp) are not (skree) what we need now, Jherek Car(roar)nelian.'

'This encounter becomes boring,' said Jherek in Amelia's ear. 'Shall we seek privacy? I have much to say.'

'Mr Carnelian – the Pweelians hope to help us!'

'But in such a dull way, Amelia. Would you belong to yet another menagerie?'

'It is not quite the same thing. As they say, we have no choice.'

'But we have. If the cities live, so may we live in them, at least for a while. We shall be free. We shall be alone.'

'You do not fear annihilation, still? For all that you have seen that wasteland – out there?'

'I am still not entirely sure what "fear" is. Come, we'll walk a little way and you can try to explain to me.'

'Well – a little way ...' Her hand was still in his. They began to leave.

'Where (skree) are you going?' shrieked Yusharisp in astonishment.

'Perhaps we'll rejoin you later,' Jherek told him. 'We have something we wish to discuss.'

'There is no time! (Roar). There is no (yelp) time left!'

But Jherek ignored him. They headed for the city, where Harold Underwood and Sergeant Sherwood had already disappeared, not long since.

'This is (skree) insane!' cried Yusharisp. 'Do you reject

our (roar) help, after all our efforts? After all we have (yelp) *forgiven* you!'

'We are still a little confused,' Jherek said, remembering his manners, 'as to the exact nature of the catastrophe. So —'

'Confused! Isn't it (skree) obvious?'

'You seem a trifle insistent that there is only one answer.'

'I warned you, Jherek,' said Mongrove. 'There are no more options!'

'Aha.' Jherek continued to draw Amelia towards the city.

'It is the very End of Time. The End of Matter!' Mongrove had gone a very odd colour. 'There may be only a few seconds left!'

'Then I think we should like to spend them as peacefully as possible,' Jherek told him. He put his arm round his Amelia's shoulders. She moved closer to him. She smiled up into his face. He bent to kiss her, as they turned a corner of a ruined building.

'Oh, there you are, at last,' said an amiable voice. 'I'm not too late, after all.'

This time, Jherek did not respond to the newcomer until he had kissed Amelia Underwood warmly upon her welcoming lips.

CHAPTER EIGHTEEN

IN WHICH TRUTHS ARE REVEALED AND CERTAIN RELATIONSHIPS ARE DEFINED

A burst of red, flickering light threw the figure of the time-traveller (for it was he) into silhouette. The city gibbered for a moment, as if, in its senility, it had just become aware of danger. Voices began to sound from a variety of places as memory banks were activated, one by another. The near querulous babble became quite disturbing before it subsided. Amelia's kiss at length betrayed awareness of her surroundings, of an observer. Their lips withdrew, they smiled and shared a glance, and then they moved their heads to acknowledge the time-traveller, who waited, non-chalantly studying some detail of a lichen-covered structure, until they had finished.

'Forgive us,' said Jherek, 'but with the uncertainty of our future . . .'

'Of course, of course.' The time-traveller had not heard Jherek's words. He waved an airy hand. 'I must admit I did not know if – phew – you'll never believe the devil of a job I had to get those passengers back before coming on here. It couldn't be more than a couple of hours, eh? A pretty fine balance. Has everyone else turned up?'

Jherek could tell by Amelia's expression that she disapproved of the time-traveller's insouciance. 'The world ends, did you know, sir? In a matter of minutes, we gather.'

'Um.' He nodded an acknowledgement but did not judge the statement interesting.

'The Duke of Queens is here.' Jherek wondered at a sudden fresh breeze bearing the scent of hyacinths. He sought the source, but the breeze subsided. 'And Yusharisp, from space, and Inspector Springer, and Lord Mongrove, and Captain Mubbers and the rest.'

Almost blankly, the time-traveller frowned. 'No, no – Society people I mean.'

'Society?' enquired Mrs Underwood, for the moment back in Bromley. Then she realized his meaning. 'The Guild! They are due here? They hope to save something of the world?'

'We arranged a meeting. This seemed the most convenient spot. On an ordinary course one can, after all, go no further!' The time-traveller walked the few yards to where his large and somewhat battered machine rested, its crystalline parts smouldering with dark, shifting colours, its brass reflecting the red light from the city. 'Heaven knows what damage this jockeying about has done to my machine. It was never properly tested, you see. My main reason for being here is to get information from some Guild member, both as regards the obtaining of spare parts and so that I may, with luck, get back into my own universe.' He tapped the ebony framework. 'There's a crack there that will last no more than another couple of long journeys.'

'You do not come to witness the End of the World, then?' Jherek wished that his power-rings were working and that he could make himself a warmer coat. He felt a chill enter his bones.

'Oh, no, Mr Carnelian! I've seen that more than once!' The time-traveller was amused. 'This is merely a convenient "time-mark", if you take my meaning.'

'But you could rescue Inspector Springer and his men,

and my husband – take them back, surely?' Mrs Underwood said. 'You did, after all, bring them here.'

'Well, I suppose that morally I have contributed to their predicament. However, the Home Secretary requisitioned my machine. I was unwilling to use it. Indeed, Mrs Underwood, I was intimidated. I never thought to hear such threats from the lips of British Civil Servants! And it was Lord Jagged who gave me away. I was working in secret. Of course, recognizing him, I confided something of my research to him.'

'You recognized Lord Jagged?'

'As a fellow time-traveller, yes.'

'So he is still in the nineteenth century!'

'He was. He vanished shortly after I was contacted by the Home Secretary. I think initially he had hoped to requisition my machine for his own use, and took advantage of his acquaintance with various members of the government. His own machine had failed him, you see.'

'Yet he was no longer in 1896 when you left?' Jherek became eager for news of his friend's safety. 'Do you know where he went?'

'He had some theory he wanted to test. Time-travel without machinery. I thought it dangerous and told him as much. I don't know what he was plotting. I must say I didn't care for the fellow. An unhealthy sort of chap. Too full of himself. And he did *me* no good, involving me in his complicated schemes, as he did.'

Jherek would not listen to this criticism. 'You do not know him well. He has been a great help to me on more than one occasion.'

'Oh, I'm sure he has his virtues, but they are of the proud sort, the egocentric sort. He plays at God, and that's what I can't abide. You meet the odd time-traveller like that. Generally speaking, they come to a sticky end.'

'You think Lord Jagged is dead, then?' Mrs Underwood asked him.

'More than likely.'

Jherek was grateful for the hand she slipped into his. 'I

154

believe this sensation must be very close to the "fear" you were talking about, Amelia. Or is it "grief", I wonder?'

She became remorseful. 'Ah, it is my fault. I teach you of nothing but pain. I have robbed you of your simple joyfulness!'

He was surprised. 'If joy flees, Amelia, it is in the face of experience. I love you. And it seems there is a price to pay for that ecstasy I feel.'

'Price! You never mentioned such things before. You accepted the good and had no understanding of the evil.' She spoke in an undertone, conscious of the time-traveller's proximity.

Jherek raised her hand to his lips, kissing the clenched fingers. 'Amelia, I mourn for Jagged, and perhaps my mother, too. There is no question...'

'I became emotional,' she said. 'It is hard to know whether such a state of mind is suitable to the occasion...' And she laughed, though her eyes blinked at tears. She cleared her throat. 'Yes, this is mere hysteria. However, not knowing if death is a heartbeat hence or if we are to be saved...'

He drew her to him. He kissed her eyes. Very quickly, then, she recovered herself, contemplating the city with a worried, unhappy gaze.

The city had every appearance of decline, and Jherek himself no longer believed the assurances he had given her, that the changes in it were merely superficial. Where once it had been possible to see for distances of almost a mile, down vistas of statuary and buildings, now there was only sufficient light (and that luridly unpleasant) to see a hundred yards or so. He began to entertain thoughts of begging the time-traveller to rescue them, to take them back to 1896, to risk the dangers of the Morphail Effect (which, anyway, did not seem to operate so savagely upon them as it did upon others).

'All that sunshine,' she said. 'It was false, as I told you. There was no real sun ever in your sky – only that which the cities made for you. They kept a shell burning and this barren cinder of a planet turning about it. Your whole world, Jherek, it was a lie!'

'You are too critical, Amelia. Man has an instinct to sustain his own environment. The cities were created in response to that instinct. They served it well.'

Her mood changed. She started away from him. 'It is so cruel that they should fail us now.'

'Amelia . . .' he moved to follow.

It was then that the sphere appeared, without warning, a short distance from the time-traveller's 'Chronomnibus'. It was black, and distorted images of the surrounding city could be seen in its gleaming hull.

Jherek joined her and together they watched as a hatch whirled and two black-clad figures emerged, pushing back their breathing-apparatus and goggles to become recognizable as Mrs Una Persson and Captain Oswald Bastable.

Captain Bastable smiled as he saw them. 'So you did arrive safely. Excellent.'

The time-traveller approached, shaking hands with the young captain. 'Glad you were able to keep the rendezvous, old man. How do you do, Mrs Persson? How pleasant to see you again.'

Captain Bastable was in high spirits. 'This should be worth witnessing, eh?'

'You have not been present at the end before?'

'No, indeed!'

'I was hoping that you could give me some advice.'

'Of course, if we can help. But the man you really need is Lord Jagged. It was he who —'

'He is not here.' The time-traveller placed both hands in the pockets of his Norfolk. 'There is some doubt that he survives.'

Una Persson shook out her short hair. She glanced idly around as a building seemed to dance a few feet towards her and then collapsed in on itself, rather like a concertina. 'I've never much cared for these places. Is this Tanelorn?'

'Shanalorm, I think.' Jherek held back, though he was

156

desperate for news of his friend.

'Even the names are confusing. Will it take long?'

Believing that he interpreted her question, Jherek told her: 'Mongrove estimates a matter of moments. He says the very planet crumbles.'

Mrs Persson sighed and rubbed at a weary eye. 'We have Shifter co-ordinates which require working out, Captain Bastable. The conditions are so good. Such a pity to waste —'

'The information we stand to gain ...' Evidently Captain Bastable had wanted to keep this appointment more than had she. He shrugged apologetically. 'It isn't every day we have the chance to see something as interesting ...'

She gestured with a gauntleted hand. 'True. Pay no attention to me. I'm not quite recovered.'

'I am trying to get back to my own universe,' began the time-traveller. 'It was suggested to me that you could help, that you have experience of such problems.'

'It's a matter of intersections,' she told him. 'That was why I wanted to concentrate on the Shifter. Conditions are excellent.'

'You can still help?'

'Hopefully.' She did not seem ready to discuss the matter. Politely, yet reluctantly, the time-traveller checked his eagerness and became silent.

'You are all taking this situation very casually.' Amelia Underwood cast a critical eye over the little group. 'Even selfishly. There is a possibility that at least some of those here could be evacuated, taken back through time. Have you no sense of the import – of the tragedy taking place. All the aspirations of our race vanishing as if they had never existed!'

Una Persson seemed to express a certain weary kindness when she replied. 'That is, Mrs Underwood, a somewhat melodramatic interpretation ...'

'Mrs Persson, the situation seems to be rather more than "melodramatic". This is extinction!'

'For some, possibly.'

'Not for you time-travellers, perhaps. Will you make no effort to help others?'

Mrs Persson did her best to stifle a yawn. 'I think our perspectives must be very different, Mrs Underwood. I assure you that I am not without a social conscience, but when you have experienced so much, on such a scale, as we have experienced, issues take on a different colouring. Besides, I do not think – Good heavens! What is that?'

They all followed her gaze towards a low line of ruins; recently crumbled. In the semi-darkness there bobbed, apparently along the top of the ruins, a procession of about a dozen objects, roughly dome-shaped. They were immediately familiar to Jherek and Amelia as the helmets of Inspector Springer's constables. They heard the faint sound of a whistle.

Within a few seconds, as a break appeared in the ruins, it was apparent to all that they witnessed a chase. The Lat were attempting to escape their captors. Their little pear-shaped bodies scuttled rapidly over the fallen masonry, but Springer's men were not far behind. They could hear the cries of the Lat and the police quite clearly now.

'Hrunt mibix ferkit!'

'Stop! Stop in the name of the law! Collar 'im, Weech!'

The Lat stumbled and fell, but managed to keep ahead of their pursuers, for all that most of them, save Captain Mubbers and perhaps Rokfrug, still wore handcuffs.

The whistles shrilled again. There was a great waving of truncheons. The Lat disappeared from view, but emerged again not far from Mrs Persson's time-sphere, saw the group of humans and hesitated before dodging off in the opposite direction.

The policemen, who would remain solidly conscious of their duty until the Crack of Doom sounded at last, and the very ground fell away from beneath their pounding boots, continued implacably after their prey.

Soon both Lat and police were out of sight and earshot again, and the conversation could resume.

Mrs Persson lost something of her weary manner and

seemed amused by the incident. 'I had no idea there were others here! Were not those the aliens we sent on? I would have thought that they would have left the planet by now.'

'They wanted to loot and rape everything first,' Jherek explained. 'But then the Pweelians stopped them. The Pweelians seem to take pleasure in stopping almost everyone from doing almost everything! This is their hour of triumph, I suppose. They have waited for it for a long time, of course, so it seems niggardly to criticize ...'

'You mean there is still another race of space-travellers in the city?' Captain Bastable asked.

'Yes. The Pweelians, as I said. They have some sort of plan for survival. But I did not find it agreeable. The Duke of Queens ...'

'He is here!' Mrs Persson brightened. Captain Bastable frowned a little circumspectly to himself.

'You know the Duke?'

'Oh, we are old friends.'

'And Lord Mongrove?'

'I have heard of him,' said Mrs Persson, 'but I have never had the pleasure of meeting him. However, if there is an opportunity ...'

'I should be delighted to introduce you. Always assuming that this little oasis, as Mongrove called it, doesn't disintegrate before I have the chance.'

'Mr Carnelian!' Amelia tugged at his sleeve. 'I would remind you that this is no time for social chat. We must attempt to prevail upon these people to rescue as many of those here as is possible!'

'I was forgetting. It is so nice to know that Mrs Persson is a friend of the Duke of Queens. Do you not think, dearest Amelia, that we should try to find him. He would be glad to resume the acquaintance, I am sure!'

Mrs Amelia Underwood shrugged her beautiful shoulders and sighed a really rather shallow sigh. She was beginning to lose interest, it seemed, in the whole business.

CHAPTER NINETEEN

IN WHICH DIFFERENCES OF OPINION ARE EXPRESSED AND RELATIONSHIPS FURTHER DEFINED

Becoming aware of Amelia's displeasure, and seeking to respond to events as she wished, Jherek recalled some Wheldrake.

> *Thus is the close upon us*
> > *(Corpse calls to corpse and chain echoes chain).*
> *Now the bold paint flakes upon the cheek*
> > *(And our pain lends point to pain).*
> *Now there are none among us*
> > *Need seek for Death's domain ...*

Captain Bastable joined in the last line, looking for approval not to Jherek but to Mrs Underwood.

'Ah, Wheldrake,' he began, 'ever apt ...'

'Oh, bother Wheldrake!' said Mrs Underwood, and she stalked off in the direction from which she and Jherek had originally come, but she paused suddenly as a cheerful voice called out:

'There you are, Amelia! Sergeant Sherwood and I were just on the point of Woman's contribution to Sin. It would be worth having any comments, from the horse's mouth, as you might say.'

'And damn you, Harold!'

She gasped at her own language. Then she grinned. 'Oh, dear ...'

If Harold had noticed he doubtless accepted her oath as further evidence of their situation. He smiled vaguely at her. 'Well, perhaps later ...' His pince-nez glittered so that his eye-sockets appeared to contain flame. Chatting, he and the police sergeant strolled on.

Jherek caught up with her. 'I have offended you, my dear. I thought ...'

'Perhaps I, too, am mad,' she told him. 'Since nobody else is taking the end of the world seriously, then it is evident that I should not, either.' But she was not convinced.

'Yusharisp and the Pweelians take it seriously, dearest Amelia. And Lord Mongrove. But it seems to me that you have no real leaning in their direction.'

'I do what I think is right.'

'Yet it conflicts with your temperament, you would admit?'

'Oh, this is unfair!' She paced on. Now they could see the Pweelian spacecraft where they had left it. Inspector Springer and the Duke of Queens held their hands in the air.

Standing on three legs, Yusharisp, or one of his comrades, held an object in his fourth foot (or hand) with which he menaced Inspector Springer and the Duke of Queens.

'My goodness!' Amelia hesitated. 'They are using force! Who would have suspected it?'

Lord Mongrove seemed put out by the turn of events. He stood to one side, muttering to himself. 'I am not sure. I am not sure.'

'We have decided (skree) to act for your own (roar) good,' Yusharisp told the two men. 'The others will be rounded up in time. Now, if you will kindly, for the moment, board the spaceship ...'

161

'Put that gun away!' The ringing command issued from the lips of Amelia Underwood. Even she seemed surprised by it. 'Does the end of the world mean the end of the Rule of Law? What point is there in perpetuating intelligent life if violence is to be the method by which we survive? Are we not above the beasts?'

'I think (skree) madam that you (yelp) fail to understand the urgency (skree) of the situation (roar).' Yusharisp was embarrassed. The weapon wavered. Seeing this the Duke of Queens immediately lowered his hands.

'We (skrrreee) did not intend to continue to threaten anyone (roar) after (yelp) the immediate danger was (skree) avoided,' said another Pweelian, probably CPS Shushurup. 'It is not in (skree) our nature to approve of (skree) violence or (roar) threats.'

'You have been threatening everyone since you arrived!' she told them. 'Bullying us not, until now, with weapons, but with moral arguments which begin to seem increasingly specious to me and which have never convinced the denizens of this world (it is not mine, I might add, and I do not approve of their behaviour any more than do you). Now you give us evidence of the weakness of your arguments – you bring forth your guns and your bald threats of violence!'

'It is not (skree) anything like so (roar) simple, madam. It is a question of (yelp) survive or die . . .'

'It seems to me,' she said calmly, 'that it is you who simplify, Mr Yusharisp.'

Jherek looked admiringly on. As usual, the arguments were inclined to confuse him, but he thought Amelia's assumption of authority was magnificent.

'I would suggest,' she continued, 'that you leave these people to their own solutions to their problems, and that you do, for yourselves, whatever you think best.'

'Lord Mongrove (yelp) invited our (skree) help,' said CPS Shushurup in an aggrieved whine. 'Do not listen (skree) to her (yelp), Yusharisp. We must continue (roar) with our work!'

162

The limb holding the gun became steadier. Slowly, the Duke of Queens raised his hands, but he winked at Jherek Carnelian.

Lord Mongrove's gloomy boom interrupted the dispute. 'I have, I must admit, Yusharisp, been having second thoughts ...'

'*Second thoughts!*' Yusharisp was beside himself. 'At this (skree) stage!'

The little alien gestured with his weapon. 'Look (skree) out there at that — that (roar) nothingness. Can you not feel (yelp) the city breaking apart? Lord Mongrove, of all (skree) people, I would have thought that you (roar) could not change your mind. Why (skree) — why?'

The giant shuffled his feet in the rust and the dust. He scratched his huge head. He fingered the collar of his robe of funereal purple. 'As a matter of fact, Yusharisp, I, too, am becoming just a jot bored with this — um — drama.'

'Drama! Skrrreeeee! It is not a game (yelp) Lord Mongrove. You, yourself, said as (skree) much!'

'Well, no ...'

'There, you see, Sergeant Sherwood. It cannot be argued any longer, I think, that there are no devils in Hell. Look at those chaps there. Devils, if ever I saw some!' It was Harold Underwood, emerging from behind the Pweelian's spaceship. 'So much for the sceptics, eh? So much for the Darwinians, hm? So much, Sergeant Sherwood, for your much vaunted Science! Ha!' He approached Yusharisp with some curiosity. He inspected him through his pince-nez. 'What a distortion of the human body — revealing, of course, the distortion of the spirit within.' He straightened up, linking arms, again, with his disciple. 'With luck, Sergeant Sherwood, we shall soon get a look at the Arch Fiend Himself!' Nodding to those of the company he recognized, Harold Underwood wandered off again.

Mrs Underwood watched her husband disappear. 'I must say, I have never known him so agreeable. What a shame he could not have been brought here before.'

'I wash my (skree) feet of you all!' said Yusharisp. He

appeared to be sulking as he went to lean against the noxious side of his spaceship. 'Most of them have run away, already.'

'Shall we lower our hands?' asked the Duke of Queens.

'Do what you (skree) like ...'

'I wonder if my men 'ave caught them Latvians yet,' said Inspector Springer. 'Not, I suppose, that it matters a lot now. On the other 'and, I 'ate to leave things unfinished. Know what I mean, Duke?' He looked at his watch.

'Oh, I do, very much, Inspector Springer. I had plans for a party that would have made all other parties seem drab, and I was about to embark on my new project – a life-size reproduction of the ancient planet, Mars, complete with reproductions of all its major cities, and a selection of different cultures from its history. But with things as they are ...' He contemplated the blackness of infinity beyond the city, he contemplated the ruin within. 'There aren't the materials any longer, I suppose.'

'Or the means,' Mongrove reminded him. 'Are you sure, Duke, that you don't want to take part in this Salvation scheme?'

The Duke sat down upon a half-melted metal cube. 'It doesn't have much to recommend it, dear Mongrove. And one cannot help feeling, well, interfered with ...'

The cube on which he sat began to grumble. Apologetically he stood up.

'It is Fate which interferes with your useless idyll!' said Yusharisp, in some exasperation. 'Not (skree) the people of Pweeli. We acted (roar) from the noblest of motives.'

Once more losing interest in the conversation, Jherek made to lead Amelia away. She resisted his tugging hand for only a moment before going with him.

'The time-travellers and the space-travellers do not, as yet, seem to be aware of one another's presence,' she said. 'Should we tell them? After all, only a few yards separate them!'

'Let us leave them all, Amelia. Initially we sought privacy.'

Her expression softened. She moved closer to him. 'Of course, dear Jherek.'

He swelled with pleasure.

'It will be so sad,' she said a little later, in a melancholy tone, 'to die, when we have at last both admitted our feelings.'

'To die, Amelia?'

Something like a dead tree, but made of soft stone, started to flicker. A screen appeared in its trunk. The image of a man began to speak, but there was no sound. They watched it for a little while before continuing.

'To die?' he said.

'Well, we must accept the inevitable, Jherek.'

'To be called by my first name! You do not know, Amelia, how happy you make me!'

'There seemed no further point in refusing you the true expression of my feelings, since we have such a short time together.'

'We have eternity!'

'In one sense, possibly. But all are agreed that the city must soon perish.'

As if to deny her words, a steady throbbing began to pulse beneath their feet. It had strength and signified the presence of considerable energy, while the glow from the surrounding ruins suddenly took on a healthier colour, a sort of bright blue.

'There! The city recovers!' Jherek exclaimed.

'No. Merely the appearance of recovery which always precedes death.'

'What is that golden light over there?' He pointed beyond a line of still rotating cylinders. 'It is like sunshine, Amelia!'

They began to run towards the source of the light. Soon they could see clearly what lay ahead.

'The city's last illusion,' said Jherek. They were both overawed, for the vision was so simple yet so much at odds with its surroundings. It was a little grassy glade, full of wild flowers, warm and lovely in the sun, covering a space of only thirty feet or so, yet perfect in every detail, with butterflies, bees, and a bird perching in a delicate elm. They could hear the bird singing. They could smell the grass.

Hand in hand, they stepped into the illusion.

'It is as if the city's memory conjures up a final image of Earth at her loveliest,' said Amelia. 'A sort of monument.'

They seated themselves on a hillock. The ruins and the livid lights were still plainly visible, but they were able to ignore them.

Mrs Underwood pointed a little way ahead to where a red and white chequered clōth had been spread on the grass, under the tree. On the cloth were plates, flasks, fruits, a pie. 'Should we see if the picnic is edible?'

'In a moment.' He leaned back and breathed the air. Perhaps the scent of hyacinths he had detected earlier had come from here.

'It cannot last,' she reminded him. 'We should take advantage of it while we may.' She stretched herself, so that her head lay in his lap. He stroked her hair and her cheek. He stroked her neck. She breathed deeply and luxuriously, her eyes closed as she listened to the insects, feeling the warmth of that invisible, non-existent sun upon her skin. 'Oh, Jherek ...'

'Amelia.' He bent his head and kissed her tenderly upon the lips for the second time since they had come to the city, and without hesitation she responded, and his touch upon her bared shoulder, her waist, only made her cling to him the closer and kiss him more deeply.

'I am like a young girl,' she said, after a while. 'It is as it should have been.'

He was baffled by this reference, but he did not question her. He merely said: 'Now that you have called me by my first name, Amelia, does that mean that we are married, that we can ...'

She shook her head sadly. 'We can never – never be husband and wife. Not now.'

'No?'

'No, Jherek, dear. It is too late for that.'

'I see.' Wistfully, he pulled up a blade of grass.

'The divorce, you see, has not taken place. And no ceremony binds us. Oh, there is much I could explain, but let us not waste the minutes we have.'

'These – these conventions. They are important enough to deny us the expression of our love?'

'Oh, do not mistake me, my dear. I know now that those conventions are not universal – that they have no usefulness here – but you forget – for years I have obeyed them. I cannot, in my own self, rebel against them in so short a time. As it is, I quell a tide of guilt that threatens to flood through me.'

'Guilt, again?'

'Yes, dearest. If I went so suddenly against my training, I suspect that I should break down completely. I should not be the Amelia Underwood you know!'

'Yet, if there were more time ...'

'Oh, I know that eventually I should have been able to overcome the guilt ... That is the awful irony of it all!'

'It is ironic,' he agreed. He rose, helping her to her feet. 'Let us see what the picnic can offer us.'

The song of the bird (it was some sort of macaw) continued to sound from the tree as they approached the red and white chequered cloth, but another noise began to break through, a sort of shrilling which was familiar to both of them. Then, bursting from the gloom of the city into the sunlight of the illusion, Captain Mubbers, Rokfrug and the other Lat appeared. They were badly out of breath and sweating; they had something of the appearance of bright red, animated turnips. Their three pupils rolled wildly in their eyes as they sighted Jherek and Amelia and came to a confused halt.

'Mibix?' said Rokfrug, recognizing Jherek. 'Drexim flug roodi?'

'You are still, I take it, pursued by the police.' Amelia was impatient, more than cool towards the intruders. 'There is nowhere to hide here.'

'Hrunt krufroodi.' Captain Mubbers glanced behind him as there came a thundering of boots and the dozen identically clad police officers, evidently as weary as the Lat, burst into the pastoral illusion, paused, blinked, and began to advance towards their quarry, whereupon Captain Mubbers uttered a strangled 'Ferkit!' and turned at bay, ready to do battle against their overwhelming numbers.

'Oh, really!' cried Amelia Underwood. 'Officer, this will not do!' She addressed the nearest policeman.

The policeman said steadily: 'You're all under arrest. You might as well come quietly.'

'You intend to arrest us, as well?' Mrs Underwood bridled.

'Strictly speakin', ma'am, you've been under arrest from the start. All right, lads ...' But he hesitated when two loud popping noises sounded, close together, and Lord Jagged of Canaria, the Iron Orchid upon his arm, materialized on the hillock.

Lord Jagged was resplendent in his favourite pale yellow robes, his tall collar framing his patrician features. He seemed in high spirits. The Iron Orchid, at her most stately and beautiful, wore billowing white of an untypical cut and was as happy as her escort.

'At last!' said Lord Jagged, apparently in some relief. 'This must be the fiftieth attempt!'

'The forty-ninth, indefatigable Jagged,' crooned the Orchid. 'I intended to give up on the fiftieth.'

Jherek ran towards his friend and his mother. 'Oh, Jagged! Cryptic, magnificent, darling Jagged! We have worried about you so much! And Iron Orchid, you are delicious. Where, where have you been?'

The kiss from Jagged's lips on Jherek's was less than chaste and was equalled by the Iron Orchid's. Standing back from them, Mrs Underwood permitted herself a sniff, but came forward reluctantly as the radiant Orchid beckoned.

'My dears, you will be so delighted by our news! But you seem distraught. What has been happening to you?'

'Well,' said Mrs Underwood with some pleasure, 'we are currently under arrest, although the charge is not altogether clear.'

'You seem to have a penchant, you two, for falling foul of the law,' said Jagged, casting a languid eye over the company. 'It's all right, constable. I think you know who I am.'

The leading constable saluted, but stood his ground. 'Yes, sir,' he said uncertainly. 'Though we do 'ave orders, direct from the 'Ome Secretary ...'

'The Home Secretary, constable, takes his advice from me, as no doubt you are aware ...'

'I 'ad 'eard something to that effect, sir.' He fingered his chin. 'What about these Latvians?'

Lord Jagged shrugged. 'I don't think they offer a threat to the Crown any longer.'

Jherek Carnelian was overjoyed by his friend's performance. 'Excellent, dear Jagged! Excellent!'

'And then, sir, there's some question about it being the end o' the world,' continued the constable.

'Don't concern yourself with that, my good man. I'll look into it, the first chance I get.'

'Very well, sir.' As one in a dream, the policeman signed to his colleagues. 'We'd better be getting back, then. Shall we tell Inspector Springer you're in charge now, sir?'

'You might as well, constable.'

The policemen wandered out of the illusion and disappeared in the darkness of the city, leaving the Lat somewhat nonplussed. Captain Mubbers looked enquiringly up at Lord Jagged but received a dismissive glance.

Rokfrug had found the food and was cramming his mouth with pie. 'Groodnix!' he said. 'Trimpit dernik, queely!'

The rest of the Lat seated themselves around the cloth and were soon feasting with gusto.

'So, most miraculous of mothers, you knew all along where to find Lord Jagged!' Jherek hugged her again. 'You played the same game, eh?'

'Not at all!' She was offended. 'We met quite by accident. I had, it is true, grown so bored with our world that I sought one which would prove more agreeable and some, I'll admit, were interesting, but the Morphail Effect gave me difficulties. I kept being thrown out of one era and into another almost before I knew it. Brannart had warned me, but your experiences had caused me to disbelieve him.' She inspected her son from head to foot and her look towards Amelia Underwood was not as critical as it had once been. 'You are both pale. You need to replenish your bloom.'

'Now we bloom, opulent Orchid! We feared so much for your well-being. Oh, and since you have been gone the world has grown dark ...'

'Death, we are told, has come to the universe,' put in Amelia, returning the Iron Orchid's glance.

Lord Jagged of Canaria smiled a wide, soft smile. 'Well, so we are returned at an opportune moment.'

'It depends what you mean by opportune, Lord Jagged.' Amelia Underwood pointed out into the darkness. 'Even the city dies now.'

'Of all our friends,' Jherek continued sorrowfully, 'only Lord Mongrove and the Duke of Queens survive. The rest are memories only!'

'Memories are sufficient, I think,' said Jagged. 'They will do.'

'You are callous, sir!' Mrs Underwood adjusted a button at her throat.

'Call me so.'

'We expected you to be waiting for us, Jagged,' said Jherek Carnelian, 'when we returned to the End of Time. Did you not promise to be here – to explain?'

'I arrived, but had to leave again almost at once.

Through no fault of my own, I was delayed. My machine failed me. I had to make some experiments. It was in the course of these experiments that I happened to meet your mother and she prevailed upon me to satisfy a whim.'

'A whim?' Mrs Underwood turned away in disgust.

'We are married,' said the Iron Orchid almost demurely. 'At last.'

'Married. I envy you! How did this come about?'

'It was a simple ceremony, Jherek, my juice.' She stroked the white material of her gown. It seemed that she blushed.

Curiosity made Amelia Underwood turn back.

'It was in the fifty-eighth century, I think,' the Iron Orchid said. Their customs are very moving. Simple, yet profound. The sacrifice of the slaves had, happily, become optional by the middle of what I believe they called the "Wet Prince" period. We had little else to do, you see, since we were waiting for the right moment to try to transfer ...'

'Sans machine,' said Jagged, with a certain quiet pride. 'We have learned to travel, perforce, without gadgetry. It was always theoretically possible.'

'By a coincidence difficult to credit,' she continued, 'Lord Jagged found me a prisoner of some extra-terrestrial creatures temporarily in control of the planet —'

'The Flerpian Conquests of 4004–6,' explained Jagged in an aside.

'– and was able to rescue me before I could experience an interesting method of torture they had devised, where the shoulders are exposed to —' She broke off. 'But I digress. From there we continued to move forward as best we could, by a series of stages. I could not, of course, have done it on my own. And some of the natives were obstructive. But your father handled them so well. He is very good with natives, don't you think?'

Jherek said in a small voice. 'My father?'

'Lord Jagged, of course! You must have guessed!' She laughed fulsomely. 'You must have guessed, my egg!'

'I thought there was a rumour concerning Sweet Orb Mace ...'

'Your father wished to make a secret of it, for reasons of his own. It was so long ago. He had some scientific obsession, then, concerning his own genes and how best to perpetuate them. He thought this method the most satisfactory.'

'As it proved.' Lord Jagged put a slim-fingered hand upon his son's head and affectionately ruffled his hair. 'As it proved.'

Again, Jherek embraced Lord Jagged. 'Oh, I am so pleased, Jagged, that it is you! This news is a gift that makes all the waiting worthwhile.' He reached to take his shy Amelia's hand. 'This is, indeed, the happiest of days!'

Mrs Underwood was reserved, though she did not deny him her hand. She stood in that smiling company and she tried to speak. She failed, and now the Iron Orchid hugged her. 'Tell me, dearest Amelia, that you are to be our new daughter!'

'As I explained to Jherek, it might have been possible.'

'In the past?'

'You seem to forget, Iron Orchid, that there is nothing *but* the past. There is no future left to us.'

'No future?'

'She is quite right.' Lord Jagged took his hands from his son's shoulders.

'Oh!' A knuckle rose to Amelia's mouth. 'I had hoped you brought a reprieve. It was foolish ...'

Arranging his yellow robes about him, Lord Jagged of Canaria seated himself upon the hillock, indicating that they should join him. 'The information I have is probably not altogether palatable,' he began, 'but since I promised an explanation when last we parted, I feel obliged to fulfil that promise. I trust I will not bore you.' And he began to speak.

CHAPTER TWENTY

IN WHICH LORD JAGGED OF CANARIA EXHIBITS A FRANKNESS NOT PREVIOUSLY DISPLAYED

'I suppose, my dears, that I had best begin by admitting that I was not originally from the End of Time,' said Lord Jagged. 'My origins are not too far from your own, Amelia (if I may call you Amelia) – in the twenty-first century, to be exact. After a number of adventures, I arrived here, some thousand or so years ago and, not wishing to spend my life in a menagerie, set myself up as a self-created personality. Thus, though trapped by the Morphail Effect, I was able to continue my research and experiments into the Nature of Time, discovering, in fact, that I could, by exercising certain disciplines, remain for long periods in one era. It even became apparent that I could, if I wished, settle in certain unpopulated periods. During the course of these experiments, I met other time-travellers, including Mrs Persson (perhaps the most experienced chrononaut we have), and was able to exchange information, concluding, at last, that I was something of a sport, for no other time-traveller was as little influenced as was I by the Morphail Effect. At last I concluded that I was, under certain conditions, impervious to the Effect so long as I took particular precautions (which included settling very thoroughly in one period and producing no anachronisms whatsoever). Further research showed that my ability had only so much to do with self-discipline and a great deal to do with my particular genes.'

'Aha!' said Jherek. 'Others spoke of genes to us.'

'Quite so. Well, in the course of my various expeditions through the millennia I became aware, long before that alien brought the news to us, that the End of Time was close. Having learned so much, it seemed to me then that I might be able to save something of our culture and, indeed, ensure the survival of our race, by making a kind of loop. It must be obvious to you what I hoped to do – to take certain people from the End of Time and put them at the Beginning, with all their knowledge (or as much as could be taken) and their civilization intact. Science would build us new cities, I thought, and we should have billions more years ahead of us. However, one factor emerged very early and that concerned the Morphail Effect. It would not permit my plan, no matter how far back in Time I went. Only those with genes like mine might colonize the past. Therefore I modified my scheme. I would find a new Adam and Eve, who could breed together and produce a race unfettered by Time (or at least the irritating Morphail Effect). To do this I had to find a man and a woman who shared the same characteristics as myself. At length I gave up my search, discovered, through experiments, that your mother, Jherek, the Iron Orchid, was the only creature I had ever found who had genes even beginning to resemble mine. That was when I put to her, without her knowledge of my intentions, that we should conceive a child together.'

'It seemed such an amusing idea,' said the Iron Orchid. 'And no one had done anything like it for millennia!'

'Thus, after some difficulties, you were born, my boy. But I still needed to find a wife for you, one who could remain, say, in the Palaeozoic (where a station, as I think you now know, already exists) without suddenly being whisked out of it again. I searched from the beginning of

174

history, trying subject after subject, until at last, Amelia Underwood, I found my Eve – you!'

'If you had consulted me, sir ...'

'I could tell you nothing. I have explained that I had to work in secrecy, that my method of countering the Morphail Effect was so delicate that I could not, then, afford a single tiny anachronism. To consult you, would have been to reveal something of my own identity. An impossibility then – a dangerous thought! I had to kidnap you and bring you here. Then I had to introduce you to Jherek, then I had to hope that you would be attracted to one another. Everything in fact seemed to go reasonably well. But I reckoned without the complications – My Lady Charlotina, you'll recall, interfered, piqued by the manner in which she had been deceived by us.'

'And when I went to seek your help, you were not there, Jagged! You were about your temporal adventurings, then!'

'Exactly, Jherek. By bad chance I was not able to forestall your going to Brannart, borrowing a machine and returning to the nineteenth century. I was, I assure you, as surprised to encounter you there as you were surprised to see me! Luckily, in one of my rôles, as High Court Judge, I arranged to preside at your trial ...'

'... and you could not acknowledge me, because of the Morphail Effect!'

'Yes. But I did arrange for the Effect to work at the very moment of your apparent execution. This led me to make other discoveries about the Nature of Time, but I could not afford, even then, to tell you of my plans. Mrs Underwood had to remain where she was (itself regarded as an impossibility by Brannart) while I worked. I returned here, as soon as possible, desperately trying to remedy matters but gradually learning more and more things which conflicted with Brannart's theories. I was able to contact Mrs Persson and she was of considerable help to me. I arranged to meet her here, by the by ...'

'She has arrived,' Amelia Underwood told him.

'I am very pleased. She wishes to watch – but I move ahead of myself. The next thing I learned, on my return, was that you had again vanished, Jherek. But you had made a discovery which was to alter my whole research. I had heard rumours about a method of recycling Time, but had dismissed them. The Nursery you discovered not only proved that it was possible, but showed *how* it was possible. It meant that much of what I had been doing was no longer necessary. But you, of course, were still stranded. I risked much to return and rescue you all, exposing myself to the Morphail Effect and, indeed, suffering from it. I became stranded in the nineteenth century, and if it had not been for that time-travelling fellow, what's-his-name, arriving out of the blue, I might never have hit upon the solution to my problem. He was able to give me a great deal of information about alternate time-cycles – he was from one himself, of course – and I regret that, in order to save myself embarrassment (for by then I had exposed myself too far and my disguises, as it were, were wearing rather thin) I had to go along with the Home Secretary's scheme for commandeering his time-craft and sending it after you. I did not imagine the complications I have witnessed ...'

'It seems to me, Lord Jagged,' murmured Amelia Underwood, 'that your problems would not have arisen at all, had you anticipated certain ordinary human factors ...'

'I bow to your criticism, Amelia. I deserve it. But I was a man obsessed – and needing to act, I thought, with great urgency. All the various fluctuations created in the mega-flow – largely because of me, I'll admit – were actually contributing to the general confusion. The present condition of this universe would not have manifested itself for a while yet, but for the energy used by the cities in our various schemes. But all that will change now, with luck.'

'Change? You say it is too late.'

'Did I give you that impression? I am sorry. I wish that you had not had to suffer so much, particularly since it now appears that my whole experiment was pointless.'

'Then we cannot settle in the past, as you planned?' said Jherek.

'Pointless!' Amelia gasped with indignation.

'Well, yes and no.'

'Did you not deliberately place us in the Palaeozoic as part of your experiment, Lord Jagged?'

'No, Amelia. I was not deceiving you. I thought I sent you here.'

'Instead we went back.'

'That is what I am coming to. You did not, strictly speaking, go back. You went *forward*, and thus countered the Morphail Effect at core!'

'How so?'

'Because you completed a circle. If Time is a circle (and it is only one way of looking at it) and we travel it round, we go, of course, from the End to the Beginning quite swiftly, do you see? You overshot the End – you went completely round and back to the Beginning.'

'And deceived the Morphail Effect!' said Jherek, clapping his hands together.

'In a word, yes. It means that we can, if we so desire, all escape the End of Time merely by jumping forward to the Beginning. The disadvantages, however, are considerable. We should not, for one thing, have the power of the cities ...'

But Jherek's excitement dismissed these quibbles. 'And so, like Ovid, you return to lead us from Time's captivity into the promised land – forward, as you might put it, Jagged, into the past!'

'Not so.' His father laughed. 'There is no need for any of us to leave this planet or this period.'

'But final destruction looms, if it is not already upon us.'

'Nonsense – what has given you that impression?'

'Come,' said Jherek beginning to rise, 'I'll show you.'

'But I have much more to tell you, my son.'

'Later – when you have seen.'

'Very well.' With a swirl of his robes, Lord Jagged of Canaria helped first Amelia, then his wife, to their feet. 'It would probably be a good idea, anyway, to seek out Mrs Persson and the others. But really, Jherek, this uncharacteristic alarmism is scarcely called for.'

From their picnic Captain Mubbers and Rokfrug looked up. 'Trorf?' said the leader of the Lat through a mouthful of plumcake; but his lieutenant calmed him. 'Grushfalls, hrunt fresha.' They gave their attention back to the food and scarcely noticed as the four humans stepped carefully out of the little pastoral glade and into the lurid, flickering light of that vast expanse of ruins whose very atmosphere, it now seemed to Jherek, gave off a faint, chilly scent of death.

CHAPTER TWENTY-ONE

A QUESTION OF ATTITUDES

'I must say,' Jagged paused in his rapid, stately stride, 'the city suffers a certain lassitude ...'

'Oh, Jagged, you understate!' His son was beside him, while the ladies, in conference, came a little way behind.

Streamers of half-metallic, half-organic matter, of a dusty lavender shade, wriggled across their path as if withdrawn by the squat building on their right. In the gloom, it was impossible to tell their nature.

'But it revives,' Jagged said. 'Look there, is that not a newly created conduit?' The pipe he indicated, running to left and right of them, did seem new, though very ordinary.

'It is no sign, paternal Jagged. The illusions proliferate.'

His father was insouciant. 'If you'll have it so.' There was a glint in his eye. 'Youth was ever obstinate.'

Jherek Carnelian detected irony in his father, his friend. 'Ah, sardonic Jagged, it is so good to have your companionship again! All trepidation vanishes!'

'Your confidence warms me.' Jagged's gesture was expansive. 'What, after all, is a father for but to give comfort to his children?'

'Children?'

A casual wave. 'One forms attachments, here and there, in Time. But you, Jherek, are my only heir.'

'A song?'

'A son, my love.'

As they advanced through the glowing semi-darkness, Jherek, infected by Jagged's apparently causeless optimism, sought for signs which would indicate that the city came back to life. Perhaps there were indeed signs of this revivification : that light which, as he had seen, glowed a robust blue, and light which now burned steady crimson; moreover, the regular pounding from beneath his feet put him in mind of the beat of a strengthening heart. But, no. How could it be?

Fastidious as ever, Lord Jagged folded back one of his sleeves so that it should not trail in the fine rust which lay everywhere upon the ground. 'We can rely upon the cities,' he said, 'even if we cannot ever hope fully to understand them.'

'You speculate, Jagged. The evidence is all to the contrary. Their sources of power have dissipated.'

'The sources exist. The cities have discovered them.'

'Even you, Jagged, cannot be so certain.' But Jherek spoke now to be denied.

'You are aware, then, of all the evidence?' Jagged paused, for ahead of them was darkness. 'Have we reached the outskirts?'

'It seems so.'

They waited for the Iron Orchid and Amelia Underwood, who had fallen some distance behind. To Jherek's surprise the two women appeared to be enjoying one another's company. No longer did they glare or make veiled attacks. They might have been the oldest of friends. He wondered if he would ever come to understand these subtle shifts of attitude in women; yet he was pleased. If all were to perish, it would be as well to be on good terms at the end. He hailed them.

Here the city shed a wider shaft of light into the landscape beyond: a pale, cracked, barren expanse no longer deserving the appellation 'earth'; a husk that might crumble to invisible dust at a touch.

The Iron Orchid twisted a white pleat. 'Dead.'

'And in the last stages of decay.' Amelia was sympathetic.

The Orchid put her back to the scene. 'I cannot accept,' she said levelly, 'that this is my world. It was so vital.'

'It's vitality was stolen, so Mongrove says.' Jherek contemplated the darkness which his mother refused.

'That's true of all life, in a sense.' Lord Jagged touched, for a second, his wife's hand. 'Well, the core remains.'

'Is it not already rotten, Lord Jagged?' Perhaps Amelia regretted her remorselessness as she glimpsed the Orchid's face.

'It can be revived, one supposes.'

'It is cold ... complained the Iron Orchid, moving further away, towards the interior.

'We drift, surely,' Jherek said. 'There is no sun. Not another star survives. Not a single meteorite. We drift in eternal darkness — and that darkness must, dear parent, shortly engulf us, too!'

'You over-dramatize, my boy.'

'Possibly he does not.' The Orchid's voice lacked timbre.

They followed her and, almost immediately, came upon the machines used by the time-traveller and by Mrs Persson and Captain Bastable.

'But where are our friends?' mused Lord Jagged.

'They were here not long since,' Jherek told him. 'The Morphail Effect?'

'Here!' Lord Jagged's look was frankly sceptical.

'Could they be with Yusharisp and the others?' Jherek smiled vaguely at Amelia and his mother, who had linked arms. He was still puzzled by the change in them. It had something to do, he felt, with the Iron Orchid's marriage to Lord Jagged, this banishment of the old tension. 'Shall we seek them out, venturesome Jagged?'

'You know where to look?'

'Over there.'

'Then lead on, my innocent!' Lord Jagged, as had often been his way in the old days, appeared to be relishing a private joke. He stood aside for Jherek.

The light from the city glittered, for a moment sharp rather than murky, and a building that had been a ruin now seemed whole to Jherek, but elsewhere there were creakings and murmurings and groanings, all suggestive of the city's decline. Again they emerged at the edge, and here the light was very dim indeed. It was not until he heard a sound that Jherek was able to advance.

'If (skree) you would take back to their (yelp) own time this (skree) group, it would at least (roar) reduce the problem to tidier proportions, Mrs (yelp) Persson.'

They were all assembled, now, about the Pweelian spacecraft – Inspector Springer and his constables, the Duke of Queens, huge, melancholy Mongrove, the time-traveller in his Norfolk jacket and plus-fours, Mrs Persson and Captain Bastable in their black uniforms, gleaming like sealskin. Only Harold Underwood, Sergeant Sherwood and the Lat were missing. Against the mould-like exterior of the Pweelian spaceship the Pweelians themselves were hard to distinguish. Beyond the group lay the now-familiar blackness of the infinite void.

They heard Mrs Persson. 'We made no preparations for passengers. As it is, we are anxious to return to our base to begin certain important experiments needed to verify our understanding of the multiverse's intersections . . .'

Lord Jagged, his pale yellow robes in contrast to the general nocturnal colouring of his surroundings, strolled into the group, leaving Jherek and the two women to follow. Jagged's private mirth was unabated. 'You are as anxious as ever, my dear Yusharisp.' Though it must have been some time since last he had seen the alien, Jagged had no difficulty in identifying him. 'And so you persist in taking the narrower view?'

The little creature's many eyes glared distastefully at

the newcomer. 'I should have (roar) thought, Lord Jagged, that no broader view (yelp) existed!' He became suspicious. 'Have you (skree) been here all along?'

'Only recently returned.' Lord Jagged performed a brief bow. 'I apologize. There were difficulties. A fine judgement is required, so close to the end of all things, if one is to arrive with matter beneath one's feet or find oneself in absolute vacuum!'

'At least (roar) you'll admit ...'

'Oh, I don't think we need disagree, Mr Yusharisp. Let us accept the fact that we shall always be temperamentally at odds. This is the moment for realism, is it not?'

Yusharisp, whilst remaining suspicious, subsided.

CPS Shushurup intervened. 'Everything is settled (skree). We intend to requisition (skree) whatever we can salvage from the (roar yelp) city in order to further our survival plans. If you wish to (yelp) help, and share the subsequent benefit (skree) of our work ...'

'Requisition? Salvage?' Lord Jagged raised a cool eyebrow. It seemed that his tall collar quivered. 'Why should that be necessary?'

'We have (skree) not the time to (roar) spare to (skree) explain again!'

Lord Mongrove lifted his heavy head, contemplating Jagged through dismal eyes, his voice as doom-laden as ever, though he spoke as if he had never associated himself with the extra-terrestrials. 'They have this scheme, equivocal Jagged, to build a self-contained environment which will outlast the final collapse of the cities.' He was a bell, tolling the futility of struggle. 'It has certain merits.'

Lord Jagged was openly dismissive. He was dry. He was contemptuous. 'I am sure it would suit the Pweelian preference for tidiness as opposed to order. For simplification as opposed to multiplicity of choice.' The patrician features displayed stern dismay. 'But they have no business, Lord Mongrove, interfering with the workings of our city (which I am sure they understand poorly).'

'Do any of us ...?' But Mongrove was already quelled.

'Besides,' continued the chrononaut, 'it is only recently that I installed my own equipment here. I should be more than a little upset if, however inadvertently, it were tampered with.'

'What?' The Duke of Queens was lifted from apathy. He stared about him, as if he would see the machinery. He became hopeful and expectant. 'Your own equipment, sagacious Jagged? Oho!' He stroked his beard and, as he stroked, a smile began to appear. 'Aha!'

They formed an audience for the lord in yellow. He gave them his best, all subtlety and self-control, with just a hint of self-mockery, enough to win the full attention of even the mistrustful time-traveller.

'Installed not long since with the help of your friend, Jherek, who enabled you to reach the nineteenth century on your last visit.'

'Nurse?' Affection warmed him.

'The same. She was invaluable. Her programmes contained every scrap of information needed. It was merely a question of refreshing her memory. She is the most sophisticated of any ancient automaton I have ever encountered. I was soon able to put our problem to her and suggest the solution. Much of the rest of the work was hers.'

The Iron Orchid evidently knew nothing of this. 'The work, heroic husband?'

'Needed to install the equipment I mentioned. You will have noticed that, of late, the city has been conserving its power, in unison with all our other cities.'

'Con(skree)serving! Bah (roar)!' Yusharisp's translation box uttered something resembling a bitter laugh. 'Ex(skree)pending its last (roar), you mean!'

Lord Jagged of Canaria ignored the Pweelian, turning instead to the Duke of Queens. 'It was fortunate that when I returned to the End of Time, seeking Jherek and Amelia, I heard of the discovery of the Nursery and was able to invite Nurse to Castle Canaria.'

'So that is where she disappeared to – she's in your

menagerie, devious Jagged!'

'Not exactly. I doubt if much of my menagerie, such as it was, survives. Nurse is now in one of the other cities. She should be finishing off a few minor adjustments.'

'You have a plan, then, to save a whole city?' Lord Mongrove glanced behind him. 'Surely not this one. See how it perishes, as we watch!'

'This is needless pessimism, Lord Mongrove. The city transforms itself, that is all.'

'But the light . . .' began the Duke of Queens.

'Conserved, as I said.'

'And out there?' Mongrove gestured towards the void.

'You could populate it. There is room for a good-sized sun.'

'You see, Jagged,' explained the Duke of Queens, 'our power-rings do not work. It suggests that the city cannot give us the energy we require.'

'You have tried?'

'We have.'

'Not two hours since,' said Amelia Underwood.

'While the city was in flux. But now?'

'They will not work, Lord Jagged.' Lord Mongrove stroked the dark stones on his fingers. 'Our inheritance is spent forever.'

'Oh, you are too doleful, all of you. It is merely a question of attitude.' Lord Jagged stretched his left hand out before him and with his right he began to twist a ruby, staring into the sky the while, still half-conscious of his audience.

Overhead there appeared what might have been a small, twinkling star; but it was already growing. It became a fiery comet, turning the stark landscape jet black and glaring white. It grew again and it was a sun illuminating the featureless world for as far as their wincing eyes could see.

'That will do, I think.' Jagged was quietly satisfied. 'The conventional orbit.' Another touch of the same ring. 'And a turning world.'

Amelia murmured: 'You are the Master Conjuror, dear

Lord Jagged. A veritable Mephistopheles. Is that sun the size of the old one?'

'A trifle smaller, but it is all we need.'

'Skree,' said Yusharisp in alarm, all his eyes slitted to resist the glare. 'Skree, skree, skree!'

Jagged chose to take the remark as a compliment. 'Just a simple beginning or two,' he murmured modestly. He swirled the great yellow cloak about him. He touched another ring and the glare became less blinding, diffused as it was, now, by the shimmering atmosphere existing everywhere beyond the city. The sky became a greenish blue and the white landscape, with its deep, black fissures, became a dull grey, seamed with brown cracks; yet still it stretched to every horizon.

'How unsightly is our Earth without its images.' The Iron Orchid was disdainful.

As if apologizing for it, Jagged said: 'It is a very old planet, my dear. But you must all regard it as a new canvas. Everything you wish for can be re-created. New scenes can be created, just as it has always been. Rest assured that the cities will not fail us.'

'So Judgement Day is resisted, after all.' The time-traveller had his head on one side as he looked, with new eyes, at Lord Jagged of Canaria. 'I congratulate you, sir. You command enormous power, it seems.'

'I borrow the power,' said Jagged, to him, his voice soft. 'It comes from the cities.'

CPS Shushurup cried: 'It cannot be real! This man confounds us with an illusion (skree)!'

Lord Jagged affected not to hear him and turned, instead, to Mrs Persson who watched him, her expression analytical. 'The cities conserved their energies because I need them for what, I am confident, will be a successful experiment. Of course, not everyone will consider my plan a perfect one, but it is a beginning. It is what I mentioned to you, Mrs Persson.'

'It is why we are here.' Her smile was for Captain Bastable. 'To see if it should work. Certainly I am convinced by the preliminaries.'

The huge and healthy sun shone down on them all, its light spreading through the city, casting great, mellow shadows. The city continued to throb quietly and steadily; an engine waiting to be used.

'It's extremely impressive, sir,' said Bastable. 'When do you intend to make the loop?'

'In about a month.'

'You cannot,' said Mrs Persson, 'sustain this state indefinitely?'

'It would be preferable, of course, but uneconomic.'

They shared amusement.

CPS Shushurup waddled up, waving a leg. 'Do not let (skree) yourselves be (roar) convinced by this (skree) illusion. For (roar) illusion is all that it is!'

Lord Jagged said mildly: 'It depends, does it not, upon your interpretation of the word "illusion"? It is a warming sun, a breathable atmosphere, the planet turns on its orbit, it circles that sun.'

Yusharisp joined the Chief Public Servant. The bright sunlight emphasized the warts and blotches on his little round body. 'It is illusion (skree), Lord Jagged, because (roar) it cannot last the (yelp) disintegration (skree) of the universe!'

'I think it will, Mr Yusharisp.' Lord Jagged made to address his son, but the Pweelians refused to content themselves with his answer.

'Energy (skree) is needed to produce (roar) such "miracles" – you will (skree) agree to that?'

Lord Jagged inclined his head.

'There must (roar) therefore be a source (skree) – perhaps a planet (skree) or two which (yelp) have escaped the (skree) catastrophe. That source (roar) will be used up soon (yelp) enough!'

It seemed that Lord Jagged of Canaria spoke to everyone but his questioner. He retained the same mild, but slightly icy, expression. 'I fear that you cannot draw satisfaction even from that idea, my dear Yusharisp. Morals

187

may be drawn, but by a more liberal intelligence.'

'Morals (skree)! You know (roar) nothing of such (yelp) things!'

Lord Jagged continued to speak to them all, now more directly than before. 'Such is the character of one prone to morbid anxiety that he would rather *experience* the worst of things than *hope* for the best. It is a particular and puritanical mentality, and one to which I can respond with scant sympathy. Why have such conclusions been drawn? Because that kind of mentality would prefer to bring on catastrophe rather than live forever in fear of its *possibility*. Suicide rather than uncertainty.'

'You are not (roar) suggesting that (skree) this problem was merely (yelp) in our own (skree) minds, Lord Jagged?' Again the strange, mechanical laughter from CPS Shushurup.

'Was it not the people of Pweeli who took it upon themselves to spread the bad news throughout the galaxy? Did you not preach your despair wherever you could find hearers? The facts were plain enough to all, but your response to them was scarcely positive. Therefore, yes – to some degree the problem was merely in your own minds. You have not investigated all the possibilities. Your case depends, for one thing, upon a firm belief in a finite universe, with finite resources. However, as the time-traveller here will tell you and as Mrs Persson and Captain Bastable will confirm, the universe is not finite.'

'Words (skree) and nothing more ...'

The time-traveller spoke earnestly. 'I may not agree with Lord Jagged in most things, but he speaks the truth. There are a multiplicity of dimensions to the universe which you, Mrs Persson, refer to I believe as "the multiverse". This is merely one such dimension, although, indeed, all experience the same fate as this one, but not simultaneously.'

Lord Jagged acknowledged the time-traveller's support. 'Therefore, by drawing its resources from any part of the multiverse at any point in time – *which will not be a parallel point* – this planet can be sustained forever, if need be.'

'The notion (yelp) is quite without foundation,' said Yusharisp dismissively.

Lord Jagged drew his high collar about his face and stretched an elegant hand towards the sun. 'There is my proof, gentlemen.'

'Illusion,' said Yusharisp obstinately, '(yelp).'

'Pseudo-science (skree),' agreed Shushurup.

Lord Jagged made an acquiescent gesture and would respond no more, but Mrs Persson remained sympathetic to the aliens in their great distress. 'We have discovered,' she said gently, 'that the "real" universe is infinite. In-finite, timeless and still. It is a tranquil pool which will re-flect any image we conceive.'

'Meta(skree)physical poppy(roar)cock!'

Captain Bastable came to her aid. 'It is *we* who popu-late the universe with what we call Time and Matter. Our intelligence moulds it; our activities give it detail. If, sometimes, we imprison ourselves, it is perhaps because our humanity is at fault, or our logic ...'

'How can we (skree) take seriously such notions?' Yusharisp's many eyes blinked contemptuously. 'You people make a playground of the universe and justify your actions with arguments so (roar) preposterous that no (skree) intelligent being (yelp) could believe them for a moment. You deceive (skree) yourselves so that you may (yelp) remain unembarrassed by any morality ...'

Lord Jagged seemed more languid than ever and his voice was sleepy. 'The infinite universe is just that, Yusharisp. It is all a playground.' He paused. 'To "take it seriously" is to demean it.'

'You will (roar) not respect the very stuff of (skree) life?'

'To respect it is quite another thing to "taking it seriously".'

'There is (skree) no difference!' The alien was smug; his comrades seemed to congratulate him.

'Ah,' said Lord Jagged, his smile small. 'You emphasize the very difference in our viewpoints, by insisting on this difference.'

'Bah (skree)!' Yusharisp glowered.

As if apologizing for his one-time friend, Lord Mongrove droned: 'I think he is upset because he places such importance on the destruction of the universe. Its end confirmed his moral understanding of things. I felt much as he did, at one stage. But now I grow weary of the ideas.'

'Turn(yelp)coat!' said CPS Shushurup. 'It was on your invitation (skree) Lord Mongrove that (yelp) we came (skree) here!'

'There was surely nowhere else to go.' Mongrove was faintly astonished. 'This is, after all, the only bit of matter left in the universe.'

With dignity, CPS Shushurup raised an admonishing hand (or foot). 'Come, Yusharisp, fellow Pweelians. There is (skree) no more use in (roar) trying to do (yelp) anything (roar) more for these fools!' The entire deputation, the Last of the Pweelians, began to waddle back in single-file into their unwholesome spacecraft.

Mongrove, remorseful, made to follow. 'Dear friends – fellow intelligences – do nothing drastic, please ...' But the hatch squelched shut in his melancholy face and he uttered a lugubrious sigh. The ship did not take-off. It remained exactly where it had landed, in silent accusation. Moodily Mongrove began to pick at a piece of mould on its surface. 'Oh, this is truly a Hell for the serious-minded!'

Inspector Springer removed his bowler hat to wipe his forehead in a characteristic gesture. 'It *'as* become rather warm, sir, all of a sudden. Nice to see the sun again, though, I suppose.' He turned to his sweltering men. 'You can loosen your collars, lads, if you wish. 'E's quite right. As 'ot as 'ell. I'm beginning to believe it meself.' The constables began to unbutton the tops of their tunics. One or two went so far as to remove their helmets and were not admonished.

A moment later, Inspector Springer removed his jacket.

'And the preliminaries are now complete. There is a sun, an atmosphere, the planet revolves.' Una Persson's words were clipped as she spoke to Lord Jagged.

Lord Jagged had been lost in thought. He raised his eyes and smiled. 'Ah, yes. As I said. They are over. The rest must be dealt with later, when I activate my equipment.'

'You said you are certain of success.' The time-traveller was cool, still critical. He was not disposed to support Lord Jagged's view of himself. 'The experiment seems somewhat grandiose to me.'

Lord Jagged accepted the criticism. 'I make no claims, sir. The technology is not of my invention, as I said. But it will do its job, with Nurse's help.'

'You will re-cycle Time!' exclaimed Captain Bastable. 'I do hope we can return in order to witness that stage of the experiment.'

'It will be safe enough, during the first week,' said Jagged.

'Is that how you intend to preserve the planet, Jagged?' Jherek asked in excitement. 'To use the equipment I found in the Nursery?'

'It is similar equipment, though more complex. It should preserve our world for eternity. I shall make a loop of a seven-day period. Once made, it will be inviolable. The cities will become self-perpetuating; there will be no threats either from Time or from Space, for the world will be closed off, re-living the same seven days over and over again.'

'We shall re-live the same short period for eternity?' The Duke of Queens shook his head. 'I must say, Jagged, that your scheme has no more attraction than Yusharisp's.'

Lord Jagged was grave. 'If you are conscious of what is happening, then you will not repeat your actions during that period. But the time will remain the same, even though it seems to change.'

'We shall not be trapped – condemned to a mere week

191

of activity which we shall not be able to alter?'

'I think not.' Lord Jagged looked out across the miles and miles of wasteland. 'Ordinary life, as we know it at the End of Time, can continue as it has always done. The Nursery itself was deliberately limited – a kind of temporal deep-freeze to preserve the children.'

'How quickly one would become bored, if one had the merest hint that that was happening.' The Iron Orchid did her best to hide any anxiety she might display.

'Again, it is a question of attitudes, my dear. Is the prisoner a prisoner because he lives in a cage or because he *knows* that he lives in a cage?'

'Oh, I shall not attempt to discuss such things!'

He spoke fondly. 'And there, my dear, lies your salvation.' He embraced her. 'And now there is one more thing I must do here. The equipment must be supplied with energy.'

While they watched, he walked a little way into the city and stood looking about him. His pose was at once studied and casual. Then he seemed to come to a decision and placed the palm of his right hand across all the rings on his left.

The city gave out one high, almost triumphant, yell. There came a pounding roar as every building shook itself. Blue and crimson light blended in a brilliant aura overhead, blotting the sun. Then a deep sound, comforting and powerful, issued from the very core of the planet. There was a rustling from the city, familiar murmurings, the squeak of some half-mechanical creature.

Then the aura began to grow dim and Jagged became tense, as if he feared that the city could not, after all, supply the energy for his experiment.

There came a whining noise. The aura grew strong again and formed a dome-shaped cap hovering a hundred feet or more over the whole of the city. Then Lord Jagged of Canaria seemed to relax, and when he turned back to them there was a suggestion of self-congratulation in his features.

Amelia Underwood was the first to speak as he returned. 'Ah, Mephistopheles. Are you capable, now, of creation?'

He was flattered by the reference this time. He shared a private glance. 'What's this, Mrs Underwood? Manicheanism?'

'Oh, dear! Perhaps!' A hand went to her mouth, but she parodied herself.

He added: 'I cannot create a world, Amelia, but I can revive an existing one, bring the dead to life. And perhaps I once hoped to populate another world. Oh, you are right to think me prideful. It could be my undoing.'

On Jagged's right, from behind a gleaming ruin of gold and steel, came Harold Underwood and Sergeant Sherwood. They sweated, both, but seemed unaware of the heat. Mr Underwood indicated the sunny sky, the blue aura. 'See Sergeant Sherwood, how they tempt us now.' He pushed his pince-nez more firmly onto his nose as he approached Lord Jagged who towered over him, his extra height given emphasis by his face-framing collar. 'Did I hear right, sir?' said Mr Underwood. 'Did my wife – perhaps my ex-wife, I am not sure – refer to you by a certain name?'

Lord Jagged, smiling, bowed.

'Ha!' said Harold Underwood, satisfied. 'I must congratulate you, I suppose, on the quality of your illusions, the variety of your temptations, the subtlety of your torments. This present illusion, for instance, could well deceive some. What seemed to be Hell now resembles Heaven. Thus, you tempted Christ, on the mountain.'

Even Lord Jagged was nonplussed. 'The reference was a joking one, Mr Underwood ...'

'Satan's jokes are always clever. Happily, I have the example of my Saviour. Therefore, I bid you good-day, Son of the Morning. You may have claimed my soul, but you shall never own it. I trust you are thwarted as often as possible in your machinations.'

'Um ...' said Lord Jagged.

Harold Underwood and Sergeant Sherwood began to head towards the interior, but not before Harold had addressed his wife: 'You are doubtless already Satan's slave, Amelia. Yet I know we can still be saved, if we are genuinely repentant and believe in the Salvation of Christ. Be wary of all this, Amelia. It is merely a semblance of life.'

'Very convincing, on the surface, though, isn't it, sir?' said Sergeant Sherwood.

'He is the Master Deceiver, Sergeant.'

'I suppose 'e is, sir.'

'But –' Harold flung an arm around his disciple – 'I was right in one thing, eh? I said we should meet Him eventually.'

Amelia sucked at her lower lip. 'He is quite mad, Jherek. What should we do for him? Can he be sent back to Bromley?'

'He seems very much at ease here, Amelia. Perhaps so long as he receives regular meals which the city, after all, can be programmed to provide, he could stay here with Sergeant Sherwood.'

'I should not like to abandon him.'

'We can come and visit him from time to time.'

She remained dubious. 'It has not quite impinged upon me,' she said, 'that it is not the end of the world!'

'Have you ever seen him more relaxed?'

'Never. Very well, let him stay here, for the moment at least, in his – his Eternal Damnation.' She uttered a peculiar laugh.

Inspector Springer approached Lord Jagged with due deference. 'So things are more or less back to normal then, are they sir?'

'More or less, Inspector.'

Inspector Springer sucked at a tooth. 'Then I suppose we'd better get on with the job then, sir. Roundin' up the suspects and that ...'

'Most of them are in the clear now, Inspector.'

'The Latvians, Lord Jagged?'

'I suppose you could arrest them, yes.'

'Very good, sir.' Inspector Springer saluted and returned his attention to his twelve constables. 'All right, lads. Back on duty again. What's Sherwood up to? Better give 'im a blast on your whistle, Reilly, see if 'e answers.' He mopped his forehead. 'This *is* a very peculiar place. If I was a dreamin' man, I'd be 'alf inclined to think I was in the middle of a bloomin' nightmare. Har, har!' The answering laughter of some of his men as they plodded behind him was almost hollow.

Una Persson glanced at one of several instruments attached to her arm. 'I congratulate you, Lord Jagged. The first stages are a great success. We hope to be able to return to witness the completion.'

'I would be honoured, Mrs Persson.'

'Forgive me, now, if I get back to my machine. Captain Bastable . . .'

Bastable hovered, evidently reluctant to go.

'Captain Bastable, we really must —'

He became attentive. 'Of course, Mrs Persson. The Shifter and so forth.' He waved a cheerful hand to them all. 'It's been an enormous pleasure. And thank you so much, Lord Jagged, for the privilege . . .'

'Not at all.'

'I suppose, unless we do return just before the loop is finally made, we shall not be able to meet —'

'Come along, Oswald!' Mrs Persson was marching through the mellow sunshine to where they had left their machine.

'Oh, I don't know.' Lord Jagged waved in reply. 'A pleasant journey to you.'

'Thanks most awfully, again.'

'Captain Bastable!'

'— because of the drawbacks you mentioned,' shouted Bastable breathlessly, and ran to join his co-chrononaut.

When they had gone, Amelia Underwood looked almost suspiciously at the man Jherek one day hoped to make her father-in-law. 'The world is definitely saved, is it, Lord Jagged?'

'Oh, definitely. The cities have ample energy. The time-loop, when it is made, will re-cycle that energy. Jherek has told you of his adventures in the Nursery. You understand the principle.'

'Sufficiently, I hope. But Captain Bastable spoke of drawbacks.'

'I see.' Lord Jagged pulled his cloak about him. Now Mongrove and the Duke of Queens, the time-traveller and the Iron Orchid, Jherek and Amelia were all that remained of his audience. He spoke more naturally. 'Not for all, Amelia, those drawbacks. After a short period of re-adjustment, say a month, in which Nurse and I will test our equipment until we are satisfied with its functioning, the world will be in a perpetually closed circuit, with both past and future abolished. A single planet turning about a single sun will be all that remains of this universe. It will mean, therefore, that both time-travel and space-travel will be impossible. The drawback will be (for many of us) that there is no longer any intercourse between our world of the End of Time and other worlds.'

'That is all?'

'It will mean much to some.'

'To me!' groaned the Duke of Queens. 'I do wish you had told me, Jagged. I'd hoped to re-stock my menagerie.' He looked speculatively at the Pweelian spaceship. He fingered a power-ring.

'A few time-travellers may yet arrive, before the loop is made,' comforted Jagged. 'Besides, doleful Duke, your creative instincts will be fulfilled for a while, I am sure, by helping in the resurrection of all our old friends. There are dozens. Argonheart Po . . .'

'Bishop Castle. My Lady Charlotina. Mistress Christia. Sweet Orb Mace. O'Kala Incarnadine. Doctor Volospion.' The Duke brightened.

'The long-established time-travellers, like Li Pao, may also still be here – or will re-appear, thanks to the

Morphail Effect.'

'I thought you had proved that a fallacy, Lord Jagged.' Mongrove spoke with interest.

'I have proved it a Law — but not the only Law — of Time.'

'We shall resurrect Brannart and tell him!' said the Iron Orchid.

Amelia was frowning. 'So the planet will be completely isolated, for eternity, in time and space.'

'Exactly,' said Jagged.

'Life will continue as it has always done,' said the Duke of Queens. 'Who shall you resurrect first, Mongrove?'

'Werther de Goethe, I suppose. He is no real fellow spirit, but he will do for the moment.' The giant cast a glance back at the Pweelian spaceship as he began to move his great bulk forward. 'Though it will be a travesty, of course.'

'What do you mean, melancholy Mongrove?' The Duke of Queens turned a power-ring to rid himself of his uniform and replace it with brilliant multicoloured feathers from head to foot, a coxcomb in place of his hair.

'A travesty of life. This will be a stagnant planet, forever cycling a stagnant sun. A stagnant society, without progress or past. Can you not see it, Duke of Queens? Shall we have been spared death only to become the living dead, dancing forever to the same stale measures?'

The Duke of Queens was amused. 'I congratulate you, Lord Mongrove. You have found an image with which to distress yourself. I admire your alacrity!'

Lord Mongrove licked his large lips and wrinkled his great nose. 'Ah, mock me, as you always mock me — as you all mock me. And why not? I am a fool! I should have stayed out there, in space, while suns flickered and faded and whole planets exploded and became dust. Why remain here, after all, a maggot amongst maggots?'

'Oh, Mongrove, your gloom is of the finest!' Lord Jagged congratulated him. 'Come — you must all be my guests at Castle Canaria!'

'Your castle survives, Jagged?' Jherek asked, putting his arm round his Amelia's waist.

'As a memory, swiftly restored to reality – as shall be the entire society at the End of Time. That is what I meant, Amelia, when I told you that memories would suffice.'

She smiled a little bleakly. She had been listening intently to Mongrove's forebodings. It took some little while before she could rid herself of her thoughts and laugh with the others as they said farewell to the time-traveller, who intended, now that he had certain information from Mrs Persson, to make repairs to his craft and return to his own world if he could.

The Duke of Queens stood on the grey, cracked plain and admired his handiwork. It was a great squared-off monster of a vehicle and it bobbed gently in the light wind which stirred the dust at their feet.

'The bulk of it is the gas-container – the large rear-section,' he explained to Jherek. 'The front is called, I believe, the cab.'

'And the whole?'

'From the twentieth century. An articulated truck.'

The Iron Orchid sighed as she tripped towards it, gathering up the folds of her wedding dress. 'It looks most uncomfortable.'

'Not as bad as you'd think,' the Duke reassured her. 'There is breathing equipment inside the gas-bag.'

CHAPTER TWENTY-TWO

INVENTIONS AND RESURRECTIONS

Soon all would be as it had always been, before the winds of limbo had come to blow their world away. Flesh, blood and bone, grass and trees and stone would flourish beneath the fresh-born sun, and beauty of every sort, simple or bizarre, would bloom upon the face of that arid, ancient planet. It would be as if the universe had never died; and for that the world must thank its half-senile cities and the arrogant persistence of that obsessive temporal investigator from the twenty-first century, from the Dawn Age, who named himself for a small pet singing bird fashionable two hundred years before his birth, who displayed himself like an actor, yet disguised himself and his motives with all the consummate cunning of a Medici courtier; this fantastico in yellow, this languid meddler in destinies, Lord Jagged of Canaria.

They had already witnessed the rebuilding of Castle Canaria, at first a glowing mist, opaque and coruscating, modelled upon a wickerwork cage, some seventy-five feet high; and then its bars had become pale gold and within could be seen the floating compartments, each a room, where Jagged chose to live in certain moods (though he had had other moods, other castles). They had watched while Lord Jagged had spread the sky with tints of pink-tinged amber and cornflower blue, so that the orb of the sun burned a dull, rich red and cast shadows through the bars of that great cage so that it seemed the surrounding dust was criss-crossed by lattice: but then the dust itself was banished and turf replaced it, sparkling as it might after a shower, and there were hedges, too, and trees, and a pool of clear water, all standing in contrast to the sur-rounding landscape, thousands and thousands of miles of featureless desert. And they had been fired by this experi-ence to begin their own creations at once and Mongrove went off to build his black mountains, his cold, cloud-cloaked halls, his gloomy heights; and the Duke of Queens went in another direction to erect first mosaic pyramids, then flower-hung ziggurats, then golden moondomes and etoliated Towers of Mercury, then an ocean, as large as the Mediterranean, on which floated monstrous, baroque fish, each fish an apartment. Meanwhile the Iron Orchid, con-tent for the moment to share her husband's quarters, caused forests of slightly metallic blossoms to spring up from fields of silver snow, where cold birds, bright as steel, but electric green and engine red, clashed beaks and wings and sang human songs in the voices of machines, where robot foxes lurked and automata in scarlet, mounted on mechanical horses, hunted them – acre upon acre of ingenious animated gadgetry.

Jherek Carnelian and Amelia Underwood were more modest in their creations; first they chose an area and sur-rounded it with great breaks of poplars, cypresses and willows, so that the wasteland beyond could not be seen. Her fanciful palace was forgotten; she wished for a low Tudor house, with thatch and beams, whitewashed. A few of the windows she allowed for stained-glass, but the majority were as large as possible and leaded. Flower-beds surrounded the house and in these she put roses, holly-hocks and a variety of old, half-wild English flowers. There was a paved area, a pathway, a vegetable garden, shaded arbours of yew and climbing roses, a pond with a fountain in the centre, and goldfish, and everywhere high hedges, as if she would shield her house from the rest of the world. He admired it, but had little to do with its creation. Within were oak tables and chairs, bookcases (though the books themselves defeated her powers of creation, just as her attempts to recreate paintings failed badly — Jherek consoled her: no one could make such things, at the End of Time); there were comfortable armchairs, carpets, polished boards, vases of flowers, tapestries, figurines, candlesticks, lamps; there was a large kitchen, with tapped water, and every modern utensil, including knife-polishers, a gas-copper and a gas-stove, though she knew she would have little use for them. The kitchen looked out onto the vegetable garden where her runner-beans and cabbages already flourished. On the top floor of the house she created two sets of apartments for them, with a bedroom, dressing room, study and sitting room each. And when she had finished she looked to her Jherek for his approval and, ever enthusiastic, he gave it.

Elsewhere the creation continued: a superabundance of inventiveness. A summoning of certain particles by the Iron Orchid, and Bishop Castle, complete with crook and mitre, was born again, joining her to recreate first My Lady Charlotina of Below-the-Lake, a little bemused and her memory not what it was, and then Mistress Christia, the Everlasting Concubine, Doctor Volospion, O'Kala Incarnadine, Argonheart Po, Sweet Orb Mace, all restored to life and ready to add their own themes to the recon-structed world, to resurrect their particular friends. And Mongrove, in his rainy, thunder-haunted crags, let gloomy, romantic Werther de Goethe look on the world again and mourn, while Lord Shark the Unknown, re-sentful, unbelieving, contemptuous, stayed in Mongrove's domain for only a few moments before flinging himself from a cliff, to be restored by a solicitous Mongrove, who had assumed that he was not yet quite himself, and fussed over until, in a pet, he summoned his plain grey air-car and sailed away, to build again his square living quarters with their square rooms, each one of exactly the same proportions, and to populate them with his automata, each one exactly in his image (not to satisfy his ego but because Lord Shark was a being devoid of any sort of imagination). Lord Shark, once his residence and his servants were re-established, created nothing further, allowed the grey, cracked ground to be his only view, while in all other quarters of the planet whole ranges of mountains were flung up, great rivers rolled across lush plains, seas heaved, woods proliferated; hills and valleys, meadows and forests were filled with life of every description.

Argonheart Po made perhaps his most magnificent contribution to his world, a detailed copy of one of the ancient cities, each ruined tower and whispering dome subtly delicious to taste and smell, each chemical lake a soup of transporting exquisiteness, each jewel a bon-bon of mouth-watering delicacy, each streamer a noodle of previously undreamed of savouriness. The Duke of Queens built a fleet of flying trucks, causing them to perform complex aerobatics in the skies above his home, while below he prepared for a party on the theme of Death and Destruction, searching the memory-banks of the cities for fifty of the most famous ruins in history: Pompeii existed again on the slopes of Krakatoa, Alexandria, built all of books, burned afresh, while every few minutes a new mushroom cloud blossomed over Hiroshima, showering mushrooms almost fit to match Argonheart's culinary marvels. The grave-pits of Brighton, reduced to miniatures because of the huge amount of space needed to contain them, were heaped with tiny bodies, some of which still moved, mewling and touchingly pathetic; but perhaps his most effective creation was his liquidized Minneapolis, frozen, viscous, still recognizable, with its inhabitants turning to semi-transparent jelly even as they tried to flee the Swiss holocaust.

It was, as Bishop Castle proposed, a Renaissance. Lord

Jagged of Canaria was a hero; his exploits were celebrated. Only Brannart Morphail saw Jagged's interference as unwelcome; indeed Brannart remained sceptical of the whole theory behind the method of salvation. He looked with a jaundiced eye upon the carolling sculptures surrounding the green feather palace of My Lady Charlotina (she had renounced the underworld since the flood which had swept her from her halls), upon the pink pagodas of Mistress Christia and the ebony fortress of Werther de Goethe, warning all that the destruction had merely been averted for a little while, but none of them chose to listen to him. Doctor Volospion, a scarecrow in flaring, tattered black, his body black, his eyes red flames, made a Martian sarcophagus some thousand feet high, with a reproduction on its lid of the famous Revels of Cha'ar in which four thousand boys and girls died of exhaustion and seven thousand men and women flogged one another to death. Doctor Volospion found his home 'pretty' and filled it inside with lunatic manikins given to biting him or laying little vicious traps for him whenever they could, and this he found 'amusing'. Bishop Castle's own laser-beam cathedral, whose twin steeples disappeared in the sky, was unpretentious in comparison, though the music which the beams produced was ethereal and moving: even Werther de Goethe, impressed by but disapproving of Doctor Volospion's dwelling, congratulated Bishop Castle on his sonorous melodies, and Sweet Orb Mace actually copied the idea for (she was feminine again) her blue quartz Old New Old Old New New Old New Old New New New Old New New Versailles, which had flourished in her favourite period (the Integral Seventh Worship) on Sork, a planet of some Centauri or Beta, vanished long-since, the whole structure based on certain favourite primitive musical forms from the fiftieth century. O'Kala Incarnadine simply became a goat and trotted about in what remained of the wastelands bleating to anyone who would give him an ear that he preferred the planet unspoiled; the idea seemed to give him considerable pleasure, but he set no fashion. Indeed the only positive response he received at all was from Li Pao (who had not enjoyed, it emerged, his brief return to 2648) who judged his rôle a subtle metaphor, and from Gaf the Horse in Tears who derived much mindless glee from bleating back at him, hovering overhead in his aerial sampan and occasionally pelting him with the fruit he won from one of the thirty or so machines dotted about on the boat's fifth tier.

The time-traveller had become frustrated, for it had materialized that he still needed someone who could help him with the repairs he must make to his machine before he would risk a cross-dimension time-leap. He had found Lord Jagged too concerned with his own experiments to be helpful and Brannart Morphail now refused to speak to anyone, having been snubbed so badly in the first few days of the resurrection. For a short time he fell in with another time-traveller, returned, like Li Pao, by the Morphail Effect, calling himself Rat Oosapric, but it turned out that the man was an escaped criminal from the thirty-sixth century Stilt Cities and knew nothing at all about the principles of time-travel; he merely tried to steal the time-traveller's machine and was restrained from so doing by the fortunate arrival of My Lady Charlotina who froze him with a power-ring and sent him drifting into the upper atmosphere for a while. My Lady Charlotina, deprived of Brannart Morphail, was trying to convince the time-traveller that she should be his patron, that he should become her new Scientist. The time-traveller considered the idea but found her terms too restricting. It was My Lady Charlotina who returned from the old city, leaving the time-traveller to his brooding, with the news that Harold Underwood, Inspector Springer, Sergeant Sherwood, the twelve constables, and the Lat all seemed healthy and relatively cheerful, but that the Pweelian spacecraft had vanished. This caused the Duke of Queens to reveal his secret a little earlier than he had planned. He had re-started his menagerie and the

Pweelians were his prize, though they did not know it. He had allowed them to build their own environment – the closed one they had planned to escape the End of Time – and they now believed that they were the only living creatures in the entire universe. Anyone who wished to do so could visit the Duke's menagerie and watch them moving about in their great sphere, completely unaware that they were observed, involved in their curious activities. Even Amelia Underwood went to see them and agreed with the Duke of Queens that they seemed completely at ease and if anything rather happier than they had originally been.

This visit to the Duke was the first time Jherek and Amelia had emerged into society since they had built their new house. Amelia was astonished by the rapid changes: there were only a few small areas no longer altered, and there was a certain freshness to everything which made even the most bizarre inventions almost charming. The air itself, she said, had the sweet sharpness of a spring morn. On the way home they saw Lord Jagged of Canaria in his great flying swan, a yellowish white, with another tall figure beside him. Jherek brought his locomotive alongside and hailed him, at once recognizing the other occupant of the swan.

'My dear Nurse! What a pleasure to meet you again! How are your children?'

Nurse was considerably more coherent than she had been when Jherek had last seen her. She shook her old steel head and sighed. 'Gone, I fear. Back to an earlier point in Time – where I still operate the time-loop, where they still play as, doubtless, they will always play.'

'You sent them back?'

'I did. I judged this world too dangerous for my little ones, young Jerry. Well, I must say, you're looking well. Quite a grown man now, eh? And this must be Amelia, whom you are to marry. Ah, I am filled with pride. You have proved yourself a fine boy, Jerry.' It seemed that she still had the vague idea that Jherek had been one of her

original charges. 'I expect "daddy" is proud of you, too!'
She turned her head a full ninety degrees to look fondly
at Lord Jagged, who pursed his lips in what might have
been an embarrassed smile.

'Oh, very proud,' he said. 'Good morning Amelia.
Jherek.'

'Good morning, Sir Machiavelli.' Amelia relished his
discomfort. 'How go your schemes?'

Lord Jagged relaxed, laughing. 'Very well, I think.
Nurse and I have a couple of modifications to make to a
circuit. And you two? Do you flourish?'

'We are comfortable,' she told him.

'Still – engaged?'

'Not yet married, Lord Jagged, if that is what you ask.'

'Mr Underwood still in the city?'

'So we hear from My Lady Charlotina.'

'Aha.'

Amelia looked at Lord Jagged suspiciously, but his
answering expression was bland.

'We must be on our way.' The swan began to drift clear
of the locomotive. 'Time waits for no man, you know.
Not yet, at any rate. Farewell!'

They waved to him and the swan sailed on. 'Oh, he is
so devious,' she said, but without rancour. 'How can a
father and son be so different?'

'You think that?' The locomotive began to puff towards
home. 'And yet I have modelled myself on him for as long
as I can remember. He was ever my hero.'

She was thoughtful. 'One seeks for signs of corruption
in the son if one witnesses them in the father, yet is it not
fairer to see the son as the father, unwounded by the
world?'

He blinked but did not ask her to elaborate as, with
pensive eye, she contemplated the variegated landscape
sweeping by below.

'But I suppose I envy him,' she said.

'Envy Jagged? His intelligence?'

'His work. He is the only one upon the whole planet

who performs a useful task.'

'We made it beautiful again. Is that not "useful", Amelia?'

'It does not satisfy me, at any rate.'

'You have scarcely begun, however, to express your creativity. Tomorrow, perhaps, we shall invent something together, to delight our friends.'

She made an effort to brighten. 'I suppose that you are right. It is a question, as your father said, of attitude.'

'Exactly.' He hugged her. They kissed, but it seemed to him that her kiss was not as wholehearted as, of late, it had become.

From the next morning it was as if a strange fever took possession of Amelia Underwood. Her appearance in their breakfast room was spectacular. She was clad in crimson silk, trimmed with gold and silver, rather oriental in influence. There were curling slippers upon her feet; there were ostrich and peacock feathers decorating her hair and it was evident that she had painted or otherwise altered her face, for the eyelids were startling blue, the eyebrows plucked and their length exaggerated, the lips fuller and of astonishing redness, the cheeks glowing with what could only be rouge. Her smile was unusually wide, her kiss unexpectedly warm, her embrace almost sensual; scent drifted behind her as she took her place at the other end of the table.

'Good morning, Jherek, my darling!'

He swallowed a small piece of toast. It seemed to stick in his throat. His voice was not loud. 'Good morning, Amelia. You slept well?'

'Oh, I did! I woke up a new woman. *The* new woman, if you would have it. Ha, ha!'

He tried to clear the piece of toast from his throat. 'You seem very new. The change in appearance is radical.'

'I would scarcely call it that, dear Jherek. Merely an

aspect of my personality I have not shown you before. I determined to be less stuffy, to take a more positive view of the world and my place in it. Today, my love, we *create*!'

'Create?'

'It is what you suggested we do.'

'Ah, yes. Of course. What shall we create, Amelia?'

'There is so much.'

'To be sure. As a matter of fact, I had become fairly settled – that is, I had not intended ...'

'Jherek, you were famous for your invention. You set fashion after fashion. Your reputation demands that you express yourself again. We shall build a scene to excel all those we have so far witnessed. And we shall have a party. We have accepted far too much hospitality and offered none until now!'

'True, but ...'

She laughed at him, pushing aside her kedgeree, ignoring her porridge. She sipped at her coffee, staring out through the window at her hedges and her gardens. 'Can you suggest anything, Jherek?'

'Oh – a small "London" – we could make it together. As authentic as anything.'

'"London"? You would not repeat an earlier success, surely?'

'It was an initial suggestion, nothing more.'

'You are admiring my new dress, I see.'

'Bright and beautiful.' He recalled the hymn they had once sung together. He opened his lips and took a deep breath, to sing it, but she forestalled him.

'It is based on a picture I saw in an illustrated magazine,' she told him. 'An opera, I think – or perhaps the music hall. I wish I knew some music hall songs. Would the cities be able to help?'

'I doubt if they can remember any.'

'They are concerned these days, I suppose, with duller things. With Jagged's work.'

'Well, not entirely ...'

208

She rose from the table, humming to herself. 'Hurry, Jherek dear. The morning will be over before we have begun!'

Reluctantly, as confused by this rôle as he had been confused when first they had met, he got up, almost desperately trying to recapture a mood which had always been normal to him, until, it seemed, today.

She linked her arm in his, her step rather springier than usual, perhaps because of the elaborate boots she wore, and they left the house and entered the garden. 'I think now I should have kept my palace,' she said. 'You do not find the cottage dull?'

'Dull? Oh, no!'

He was surprised that she gave every hint of disapproving of his remark. She cast speculative eyes upon the sky, turned a power-ring, and made a garish royal blue tint where a moment ago there had been a relatively subdued sunrise. She added broad streaks of bright red and yellow. 'So!'

Beyond the willows and the cypresses was what remained of the wasteland. 'Here,' she said, 'is what Jagged told us was to be our canvas. It can contain anything – any folly the human mind can invent. Let us make it a splendid folly, Jherek. A vast folly.'

'What?' He began to cheer, though forebodings remained. 'Shall we seek to outdo the Duke of Queens?'

'By all means!'

He was dressed in modest dove-grey today; a frock-coat and trousers, a waistcoat and shirt. He produced a tall hat and placed it, jaunty, on his head. Hand went to ring. Columns of water seemed to spring from the ground, as thick as redwoods, and as tall, forming an arch that in turn became a roof through which the sun glittered.

'Oh, you are too cautious, Jherek!' Her own rings were used. Great cliffs surrounded them and over every cliff gushed cataracts of blood, forming a sea on which bobbed obsidian islands filled with lush, dark vegetation; and now the sun burned almost black above and peculiar sounds came to them across the ocean of blood, from the islands.

'It is very grand,' said Jherek, his voice small. 'But I should not have believed ...'

'It is based on a nightmare I once had.'

'A horse?'

'A dream.'

Something dark reared itself from the water. There was a brief flash of teeth, reminiscent of the creatures they had encountered in the Palaeozoic, of a snake-like and powerful body, an unpleasant rushing sound as it submerged again. He looked to her for an explanation.

'An impression,' she said, 'of a picture I saw as a girl, at the Crystal Palace I think. Oh, you would not believe some of the nightmares I had then. Until now I had forgotten them almost completely. Does the scene please you, Jherek? Will it please our friends?'

'I think so.'

'You are not as enthusiastic as I had hoped you would be.'

'I am. I am enthusiastic, Amelia. Astonished, however.'

'I am glad I astonish you, Jherek dear. It means, then, that our party has every chance of success, does it not?'

'Oh, yes.'

'I shall make a few more touches but leave the rest until later. Let us go into the world now.'

'To —?'

'To offer invitations.'

He acquiesced and called for his locomotive. They boarded her, setting course for Castle Canaria where they hoped to find the Iron Orchid.

CHAPTER TWENTY-THREE

AMELIA UNDERWOOD TRANSFORMED

'The Lat are still with us?' Mistress Christia, the Ever-lasting Concubine, licked lush lips and widened her already very wide blue eyes to assume that particular look of heated innocence so attractive to those who loved her (and who did not?). 'Oh, what splendid news, Iron Orchid! They raped me, you know, an enormous number of times. You cannot see them now, since my resurrection, but my elbows were both bright red!' Her dress, liquid crystal, coruscated as she lifted her arms. They walked together through the dripping, glassy passage in one of Mrs Underwood's obsidian islands; at the far end of the tunnel was reddish light, reflected from the bloody sea beyond. 'The atmosphere is rather good here, don't you think?'

'A trifle reminiscent of something of Werther's.'

'None the worse for that, dearest Orchid.'

'You have always found his work more attractive than I have.' (They had been rivals once, however, for sighing de Goethe.)

The light was blocked. My Lady Charlotina rustled towards them, in organdie and tulle of clashing greens. She staggered for a second as a wave struck the island and it tilted, then righted itself. 'Have you seen the *beasts*? One has eaten poor O'Kala.' She giggled. 'They are fond of goats, it seems.'

'I thought the beasts good,' agreed her friend. The Orchid had retained white as her main effect, but had added a little pale yellow (Jagged's colours) here and there. The yellow looked well on her lips, against the pallor of her skin. 'And the smell. So heavy.'

'Not too sweet?' asked Mistress Christia.

'For me, no.'

'And your *marriage*, oracular Orchid,' breathed My Lady Charlotina, giving her ears a pinch, to increase the size of the lobes. She added earrings. 'I have just heard. But should we call you Orchid still? Is it not Lady Jagged now?'

They moved back towards the opening in the passage.

'I had not considered it.' The Iron Orchid was the first to reach the open. Her son was there, leaning against a dark green palm, staring into the depths of the crimson ocean.

'With Jherek,' said My Lady Charlotina enviously, from behind her, 'you begin a dynasty. Imagine that!'

All three women emerged now and saw him. He looked up, as if he had thought himself alone.

'We interrupt a reverie ...' said Mistress Christia kindly.

'Oh, no ...' He still wore clothes his Amelia had considered suitable – a straw boater, a bright blazer, white shirt and white flannels.

'Well, Jherek?' His mother approached closer, amused. 'Shall you be presenting us with a son, you and your Amelia?'

'An air?'

'A boy, my boy!'

'Aha! I rather doubt it. We cannot marry, you see.'

'Your father and I, Jherek, were not formally married when ...'

'But she has reservations,' he told her gloomily. 'Her

husband, who is still in the city, haunts us. But perhaps she changes . . .'

'Her inventions indicate as much.'

A sigh. 'They do.'

'You do not find this lake, these cliffs, these beasts, magnificently realized?'

'Of course I do.' He raised his head to watch the blood as it roared from every edge. 'Yet I am disturbed, mother.'

'Resentful of her hidden talent, you mean!' The Iron Orchid chided him.

'Where is she?' My Lady Charlotina cast about. 'I must congratulate her. All her work, Jherek? Nothing yours?'

'Nothing.'

'Exquisite!'

'She was with Li Pao when I last saw her,' Jherek said. 'On one of the farther islands.'

'I was glad Li Pao returned in time,' the Iron Orchid said. 'I should miss him. But so many others are gone!'

'And nothing for a menagerie, save what we make ourselves,' complained My Lady Charlotina. She produced a sunshade (the fashion had been set by Amelia) and twirled it. 'We live in difficult days, audacious Orchid.'

'But challenging.'

'Oh, yes.'

'The Duke of Queens has those round aliens,' said Mistress Christia.

'By rights,' My Lady Charlotina told her bitterly, with a glance at Jherek, 'at least one of those is mine. Still, not very much of an acquisition, by any real standards. I suppose they'll be prized now, however.'

'He remains very proud of them.' Mistress Christia moved to hug Jherek. 'You seem sad, handsomest of heroes.'

'Sad? Is that the emotion? I am not sure I am enjoying it, Mistress Christia.'

'Why sad?'

'I am not at all sure.'

'You seek to rival Werther, that is it. You are in competition!'

'I had not thought of Werther.'

'Here he is!' The Iron Orchid and My Lady Charlotina pointed together. Werther had seen them from above and came circling down on his coffin-shaped car. His cape and hood were black and white checks and he had removed all the flesh from his face so that his skull was revealed and only his dark eyes, in the recesses of the sockets, gave it life. 'Where is Mrs Underwood, Jherek?' said Werther. 'I must honour her. This is the most beautiful creation I have seen in a millennium!'

They were slow to answer. Only Jherek pointed to a distant island.

'Oho!' said Mistress Christia, and she winked at the Iron Orchid. 'Amelia makes another conquest.'

Jherek kicked at a piece of rock. It resisted his foot. Again, he sighed. His boater fell from his head. He stooped and picked it up.

The women linked arms and rose together into the air. 'We go to Amelia,' called back the Iron Orchid. 'Shall you join us, Jherek?'

'In a moment.'

He had only recently escaped the press of guests who flocked about his intended bride, for she was at the centre and all congratulated her on her creation, her costume, her comportment and if they spoke to him, it was to praise Amelia. And over there on the other island, she chattered, she was witty, she held them but – and he could define it no better – she was not his Amelia.

He turned, at the sound of a footfall, and it was the time-traveller, hands in pockets, looking quite as glum as he did himself. 'Good afternoon to you, Jherek Carnelian. My Lady Charlotina passed on your invitation. Lord Mongrove brought me. This is all very fanciful. You must have journeyed further inland, during your stay in the Palaeozoic, than I realized.'

'To the creek?'

'Beyond the creek there are landscapes very similar to this – wild and beautiful, you know. I assumed this to be a perverse version. Ah, to see again the rain falling through sunshine on a Palaeozoic morning, near the great waterfalls, with the ferns waving in a light wind which ripples the waters of the lake.'

'You make me envious.' Jherek stared at his reflection, distorted in the blood. 'I sometimes regret our return, though I know now we should have starved.'

'Nonsense. With decent equipment and a little intelligence one could live well in the Palaeozoic.' The time-traveller smiled. 'So long as one resisted the urge to swim in the creeks. That fish, by the by, is very tasty. Sweet, you know. Like a kind of ham.'

'Um,' said Jherek, looking towards the island where Amelia Underwood held court.

'It seems to me,' murmured the time-traveller after a pause, 'that all the romance has gone out of time-travel since I first began. I was one of the first, you know. Perhaps the very first.'

'A pioneer,' Jherek confirmed.

'Quite so. It would be a terrible irony indeed if I were to be marooned here, when your Lord Jagged puts his time-recycling plan into operation. I crossed eons, crossed the barriers between the worlds, and now I am threatened with being imprisoned forever in the same week, repeated over and over again, throughout eternity.' He uttered something resembling a staccato snort. 'Well, I shall not allow it. If I cannot get help with repairs to my craft, I shall risk the journey back and ask for the support of the British Government. It will be better than this.'

'Brannart refuses his aid?'

'He is involved, I gather, in building a machine of his own. He refuses to accept Lord Jagged's theories or his solutions.'

Jherek's smile was faint. 'For thousands of years Brannart was the Lord of Time. His Effect was one of the few laws known to that imprecise science. Suddenly he is

dethroned, without authority. It is no wonder that he be-
came so agitated recently, that he still utters warnings.
Yet there would be much he could continue to do. Your
Guild would welcome his knowledge, would it not?'

'Possibly. He is not what I would call a true scientist.
He imposes his imagination upon the facts, rather than
using that imagination to investigate. It is probably not
his fault, for you all do that, and with considerable success. In most cases you are in the position to alter all the
Laws of Nature which, in my own time, were regarded as
unalterable.'

'I suppose that's so.' Jherek saw more new arrivals heading for Amelia's island.

'Enviable, of course. But you have lost the scientific
method. You solve problems by changing the facts. Magic,
we'd call it.'

'Very kind of you.' Absently.

'Fundamentally different attitudes. Even your Lord
Jagged is to some extent infected.'

'Infected?' He saw Argonheart Po's shortcake space-
shuttle spiralling above the cliffs. It, too, made for the
island which had his attention.

'I employed the word without criticism. But for someone like myself used to getting to grips with a problem by
means of analytical method . . .'

'Naturally.'

'Natural to me. I was trained to despise any other
method.'

'Aha.' It was useless to hold himself in check any longer.
He twisted a power-ring. He rose into the air. 'Forgive me
– social commitments – perhaps we'll have a chance to
chat later.'

'I say,' said the time-traveller urgently, 'you couldn't
give me a lift, I suppose? I have no means of crossing . . .'

But Jherek was already out of earshot, leaving the time-
traveller abjectly staring at the pink-flecked foam wash-
ing the rocking obsidian shore, stranded until some other
guest arrived to help him to the mainland. Something

black and somewhat phallic pushed itself above the surface of the crimson sea and stared at him, smacking its tiny
lips before losing interest and swimming away in the
direction Jherek had taken. Removing his hands from his
pockets, the time-traveller turned, seeking the highest
point of the island where, with luck, he would be safe
from the beasts and be able to signal for help.

She was surrounded. Jherek could just see her head and
shoulders at the centre of the crowd; she was struggling
with a cigarette. In imitation, Sweet Orb Mace, all mauve
fluff, puffed smoke from her ears, while Bishop Castle
decorously swung his huge headdress back to avoid
collision with the holder. The Iron Orchid, Mistress
Christia, My Lady Charlotina and Werther de Goethe
were closest to her and their words came to Jherek through
the general babble.

'Even you, Amelia, would admit that the nineteenth
century is rather passé ...'

'Oh, but you have proven it, my love, with all this.
It is so wonderfully original ...'

'And yet so simple —'

'The best ideas, Mistress Christia, are always simple ...'

'Truly, sweetest Orchid — the ones you wish you'd conceived yourself, but never did ...'

'But *serious*, withal. If Man were still mortal — ah,
and what he loses! — what a comment on that mortality!'

'I see it merely as beauty, Werther, and nothing more.
Surely, Amelia, the creation is not intended ...'

'There was no conscious intention.'

'You must have planned for days —?'

'It came spontaneously.'

'I knew it! It's so vital ...'

'And the monsters! Poor O'Kala ...'

'We must remember to revive him.'

'At the end. Not before.'

'Our first post-Resurrection resurrection! Here's the Duke of Queens.'

'Come to pay my compliments. I bow to a master. Or should it be mistress?'

'Master will do, Duke of Queens.'

'Mistress of my heart!'

'Really Werther, you embarrass me!' A burst of laughter such as she had never uttered before. Jherek pushed forward.

'Oh, Amelia, but if you would give me just the smallest encouragement . . .'

'Jherek! Here at last!'

'Here,' he said. A silence seized him. It threatened to spread through the throng, for it was that kind, but Bishop Castle wagged his crook.

'Oho, Werther. You were overheard. Will this mean a duel, I wonder?'

'A *duel*!' The Duke of Queens saw an opportunity to strike a pose. 'I will advise you. My own skill with the foil is considered not unremarkable. I am sure Lord Shark would agree . . .'

'Boasting Duke!' The Iron Orchid put a pale yellow hand upon Amelia's naked shoulder and a white one upon Jherek's Joseph-coat. 'I am sure that we are as tired of the fashion for duelling as we are of the nineteenth century. Amelia must have seen enough of such sport in her native Burnley.'

'Bromley,' said Jherek.

'Forgive me. Bromley.'

'Oh, but the idea is appealing!' cawed Doctor Volospion, his pointed chin thrust forward from beneath the brim of his hat. He cocked an eye first at Jherek, then at Werther. 'The one so fresh and healthy, the other so stale and deathly. It would suit you, Werther, eh? With your penchant for parable. A duel between Life and Death. Whoever shall win shall decide the fate of the planet!'

'I could not undertake such a responsibility, Doctor Volospion.' It was impossible to tell either from Werther's tone or from his expression (a skull's are limited at the best of times) if he jested or was in earnest.

Jherek, who had never much cared for Doctor Volospion (the doctor's jealousy of Lord Jagged was notorious), affected not to have heard. His suspicion of Volospion's motives was confirmed with the next remark.

'Is it only Jagged then who is allowed to decide Man's fate?'

'We choose our own!' Jherek defended his absent father. 'Lord Jagged merely supplies us with the means of choice. We should have none at all without him!'

'So the old dog is barked for by the pup.' Doctor Volospion's malice was at its sharpest.

'You forget, Doctor Volospion,' said the Iron Orchid sweetly, 'that the bitch is here, too.'

Volospion bowed to this; a withdrawal.

In a loud voice Amelia Underwood declared: 'Shall we repair to the largest island? Refreshment awaits us.'

'I anticipate inspiration,' said Argonheart Po, with weighty gallantry.

The guests became airborne.

For a second Jherek and Amelia were left alone, confronting one another. His face was a question which she ignored. He made a movement towards her, certain that he saw pain and bewilderment behind those painted, unblinking eyes.

'Amelia . . .'

She was already rising.

'You punish me!' His hand went up, as if to catch at her fluttering gown.

'Not you, my love.'

CHAPTER TWENTY-FOUR

THE VISION IN THE CITY

'We hear you have command of so many ancient arts, Mrs Underwood. You read I understand?' Agape, Gaf the Horse in Tears, all foliage save for his face, one of Amelia's swiss rolls filling the twigs at the end of his left bough, rustled with enthusiasm. 'And write, eh?'

'A little.' Her amusement was self-conscious.

'And play an instrument?'

She inclined an artificial curl or two. 'The harmonium.'

The guests, each with a costume more outrageous than the next, filed in to stand on both sides of the long trestle tables, sampling the cups of tea, the cucumber sandwiches, the roast ham, the cold sausages, the strawberry flan, the battenbergs, the ginger cakes, the lettuce and the cress, all under the shade of the tall red and white striped marquee. Jherek, in a corner of the tent, nibbled a pensive teacake, ignored by all save Li Pao, who was complaining of his treatment during his brief return home. 'They called *me* decadent, you know . . .'

'And you sew. Embroider, is it?' Bishop Castle carefully replaced a rattling, scarcely tasted, cup upon the trestle.

'I used to. There is little point, now . . .'

'But you must demonstrate these arts!' The Iron Orchid signalled to Jherek. 'Jherek. You told us Amelia *sang*, did you not?'

'Did I tell you that? She does.'

'You must persuade her to give us an air.'

'A son?'

'A song, my seed!'

He looked miserably over to where Amelia gesticulated, laughing with Doctor Volospion. 'Will you sing a hymn for us, Amelia?'

Her answering smile chilled him. 'Not now, I think.' The crimson-clad arms spread wide. 'Has everyone enough tea?'

A murmur of satiation.

Werther advanced again, hovering, a white hand holding a silver cake-stand from which he helped himself, popping one pastry at a time into his clacking jaws. 'Queen of Melancholy, come with me to my Schloss Dolorous, my dear and my darling to be!'

She flirted. At least, she attempted to flirt. 'Oh, chivalrous Knight of Death, in whose arms is eternal rest – would that I were free.' The eyelids fluttered. Was there a tear? Jherek could bear no more. She was glancing towards him, perhaps to test his reaction, as he bowed and left the tent.

He hesitated outside. The red cascades continued to fall from all sides into the lake. The obsidian islands slowly drifted to the centre, some of them already touching. In the distance he could see the time-traveller gingerly leaping from one to another.

He had a compulsion to seek solitude in the old city, where he had sought it as a boy. It was possible that he would find his father there and could gain advice.

'Jherek!'

Amelia stood behind him. There was a tear on either scarlet cheek. 'Where are you going? You are a poor host today.'

'I am ignored. I am extraneous.' He spoke as lightly as he could. 'Surely I am not missed. All the guests join your entourage.'

'You are hurt?'

'I merely had it in mind to visit the city.'

'Is it not bad manners?'

'I do not understand you fully, Amelia.'

'You go now?'

'It occurred to me to go now.'

She paused. Then: 'I would go with you.'

'You seem content' – a backward look at the marquee – 'with all this.'

'I do it to please you. It was what you wanted.' But she accused him. The tears had fallen: no more followed.

'I see.'

'And you find my new rôle unattractive?'

'It is very fine. It is impressive. Instantly, you rank with the finest of fashion-setters. The whole of society celebrates your talents, your beauty. Werther courts you. Others will.'

'Is that not how life is led, at the End of Time – with amusements, flirtations?'

'I suppose that it is.'

'Then I must learn to indulge in such things if I am to be accepted.' Again that chilling smile. 'Mistress Christia would have you for a lover. You have not noticed?'

'I want only you. You are already accepted. You have seen that today.'

'Because I play the proper game.'

'If you'll have it so. You'll stay here, then?'

'Let me and I'll come with you. I am unused to so much attention. It has an effect upon the nerves. And I would satisfy myself that Harold fares well.'

'Oh, you are concerned for him.'

'Of course.' She added: 'I have yet to cultivate that particular insouciance characteristic of your world.'

Lord Jagged's swan was drifting down. The pale yellow draperies billowed; he was somewhere amongst them –

they heard his voice.

'My dears. How convenient. I did not wish to become involved with your party, but I did want to make a brief visit, to congratulate you upon it. A beautiful ambience, Amelia. It is yours, of course.'

She acknowledged it. The swan began to hover, Lord Jagged's face now distinct, faintly amused as it often was, looking down on them. 'You are more at ease, I see, with the End of Time, Amelia.'

'I begin to understand how one such as I might learn to live here, Mephistopheles.'

The reference brought laughter, as it always did. 'So you have not completely committed yourself. No wedding, yet?'

'To Jherek?' She did not look at Jherek Carnelian, who remained subdued. 'Not yet.'

'The same reasons?'

'I do my best to forget them.'

'A little more time, that is all you need, my dear.' Jagged's stare gained intensity, but the irony remained.

'I gather there is only a little left.'

'It depends upon your attitude, as I say. Life will continue as it has always done. There will be no change.'

'No change,' she said, her voice dropping. 'Exactly.'

'Well, I must continue about my work. I wish you well, Amelia – and you, my son. You have still to recover from all your adventures. Your mood will improve, I am sure.'

'Let us hope so, Lord Jagged.'

'Hi! I say there. Hi!' It was the time-traveller, from a nearby island. He waved at Jagged's swan. 'Is that you, Jagged?'

Lord Jagged of Canaria turned a handsome head to contemplate the source of this interruption. 'Ah, my dear chap. I was looking for you. You need help, I gather.'

'To get off this damned island.'

'And to leave this damned era, too, do you not?'

'If you are in a position ...'

'You must forgive me for my tardiness. Urgent prob-

lems. Now solved.' The swan began to glide towards the
time-traveller, settling on the rocky shore so that he could
climb aboard. They heard the time-traveller say: 'This
is a great relief, Lord Jagged. One of the quartz rods
requires attention, also two or three of the instruments
need adjusting . . .'

'Quite so,' came Jagged's voice. 'I head now for Castle
Canaria where we shall discuss the matter in full.'

The swan rose high into the air and disappeared above
one of the cliffs, leaving Jherek and Amelia staring after
it.

'Was that Jagged?' It was the Iron Orchid, at the entrance to the tent. 'He said he might come. Amelia, everyone is remarking on your absence.'

Amelia went to her. 'Dearest Orchid, be hostess for a
little while. I am still inexperienced. I tire. Jherek and I
would rest from the excitement.'

The Iron Orchid was sympathetic. 'I will give them
your apologies. Return soon, for our sakes.'

'I will.'

Jherek had already summoned the locomotive. It
awaited them, blue and white steam drifting from its
funnel, emeralds and sapphires winking.

As they climbed into the air they looked down on the
scene of Amelia's first social creation. Against the surrounding landscape it resembled some vast and terrible
wound; as if the Earth were living flesh and a gigantic
spear had been driven into its side.

Shortly, the city appeared upon the horizon, its oddly
shaped, corroded towers, its varicoloured halo, its drifting
streamers and clouds of chemical vapour, its little grumb-
lings and murmurings, its peculiar half-organic, half-
metallic odour, filling them both with a peculiar sense of
nostalgia, as if for happier, simpler days.

They had not spoken since they had left; neither, it
seemed, was capable of beginning a conversation; neither
could come to terms with feelings which were, to Jherek
at least, completely unfamiliar. He thought that for all her

gaudy new finery he had never known her so despairing. She hinted at this despair, yet denied it when questioned. Used to paradox, believing it the stuff of existence, he found this particular paradox decidedly unwelcome.

'You will look for Mr Underwood?' he asked, as they approached the city.

'And you?'

He knew foreboding. He wished to volunteer to accompany her, but was overwhelmed by unusual and probably unnecessary tact.

'Oh, I'll seek the haunts of my boyhood.'

'Isn't that Brannart?'

'Where?' He peered.

She was pointing into a tangle of ancient, rotten machinery. 'I thought in there. But he has gone. I even glimpsed one of those Lat, too.'

'What would Brannart want with the Lat?'

'Nothing, of course.'

They had flown past, but though he looked back, he saw no sign either of Brannart Morphail or the Lat. 'It would explain why he did not attend the party.'

'I assumed that was pique, only.'

'He could never resist an opportunity in the past to air his portentous opinions,' said Jherek. 'I am of the belief that he still works to thwart our Lord Jagged, but that he cannot be successful. The time-traveller was explaining to me, as I recall, why Brannart's methods fail.'

'So Brannart is out of favour,' said she. 'He did much to help you at first.' She chided him.

'By sending you back to Bromley? He forgets, when he berates us for our meddling with Time, that a great deal of what happened was because of his connivance with My Lady Charlotina. Waste no sympathy on Brannart, Amelia.'

'Sympathy? Oh, I have little of that now.' She had returned to her frigid, sardonic manner.

This fresh ambiguity caused further retreat into his own thoughts. He had surprised himself with his criticisms, having half a notion that he did not really intend to attack Brannart Morphail at all. He was inexpert in this business of accusation and self-immolation: a novice in the expression of emotional pain, whereas she, it now seemed, was a veteran. He floundered, he who had known only extrovert joy, innocent love; he floundered in a swamp which she in her ambivalence created for them both. Perhaps it would have been better if she had never announced her love and retained her stern reliance upon Bromley and its mores, left him to play the gallant, the suitor, with all the extravagance of his world. Were his accusations really directed at her, or even at himself? And did she not actually rack her own psyche, all aggression turned upon herself and only incidentally upon him, so that he could not react as one who is threatened, must thresh about for an object, another person, upon whom to vent his building wrath, as a beaten dog snaps at a neutral hand, unable to contemplate the possibility that it is its master's victim?

All this was too much for Jherek Carnelian. He sought relief in the outer world; they flew across a lake whose surface was a rainbow swirl, bubbling and misty, then across a field of lapis lazuli dotted with carved stone columns, the remnants of some peculiar two hundred thousandth-century technology. He saw, ahead, the mile-wide pit where not long since they had awaited the end of the world. He made the locomotive circle and land in the middle of a group of ruins wreathed in bright orange fire, each flame an almost familiar shape. He helped her from the footplate and they stood in frozen attitudes for a second before he looked deliberately into her kohl-circled eyes to see if she guessed his thoughts, for he had no words to express them; the vocabulary of the End of Time was rich only in hyperbole. He reflected then that it had been his original impulse to expand his own vocabulary, and consequently his experience, that had led him to this present pass. He smiled.

'Something amuses you?' she said.

'Ah, no, Amelia. It is only that I cannot say what I wish to say —'

'Do not be constrained by good manners. You are disappointed in me. You love me no longer.'

'You wish me to say so?'

'It is true, is it not? You have found me out for what I am.'

'Oh, Amelia, I love you still. But to see you in such misery – it makes me dumb. The Amelia I now see is not what you are!'

'I am learning to enjoy the pleasures of the End of Time. You must allow me an apprenticeship.'

'You do not enjoy them. You use them to destroy yourself.'

'To destroy my old-fashioned notions. Not myself.'

'Perhaps those notions are essential. Perhaps they *are* the Amelia Underwood I love, or at least part of her ...' He subsided; words again failed him.

'I think you are mistaken.' Did she deliberately put this distance between them? Was it possible that she regretted her declaration of love, felt bound by it?

'You love me, still ...?'

She laughed. 'All love all at the End of Time.'

With an air of resolve, she broke the ensuing silence. 'Well, I will look for Harold.'

He pointed out a yellow-brown metal pathway. 'That will lead you to the place where you left him.'

'Thank you.' She set off. The dress and the boots gave her a hobbling motion; her normal grace was almost entirely gone. His heart went to her, but his throat remained incapable of speech, his body incapable of movement. She turned a corner, where a tall machine, its casing damaged to expose complicated circuits, whispered vague promises to her as she passed but became inaudible, a hopeless whore, quickly rebuffed by her lack of interest.

For a moment Jherek's attention was diverted by the sight of three little egg-shaped robots on caterpillar tracks trundling across a nearby area of rubble deep in a conversation held in a polysyllabic, utterly incomprehensible language; he looked back to the road. She was gone.

He was alone in the city, but the solitude was no longer palatable. He wanted to pursue her, to demand her own analysis of her mood, but perhaps she was as incapable of expressing herself as was he. Did Bromley supply a means of interpreting emotion as readily as it supplied standards of social conduct?

He began to suspect that neither Amelia's society nor his, for all their differences, concerned themselves with anything but the surface of things. Now that he was in the city it might be that he could find some still functioning memory bank capable of recalling the wisdom of one of those eras, like the Fifth Confucian or the Zen Commonwealth, which had placed rather exaggerated emphasis on self-knowledge and its expression. Even the strange, neurotic refinements of that other period with which he had a slight familiarity, the Saint-Claude Dictatorship (under which every citizen had been enjoined to supply three distinctly different explanations as to their psychological motives for taking even the most minor decisions), might afford him a clue to Amelia's behaviour and his own reactions. It occured to him that she might be acting so strangely because, in some simple way, he was failing to console her. He began to walk through the ruins, in the opposite direction to the one she had taken, trying to recall something of Dawn Age society. Could it be that he was supposed to kill Mr Underwood? It would be easy enough to do. And would she permit her husband's resurrection? Should he, Jherek, change his appearance, to resemble Harold Underwood as much as possible? Had she rejected his suggestion that he change his name to hers because it was not enough? He paused to lean against a carved jade post whose tip was lost in chemical mist high above his head. He seemed to remember reading of some ritual formalizing the giving of oneself into another's power. Did she pine because he did not perform it? Or did the reverse apply? Did kneeling have something to do with it, and if so who knelt to whom?

'Om,' said the jade post.

'Eh?' said Jherek, startled.

'Om,' intoned the post. 'Om.'

'Did you detect my thoughts, post?'

'I am merely an aid to meditation, brother. I do not interpret.'

'It is interpretation I need. If you could direct me...'

'Everything is as everything else,' the post told him. Everything is nothing and nothing is everything. The mind of man is the universe and the universe is the mind of man. We are all characters in God's dreams. We are all God.'

'Easily said, post.'

'Because a thing is easy does not mean that it is difficult. Because a thing is difficult does not mean that it is easy.'

'Is that not a tautology?'

'The universe is one vast tautology, brother, yet no one thing is the same as another.'

'You are not very helpful. I sought information.'

'There is no such thing as information. There is only knowledge.'

'Doubtless,' said Jherek doubtfully. He bade good day to the post and retreated. The post, like so many of the city's artefacts, seemed to lack a sense of humour, though probably, if taxed, it would – as others here did – claim a 'cosmic sense of humour' (this involved making obvious ironies about things commonly observed by the simplest intelligence).

In the respect of ordinary, light conversation, machines, including the most sophisticated, were notoriously bad company; more literal-minded even than someone like Li Pao. This thought led him, as he walked on, to ponder the difference between men and machines. There had once been very great differences, but these days there were few, in superficial terms. What were the things which distinguished a self-perpetuating machine, capable of almost any sort of invention, from a self-created human being, equally capable? There *were* differences – perhaps emotional. Could it not be true that the less emotion the entity possessed the poorer its sense of humour – or the more emotion it repressed the weaker its capacity for original irony?

These ideas were scarcely leading him in the direction he wished to go, but he was beginning to give up hope of finding any solution to his dilemma in the city, and at least he now felt he understood the jade post better.

A chromium tree giggled at him as he entered a paved plaza. He had been here several times as a boy. He had a great deal of affection for the giggling tree.

'Good afternoon,' he said.

The tree giggled as it had giggled without fail for at least a million years, whenever addressed or approached. Its function seemed merely to amuse. Jherek smiled, in spite of the heaviness of his thoughts.

'A lovely day.'

The tree giggled, its chromium branches gently clashing.

'Too shy to speak, as usual?'

'Tee hee hee.'

The tree's charm was very hard to explain, but it was unquestionable.

'I believe myself, old friend, to be "unhappy" – or worse!'

'Hee hee hee.' The tree seemed helpless with mirth. Jherek began to laugh, too. Laughing, he left the plaza, feeling considerably more relaxed.

He had wandered close to the tangle of metal where, from above, Amelia had thought she had seen Brannart Morphail. Curiosity led him on, for there were, indeed, lights moving behind the mass of tangled girders, struts, hawsers, cables and wires, though they were probably not of human origin. He approached closer, but cautiously. He peered, thinking he saw figures. And then, as a light flared, he recognized the unmistakable shape of Brannart Morphail's quaint body, an outline only, for the light half-blinded him. He recognized the scientist's voice, but it was not speaking its usual tongue. As he listened, it dawned on Jherek that Brannart Morphail was, however, using a language familiar to him.

'Gerfish lortooda, mibix?' said the scientist to someone beyond the pool of light. 'Derbi kroofrot!'

Another voice answered and it was equally unmistakable as belonging to Captain Mubbers. 'Hrunt, arragak fluzi, grodsink Morphail.'

Jherek regretted that he no longer habitually carried his translation pills with him, for he was curious to know why Brannart should be conspiring with the Lat, for conspiring he must be – there was a considerable air of secrecy to the whole business. He resolved to mention his discovery to Lord Jagged as soon as possible. He considered attempting to see more of what was going on but decided not to risk revealing his presence; instead he turned and made for the cover of a nearby dome, its roof cracked and gaping like the shell of an egg.

Within the dome he was delighted to find brilliantly coloured pictures, all as fresh as the day they were made, and telling some kind of story, though the voices accompanying them were distorted. He watched the ancient programme through until it began again. It described a method of manufacturing machines of the same sort as the one on which Jherek watched the pictures, and there were fragments, presumably demonstrating other programmes, of scenes showing a variety of events – in one a young woman in a kind of luminous net made love underwater to a great fish of some description, in another two men set fire to themselves and ran through what was probably the airlock of a spaceship, making the spaceship explode, and in another a large number of people wearing rococo metal and plastic struggled in free fall for the possession of a small tube which, when one of them managed to take hold of it, was hurled towards one of several circular objects on the wall of the building in which they floated. If the tube struck a particular point on the circular object there would be great exultation from about half the people and much despondency displayed by the other half, but Jherek was particularly interested in the fragment which seemed to be demonstrating how a man and a woman might copulate, also in free fall. He found the ingenuity involved extremely touching and left the dome in a rather more positive and hopeful spirit than when he had entered it.

It was in this mood that he determined to seek out Amelia and try to explain his discomfort with her own behaviour and his. He sought for the way he had come, but was already lost, though he knew the city well; but he had an idea of the general direction and he began to cross a crunching expanse of sweet-smelling green and red crystals, almost immediately catching sight of a landmark ahead of him – a curving, half-melted piece of statuary suspended, without visible support, above a mechanical figure which stretched imploring arms to it, then scooped little golden discs in its hands and flung them into the air, repeating these motions over and over again, as they had been repeated ever since Jherek could remember. He passed the figure and entered an alley poorly illuminated with garish amber and cerise; from apertures on both sides of the alley little metal snouts emerged, little machine-eyes peered inquisitively at him, little silver whiskers twitched. He had never known the function of these platinum rodents, though he guessed that they were information-gatherers of some kind for the machines housed in the great smooth radiation-splashed walls of the alley. Two or three illusions, only half tangible, appeared and vanished ahead of him – a thin man, eight feet tall, blind and warlike; a dog in a great bottle on wheels, a yellow-haired porcine alien in buff-coloured clothing – as he hurried on.

He came out of the alley and pushed knee-deep through soft black dust until the ground rose and he stood on a hillock looking down on pools of some glassy substance, each perfectly circular, like the discarded lenses of some gigantic piece of optical equipment. He skirted these, for he knew from past experience that they were capable of movement and could swallow him, subjecting him to hallucinatory experiences which, though entertaining, were time-consuming, and a short while later he saw ahead the pastoral illusion where they had met Jagged on his return. He crossed the illusion, noticing that a fresh picnic had been laid and that there was no trace of the Lat having been here (normally they left a great deal of litter behind them), and would have continued on his way towards the mile-wide pit had he not heard the sound, to his left, of voices raised in song.

> *Who so beset him round*
> *With dismal stories,*
> *Do but themselves confound —*
> *His strength the more is.*

He crossed an expanse of yielding, sighing stuff, almost losing his balance so that on several occasions he was forced to take to the air as best he could (there was still some difficulty, it seemed, with the city's ability to transmit power directly to the rings). Eventually, on the other side of a cluster of fallen arcades, he found them, standing in a circle around Mr Underwood, who waved his arms with considerable zest as he conducted them — Inspector Springer, Sergeant Sherwood and the twelve constables, their faces shining and full of joy as they joined together for the hymn. It was not for some moments that Jherek discovered Mrs Underwood, a picture of despairing bewilderment, her oriental dress all dusty, her feathers askew, seated with her head in her hand, watching the proceedings from an antique swivel chair, the remnant of some crumbled control room.

She lifted her head as he approached, on tip-toe, so as not to disturb the singing policemen.

'They are all converted now,' she told him wearily. 'It seems they received a vision shortly before we arrived.'

The hymn was over, but the service (it was nothing less) continued.

'And so God came to us in a fiery globe and He spoke to us and He told us that we must go forth and tell the world of our vision, for we are all His prophets now. For he has given us the means of grace and the hope of glory!' cried Harold Underwood, his very pince-nez aflame with fervour.

'Amen,' responded Inspector Springer and his men.

'For we were afraid and in the very bowels of Hell, yet still He heard us. And we called unto the Lord – Our help is in the name of the Lord who hath made heaven and earth. Blessed be the name of the Lord; henceforth, world without end. Lord, hear our prayers; and let our cry come unto thee.'

'And He heard us!' exulted Sergeant Sherwood, the first of all these converts. 'He heard us, Mr Underwood!'

'Hungry and thirsty: their soul fainted in them,' continued Harold Underwood, his voice a holy drone:

'So they cried unto the Lord in their trouble: and he delivered them forth from their distress.

He led them forth by the right way: that they might go to the city where they dwelt.

O that men would therefore praise the Lord for His goodness; and declare the wonders that he doeth for the children of men!

For He satisfieth the empty soul: and filleth the hungry soul with goodness.

Such as sit in darkness, and in the shadow of death: being fast bound in misery and iron;

Because they rebelled against the words of the Lord: and lightly regarded the counsel of the most Highest.'

'Amen,' piously murmured the policemen.

'Ahem,' said Jherek.

But Harold Underwood passed an excited hand through his disarranged hay-coloured hair and began to sing again.

234

'Yea, though I walk in death's dark vale,
  yet will I fear none ill ...'

'I must say,' said Jherek enthusiastically to Mrs Underwood, 'it makes a great deal of sense. It is attractive to me. I have not been feeling entirely myself of late, and have noticed that you —'

'Jherek Carnelian, have you no conception of what has happened here?'

'It is a religious service.' He was pleased with the precision of his knowledge. 'A conspiracy of agreement.'

'You do not find it strange that all these police officers should suddenly become pious – indeed, fanatical! – Christians?'

'You mean that something has happened to them while we have been away?'

'I told you. They have seen a vision. They believe that God has given them a mission, to return to 1896 – though how they intend to get there Heaven alone knows – to warn everyone of what will happen to them if they continue in the paths of sinfulness. They believe that they have *seen* and *heard* God Himself. They have gone completely mad.'

'But perhaps they have had this vision, Amelia.'

'Do you believe in God now?'

'I have never disbelieved, though I, myself, have never had the pleasure of meeting Him. Of course, with the destruction of the universe, perhaps He was also destroyed ...'

'Be serious, Jherek. These poor people, my husband amongst them (doubtless a willing victim, I'll not deny) have been duped!'

'Duped?'

'Almost certainly by your Lord Jagged.'

'Why should Jagged – you mean that Jagged is God?'

'No. I mean that he plays at God. I suspected as much. Harold has described the vision – they all describe it. A fiery globe announcing itself as "The Lord thy God" and calling them His prophets, saying that He would release them from this place of desolation so that they could return to the place from which they had come to warn others – and so on and so on.'

'But what possible reason would Jagged have for deceiving them in that way?'

'Merely a cruel joke.'

'Cruel? I have never seen them happier. I am tempted to join in. I cannot understand you, Amelia. Once you tried to convince me as they are convinced. Now I am prepared to be convinced, you dissuade me!'

'You are deliberately obtuse.'

'Never that, Amelia.'

'I must help Harold. He must be warned of the deception.'

They had begun another hymn, louder than the first.

> *There is a dreadful Hell,*
> *And everlasting pains;*
> *There sinners must with devils dwell*
> *In darkness, fire, and chains.*

He tried to speak through it, but she covered her ears, shaking her head and refusing to listen as he implored her to return with him.

'We must discuss what has been happening to us . . .' It was useless.

> *O save us, Lord, from that foul path,*
> *Down which the sinners tread;*
> *Consigned to flames like so much chaff;*
> *There is no greater dread.*

Jherek regretted that this was not one of the hymns Amelia Underwood had taught him when they had first lived together at his ranch. He should have liked to have joined in, since it was not possible to communicate with her. He hoped they would sing his favourite – *All Things Bright and Beautiful* – but somehow guessed they would not. He found the present one not to his taste, either in tune (it was scarcely more than a drone) or in words which, he thought, were somewhat in contrast to the expressions on the faces of the singers. As soon as the hymn was over, Jherek lifted up his head and began to sing in his high, boyish voice:

> *'O Paradise! O Paradise!*
> *Who doth not crave for rest?*
> *Who would not seek the happy land*
> *Where they that loved are blest;*
> *Where loyal hearts and true*
> *Stand ever in the light,*
> *All rapture through and through,*
> *In God's most holy sight.*
>
> *O Paradise! O Paradise!*
> *The world is growing old;*
> *Who would not be at rest and free*
> *Where love is never cold ...'*

'Excellent sentiments, Mr Carnelian.' Harold Underwood's tone denied his words. He seemed upset. 'However, we were in the middle of giving thanks for our salvation ...'

'Bad manners? I am deeply sorry. It is just that I was so moved ...'

'Ha!' said Mr Underwood. 'Though we have witnessed a miracle today, I cannot believe that it is possible to convert one of Satan's own hierarchy. You shall not deceive us now!'

'But you *are* deceived, Harold!' cried his wife. 'I am sure of it!'

'Listen not to temptation, brothers,' Harold Underwood told the policemen. 'Even now they seek to divert us from the true way.'

'I think you'd better be getting along, sir,' said Inspector Springer to Jherek. 'This is a private meeting and I shouldn't be surprised if you're not infringing the Law of

Trespass. Certainly you could be said to be Causing a Disturbance in a Public Place.'

'Did you really see a vision of God, Inspector Springer?' Jherek asked him.

'We did, sir.'

'Amen,' said Sergeant Sherwood and the twelve constables.

'Amen,' said Harold Underwood. 'The Lord has given us the Word and we shall take the Word unto all the peoples of the world.'

'I'm sure you'll be welcome everywhere.' Jherek was eager to encourage. 'The Duke of Queens was saying to me only the other day that there was a great danger of becoming bored, without outside stimulus, such as we used to get. It is quite possible, Mr Underwood, that you will convert us all.'

'We return to our own world, sir,' Sergeant Sherwood told him mildly, 'as soon as we can.'

'We have been into the very bowels of Hell and yet were saved!' cried one of the constables.

'Amen,' said Harold Underwood absently. 'Now, if you'll kindly allow us to continue with our meeting ...'

'How do you intend to return to 1896, Harold?' implored Mrs Underwood. 'Who will take you?'

'The Lord,' her husband told her, 'will provide.' He added, in his old, prissy voice: 'I see you appear at last in your true colours, Amelia.'

She blushed as she stared down at her dress. 'A party,' she murmured.

He pursed his lips and looked away from her so that he might glare at Jherek Carnelian. 'Your master still has power here, I suppose, so I cannot command you ...'

'If we're interrupting, I apologize again.' Jherek bowed. 'I must say, Mr Underwood, that you seemed rather happier, in some ways, before your vision.'

'I have new responsibilities, Mr Carnelian.'

'The 'ighest sort,' agreed Inspector Springer.

'Amen,' said Sergeant Sherwood and the twelve constables. Their helmets nodded in unison.

'You are a fool, Harold!' Amelia said, her voice trembling. 'You have not seen God! The one who deceives you is closer to Satan!'

A peculiar, self-congratulatory smile appeared on Harold Underwood's features. 'Oh, really? You say this, yet you did not experience the vision. We have been chosen, Amelia, by God to warn the world of the terrors to come if it continues in its present course. What's this? Are you jealous, perhaps, that you are not one of the chosen, because you did not keep your faith and failed to do your duty?'

She gave a sudden cry, as if physically wounded. Jherek took her in his arms, glaring back at Underwood. 'She is right, you know. You are a cruel person, Harold Underwood. Tormented, you would torment us all!'

'Ha!'

'Amen,' said Inspector Springer automatically. 'I really must warn you again that you're doing yourself no good if you persist in these attempts to disrupt our meeting. We are empowered, not only by the 'Ome Secretary 'imself, but by the 'Osts of 'Eaven, to deal with would-be troublemakers as we see fit.' He gave the last few words special emphasis and placed his fists on his waistcoated hips (his jacket was not in evidence, though his bowler hat was still on his head). 'Get it?'

'Oh, Jherek, we must go!' Amelia was close to tears. 'We must go home.'

'Ha!'

As Jherek led her away the new missionaries stared after them for only a moment or two before returning to their service. They walked together up the yellow-brown metal pathway, hearing the voices raised again in song:

> *Christian! seek not yet repose,*
> *Hear thy guardian Angel say;*
> *Thou art in the midst of foes;*
> *Watch and pray.*

239

Principalities and powers,
Mustering their unseen array,
Wait for thy unguarded hours;
Watch and pray.

Gird thy heavenly armour on,
Wear it ever night and day;
Ambush'd lies the evil one;
Watch and pray ...

They came to where they had left the locomotive and, as she clambered onto the footplate, her hem in tatters, her clothes stained, she said tearfully. 'Oh, Jherek, if there is a Hell, then surely I deserve to be consigned there ...'

'You do not blame yourself for what has happened to your husband, Amelia?'

'Who else shall I blame?'

'You were blaming Jagged,' he reminded her.

'Jagged's machinations are one thing; my culpability is another. I should never have left him. I have betrayed him. He has gone mad with grief.'

'Because he loses you?'

'Oh, no – because his pride is attacked. Now he finds consolation in religious mania.'

'You have offered to stay with him.'

'I know. The damage is done, I suppose. Yet I have a duty to him, perhaps more so, now.'

'Aha.'

They began to rise up over the city. Another silence had grown between them. He tried to break it:

'You were right, Amelia. In my wanderings I found Brannart. He plots something with the Lat.'

But she would not reply. Instead, she began to sob. When he went to comfort her, she shrugged him away.

'Amelia?'

She continued to sob until the scene of her party came in sight. There were still guests there, Jherek could see, but few. The Iron Orchid had not been sufficient to make

240

them stay – they wanted Amelia.

'Shall we rejoin our guests . . .?'

She shook her head. He turned the locomotive and made for the thatched roof of their house, visible behind the cypresses and the poplars. He landed on the lawn and immediately she ran from the locomotive to the door. She was still sobbing as she ran up the stairs to her apartment. Jherek heard a door close. He sat at the bottom of the stairs pondering on the nature of this new, all-consuming feeling of despair which threatened to rob him of the ability to move, but he was incapable of any real thought. He was wounded, he knew self-pity, he grieved for her in her pain and he, who had always expressed himself in terms of action (her wish had ever been his command, even if he had misinterpreted her occasionally), could think of nothing, not the simplest gesture, which might please her and ease their mutual misery.

After some time he went slowly to his bed.

Outside, beyond the house, the great rivers of blood still fell with unchecked force over the black cliffs, filling the swirling lake where cryptic monsters swam and on which obsidian islands still bobbed, their dark green fleshy foliage rustling in a hot, sweet wind; but Mrs Amelia Underwood's pièce-de-résistance had been abandoned long since by her forgotten guests.

CHAPTER TWENTY-FIVE

THE CALL TO DUTY

For the first time in his long life Jherek Carnelian, whose
body could always be modified so that it did not need
sleep, knew insomnia. Oblivion was his only demand, but
it refused to come. Line after line of thought developed
in his brain and each line led nowhere and had to be cut
off. He considered seeking Jagged out, yet something
stopped him. It was Amelia, only Amelia – Amelia was the
only company he desired and yet (he must admit this to
himself, here in the dark) presently he feared her. Thus
in his mind he performed a forward step only, immediately thereafter, to take a backward – forward, backward
– a horrid little dance of indecision which brought, in
due course, his first taste of self-disgust. He had always
followed his impulses, without a grain of self-consciousness,
without the suggestion of a question, as did his peers at
the End of Time. Yet now it seemed he had two impulses;
he was caught like a steel ball between magnets, equi-
distant. His identity and his actions had hitherto been
one – so now his identity came under siege. If he had two
impulses, why, he must be two people. And if he were two
people, then which was the worthwhile one, which should

be abandoned as soon as possible? So Jherek discovered the old night-game of see-saw, in which a third Jherek, none too firm in his resolves, tried to hold judgement on two others, sliding first this way, then the other – 'I shall demand from her ...' and 'She deserves better than I ...' were two beginnings new to Jherek, though doubtless familiar to many of Mrs Underwood's contemporaries, particularly those who were frustrated in their relationships with the object of their affections, or were in a position of having to choose between old loyalties and fresh ones, between an ailing father, say, and a handsome suitor or, indeed, between an unlovable husband and a lover who offered marriage. It was halfway through this exercise that Jherek discovered the trick of transference – what if she experienced these torments, even as he experienced them? And immediately self-pity fled. He must go to her and comfort her. But no – he deceived himself, merely wishing to influence her, to focus her attention on to his dilemma. And so the see-saw swung again, with the judging Jherek poorly balanced on the pivot.

And so it might have continued until morning, had not she softly opened his door with a murmured query as to his wakefulness.

'Oh, Amelia!' He sat up at once.

'I have done you an injury,' she whispered, though there was none to overhear. 'My self-control deserted me today.'

'I am not quite sure what it is that you describe,' he told her, turning on the lamp by his bed so that it shed just a fraction more light and he could see her haggard face, red with crying, 'but you have done me no injury. It is I who have failed. I am useless to you.'

'You are brave and splendid – and innocent. I have said it before, Jherek: I have robbed you of that innocence.'

'I love you,' he said. 'I am a fool. I am unworthy of you.'

'No, no, my dear. I am a slave to my upbringing and I know that upbringing to be narrow, unimaginative, even brutalizing – ah, and it is essentially cynical, though I could never have admitted it. But you, dearest, are without a grain of cynicism, though I thought at first you and your world were nothing else but cynical. And now I see I am on the verge of teaching you my own habits – cynicism, hypocrisy, fear of emotional involvement disguised as self-denial – ah, there is a monstrous range ...'

'I asked you to teach me these things.'

'You did not know what you asked.'

He stretched a hand to her and she took it, though she remained standing. Her hand was cold, and it shook a little.

'I am still unable to understand all that you say,' he told her.

'I pray that you never shall, my dear.'

'You love me? I was afraid I had done something to destroy your love.'

'I love you, Jherek.'

'I wish only to change for you, to become whatever you wish me to be ...'

'I would not have you change, Jherek Carnelian.' A little smile appeared.

'Yet, you said ...'

'You accused me, earlier, of not being myself.' With a sigh she sat down upon the edge of his bed. She still wore the tattered oriental dress, but she had removed her feathers from her hair, which was restored to its natural colour, though not its original cut. Most of the paint was gone from her face. It was evident to him that she had slept no better than had he. His hand squeezed hers and she sighed for a second time. 'Of not being your Amelia,' she added.

'Not accused – but I was confused ...'

'I tried, I suppose, to please you, but could not please myself. It seemed so wicked ...' This smile was broader and it mocked her own choice of words. 'I have been trying so hard, Jherek, to enjoy your world for what it is. Yet I am constantly haunted first by my own sense of duty, which I have no means of expressing, and second by the knowledge of what your world is – a travesty, artificially maintained, denying mortality and therefore defying destiny.'

'Surely that is only one way of seeing it, Amelia.'

'I agree completely. I describe only my emotional response. Intellectually I can see many sides, many arguments. But I am, in this, as in so many other things, Jherek, a child of Bromley. You have given me these power-rings and taught me how to use them – yet I am filled with a desire to grow a few marigolds, to cook a pie, to make a dress – oh, I feel embarrassed as I speak. It seems so silly, when I have all the power of an Olympian god at my disposal. It sounds merely sentimental, to my own ears. I cannot think what you must feel ...'

'I am not sure what sentimentality is, Amelia. I wish you to be happy, that is all. If that is where fulfilment lies for you, then do these things. They will delight me. You can teach me these arts.'

'They are scarcely arts. Indeed, they are only desirable when one is denied the opportunity to practise them.' Her laughter was more natural, though still it shook. 'You can join in, if you wish, but I would not have you miserable. You must continue to express yourself as you wish, in ways that fulfil your instincts.'

'As long as I can express myself the means is unimportant, Amelia. It is that frozen feeling that I fear. And it is true that I live for you, so that what pleases you pleases me.'

'I make too many demands,' she said, pulling away. 'And offer nothing.'

'Again you bewilder me.'

'It is a bad bargain, Jherek, my dear.'

'I was unaware that we bargained, Amelia. For what?'

'Oh ...' she seemed unable to answer. 'For life itself, perhaps. For something ...' She gasped, as if in pain, but then smiled again, gripping his hand tighter. 'It is as if a tailor visits Eden and sees an opportunity for trade. No,

I am too hard upon myself, I suppose. I lack the words...'

'As do I, Amelia. If only I could find adequate phrases to tell you what I feel! But of one thing you must be certain. I love you absolutely.' He flung back the bed-clothes and sprang up, taking her hand to his breast. 'Amelia, of that you must be assured!'

He noticed that she was blushing, trying to speak, swallowing rapidly. She made a gulping noise.

'What is it, my dear?'

'Mr Carnelian – Jherek – you – you ...'

'Yes, my love?' Solicitously.

She broke free, making for the door. 'You seem unaware that you are – Oh, heavens!'

'Amelia!'

'You are quite naked, my dear.' She reached the door and sped through. 'I love you, Jherek. I love you! I will see you in the morning. Goodnight.'

He sat down heavily upon his bed, scratching his knee and shaking his head, but he was smiling (if somewhat bewilderedly) when he stretched out again and pulled the sheets over himself and fell into a deep sleep.

In the morning they breakfasted and were happy. Both had slept well, both chose to discuss little of the previous day's events, although Amelia expressed an intention of trying to discover if, in any museum in any of the old cities, there might be preserved seeds which she could plant. Jherek thought that there were one or two likely places where they could look.

Shortly after breakfast, as she boiled water to wash the dishes, two visitors arrived. The Iron Orchid – in a sur-prisingly restrained gown of dark blue silk against which living butterflies beat dark blue wings, upon the arm of the bearded time-traveller, dressed, as always, in his Nor-folk jacket and tweed plus-fours. That Amelia had set more than one fashion was obvious from the way in which the Iron Orchid demurely knocked upon the door and waited until Amelia, her hands quickly dried, her sleeves rolled down, answered it and smilingly admitted them to the sitting room.

'I am so sorry, Iron Orchid, for yesterday's rudeness,' began Amelia. 'An instinct, I suppose. I was worried about Harold. We visited the city and were longer than we expected.'

The Iron Orchid listened patiently and with a hint of sardonic pleasure while Amelia's apologies ran their course.

'My dear, I told them nothing. Your mysterious disappearance only served to give greater spice to a wonderful creation. I see that you have not yet disseminated it ...'

'Oh, dear. I shall do so presently.'

'Perhaps it should be left? A kind of monument?'

'So close to the garden? I think not.'

'Your taste cannot be questioned. I merely suggested ...'

'You are very kind. Would you care for some tea?'

'Excellent!' said the time-traveller. He appeared to be in fine spirits. He rubbed his hands together. 'A decent cup of English tea would be most welcome, dear lady.'

They waited expectantly.

'I will put the kettle on.'

'The kettle?' The Iron Orchid looked questioningly at the time-traveller.

'The kettle!' he breathed, as if the words had mystic significance for him. 'Splendid.'

In poorly disguised astonishment (for she had expected the tea to appear immediately), the Iron Orchid watched Amelia Underwood leave for the kitchen, just as Jherek came in.

'You are looking less pensive today, my boy.'

'Most maternal of blossoms, I am completely without care! What a pleasure it is to see you. Good morning to you, sir.'

'Morning,' said the time-traveller. 'I am staying, presently, at Castle Canaria. The Iron Orchid suggested that I accompany her. I hope that I do not intrude.'

'Of course not.' Jherek was still in a woollen dressing gown and striped nightshirt, with slippers on his feet. He signed for them to sit down and sat, himself, upon a nearby sofa. 'Do the repairs to your craft progress well?'

'Very well! I must say – for all my reservations – your Lord Jagged – your father, that is – is a brilliant scientist. Understood exactly what was needed. We're virtually finished and just in time it seems – just waiting to test a setting. That's why I decided to drop over. I might not have another chance to say goodbye.'

'You will continue your travels?'

'It has become a quest. Captain Bastable was able to give me a few tips, and if I get the chance to return to the Palaeozoic, where they have a base, I gather they'll be able to supply me with further information. I need, you see, to get back onto a particular track.' The time-traveller began to describe complicated theories, most of them completely hypothetical and absolutely meaningless to Jherek. But he listened politely until Amelia returned with the tea-tray; he rose to take it from her and place it upon the low table between them and their guests.

'We have yet to solve the servant problem,' Amelia told them as she poured the tea.

The Iron Orchid, to her credit, entered into the spirit of the thing. 'Jherek had – what did you call them, dear? – serbos.'

'Servos – mechanical servants in human form. But they were antiques, or at least of antique design.'

'Well,' said Amelia, handing out the cups, 'we shall manage for a while, at any rate. All we had in Bromley was a maid and a cook (and she did not live in) and we coped perfectly.' As the time-traveller accepted his cup she said, 'It would be such a pleasure for me to be able to return your kindness to us, when we were stranded. You must, at least, come to dinner soon.'

He was cheered as well as embarrassed. 'Thank you, dear lady. You cannot, I think, realize what a great consolation it is for me to know that there are, in this peculiar world, at least a few people who maintain the old-fashioned virtues. However, as I was saying to Mr Carnelian, I shall soon be on my way.'

'Today?'

'Tomorrow morning, probably. It must be so, I fear, for Lord Jagged completes the circuit shortly and then it will be impossible either to leave or to return to this world.'

She sipped and reflected. 'So the last brick of the gaol is about to be cemented in place,' she murmured.

'It is unwise to see it in those terms, dear lady. If you are to spend eternity here ...'

She drew a deep breath. Jherek was disturbed to see something of a return to yesterday's manner.

'Let us discuss a different topic,' he suggested brightly.

'It is scarcely a prison, dear,' said the Iron Orchid pinching, with finger and thumb, the wing of a straying butterfly tickling her chin.

'Some would call it Heaven,' tactfully said the time-traveller. 'Nirvana.'

'Oh, true. Fitting reward for a dead Hindu! But I am a live Christian.' Her smile was an attempt to break the atmosphere.

'Speaking of that,' said the time-traveller, 'I am able to do one last favour for Lord Jagged, and for you all, I dare say.' He laughed.

'What is it?' said Jherek, grateful for the change of subject.

'I have agreed to take Mr Underwood and the policemen back to 1896 before I continue on my journey.'

'What?' It was almost a breath from Amelia, slow and soft.

'You probably do not know that something happened in the city quite recently. They believe that God appeared to them and are anxious to return so that they might ...'

'We have seen them,' Jherek told him anxiously.

'Aha. Well, since I was responsible for bringing them

249

here, when Lord Jagged suggested that I take them back —'

'Jagged!' exclaimed Amelia Underwood rising. 'This is all his plot.'

'Why should Jagged "plot"?' The Iron Orchid was astonished. 'What interest has he in your husband, my dear?'

'None, save where it concerns me.' She turned upon the disconcerted Jherek. 'And you, Jherek. It is an extension of his schemings on our behalf. He thinks that with Harold gone I shall be willing to —' she paused. 'To accept you.'

'But he has abandoned his plans for us. He told us as much, Amelia.'

'In one respect.'

Mildly the Orchid interjected. 'I think you suspect Jagged of too much cunning, Amelia. After all, he is much involved with a somewhat larger scheme. Why should he behave as you suggest?'

'It is the only question for which I have no ready answer.' Amelia raised fingers to her forehead.

A knock at the front door. Jherek sprang to answer, glad of respite, but it was his father, all in voluminous lemon, his features composed and amused. 'Good morning to you, my boy.'

Lord Jagged of Canaria stepped into the sitting room and seemed to fill it. He bowed to them all and was stared at.

'Do I interrupt? I came to tell you, sir,' addressing the time-traveller, 'that the quartz has hardened satisfactorily. You can leave in the morning, as you planned.'

'With Harold and Inspector Springer and the rest!' almost shouted Amelia.

'Ah, you know.'

'We know everything —' her colour was high, her eyes fiery —. 'save why you arranged this!'

'The time-traveller was good enough to say that he would transport the gentlemen back to their own period.

It is their last chance to leave. No other will arise.'

'You made sure, Lord Jagged, that they should wish to leave. This ridiculous vision!'

'I fear that I do not follow your reasoning, beautiful Amelia.' Lord Jagged looked questioningly at Jherek.

Amelia sank to the sofa, teeth in knuckles.

'It seems to us,' Jherek loyally told his father, 'that you had something to do with Harold Underwood's recent vision in which God appeared to him in a burning sphere and ordered him to return to 1896 with a mission to warn his world of terrors to come.'

'A vision, eh?' Jagged smiled. 'But he will be considered mad if he tries to do that. Are they all so affected?'

'All!' mumbled Amelia viciously from behind her fist.

'They will not be believed, of course.' Jagged seemed to muse, as if all this news were new.

'Of course!' Amelia removed her knuckles from her mouth. 'And thus they will be unable to affect the future. Or, if they are caught by the Morphail Effect, it will be too late for them to return here. This world will be closed to them. You have staged everything perfectly, Lord Jagged.'

'Why should I stage such scenes?'

'Could it be to ensure that I stay with Jherek?'

'But you *are* with him, my dear.' Innocent surprise.

'You know what I mean, I think, Lord Jagged.'

'Are you concerned for your husband's safety if he returns?'

'I think his life will scarcely change at all. The same might not be said for poor Inspector Springer and his men, but even then, considering what has already happened to them, I have no particular fears. Quite likely it is the best that could happen. But I object to your part in arranging matters so – so suitably.'

'You do me too much credit, Amelia.'

'I think not.'

'However, if you think it would be best to keep Harold Underwood and the policemen in the city, I am sure that the time-traveller can be dissuaded ...'

'You know it is too late. Harold and the others want nothing more than to return.'

'Then why are you so upset?'

Jherek interposed. 'Ambiguous parent, if you are the author of all this – if you have played God as Amelia suggests – then be frank with us.'

'You are my family. You are all my confidants. Frankness is not, admittedly, my forte. I am not prone to making claims or to denying accusations. It is not in my nature, I fear. It is an old time-travelling habit, too. If Harold Underwood experienced a vision in the city and it was not a hallucination – and you'll all admit the city is riddled with them, they run wild there – then who is to argue that he has not seen God?'

'Oh, this is the rankest blasphemy!'

'Not quite that, surely,' murmured the time-traveller. 'Lord Jagged has a perfectly valid point.'

'It was you, sir, who first accused him of playing at God!'

'Ah. I was upset. Lord Jagged has been of considerable help to me, of late ...'

'So you have said.'

As the voices rose, only the Iron Orchid remained where she had been sitting, watching the proceedings with a degree of quiet amusement.

'Jagged,' said his son desperately, 'do you categorically deny—'

'I have told you, my boy, I am incapable of it. I think it is a kind of pride.' The lord in yellow shrugged. 'We are all human.'

'You would be more, sir, it seems!' accused Amelia.

'Come now, dear lady. You are over-excited. Surely the matter is not worth ...' The time-traveller waved his hands helplessly.

'My coming seems to have created some sort of tension,' said Lord Jagged. 'I only stopped by in order to pick up my wife and the time-traveller, to see how you were settling down, Amelia ...'

'I shall settle down, sir – if I do – in my own way and in my own time, without help from you!'

'Amelia,' Jherek implored, 'there is no need for this!'

'You will calm me, will you!' Her eyes were blazing on them all. All stepped back. 'Will you?'

Lord Jagged of Canaria began to glide towards the door, followed by his wife and his guest.

'Machiavelli!' she cried after him. 'Meddler! Oh, monstrous, dandified Prince of Darkness!'

He had reached the door and he looked back, his eyes serious for a fraction of a moment. 'You honour me too much, madam. I seek only to correct an imbalance where one exists.'

'You'll admit your part in this?'

Already his shoulder had turned and the collar hid his face. He was outside, floating to where his great swan awaited him. She watched from the window. She was breathing heavily, was reluctant, even, to let Jherek take her hand.

He tried to excuse his father. 'It is Jagged's way. He means only good ...'

'He can judge?'

'I think you have hurt his feelings, Amelia.'

'I hurt his? Oho!' She removed the hand from his grasp and folded both under her heaving breast. 'He makes fools of all!'

'Why should he wish to? Why should he, as you say, play God?'

She watched the swan as it disappeared in the pale blue sky. 'Perhaps he does not know, himself,' she said softly.

'Harold can be stopped. Jagged said so.'

She shook her head and moved back into the room. Automatically, she began to gather up the cups and place them on the tray. 'He will be happier in 1896, without question. Now, at any rate. The damage is done. And he has a mission. He has a duty to perform, as he sees it. I envy him.'

He followed her reasoning. 'We shall go to seek for seeds today. As we planned. Some flowers.'

She shrugged. 'Harold believes he saves the world. Jagged believes the same. I fear that growing flowers will not satisfy my impulses. I cannot live, Jherek, unless I feel my life is useful.'

'I love you,' was all he could answer.

'But you do not need me, my dear.' She put down the tray and came to him. He embraced her.

'Need?' he said. 'In what respect?'

'It is the woman that I am. I tried to change, but with poor success. I merely disguised myself and you saw through that disguise at once. Harold needed me. My world needed me. I did a great deal of charitable work, you know. Missionary work, of sorts, too. I was not inactive in Bromley, Jherek.'

'I am sure that you were not, Amelia, dearest . . .'

'Unless I have something more important than myself to justify —'

'There is nothing more important than yourself, Amelia.'

'Oh, I understand the philosophy which states that, Jherek —'

'I was not speaking philosophically, Amelia. I was stating fact. You are all that is important in my life.'

'You are very kind.'

'Kind? It is the truth!'

'I feel the same for you, as you know, my dear. I did not love Harold. I can see that I did not. But he had certain weaknesses which could be balanced by my strengths. Something in me was satisfied that is satisfied no longer. In your own way, in your very confidence, your innocence, you are strong . . .'

'You have — what is it? — character? — which I lack.'

'You are free. You have a conception of freedom so great that I can barely begin to sense it. You have been brought up to believe that nothing is impossible, and your experience proves it. I was brought up to believe that almost everything was impossible, that life must be suffered, not enjoyed.'

'But if I have freedom, Amelia, you have conscience. I give you my freedom. In exchange, you give me your conscience.' He spoke soberly. 'Is that not so?'

She looked up into his face. 'Perhaps, my dear.'

'It is what I originally sought in you, you'll recall.'

She smiled. 'True.'

'In combination, then, we give something to the world.'

'Possibly.' She returned to her tea-cups, lifting the tray. He sprang to open the door. 'But does this world want what, together, we can give it?'

'It might need us more than it knows.'

She darted him an intelligent look as he followed her into the kitchen. 'Sometimes, Jherek Carnelian, I come close to suspecting that you have inherited your father's cunning.'

'I do not understand you.'

'You are capable of concocting the most convincing of arguments, on occasion. Do you deliberately seek to mollify me?'

'I stated only what was in my mind.'

She put on a pinafore. She was thoughtful as she washed the tea-cups, handing them to him as each one was cleaned. Unsure what to do with them, he made them weightless so that they drifted up to the ceiling and bobbed against it.

'No,' she said at last, 'this world does not need me. Why should it?'

'To give it texture.'

'You speak only in artistic terms.'

'I know no others. Texture is important. Without it a surface quickly loses interest.'

'You see morality only as texture?' She looked about for the cups, noted them on the ceiling, sighed, removed her pinafore.

'The texture of a painting is its meaning.'

'Not the subject?'

'I think not. Morality gives meaning to life. Shape at any rate.'

'Texture is not shape.'

'Without texture the shape is barren.'

'You lose me. I am not used to arguing in such terms.'

'I am scarcely used to arguing at all, Amelia!'

They returned to the sitting room, but she would advance into the garden. He went with her. Many flowers sweetened the air. She had recently added insects, a variety of birds to sing in the trees and hedges. It was warm; the sun relaxed them both. They went hand-in-hand along a path between rose trellises, much as they had wandered once in their earliest days together. He recalled how she had been snatched from him, as he had been about to kiss her. A hint of foreboding was pushed from his mind. 'What if these hedges were bare,' he said, 'if there was no smell to the roses, no colour to the insects, they would be unsatisfying, eh?'

'They would be unfinished. Yet there is a modern school of painting – was such a school, in my time – that made a virtue of it. Whistlerites, I believe they were called. I am not too certain.'

'Perhaps the leaving out was meant to tell us something too, Amelia? What was important was what was absent.'

'I don't think these painters said anything to that effect, Jherek. I believe they claimed to paint only what the eye saw. Oh, a neurotic theory of art, I am sure ...'

'There! Would you deny this world your common sense? Would you let it be neurotic?'

'I thought it so, when first I came. Now I realize that what is neurotic in sophisticated society can be absolutely wholesome in a primitive one. And in many respects, I must say, your society shares much in common with some of those our travellers experienced when first landing upon South Sea islands. To be sinful, one must have a sense of sin. That is my burden, Jherek, and not yours. Yet, it seems, you ask me to place that burden on you, too. You see, I am not entirely selfish. I do you little good.'

'You give meaning to my life. It would have none without you.' They stood by a fountain, watching her goldfish swimming. There were even insects upon the surface of the water, to feed them.

She chuckled. 'You can argue splendidly, when you wish, but you shall not change my feelings so quickly. I have already tried to change them myself for you. I failed. I must think carefully about my intentions.'

'You consider me bold, for declaring myself while your husband is still in our world?'

'I had not quite considered it in those terms.' She frowned. She drew away from him, moving around the pool, her dress dappled with bright spots of water from the fountain. 'I believe you to be serious, I suppose. As serious as it is possible for you to be.'

'Ah, you find me superficial.' He was saddened.

'Not that. Not now.'

'Then —?'

'I remain confused, Jherek.'

They stood on opposite sides of the pool, regarding each other through the veil of falling silvery water. Her beauty, her auburn hair, her grey eyes, her firm mouth, all seemed more desirable than ever.

'I wish only to honour you,' he said, lowering his eyes.

'You do so, already, my dear.'

'I am committed to you. Only to you. If you wished, we could try to return to 1896 ...'

'You would be miserable there.'

'Not if we were together, Amelia.'

'You do not know my world, Jherek. It is capable of distorting the noblest intentions, of misinterpreting the finest emotions. You would be wretched. And I would feel wretched, also, to see one such as you transformed.'

'Then what is to be the answer?'

'I must think,' she said. 'Let me walk alone for a while, my dearest.'

He acknowledged her wish. He strode for the house, driving back the thoughts that suggested he would never see her again, shaking off the fear that she would be snatched from him, as she had been snatched once before, telling himself that it was merely association and that circumstances had changed. But how radically, he wondered, had they changed?

He reached the house. He closed the door behind him. He began to wander from room to room, avoiding only her apartments, the interior of which he had never seen, though he retained a deep curiosity about them, had often restrained an impulse to explore.

It came to him, as he entered his own bedroom and lay down upon the bed, still in his nightshirt and dressing gown, that perhaps all these new feelings were new only to him. Jagged, he felt sure, had known such feelings in the past – they had made him what he was. He vaguely recollected Amelia saying something about the son being the father, unwounded by the world. Did he grow more like Jagged? The thoughts of the previous night came back to him, but he refused to let them flourish. Before long, he had fallen asleep.

He was awakened by the sound of her footfall as she came slowly upstairs. It seemed to him that, on the landing, she paused at his door before her own door opened and she entered her rooms. He lay still for a little while, perhaps hoping that she would return. He got up, disseminating his night-clothes, naked as he listened; she did not come back. He used one of his power-rings to make a loose blouse and long kilt, in dark green. He left the bedroom and stood on the landing, hearing her moving about on the other side of the wall.

'Amelia?'

There was no reply.

He had grown tired of introspection. 'I will return soon, my dear,' he called.

Her voice was muffled. 'Where do you go?'

'Nowhere.'

He descended, passing through the kitchen and into the garden at the back, where he normally kept his locomotive. He boarded the craft, whistling the tune of *Carrie Joan*, feeling just a hint of nostalgia for the simpler days before he had met Amelia at the party given by the Duke of Queens. Did he regret the meeting? No.

The locomotive steamed into the sky, black, silver and gold now. He noticed how strange the two nearby scenes looked – the thatched house and its gardens, the lake of blood. They clashed rather than contrasted with each other. He wondered if she would mind if he disseminated the lake, but decided not to interfere.

He flew over transparent purple palaces and towering, quivering pink and puce mounds of unremarkable workmanship and imprecise invention, over a collection of gigantic prone figures, apparently entirely made of chalk, over a half-finished forest, and under a black thunderstorm whose lightning, in his opinion, was thoroughly overdone, but he refused to let the locomotive bear him back towards the city, to which his thoughts constantly went these days, perhaps because it was the city of his conception, perhaps because Lord Jagged and Nurse worked there (if they did), perhaps because he might study the man who remained his rival, at least until the next morning. He had no inclination to visit any of the friends whose company would normally give him pleasure; he considered going to Mongrove's rainy crags, but Mongrove would be of no help to him. Perhaps, he thought, he should choose a site and make something, to exercise his imagination in some ordinary pursuit, rather than let it continue to create impossible emotional dilemmas for him. He had just decided that he would try to build a reproduction of the Palaeozoic seashore and had found a suitable location when he heard the voice of Bishop Castle above him.

The bishop rode in a chariot whose wheels rotated, red and flaming, but which was otherwise of ordinary bronze, gold and platinum. His hat, one of his old crenellated kind, was immediately visible over the side of the chariot, but it was a moment before Jherek noticed his friend's face.

'I am so glad to see you, Jherek. I wished to congratulate you – well, Amelia, really – on yesterday's party.'

'I will tell her, ebullient Bishop.'

'She is not with you?'

She remains at home.'

'A shame. But you must come and see this, Jherek. I don't know what Brannart has been trying, but I would say it had gone badly wrong for him. Would you be amused for a few minutes?'

'I can think of nothing I should want more.'

'Then follow me!'

The chariot banked away, flying north, and obediently Jherek set a course behind it.

In a moment Bishop Castle was laughing and shouting, pointing at the ground. 'Look! Look!'

Jherek saw nothing but a patch of parched, unused earth. Then dust swirled and a conical object appeared, its outer casing whirling counter to another within. The whirling stopped and a man emerged from the cone. For all that he wore breathing equipment and carried a large bag, the man was recognizable as Brannart Morphail by his hump and his club foot. He turned, as if to tell the other occupants of the cone not to leave, but already a number of small figures had tumbled out and stood there, hands on hips, looking around them, glaring through their goggles. It was Captain Mubbers and the remnants of his crew. He gesticulated at Brannart, tapping his elbow several times. Wet, smacking noises could be heard, even from where Jherek and Bishop Castle hovered watching.

At length, after an argument, they all crowded back into the cone. The two shells whirled again and the cone vanished. Bishop Castle was beside himself with laughter, but Jherek could not see why he was so amused.

'They have been doing that for the past four hours, to my knowledge!' roared Bishop Castle. 'The machine appears. It stops. They disembark, argue, and get back in again. All exactly the same. Wait ...'

Jherek waited and, sure enough, the dust swirled, the cone reappeared, Brannart and then Captain Mubbers and his men got out, they argued and returned to the ship. Each movement had been the same.

'What is happening, Bishop?' Jherek asked, as soon as the next wave of laughter had subsided.

'Some sort of time-loop, evidently. I wondered what Brannart was up to. He schemed, I gather, with the Lat – offering to take them back to a period when their space-ship – and space – still existed – if they would help him. He swore me to secrecy, but it cannot matter now.'

'What did he plan?' In the confusion Jherek realized he had forgotten to warn Jagged of what he had seen.

'Oh, he was not too clear. Wished to thwart Jagged in some way, of course. Go back in time and change events.'

'Then what has happened to him now?'

'Isn't it obvious? Ho, ho, ho!'

'Not to me.'

'He's hoist by his own petard – caught in a particularly unpleasant version of the Morphail Effect. He arrives in the past, certainly, but only to be flung back to the present immediately. As a result he's stuck. He could go round and round for ever, I suppose ...'

'Should we not try to rescue him?'

'Jagged is the only one qualified to do that, Jherek, I'd say. If we tried to help we might find ourselves caught in the loop, too.'

Jherek watched as the cone appeared for the third time and the figures went through their set ritual. He tried to laugh, but he could not find it as amusing as did his friend.

'I wonder if Jagged knew of this,' continued Bishop Castle, 'and trapped Brannart into the situation. What a fine revenge, eh?'

Everyone, it seemed, suspected his father of a scheme. However, Jherek was not in a mood to defend Lord Jagged again today.

Bishop Castle brought his chariot closer to Jherek's locomotive. 'By the by, Jherek, have you seen Doctor Volospion's latest? It's called "The History of the World in Miniature" – the entire history of mankind from start to finish, all done with tiny reproductions at incredible speed – it can be slowed down to observe details of any particular millennium – it lasts a full week!'

'It is reminiscent, is it not, of something of Jagged's?'

'Is it? Well, Volospion always saw himself as a rival to Jagged, and perhaps hopes to fill his shoes, now that he is occupied with other things. O'Kala Incarnadine has been safely resurrected, by the by, and has lost interest in being a goat. He has become some kind of leviathan, with his own lake. Now that *is* a copy – of Amelia's creation. Well, if you'll forgive me, I'll be on my way. Others will want to see this.'

For the fourth time, the whirling cone appeared, Brannart and the Lat emerged. As Bishop Castle flew off Jherek dropped closer. He was still unable to understand them.

'Hrunt!' cried Captain Mubbers.

'Ferkit!' declared Brannart Morphail.

Blows were exchanged. They returned to the craft.

Jherek wondered if he should not continue on to Castle Canaria and tell Lord Jagged what was happening, but the sight had distressed him too much and he did not relish a further encounter with his father and mother today. He decided to return with the news to Amelia.

It was almost twilight as he directed the locomotive home. The darkness seemed to come quicker than usual and it was beneath a starless, moonless sky that he eventually located the house where only one light burned at a single window.

He was surprised, as he landed, to note that the window was not Amelia's but his own. He did not recall leaving a light there. He felt alarm as he entered the house and ran upstairs. He knocked at her door. 'Amelia! Amelia!' There was no reply. Puzzled, he opened his door and went in. The lamp burned low, but there was sufficient light to

see that his Amelia occupied the bed, her face turned
away from him, the great sable sheet drawn tightly around
her body so that only her head was visible.

'Amelia?'

She did not turn, though he could see that she was not
asleep. He could do nothing but wait.

Eventually, she spoke in a small, unsteady voice. 'As a
woman, I shall always be yours.'

'Are we —? Is this marriage?'

She looked up at him. There were tears in her eyes; her
expression was serious. Her lips parted.

He kneeled upon the bed; he took her head in his
hands. He kissed her eyes. She moved convulsively and he
thought he alarmed her until he realized that she was
struggling free of the sheet, to open her arms to him, to
hold him, as if she feared to fall. He took her naked shoulders in his arm, he stroked her cheek, experiencing a
sensation at once violent and tender – a sensation he had
never felt before. The smell of her body was warm and
sweet.

'I love you,' he said.

'I shall love you for ever, my dear,' she replied. 'Believe
me.'

'I do.'

Her words seemed subtly inappropriate and the old
sense of foreboding came and went. He kissed her. She
gasped and her hands went beneath his blouse; he felt her
nails in his flesh. He kissed her shoulder. She drew him to
her.

'It is all I can give you . . .' She seemed to be weeping.

'It is everything.'

She groaned. With a touch of a power-ring he disrobed,
stroking the tears on her cheek, kissing her trembling
shoulder, until at last he drew back the sheet and pressed
himself upon her.

'The lamp,' she said. He caused it to vanish and they
were in complete darkness.

'Always, Jherek.'

'Oh, my dearest.'

She hugged him. He touched her waist. 'Is this what you do?' he asked. 'Or is it this?'

Then they made love; and in the fullness of time they slept.

The sun had risen. He felt it upon his eyelids and he smiled. At last the future, with its confusion and its fears, was banished; nothing divided them. He turned, so that his first sight of the morning would be of her; but even as he turned the foreboding came back to him. She was not there. There was a trace of her warmth, little more. She was not in the room. He knew that she was not in the house.

'Amelia!'

This was what she had decided. He recalled her anecdote of the young man who had only dared declare his love when he knew he would never see her again. All his instincts had told him, from that moment by the fountain, that it was her intention to answer her Victorian conscience, to go back with Harold Underwood to 1896, to accept her responsibilities. It was why she had said what she said to him last night. As a woman, she would always be his, but as a wife she was committed to her husband.

He plunged from his bed, opening the window, and, naked, flung himself into the dawn sky, flying as rapidly as his power-rings could carry him, rushing towards the city, her name still on his lips, like the mad cry of a desolate seabird.

'Amelia!'

Once before he had followed her thus, coming too late to stop her return to her own time. Every sensation, every thought was repeated now, as the air burned his body with the speed of his flight. Already he planned how he might pursue her back to Bromley.

He reached the city. It seemed to sleep, it was so still.

And near the brink of the pit he saw the great open structure of the time-machine, the chronomnibus. Aboard he could see the time-traveller at the controls, and the policemen, all in white robes, with their helmets upon their heads, and Inspector Springer, also in white, wearing his bowler, and Harold Underwood with his hay-coloured hair and his pince-nez twinkling in the early sun. And he glimpsed Amelia, in her grey suit, seemingly struggling with her husband. Then the outlines of the machine grew faint, even as he descended. There was a shrill sound, like a scream, and the machine faded away and was gone.

He reached the ground, staggering.

'Amelia.' He could barely see for his tears; he stood hopeless and trembling, his heart pounding, gasping for air.

He heard sobbing and it was not his own sobbing. He lifted his head.

She lay there, in the black dust of the city, her face upon her arm. She wept.

Half-sure that this was a terrible illusion, merely a recollection from the city's memory, he approached her. He fell on his knees beside her. He touched her grey sleeve.

She looked up at him. 'Oh, Jherek! He told me that I was no longer his wife ...'

'He has said as much before.'

'He called me "impure". He said that my presence would taint the high purpose of his mission, that even now I tempted him ... Oh, he said so many things. He threw me from the machine. He hates me.'

'He hates sanity, Amelia. I think it is true of all such men. He hates truth. It is why he accepts the comforting lie. You would have been of no use to him.'

'I was so full of my resolve. I loved you so much. I fought so hard against my impulse to stay with you.'

'You would martyr yourself in response to the voice of Bromley? To a cause you know to be at best foolish?' He was surprised by his words and it was plain that he surprised her, also.

'*This* world has no cause at all,' she told him, as he held her against him. 'It has no use for one such as me!'

'Yet you love me. You trust me?'

'I trust you, Jherek. But I do not trust your background, your society – all this . . .' She stared bleakly at the city. 'It prizes individuality and yet it is impossible to feel oneself an individual in it. Do you understand?'

He did not, but he continued to comfort her.

He helped her to her feet.

'I can see no future for us here,' she told him. She was exhausted. He summoned his locomotive.

'There is no future,' he agreed, 'only the present. Surely it is what lovers have always wished for.'

'If they are nothing but lovers, Jherek, my dear.' She sighed deeply. 'Well, there is scarcely any point to my complaints.' Her smile was brave. 'This is my world and I must make the best of it.'

'You shall, Amelia.'

The locomotive appeared, puffing between high, ragged towers.

'My sense of duty —' she began.

'To yourself, as I said. My world esteems you as Bromley never could. Accept that esteem without reserve; it is given without reserve.'

'Blindly, however, as children give. One would wish to be respected for – for noble deeds.'

He saw clarity, at last. 'Your going to Harold – that was "noble"?'

'I suppose so. The self-sacrifice . . .'

' "Self-sacrifice" – another. And is that "virtuous"?'

'It is thought so, yes.'

'And "modest"?'

'Modesty is often involved.'

'Your opinion of your own actions is "modest"?'

'I hope so.'

'And if you do nothing save what your own spirit tells you to do – that is "lazy", eh? Even "evil"?'

'Scarcely evil, really, but certainly unworthy . . .'

266

The locomotive came to a rest beside them, where the chronomnibus had lately been.

'I am enlightened at last!' he said. 'And to be "poor", is that frowned upon by Bromley.'

She began to smile. 'Indeed, it is. But I do not approve of such notions. In my charity work, I tried to help the poor as much as I could. We had a missionary society, and we collected money so that we could purchase certain basic comforts ...'

'And these "poor" ones, they exist so that you might exercise your own impulses towards "nobility" and "self-sacrifice". I understand!'

'Not so, Jherek. The poor – well, they just *exist*. I, and others like me, tried to ease their conditions, tried to find work for the unemployed, medicine for their sick.'

'And if they did not exist? How, then, would you express yourself?'

'Oh, there are many other causes, all over the world. Heathen to be converted, tyrants to be taught justice, and so on. Of course, poverty is the chief source of all the other problems ...'

'I could perhaps create some "poor" for you.'

'That would be terrible. No, no! I disapproved of your world before I understood it. Now I do not disapprove – it would be irrational of me. I would not change it. It is I who must change.' She began to weep again. 'I who must try to understand that things will remain as they are throughout eternity, that the same dance will be danced over and over again and that only the partners will differ ...'

'We have our love, Amelia.'

Her expression was anguished. 'But can't you see, Jherek, that it is what I fear most! What is love without time, without death?'

'It is love without sadness, surely.'

'Could it be love without purpose?'

'Love is love.'

'Then you must teach me to believe that, my dear.'

CHAPTER TWENTY-SIX

WEDDING BELLS AT THE END OF TIME

She was to be Amelia Carnelian; she insisted upon it. They found seeds and bulbs, preserved by the cities, and they planted them in her gardens. They began a new life, as man and wife. She was teaching him to read again, and to write, and if Jherek felt contentment she, at least, felt a degree more secure; his assurances of fidelity became credible to her. But though the sun shone and the days and nights came and went with a regularity unusual at the End of Time, they were without seasons. She feared for her crops. Though she watered them carefully, no shoots appeared, and one day she decided to turn a piece of ground to see how her potatoes fared. She found that they had gone rotten. Elsewhere not a single seed had put out even the feeblest root. He came upon her as she dug frantically through her vegetable garden, searching for one sign of life. She pointed to the ruined tubers.

'Imperfectly preserved, I suppose,' he suggested.

'No. We tasted them. These are the same. It is the earth that ruins them. It is not true soil at all. It is without goodness. It is barren, Jherek, as everything is fundamentally barren in this world.' She threw down the spade; she entered the house. With Jherek at her heels, she went to sit at a window looking out towards her rose-garden.

He joined her, feeling her pain but unable to find any means of banishing it.

'Illusion,' she said.

'We can experiment, Amelia, to make earth which will allow your crops to grow.'

'Oh, perhaps ...' She made an effort to free herself from her mood, then her brow clouded again. 'Here is your father, like an Angel of Death come to preside at the funeral of my hopes.'

It was Lord Jagged, stepping with jaunty tread along the crazy paving, waving to her.

Jherek admitted him. He was all bustle and high humour. 'The time comes. The circuit is complete. I let the world run through one more full week, to establish the period of the loop, then we're saved forever! My news displeases you?'

Jherek spoke for Amelia. 'We do not care to be reminded of the manner in which the world is maintained, Father!'

'You will notice no outward effects.'

'We shall have the *knowledge* of what has happened,' she murmured. 'Illusions cease to satisfy, Lord Jagged.'

'Call me Father, too!' He seated himself upon a chaise-longue, spreading his limbs. 'I should have guessed you very happy by now. A shame.'

'If one's only function is to perpetuate illusion, and one has known real life, one is inclined to fret a little,' said she with ungainly irony. 'My crops have perished.'

'I follow you, Amelia. What do you feel, Jherek?'

'I feel for Amelia,' he answered. 'If she were happy, then I would be happy.' He smiled. 'I am a simple creature, father, as I have often been told.'

'Hm,' said Lord Jagged. He eased himself upward and was about to say more when, in the distance, through the open windows, they heard a sound.

They listened.

'Why,' said Amelia, 'it is a band.'

'Of what?' asked Jherek.

'A musical band,' his father told him. He swept from the house. 'Come, let's see!'

They all ran through the walks and avenues until they reached the white gate in the fence Amelia had erected around the trees. The lake of blood had long since vanished and gentle green hills replaced it. They could see a column of people, far away, marching towards them. Even from here, the music was distinct.

'A brass band!' cried Amelia. 'Trumpets, trombones, tubas —!'

'And a silver band!' declared Lord Jagged, with unfeigned enthusiasm. 'Clarinets, flutes, saxophones!'

'Bass drums — hear!' For the moment her miseries were gone. 'Snare drums, tenor drums, timpani ...'

'A positive profusion of percussion!' added Jherek, wishing to include himself in the excitement. 'Ta-ta-ta-*ta*! Hooray!' He made a cap for himself, so that he might fling it into the air. 'Hooray!'

'Oh, look!' Amelia had forgotten her distress entirely, for the moment at least. 'So many! And is that the Duke of Queens?'

'It is!'

The band — or rather the massed bands, for there must have been at least a thousand mechanical musicians — came marching up the hill towards them, with flags flying, plumes nodding, boots and straps shining, scarlet and blue, silver and black, gold and crimson, green and yellow.

Father, son and wife hung over the white gate like so many children, waving to the Duke of Queens, who marched at the front, a long pole whirling in the air above him, two others whirling on either side, a baton in one hand, a swagger-cane in the other, a huge handle-bar moustache upon his face, and a monstrous bearskin tottering on his head, goose-stepping so high that he almost fell backwards with every movement of his legs. And the band had grown so loud, though it remained in perfect time,

270

that it was utterly impracticable to try to speak, either to the Duke of Queens or to one another.

On and on it marched, with its sousaphones, its kolaphones, its brownophones, its telophones and its gramophones, performing intricate patterns, weaving in and out of itself, making outrageously difficult steps coupled with peculiar time-signatures; with its euphoniums and harmoniums, pianos and piccolos, its banjos, its bongos and its bassoons, saluting, marking time, forming fours, bagpipes skirling, bullroarers whirling, ondes Martenot keening, cellos groaning, violins wailing, Jew's harps boinging, swannee whistles, wailing, tubular bells tolling, calliopes wheezing, guitars shrieking, synthesizers sighing, ophicleides panting, gongs booming, organs grinding, sweet potatoes warbling, xylophones clattering, serpents blaring, bones rattling, glockenspiels tinkling, virginals whispering, bombardons moaning, until it had marshalled itself before the gate. And then it stopped.

'Haydn, eh?' said Lord Jagged knowledgeably as the proud Duke approached.

'*Yellow Dog Charlie*, according to the tape reference.' The Duke of Queens was beaming from beneath his bearskin. 'But you know how mixed up the cities are. Something from your period again, Mrs Un —'

'Carnelian,' she murmured.

'— derwood. We simply can't leave it alone, can we? I've seen a craze last a thousand years, unabated.'

'Your enthusiasms always tend to prolong themselves beyond the capabilities of your contemporaries, ebullient bandsman, most carefree of capellmeisters, most glorious of gleemen!' congratulated Lord Jagged. 'Have you marched far?'

'The parade is to celebrate my first venture into connubial harmony!'

'Music?' enquired Jherek.

'Marriage.' A wink at Jherek's father. 'Lord Jagged will know what I mean.'

'A wedding? laconically supplied Jagged.

'A wedding, yes! It is all the rage. Today – I think it's today – I am joined in holy matrimony (admit my grasp of the vocabulary!) to the loveliest of ladies, the beautiful Sweet Orb Mace.'

'And who conducts the rites?' asked Amelia.

'Bishop Castle. Who else? Will you come, and be my best men and women?'

'Well . . .'

'Of course we'll come, gorgeous groom.' Lord Jagged leapt the gate to embrace the Duke before he departed. 'And bring gifts, too. Green for a groom and blue for a bride!'

'Another custom?'

'Oh, indeed.'

Amelia pursed her lips and frowned at Lord Jagged of Canaria. 'It is astonishing that so many of our old customs are remembered, sir.'

His patrician head moved to meet her eyes; he wore the faintest of smiles. 'Oh, didn't you know? In the general confusion, with the translation pills and so forth, it seems that we are all talking nineteenth-century English. It serves. It serves.'

'You arranged this?'

Blandly, he replied. 'I am constantly flattered by your suggestions, Amelia. I admire your perceptions, though it would seem to me that you are inclined to over-interpret, on occasion.'

'If you would have it so, sir.' She curtsied, but her expression was hardly demure.

Fearful of further tension between the two, Jherek said: 'So we are again to be guests at the Duke of Queens.' You are not disturbed by the prospect, Amelia?'

'We have been invited. We shall attend. If it be a mock marriage, it will certainly be an extravagant one.'

Lord Jagged of Canaria was looking at her through perceptive eyes and it was as if his mask had fallen for a moment.

She was baffled by this sudden sincerity; she avoided

that eye.

'Very well, then,' said Jherek's father briskly, 'We shall meet again soon, then?'

'Soon,' she said.

'Farewell,' he said, 'to you both.' He strode for his swan which swam on a tiny pond he had manufactured for parking purposes. He was soon aloft. A wave of yellow froth and he was gone.

'So marriage is the fashion now,' she said as they walked back to the house.

He took her hand. 'We are already married,' he said.

'In God's eyes, as we used to say. But God looks down on this world no longer. We have only a poor substitute. A poseur.'

They entered the house. 'You speak of Jagged again, Amelia?'

'He continues to disturb me. It would seem he has satisfied himself, seen all his schemes completed. Yet still I am wary of him. I suppose I shall always be wary, through eternity. I fear his boredom.'

'Not your own?'

'I have not his power.'

He let the matter rest.

That afternoon, with Jherek in morning dress and Amelia in grey and blue stripes, they set off for the wedding of the Duke of Queens.

Bishop Castle (it was evidently his workmanship) had built a cathedral specially for the ceremony, in classical subtlety, with great stained glass windows, Gothic spires and masonry, massive and yet giving the impression of lightness, and decorated on the outside primarily in orange, purple and yellow. Surrounding the area was the band of the Duke of Queens, its automata at rest for the moment. There were tall flag-masts, flying every conceivable standard still existing in the archives; there were tents and booths dispensing drinks and sweetmeats, games of chance and of skill, exhibitions of antique entertainments, through which moved the guests, laughing and talking, full of merriment.

'It's a lovely scene,' said Jherek, as he and Amelia descended from their footplate. 'A beautiful background for a wedding.'

'Yet still merely a scene,' she said. 'I can never rid myself of the knowledge that I am playing a part in a drama.'

'Were ceremonies different, then, in your day?'

She was silent for a moment. Then: 'You must think me a cheerless creature.'

'I have seen you happy, Amelia, I think.'

'It is a trick of the mind I was never taught. Indeed, I was taught to suspect an open smile, to repress my own. I try, Jherek, to be carefree.'

'It is your duty,' he told her as he joined the throng and were greeted, at once, by their friends. 'Why, Mistress Christia, the last time I saw your companions they were trapped in a particularly unpleasant dilemma, battling with Brannart.'

Mistress Christia, the Everlasting Concubine, laughed a tinkling laugh, as was her wont. She was surrounded by Captain Mubbers and his men, all dressed in the same brilliant powder-blue she wore, save for strange balloon-like objects of dull red, on elbows and knees. 'Lord Jagged rescued them, I gather, and I insisted that they be my special guests. We are to be married, too, today!'

'You – to them all!' said Amelia in astonishment. She blushed.

'They are teaching me their customs.' She displayed the elbow balloons. 'These are proper to a married Lat female. The reason for their behaviour, where women were concerned, was the conviction that if we did not wear knee- and elbow-balloons we were – um?' She looked enquiringly at her nearest spouse, who crossed his three pupils and stroked his whiskers in embarrassment. Jherek thought it was Rokfrug. 'Dear?'

'Joint-sport,' said Rokfrug almost inaudibly.

'They are so contrite!' said Mistress Christia. She moved intimately to murmur to Amelia. 'In public, at least, dear.'

'Congratulations, Captain Mubbers,' said Jherek. 'I hope you and your men will be very happy with your wife.'

'Fill it, arse-lips,' Captain Mubbers said, sotto voce, even as they shook hands. 'Sarcy fartin' knicker-elastic hole-smeller.'

'I intended no irony.'

'Then wipe it and button it, bumface, Nn?'

'You have given up any intention of going into space again?' Amelia said.

Captain Mubbers shrugged his sloping shoulders. 'Nothing there for us, is there?' He offered her a knowing look which took her aback.

'Well —' she drew a breath — 'I am sure, once you have settled down to married life ...' She was defeated in her efforts.

Captain Mubbers grunted, eyeing her elbow, visible through the silk of her dress.

'Flimpoke!' Mistress Christia had noticed. 'Well!'

'Sorry, my bone.' He stared at the ground.

'Flimpoke?' said Jherek.

'Flimpoke Mubbers,' Mistress Christia told him, with every evidence of pride. 'I am to be Mrs Mubbers, and Mrs Rokfrug, and Mrs Glopgoo ...'

'And we are to be Mr and Mr Mongrove-de Goethe!' It was Werther, midnight blue from head to toe. Midnight blue eyes stared from a midnight-blue face. It was rather difficult to recognize him, save for his voice. Beside him lounged in an attitude of dejected satisfaction the great bulk of Lord Mongrove, moody monarch of the weeping cliffs.

'What? You marry? Oh, it is perfect.'

'We think so,' said Werther.

'You considered no one else?'

'We have so little in common with anyone else,' droned Mongrove. 'Besides, who would have me? Who would spend the rest of his life with this shapeless body, this

275

colourless personality, this talentless brain ...?'

'It is a good match,' said Jherek hastily. Mongrove was inclined, once started, to gather momentum and spend an hour or more listing his own drawbacks.

'We decided, at Doctor Volospion's fairground, when we fell off the carousel together, that we might as well share our disasters ...'

'An excellent scheme.' A scent of dampness wafted from Mongrove's robes as he moved; Jherek found it unpleasant. 'I trust you will discover contentment ...'

'Reconciliation, at least,' said Amelia.

The two moved on.

'So,' said Jherek, offering his arm. 'We are to witness three weddings.'

'They are too ludicrous to be taken seriously,' she said, as if she gave her blessing to the proceedings.

'Yet they offer satisfaction to those taking part, I think.'

'It is so hard for me to believe that.'

They found Brannart Morphail, at last, in unusual finery, a mustard-coloured cloak hanging in pleats from his hump, tassels swinging from the most unlikely places on his person, his medical boot glittering with spangles. He seemed in an almost jolly mood as he limped beside My Lady Charlotina of Above-the-Ground (her new domicile).

'Aha!' cried Brannart, sighting the two. 'My nemesis, young Jherek Carnelian!' The jocularity, if forced, was at least well-meant. 'And the *cause* of all our problems, the beautiful Amelia Underwood.'

'Carnelian, now,' she said.

'Congratulations! You take the same step, then?'

'As the Duke of Queens,' agreed Jherek amicably, 'and Mistress Christia. And Werther and Lord Mongrove ...'

'No, no, no! As My Lady Charlotina and myself!'

'Ah!'

My Lady Charlotina fluttered lashes fully two inches long and produced a winsome smile. In apple-green tupperware crinoline and brown slate bonnet she had some difficulty moving even at the relatively slow pace of her husband-to-be.

'You proposed rapidly enough, you dog!' said Jherek to the scientist.

'She proposed,' Brannart grunted, momentarily returned to his usual mood. 'I owe my rescue to her.'

'Not to Jagged?'

'It was she who went to get Jagged's help.'

'You were attempting a jump backwards through time, eh?' Jherek said.

'I did my best. Given half a chance, I might have improved this disastrous situation. But I tried to move within too limited a period and, as always happens, I got caught in a kind of short-circuit. Proving, irrefutably, of course, the truth of Morphail's Law.'

'Of course,' they both consented.

'I suppose the Law still applies, at present,' Amelia suggested.

'At present, and always.'

'Always?'

'Well –' Brannart rubbed his warted nose – 'in essence. If Jagged re-cycles a seven-day period, then the Law will probably apply to the time contained within that span, d'you see.'

'Aha.' Amelia was disappointed, though Jherek did not know why. 'There is no other means of leaving this world, once the circuit is completed?'

'None at all. Isolated chronologically as well as spacially. By rights this planet has no business existing at all.'

'So we gather,' said Jherek.

'It defies all logic.'

'You have ever made a practice of that, have you not?' said Amelia.

'Have we, dear?' said My Lady Charlotina of Above-the-Ground.

'What I was taught to call logic, at any rate.' Amelia swiftly compromised.

'This will mean the death of Science,' said Brannart

cheerfully. 'Oh, yes. The death of Science, right enough. No more enquiry, no more investigation, no more analysis, no more interpretation of phenomena. Nothing for me to do.'

'There are functions of the cities which might be restored,' said Amelia helpfully.

'Functions?'

'Old sciences which could be re-discovered. There are all kinds of possibilities, I should have thought.'

'Hm,' said Brannart. Gnarled fingers crossed a pitted chin. 'True.'

'Memory banks which need their wits sharpening,' Jherek told him. 'It would take a brilliant scientist to restore them ...'

'True,' repeated Brannart. 'Well, perhaps I can do something in that direction, certainly.'

My Lady Charlotina patted his pleated hump. 'I shall be so proud of you, Brannart. And what a contribution you could make to social life, if some of those machines could be got to reveal their secrets.'

'Jagged will be so jealous!' Amelia added.

'Jealous?' Brannart brightened still further. 'I suppose he will.'

'Hideously,' said Jherek.

'Well, you of all people would know, Jherek.' The scientist seemed to do a little jig on his spangled boot. 'You think so?'

'Without question!'

'Hm.'

A small irascible voice said from just behind Jherek: 'Ah! There you are posterior-visage. I've been looking for you!'

It was Rokfrug. He continued heavily: 'If the ladies will excuse us, I'd like a middle-of-the-leg word with you, sediment-nostril.'

'I have already apologized, Lieutenant Rokfrug,' Brannart Morphail told him. 'I see no reason to go on with this —'

'You offered me rapine, loot, arson, toe-pillage, and all I get is to be a member of a smelly male harem ...'

'It was not my fault. You did not have to agree to the marriage!' Brannart began to back away.

'If it's the only way to get a bit of jointing hoo-hoo, what else am I supposed to do? Come here!'

Brannart broke into a hobbling run, pursued by Lieutenant Rokfrug who was quickly tripped by the passing Lord Jagged, who picked him up, dusted him down, pointed him in the wrong direction and continued towards them.

Brannart, followed by his bride-to-be, disappeared behind a cluster of booths, while Rokfrug vanished into a candy-striped tent. Lord Jagged seemed content.

'So the peace is kept.' He smiled at Jherek and Amelia. 'And a certain balance is maintained.'

'Perhaps I should have dubbed you "Solomon",' said Amelia acidly.

'You *must* call me "Father", my dear.' A bow to a passing O'Kala Incarnadine, recognizable only from the face at the top of the giraffe neck. For reasons best known to himself, Lord Jagged had discarded his usual robes and collars and wore, like Jherek, a simple grey morning suit, with a grey silk hat upon his noble head, a silver-topped cane in one gloved hand. The only touch of yellow was the primrose in his button-hole. 'And here is my own spouse. Iron Orchid, as delicious as only you can be!'

The Orchid acknowledged the compliment. She wore her name-flower today – orchids of every possible hue and variety clustered over her body, hugging themselves close to her as if she were the only substantial thing remaining in the universe. The scents were so strong, in combination, that they threatened to overwhelm everyone within a radius of twenty feet. Orchids formed a hood around her head, from which she peered. 'Husband mine! And dear children! All together, again. And for such a beautiful occasion! How many weedings take place today?' Her question was for Jherek.

'Weddings, mama. Three – no four – to my knowledge.'

'About twenty in all,' said Jagged. 'You know how quickly these things catch on.'

'Who else?' said Jherek.

'Doctor Volospion weds the Platinum Poppy.'

'Such a pleasant, empty creature,' sniffed the Iron Orchid, 'at least, before she changed her name.'

'And Captain Marble is to be spliced to Soola Sen Sun. And Lady Voiceless, I gather, gives herself in marriage to Li Pao.'

The Iron Orchid seemed displeased by this announcement, but she said nothing.

'And how long, I wonder, will these "marriages" last,' said Amelia.

'Oh, I should think as long as the various parties wish them to last,' murmured Lord Jagged. 'The fashion could remain with us for a thousand years, or even two. One never knows. It all depends upon the ingenuity, surely, of the participants. Something else might come along to fire society's imagination ...'

'Of course,' she said. She had become subdued. Noticing this, Jherek pressed her arm, but she was not comforted.

'I should have thought, Amelia, that you would have been pleased by this development.' Lord Jagged's lips curved a fraction. 'A tendency towards social stability, is it not?'

'I cannot rise to your jesting today, Lord Jagged.'

'You still grieve for your perished potatoes, then?'

'For what is signified by their destruction.'

'Later, we must put our heads together. There could be a solution to the problem ...'

'There can be no solution, sir, to the abiding dilemma of one who would not be a drone in a world of drones.'

'You are too hard on yourself, and on us. See it, instead, as a reward to the human race for all its millions of years of struggle.'

'I have not been part of that struggle.'

'Surely, in one sense ...'

'In one sense, sir, we have all been involved. In another, we have not. It is, as you would agree, I know, not what *is*, but how one looks at what is.'

'You will change.'

'I fear that I shall.'

'You fear cynicism in yourself?'

'Perhaps it is that.'

'Some would consider your attitude cowardly.'

'*I* consider it cowardly, Lord Jagged, you may be sure. Let us terminate this conversation. It excludes too many; it discomforts all. My problems are my own responsibility.'

'You claim more than you should, Amelia. Have I had no part in creating those problems?'

'I suppose that you would be offended if I disagreed with you on that point.'

His voice was very quiet and only for her ears. 'I have a conscience, too, Amelia. All that I have done might be seen as the result of possessing an exaggerated sense of duty.'

Her lips parted; her chin lifted a fraction. 'If I could believe that, I think I should be more reconciled to my situation.'

'Then you must believe it.'

'Oh, Jagged! Amelia is right. We become bored with all this listless talk. It lacks colour, my dears.' The Iron Orchid drew close to her husband.

Lord Jagged of Canaria raised his hat to Amelia. 'Perhaps we can continue with this later. I have a proposal of my own, which you might find satisfactory.'

'You must not concern yourself,' she said, 'with our affairs.'

Jherek made to speak, but an ear-splitting fanfare came suddenly from all directions and an unnaturally loud, somewhat distorted voice – almost certainly that of the Duke of Queens – cried from the air:

'The weddings begin!'

They joined the crowd moving towards the cathedral.

CHAPTER TWENTY-SEVEN

CONVERSATIONS AND CONCLUSIONS

Dusty varicoloured light fell from brilliant windows through the lofty shadows of the cathedral; rainbow patterns littered the marble floors, the dark oak stalls, the cool vaulted galleries, the golden pulpits, the brass and ceramic choirs; they filtered through the silver-framed squints, dappling the extravagant costumes of brides, grooms and celebrants who, together, were the whole complement of this world at the End of Time and would remain its sole denizens for eternity. At the great altar, against the radiance from the circular stained glass behind him, wearing vestments of black and red silk trimmed with woven ribbons of white and grey, a magnificent mitre swaying on his head, his aluminium crook in one gloved hand, his other hand raised to give a blessing, stood Bishop Castle, impressive and grave as through the high doors, admitting a sweep of sunshine into the main aisle, sounded the blare of a thousand instruments voicing a single note. Then there came a silence from without while the cathedral echoed, transformed the note, seeming to answer. Bishop Castle let the echoes fade before signalling Sweet Orb Mace, on the arm of Lord Jagged himself, to proceed towards the altar; then came the Duke of Queens, in uniform still, striding until he stood beside his bride-to-be, who wore white – hair, eyebrows, lashes, lips, gown bobbysox and boots. The altar itself was already piled with blue and green gifts of every description. From the chancel Jherek, Amelia and the Iron Orchid watched as, with due ceremony, Bishop Castle handed the Duke of Queens a black curved bow and a single arrow, enjoining the groom to 'show yourself worthy of this woman'. The Iron Orchid whispered that Amelia would be familiar with the ritual and would doubtless be a trifle blasé, but she, the Orchid, was thrilled. Bishop Castle motioned and twenty palm trees sprang up in the main aisle, stand-ing, one behind each other, in a perfectly straight line. The Duke of Queens placed the arrow upon the string, drew it back, and shot at the first palm tree. The arrow pierced the tree through, entered the next and pierced that, going on to the next and the next until all twenty trees were pierced. There came a yell from the distance (it seemed that Li Pao had been standing behind the last palm tree and had received the arrow directly in his eye and had been killed; with as little fuss as possible he was resurrected – meanwhile the ceremony continued), but the Duke of Queens was already handing the bow back to Bishop Castle while intoning a reference to Sugriva, Jata-yus and Disney the Destroyer and calling upon the Buddha to strike him bald if his love for Sweet Orb Mace ever faltered. This ritual progressed for some time, giving great satisfaction to the central participants, as is the nature of ritual, but tending to drag a little so far as the audience was concerned, though many admitted that the spoken parts were moving. Bishop Castle gradually brought the wedding to its conclusion. '... until such time as the afore-mentioned Parties shall deem this Agreement void and that any disputes arising from this Agreement, or the per-formance thereof, shall be determined by arbitration in the Heavenly City or its Dependencies in accordance with the rules then obtaining of the High, Middle and Low

Courts of Chance and Arbitrary Union and judgement on the award rendered may be entered in any court having jurisdiction thereof, in the name of God the Father, God the Mother or God the Next of Kin, God Bless, Good Luck and Keep Smiling.' The ceremonial chain of iron was locked about Sweet Orb Mace's neck; the huge jewelled truss was fitted onto the lower part of the Duke of Queens' torso, thumbs were cut and blood mingled, halos were exchanged, two goats were slaughtered, and a further fanfare announced that the marriage was duly sanctified. Next came Werther de Goethe and Lord Mongrove, who had chosen a shorter but rather gloomier ceremony, followed by Mistress Christia, the Everlasting Concubine, and her little group of grooms, then Doctor Volospion with Platinum Poppy (a clever, but obvious copy of the Iron Orchid, to the smallest feature). It was at this point that Lord Jagged slipped away. Probably, Jherek thought, it was because his father was quickly bored by such things and also because (it was rumoured) he had no liking for the envious Volospion. Not a few of the others had chosen group marriages, which, save for the naming of the names, took somewhat less time to complete. Amelia was becoming restless, as was the Iron Orchid; the two women whispered together and occasionally made remarks which caused one or both to repress laughter and, on certain occasions, under cover of some loud report, for instance, from a Wedding Cannon, or Clare Cyrato's perfect rising contralto shriek as her labia were pierced, or the Earl of Carbolic's nine hundredth-century bull-bellow, allowed themselves to giggle quite openly. Jherek did not feel excluded; he was relieved that their friendship flourished, though every so often he noticed a look of disapproval cross Amelia's features, as if she found her own behaviour reprehensible. Sometimes she would join in the applause which began to fill the cathedral, as more and more people, on the spur of the moment, rushed towards the tasteful web of neon that was the altar, and married one another. The proceedings were becoming extremely chaotic and Bishop Castle, who had lost his air of gravity, was waving his mitre around his head, making up more and more extravagant rituals and, like the ringmaster, putting his brides and his grooms through increasingly ludicrous paces, so that laughter now sounded from every corner of the great cathedral, bursts of clapping greeted quite unremarkable exercises (such as the four ladies who insisted on being married whilst standing on their hands). As the Iron Orchid remarked: 'The wittiest of us are already wedded – these give us only low comedy!'

They prepared to leave.

'Bishop Castle should not lend himself to such sport,' said the Orchid. 'I note that most of these people are largely of immigrant origin who have been returned, just recently, by the Morphail Effect. Is that not boorish Pereg Tralo – there in the blazing crown, with all those little girls? But what is Gaf the Horse in Tears doing to that other time-traveller, the one bending down – there?'

Amelia turned away.

The Iron Orchid patted her padded shoulder. 'I agree, my dear, it is most distasteful.'

The remaining celebrants were dancing now, in a long line which wandered in and out of the arches, up and down the stairs, along the high galleries, through deep shadows and into sudden sunlight, while Bishop Castle urged them on, his mitre swinging in time to the music of the Duke's band which came faintly from beyond the doors. 'Bless you!' he cried. 'Bless you!'

Fire bloomed now as brands were added, at the insistence, it seemed, of Trixitroxi Ro, dethroned queen of a decadent court who had been exiled, by successful revolutionaries, to the future, and who had, for hundreds of years, only one idea for a successful party – to set fire to everything.

The Iron Orchid, Jherek and Amelia, began to make their way towards the doors, moving against the crowd.

'These are the very worst aspects of the world's infancy,'

protested the Orchid as she was jostled by a brand-bearing cat-masked spring-footed Holy Electrician from a period which had prospered at least a million years before.

'You become a snob, Iron Orchid!' Amelia's mockery was good-natured.

'You relished such scenes once, Mother, it is true,' agreed Jherek.

'Oh, perhaps I grow old. Or some quality leaves life at the End of Time. I find it hard to describe.'

The doors were still a good distance from them. The dancing crowd had separated into several interweaving sections. Screams of laughter mingled with snatches of song, with shrieks and guffaws and the sound of stamping feet; bizarre masks grinned through the hagioscopes in walls and pillars, bodies, painted and unpainted, natural and remodelled, writhed on steps, in choirs, pews, pulpits and confessionals; feathers waved, spangles glittered, silks scraped on satins, jewelled cloaks and boots reflected torchlight and seemed to blaze of their own accord; skins, yellow and green and brown and red and pink and black and blue and orange, glistened; and everywhere the eyes they saw were burning, the mouths were hot.

Of the three, only Jherek laughed. 'They enjoy themselves, mother! It is a festival.'

'Danse macabre,' murmured Amelia. 'The damned, the dead, the doomed – they dance to forget their fate . . .'

This was a trifle too much even for the Orchid in her abnormal despondency. 'It is certainly vulgar,' she said, 'if nothing else. The Duke of Queens is to blame, of course. It is typical of him to allow a perfectly entertaining event to degenerate into – ah!' she fell to the flagging, bowled down by a squirming couple over whom she had tripped.

Jherek helped her up. He was smiling. 'You used to chide me for my criticisms of the Duke's taste. Well, I am vindicated at last.'

She sniffed. She noticed the face of one of the people on the ground. 'Gaf! How can you lend yourself to this?'

'Eh?' said Gaf the Horse in Tears. He extricated himself

from under his partner. 'Iron Orchid! Oh, your perfume, your petals, your delicate stamen – let them consume me!'

'We are leaving,' she said pointedly, casting a hard eye over the black and white fur which Gaf sported. 'We find the proceedings dull.'

'Dull, dearest Orchid? It is an experience. Experience of any sort is sufficient to itself!' Gaf thought she joked. From where he lay, he extended a hand. 'Come. Join us. We—'

'Perhaps another time, weeping stallion.' She perceived an opening in the throng and made towards it, but it had closed before any of them could reach it.

'They seem drunk with the prospect of their own damnation ...' began Amelia before her voice was lost in the yell of the throng. She held herself as she had when Jherek had first seen her, her mouth set, her eyes contemptuous, and all his love swept over him so that he was bound to kiss her. But her cheek was cold. She plunged away, colliding with the crowd which caught her and began to bear her from him. She was as one who had fallen into a torrent and feared drowning. He ran to her rescue, dragging her clear of the press; she gasped and sobbed against him. They were on the edge of the sunlight from the doors; escape was near. They could hear the band still playing outside. She was shouting to him, but her words were indistinct. The Iron Orchid plucked at Jherek's arm, to lead them from the cathedral and at that moment darkness descended.

The sun was gone; no light entered the doors or fell through the windows; the music died; there was silence outside. It was cold. Yet many of the revellers danced on, their way illuminated by the guttering flames of the flambeaux in their hands; many still laughed or shouted. But then the cathedral itself began to tremble. Metal and glass rattled, stone groaned.

The doors, now a black gap, could still be seen, and towards them the three fled, with Iron Orchid crying in astonishment: 'Jagged has failed us. The world ends, after all!'

Into the coldness they rushed. Behind them firelight flickered from the many windows of the building, but it was too feeble to brighten the surrounding ground, though it was possible to identify the whereabouts of the stalls and booths and tents from the voices, some familiar, calling out in bewilderment. Jherek expected the air to give way to vacuum at any moment. He clutched Amelia and now she hugged him willingly. 'If only there had been some way to live,' she said. 'And yet I think I am glad for this. I could never have changed. I would have become a hypocrite and you would have ceased to love me.'

'Never that,' he said. He kissed her. Perhaps because the surrounding air was so cold, she seemed very warm to him, almost feverish.

'What an unsatisfactory conclusion,' came the voice of the Iron Orchid. 'For once, it seems, Jagged has lost his sense of timing! Still, there'll be no one to criticize in a moment or two . . .'

Beneath their feet, the ground shook. From within the cathedral a single voice was raised in a high, sustained scream. Something fell with a rush and a crash to the ground; several of the cathedral's bells tolled, crazy and dissonant. Two or three figures, one with a brand that was now scarcely more than an ember, came to the door and stood there uncertainly.

Jherek thought he heard a howling, far off, as if of a distant hurricane, but it did not approach; instead it seemed to die away in another direction.

They all awaited death with reconciliation, trepidation, amusement, relish or incredulity, according to their temperaments. Here and there people could be heard chatting with complete lack of concern, while others moaned, crying out for impossible succour.

'At least Harold is safe,' she said. 'Did Jagged know that this could happen, do you think?'

'If he did, he made sure we should not suspect.'

'He certainly said nothing to *me*.' The Iron Orchid did not bother to hide her petulance. 'I am his wife, after all.'

'He cannot help his secretive nature, Mother,' said Jherek Carnelian in defence.

'Just as you cannot help possessing an open one, my child. Where are you? Over there, eh?'

'Here,' said Amelia.

The blind hand found her. 'He is so easily deceived,' confided the Orchid to her daughter-in-law. 'It made him entertaining, of course, before all this began – but now ... I blame myself for lacking forethought, certain sorts of perception ...'

'He is a credit to you, Mother.' Amelia wished to comfort. 'I love him for what you made him.'

Jherek was amused. 'It is always the way of women, as I was discovering, to regard men as some sort of blank creature into which one woman or another has instilled certain characteristics. This woman has made him shy – this woman has made him strong – another has driven such and such an influence (always a woman's of course) from him ... Am I merely no more than an amalgamation of women's creative imaginations? Have I no identity of my own?'

'Of course, dear.' Amelia spoke. 'Of course. You are completely yourself! I spoke only figuratively.'

The Iron Orchid's voice came again. 'Do not let him bully you, Amelia. That is his father's influence!'

'Mother, you remain as adamant as always!' Jherek said affectionately. 'A flower that can never be bent by even the strongest of winds!'

'I trust you are only jesting, Jherek. There is none more malleable than I!'

'Indeed!'

Amelia was forced to join in Jherek's laughter. The Iron Orchid, it seemed, sulked.

Jherek was about to speak again when the ground beneath his feet began to undulate violently, in tiny waves.

They held fast to one another to stop themselves from falling. There was a briny smell in the air and, for a second, a flash of violet light on the horizon.

'It is the cities,' said the Iron Orchid. 'They are destroyed!' She moved closer to Amelia.

'Do you find it colder?' his mother asked.

'Somewhat,' replied Amelia.

'Certainly,' said Jherek.

'I wonder how long . . .'

'We have already had longer than I expected,' Jherek said to her.

'I do wish it would finish. The least Jagged could do for us . . .'

'Perhaps he struggles with his machinery, still trying to save something,' suggested Jherek.

'Poor man,' murmured Amelia. 'All his plans ruined.'

'You sympathize now?' Jherek was confounded.

'Oh, well – I have always felt for the loser, you know.'

Jherek contented himself with squeezing her shoulder. There came another flash of violet light, some distance away from the first, and this lasted just a fraction longer.

'No,' said the Iron Orchid, 'it is definitely the cities. I recognize the locations. They explode.'

'It is strange that the air is still with us,' Jherek said. 'One city must continue to function, at least, to create the oxygen.'

'Unless we breathe only what is left to us,' suggested Amelia.

'I am not sure that this is the end, at all,' Jherek announced.

And, as if in response to his faith, the sun began to rise, dull red at first and then increasingly brighter until it filled the blue sky with streaks of yellow and mauve and crimson; and everywhere was cheering. And life resumed.

Only Amelia seemed discontented with this reprieve. 'It is madness,' she said. 'And I shall soon be mad myself, if I am not mad already. I desired nothing but death and now even that hope has been dashed!'

The shadow of a great swan fell across her and she looked up through red-rimmed, angered eyes. 'Oh, Lord Jagged! How you must enjoy all these manipulations!'

Lord Jagged was still in his morning suit, with his tall hat on his head. 'Forgive me, for the darkness and so on,' he said. 'It was necessary to start the first week's cycle from scratch, as we mean to begin. It is running smoothly now, as it will run for ever.'

'You do not offer even the slightest possibility that it will collapse?' Amelia was not facetious; she seemed desperate.

'Not the slightest, Amelia. It is in its nature to function perfectly. It could not exist if it were not perfect, I assure you.'

'I see ...' She began to move away, a wretched figure, careless of where she walked.

'There is an alternative, however,' said Lord Jagged laconically. 'As I mentioned.' He threw himself elegantly from his swan and landed near her, his hands in his pockets, waiting for his words to register with her. She came about slowly, like a tacking schooner, looking from Jagged to Jherek, who had approached his father.

'An alternative?'

'Yes, Amelia. But you might not find it any more to your liking and Jherek would probably consider it completely distasteful.'

'Tell me what it is!' Her voice was strained.

'Not here.' He glanced around him, withdrawing one hand from a pocket so that he might signal to his swan. The air-car moved obediently and was beside him. 'I have prepared a simple meal in pleasant surroundings. Be my guests.'

She hesitated. 'I can take little more of your mystification, Lord Jagged.'

'If decisions are to be reached, you will want to make them where you may be sure to be free of interruption, surely.'

Bishop Castle, swaying a little beneath the weight of his mitre, leaning for support upon his crook, stepped from the cathedral. 'Jagged – was this your doing?' He was bemused.

Lord Jagged of Canaria bowed to his friend. 'It was necessary. I regret causing you alarm.'

'Alarm! It was splendid. What a perfect sense of drama you have!' Yet Bishop Castle was pale and his tone was achieved with a certain difficulty.

The old half-smile crossed Lord Jagged's perfect lips. 'Are all the weddings duly solemnized?'

'I think so. I'll admit to being carried away – a captive audience, you know, easily pleased – we forget ourselves.'

From the cluster of booths came the Duke of Queens. He signalled to his band to play, but after a few seconds of the din he thought better of his decision and made the band stop. He stepped up, with Sweet Orb Mace prettily clinging to his arm. 'Well, at least my marriage wasn't interrupted, illusive Jagged, elusive Lord of Time, though I believe such interruptions were once traditional.' He chuckled. 'What a joke. I was convinced that you had blundered.'

'I had more faith,' said Sweet Orb Mace, brushing black curls from her little face. 'I knew that you would not wish to spoil the happiest day of my life, dear Jagged.'

She received a dry bow from Jherek's father.

'Well,' briskly said the Duke, 'we leave now to our honeymoon (scarcely more than an asteroid, really), and so must say farewell.'

Amelia, with a gesture Jherek found almost shocking, it was so untypical, threw her arms about the jolly Duke and kissed him on his bearded cheek. 'Farewell, dear Duke of Queens. You, I know, will always be happy.' Sweet Orb Mace, in turn, was kissed. 'And may your marriage last for a long, long while.'

The Duke seemed almost embarrassed, but was pleased by her demonstration. 'And may you be happy, too, Mrs Under —'

'Carnelian.'

'– wood. Aha! Here are our wings, my dear.' Two automata carried two large pairs of white feathered wings. The Duke helped his bride into her harness and then slipped into his own, stretching his arms to catch the loops. 'Now, Sweet Orb Mace, the secret lies in taking a good, fast run *before* you commence to beat. See!' He began to race across the ground, followed by his mate. He stumbled once, righted himself, started to flap the great wings and, eventually, succeeded in becoming wildly airborne. His wife imitated him and soon she, too, was a few feet in the air, swaying and flapping. Thus, erratically, they disappeared from view, two huge, drunken doves.

'I hope,' said Amelia gravely, 'that they do not get those wings too sticky.' And she smiled at Jherek, and she winked at him. He was glad to see that she had recovered her spirits.

Mistress Christia ran past, tittering with glee, pursued by four Lat, including Captain Mubbers who grunted happily: 'Get your balloons down, you beautiful bit of bone, you!'

She had already allowed her knee-balloons to slip enticingly half-way towards her calves.

'Cor!' retorted Lieutenant Rokfrug. 'What a lovely pair!'

'Save a bit for us!' begged the Lat furthest in the rear.

'Don't worry,' panted the second furthest, 'there's enough for everyone!'

They all rushed into the cathedral and did not emerge again.

Now, in small groups, the brides, the grooms and the guests were beginning to go their ways. Farewells were made. My Lady Charlotina and Brannart Morphail passed overhead in a blue and white enamel dish-shaped boat, but Charlotina was oblivious of them all and the only evidence of Brannart being with her was his club-foot waving helplessly over the rim of the air-car.

'What do you say, Amelia?' softly asked Lord Jagged.
'Will you accept my invitation?'

She shrugged at him. 'This is the last time I intend to
trust you, Lord Jagged.'

'It could be the last time you will have to, my dear.'

The Iron Orchid mounted the swan first, with Amelia
behind her, then Jherek and lastly Jagged. They began to
rise. Below them, near the cathedral and amongst the
tents and booths, a few determined revellers continued to
dance. Their voices, thin and high, carried up to the four
who circled above. Amelia Carnelian began to quote from
Wheldrake's longest and most ambitious poem, unfinished
at his death, *The Flagellants*. Her choice seemed inappropriate to Jherek, but she was looking directly at Lord
Jagged and seemed to be addressing him, as if only he
would understand the significance of the words.

> *So shall they dance, till the end of time,*
> *Each face a mask, each mark a sign*
> *Of pride disguised as pain.*
> *Yet pity him who must remain,*
> *His flesh unflayed, his soul untried:*
> *His pain disguised as pride.*

Lord Jagged's face was impassive, yet he gave a great
shrug and looked away from her, seemingly in annoyance.
It was the only occasion Jherek had ever detected that
kind of anger in his father. He frowned at her, questioning her, wondering at the peculiar smile on her lips – a
mixture of sympathy and triumph, and of bitterness –
but she continued to stare at Jagged, even though the lord
in yellow refused to meet that gaze. The swan sailed over
forests now, but Amelia continued with her Wheldrake.

> *I knew him when he offered all,*
> *To God, and Woman, too,*
> *His faith in life was strong,*
> *His trust in Christ was pure . . .*

Jagged's interruption was, for him, quite abrupt. 'They can be delightfully sentimental, those Victorian versifiers, can they not? Are you familiar with Swinburne, Amelia?'

'Swinburne? Certainly not, sir!'

'A shame. He was once a particular favourite of mine. Was he ever Laureate?'

'There was some talk – but the scandal. Mr Kipling refused, I heard. Mr Alfred Austin is – was – our new Poet Laureate. I believe I read a book of his about gardens.' She chatted easily, but there remained an edge to her voice, as if she knew he changed the subject and she refused to be diverted. 'I am not familiar with his poetry.'

'Oh, but you should look some out.' And in turn, Lord Jagged quoted:

> But the world has wondrously changed, Granny, since
>   the days when you were young;
> It thinks quite different thoughts from then, and
>   speaks with a different tongue.
> The fences are broken, the cords are snapped, that
>   tethered man's heart to home;
> He ranges free as the wind or the wave, and changes
>   his shore like the foam.
> He drives his furrows through fallow seas, he reaps
>   what the breakers sow,
> And the flash of his iron flail is seen mid the barns of
>   the barren snow.
> He has lassoed the lightning and led it home, he has
>   yoked it unto his need,
> And made it answer the rein and trudge as straight as
>   the steer or steed.
> He has bridled the torrents and made them tame, he
>   has bitted the champing tide,
> It toils as his drudge and turns the wheels that spin
>   for his use and pride.
> He handles the planets and weights their dust, he
>   mounts on the comet's car,

And he lifts the veil of the sun, and stares in the eyes
of the uttermost star ...

'Very rousing,' said Amelia. The swan dipped and seemed to fly faster, so that her hair was blown about her face. 'Though it is scarcely Wheldrake. A different sort of verse altogether. Wheldrake writes of the spirit, Austin, it seems, of the world. Sometimes, however, it is good for those who are much in the world to spend a few quiet moments with a poet who can offer an insight or two as to the reasons why men act and think as they do ...'

'You do not find Wheldrake's preoccupations morbid, then?'

'In excess, yes. You mentioned Swinburne ...'

'Aha! Goes too far?'

'I believe so. We are told so. The fleshly school, you know ...'

Lord Jagged pretended (there was no other word) to notice the bemused, even bored, expressions of the Iron Orchid and Jherek Carnelian. 'Look how we distress our companions, our very loved ones, with this dull talk of forgotten writers.'

'Forgive me. I began it – with a quotation from Wheldrake I found apt.'

'Those we have left are not penitents of any sort, Amelia.'

'Perhaps so. Perhaps the penitents are elsewhere.'

'Now I lose your drift entirely.'

'I speak without thinking. I am a little tired.'

'Look. The sea.'

'It is a lovely sea, Jagged!' complimented the Iron Orchid. 'Have you only just made it?'

'Not long since. On my way back. He turned to Jherek. 'Nurse sends her regards, by the way. She says she is glad to hear that you are making a sensible life for yourself and settling down and that it is often the wild ones who make the best citizens in the end.'

'I hope to see her soon. I hold her in great esteem and

affection. She re-united me with Amelia.'

'So she did.'

The swan had settled; they disembarked onto a pale yellow beach that was lapped by white foam, a blue sea. Forming a kind of miniature cove was a semi-circle of white rocks, most of them just a little taller than Jherek, apparently worn almost to spikes by the elements. The smell of brine was strong. White gulls flapped here and there in the sky, occasionally swooping to catch black and grey fish. The pale yellow beach, of fine sand, with a few white pebbles, was spread with a dark brown cloth. On pale yellow plates was a variety of brown food – buns, biscuits, beef, bacon, bread, baked potatoes, pork pies, pickles, pemmican, peppercorns, pattercakes and much more – and there was brown beer or sarsaparilla or tea or coffee to drink.

As they stretched out, one at each station of the cloth, Amelia sighed, evidently glad to relax, as was Jherek.

'Now, Lord Jagged,' Amelia began, ignoring the food, 'you said there was an alternative ...'

'Let us eat quietly for a moment,' he said. 'You will admit the common sense of becoming as calm as possible after today's events, I know.'

'Very well.' She selected a prune from a nearby dish. He chose a chestnut.

Conscious that the encounter was between Jagged and Amelia, Jherek and the Iron Orchid said little. Instead they munched and watched the seabirds wheeling while listening to the whisper of the waves on the shore.

Of the four, the Iron Orchid, in her orchids, supplied the only brilliant colour to the scene; Jherek, Amelia and Lord Jagged were still in grey. Jherek thought that his father had chosen an ideal location for the picnic and smiled drowsily when his mother remarked that it was like old times. It was as if the world had never been threatened, as if his adventures had never taken place, yet now he had gained an entire family. It would be pleasant, he thought, to make a regular habit of these picnics; surely even Amelia must be enjoying the simplicity, the sunshine, the relative solitude. He glanced at her. She was thoughtful and did not notice him. As always, he was warmed by feelings of the utmost tenderness as he contemplated her grave beauty, a beauty which showed itself at its best when she was unaware of attention, as now, or when she slept. He smiled, wondering if she would agree to a ceremony, not public or grandiose as the ones they had recently witnessed but private and plain, in which they should be properly married. He was sure that she yearned for it.

She looked up and met his eyes. She smiled briefly before speaking to his father: 'And now, Lord Jagged – the alternative.'

'It is within my power,' said Jagged, responding to her briskness, 'to send you into the future.'

She became instantly guarded again. 'Future? There is none.'

'Not for this world – and there will be none at all, when this week has passed. But we are still capable of moving back and forth in the conventional time-cycle – just for the next seven days. When I say "the future" I mean, of course, "the past" – I can send you forward to the Palaeozoic, as I originally hoped. You would go forward and therefore not be at all subject to Morphail's Law. There is a slight danger, though I would not say much. Once in the Palaeozoic you would not be able to return to this world and, moreover, you would become mortal.'

'As Olympians sent to Earth,' she said.

'And denied your god-like powers,' he added. 'The rings will not work in the Palaeozoic, as you already know. You would have to build your own shelters, grow and hunt your own food. There are no material advantages at all, though you would have the advice and help of the Time Centre, doubtless, if it remains. That, I must remind you, *is* subject to the Morphail Effect. If you intended to bear children ...'

'It would be unthinkable that I should not,' she told

him firmly.

'. . . you would not have the facilities you have known in 1896. There would be a risk, though probably slight, of disease.'

'We should be able to take tools, medicines and so forth?'

'Of course. But you would have to learn to use them.'

'Writing materials?'

'An excellent idea. There would be no problem, I think I have an *Enquire Within* and a *How Things Work* somewhere.'

'Seeds?'

'You would be able to grow most things – and think how they would proliferate, with so little competition. In a few hundred years' time, before your death almost certainly, what a peculiar ecology would develop upon the Earth! Millions of years of evolution would be by-passed. There is time-travel for you, if you like!'

'Time to create a race almost entirely lacking in primitive instincts – and without need of them!'

'Hopefully.'

She addressed Jherek, who was having difficulty coming to grips with the point of the conversation. 'It would be our trust. Remember what we discussed, Jherek, dear? A combination of my sense of duty and your sense of freedom?'

'Oh, yes!' He spoke brightly, breathlessly, as he did his best to assimilate it all.

'What splendid children they could be!'

'Oh, indeed!'

'It will be a trial for you, too,' said Jagged gently.

'Compared with the trials we have already experienced, Lord Jagged, the ones to come will be as nothing.'

The familiar smile touched his lips. 'You are optimistic.'

'Given a grain of hope,' she said. 'And you offer much more.' Her grey eyes fixed on him. 'Was this always part of your plan?'

'Plan? Call it my own small exercise in optimism.'

'Everything that has happened recently – it might have been designed to have led up to this.'

'Yes, I suppose that's true.' He looked at his son. 'I could be envious of you, my boy.'

'Of me? For what, Father?'

Jagged was contemplating Amelia again. His voice was distant, perhaps a touch sad. 'Oh, for many things ...'

The Iron Orchid put down an unfinished walnut. 'They have no time-machine,' she said tartly. 'And they have not the training to travel without one.'

'I have Brannart's abandoned machine. It is an excellent one – the best he has ever produced. It is already stocked. You can set off as soon as you wish.'

'I am not sure that life in the Palaeozoic is entirely to my taste,' said Jherek. 'I would leave so many friends behind, you see.'

'And you would age, dear,' added the Orchid. 'You would grow infirm. I cannot imagine ...'

'You said that we should have several hundred years, Lord Jagged?' Amelia began to rise.

'You would have a life-span about the same as Methusalah's, at a guess. Your genes are already affected, and then there would be the prevailing conditions. I think you would have time to grow old quite gracefully – and see several generations follow you.'

'That is worthwhile immortality, Jherek,' she said to him. 'To become immortal through one's children.'

'I suppose so ...'

'And those children would become your friends,' added his father. 'As we are friends, Jherek.'

'You would not come with us?' He had so recently gained this father, he could not lose him so soon.

'There is another alternative. I intend to take that.'

'Could not we ...?'

'It would be impossible. I am an inveterate time-traveller, my boy. I cannot give it up. There is still so much to learn.'

'You gave us the impression there was nothing left to explore,' said Amelia.

'But if one goes *beyond* the End of Time, one might experience the beginning of a whole *new* cycle in the existence of what Mrs Persson terms "the multiverse". Having learned to dispense with time-machines — and it is a trick impossible to teach — I intend to fling myself completely outside the present cycle. I intend to explore infinity.'

'I was not aware ...' began the Orchid.

'I shall have to go alone,' he said.

'Ah, well. I was becoming bored with marriage. After today, anyway, it could scarcely be called a novelty!'

Amelia went to stand beside a rock, staring landwards.

Jherek said to Jagged: 'It would mean that we should be parted forever, then — you and I, Jagged.'

'As to that, it depends upon my fate and what I learn in my explorations. It is possible that we shall meet. But it is not probable, my boy.'

'It would make Amelia happy,' said Jherek.

'And I would be happy,' Lord Jagged told him softly. 'Knowing that, whatever befalls me, you and yours will go on.'

Amelia wheeled round at this. 'Your motives are clear at last, Lord Jagged.'

'If you say so, Amelia.' From a sleeve he produced pale yellow roses and offered them to her. 'You prefer to see me as a man moved entirely by self-interest. Then see me so!' He bowed as he presented the bouquet.

'It is how you justify your decisions, I think,' She accepted the flowers.

'Oh, you are probably right.'

'You will say nothing, even now, of your past?'

'I have no past.' His smile was self-mocking. 'Only a future. Even that is not certain.'

'I believe,' said Jherek suddenly, 'that I weary of ambiguity. At least, at the Beginning of Time, there is little of that.'

'Very little,' she said, coming to him. 'Our love could flourish, Jherek dear.'

'We would be truly husband and wife?'

'It would be our moral duty.' Her smile held unusual merriment. 'To perpetuate the race, my dear.'

'We could have a ceremony?'

'Perhaps, Lord Jagged —'

'I should be glad to officiate. I seem to remember that I have civil authority, as a Registrar ...'

'It would *have* to be a civil ceremony,' she said.

'We shall be your Adam and Bede after all, Jagged!' Jherek put his arm around his Amelia's waist. 'And if we keep the machine, perhaps we could visit the future, just to see how it progressed, eh?'

Lord Jagged shook his head. 'If you go further forward, once you have stopped, you will immediately become subject to the Morphail Effect again. Therefore time travel will be impossible. You will be creating your future, but if you ever dare try to find out what the future will be like, then it will almost certainly cease to exist. You will have to reconcile yourself to making the most of one lifetime in one place. Amelia can teach you that.' He stroked his chin. 'There will be something in the genes, I suppose. And you already know much about the nature of Time. Ultimately a new race of time-travellers could exist, not subject to the Morphail Effect. It might mean the abolition of Time, as we have understood it up to now. And Space, too, would assume, therefore, an entirely different character. The experiment might mean —'

'I think that we shall try not to indulge in experiments of that sort, Lord Jagged.' She was firm.

'No, no, of course not.' But his manner remained speculative.

The Iron Orchid was laughing. She, too, had risen to her feet, her orchids whispering as she moved. 'At least, at the Beginning of Time, they'll be free from your further interference, Jagged.'

'Interference?'

'And this world, too, may go its own way, within its limitations.' She kissed her husband. 'You leave many gifts behind you, cunning Lord of Canaria!'

'One does what one can.' He put his hand into hers. 'I would take you with me, Orchid, if I could.'

'I think that temperamentally I am content with things as they are. Call me conservative, if you will, but there is a certain predictability about life at the End of Time which suits me.'

'Well, then, all our temperamental needs are satisfied. Jherek and Amelia go to work as colonists, founding a whole new culture, a new history, a new kind of race. It should prove very different, in some aspects, from the old one. I travel on, as my restless brain moves me. And you, dearest Orchid, stay. The resolution seems satisfactory.'

'There might be others here,' Amelia said, after an internal struggle with her conscience, 'who might also wish to become "colonists". Li Pao, for instance.'

'I had considered that, but it complicates matters. I am afraid that Li Pao is doomed to spend eternity in this particular paradise.'

'It seems a shame,' she said. 'Could you not —?'

He raised a hand. 'You accused me of manipulating Fate, Amelia. You are wrong — I merely offer a certain resistance to it. I win a few little battles, that is all. Li Pao's fate is now settled. He will dance with the others, at the End of Time.' He made references to her quotation and as he did so he lifted his hat as if he acknowledged some previous point she had made. Jherek sighed and was glad of his own decision for, if nothing else, it would, as he had said, mean no more of these mysteries.

'Then you condemn them all to this terrible mockery of existence.' Amelia frowned.

Jagged's laughter was frank. 'You remain, in spite of all your experiences, a woman of your time, Amelia! Our beautiful Iron Orchid finds this existence quite natural.'

'It has a simplicity, you see,' agreed the Orchid, 'which I did not find, for instance, in your age, my dear. I do not have the courage, I suppose, to confront such complications as I witnessed in 1896. Though,' she hastened to add, 'I enjoyed my short visit thoroughly. I suppose it is mortality which makes people rush about so. This world is more leisurely, probably because we are not constrained by the prospect of death. It is, I would be the first to admit, entirely a matter of taste. You choose your work, your duty, and your death. I choose pleasure and immortality. Yet, if I were in your position, I should probably make the decisions you have made.'

'You are the most understanding of mothers-in-law!' cried Amelia, hugging her. 'There will be some things I shall regret leaving here.'

The Iron Orchid touched Amelia's neck with a hand subtly coloured to match her costume; her tongue moistened her lower lip for an instant; her expression caused Amelia to blush. 'Oh, indeed,' breathed the Orchid, 'there is much we might have done together. And I shall miss Jherek, of course, as I am sure will Jagged.'

Amelia became her old, stern self. 'Well, there'll be little time to make all the arrangements necessary before we leave, if we go tomorrow.'

'Tomorrow?' said Jherek. 'I was hoping ...'

'It would be best to go as soon as possible,' she told him. 'Of course, if you have changed your mind and wish to remain with – your parents, and your friends ...'

'Never. I love you. I have followed you across a world and through Time. I will go with you wherever you choose, Amelia.'

Her manner softened. 'Oh, my dear.' She linked her arm in his.

Lord Jagged said. 'I suggest we stroll along the beach for a bit.' He offered an exquisite arm to Amelia and, after scarcely any hesitation at all, she took it. The Iron Orchid took Jherek's free arm, and thus joined, they began to walk along the pale yellow shore; as handsome and as happy a family group as any one might find in history.

The sun was starting to sink as Amelia stopped, dropped Jherek's arm and began to turn one of her power-rings, 'I could not resist a last indulgence,' she apologized.

The yellow beach became a white promenade, with green wrought-iron railings, stretching, it seemed, to infinity. The rocky interior became rolling green hills, a little golf-course. She created a red and white-striped band-stand, in which a small German band, not dissimilar to the larger one made by the Duke of Queens, began to play Strauss. She paused, then turned another ring, and there was a white and green rococo pier, with flags and bunting and variously coloured lamps decorating its iron-work, stretching out to sea. She made four deck-chairs, brilliantly striped, appear on the beach below the prom-enade. She created four large ice-cream cornets so that they had one each.

It was almost twilight now, as they continued to stroll, admiring the twinkling lights of the pier which were re-flected in the calm, dark blue sea.

'It is beautiful,' said the Iron Orchid. 'May I keep it, when you have gone?'

'Let it be my monument,' she said.

They all began to hum the tune of the waltz; Lord Jagged even danced a few jaunty steps as he finished his ice-cream, tilting his topper over one eye, and everyone laughed. They stopped when they came close to the pier. They leaned on the railings, staring out across the glisten-ing water. Jherek put his arm about her shoulders; Lord Jagged embraced his own wife, and the distant band played on.

'Perhaps,' said Jherek romantically, 'we shall be able to make something like this in the Palaeozoic – not immedi-ately of course, but when we have a larger family to build it.'

She smiled. 'It would be pleasant to dream about, at least.'

The Iron Orchid sighed. 'Your imagination will be a great loss to us at the End of Time, Amelia. But your inspiration will remain with us, at least.'

'You flatter me too much.'

'I think she is right,' said Lord Jagged of Canaria, producing a pale yellow cigarette. 'Would you mind, Amelia?'

'Of course not.'

Lord Jagged began to smoke, looking upward at the infinite blackness of the sky, his features once again controlled and expressionless, the tip of his cigarette a tiny glowing ember in the gathering twilight. The sun, which he and the cities had created, burned deepest crimson on the horizon and then was gone, leaving only a smear of dusky orange behind it; then that, too, faded.

'So you'll leave tomorrow,' said Jagged.

'If it is possible.'

'Certainly. And you have no fears? You are content with your decision?'

'We are content.' Jherek spoke for them both, to reassure her.

'I was truly divorced from Harold,' she said, 'when he refused to let me return with him. And, after you have married us, Lord Jagged, I do not think I shall feel even a hint of guilt about any of my decisions.'

'Good. And now ...' Lord Jagged drew his wife from the rail, escorting her along the promenade, leaving the lovers alone.

'It is growing a little chilly,' she said.

Jherek produced a cloak for her, of gold-trimmed ermine, and placed it around her shoulders. 'Will this do?'

'It is a trifle ostentatious.' She stroked the fur. 'But since this is our last night at the End of Time, I think I can allow myself the luxury.'

He bent to kiss her. Gently, she took his face in her hands. 'There will be so much, Jherek, that we shall have to learn together. Much that I will have to teach you. But do not ever, my dear, lose that joyous spirit. It will be a wonderful example to our children, and their children, too.'

'Oh, Amelia! How could I lose it, for it is you who

make me joyful! And I shall be a perfect pupil. You must explain it all to me again and I am sure that I shall learn it eventually.'

She was puzzled. 'What is it I must explain to you, my dear?'

'Guilt,' he said.

They kissed.